MW00882633

The Fall
of White City
Revised Edition

N. S. WIKARSKI

The Fall of White City – Revised 2020 Edition
Book One – Gilded Age Chicago Mystery Series

http://www.mythofhistory.com

All rights reserved. No portion of this book may be used or reproduced in any manner whatsoever without the express written permission of the author except in the case of brief quotations embodied in critical articles or reviews.

This is a work of fiction. Names, characters, places, and incidents either are the product of the author's imagination or are used fictitiously, and any resemblance to any persons, living or dead, business establishments, events, or locales is entirely coincidental.

Copyright © 2011, 2020 N. S. Wikarski

All rights reserved.

ISBN: 9781468147094

EPIGRAPH

Justice is always Violence to the party offending!
For every man is innocent in his own eyes.

--Daniel DeFoe
The Shortest Way with the Dissenters

TABLE OF CONTENTS

PREFACE TO THE 2020 REVISED EDITION

Nearly two decades ago when I was writing my first book, an established author advised me to "sin boldly." At the time, I was agonizing over whether to use real historical names and places or fictional ones in my 1890s Chicago series. She thought I should use real names. Being a self-doubting newbie, I failed to heed her advice. It seemed to me that I would be taking liberties with figures from the past by weaving them into the imaginary world I was creating.

However, I've since discovered that fellow historical mystery authors aren't as excruciatingly punctilious as I am. They don't lose any sleep at night after casting founding fathers in the role of amateur sleuths or dead presidents as vampire hunters. Because any liberties I'm taking with historic figures pale in comparison, I no longer feel that I'm hijacking history by naming names in my own work.

After a very long hiatus, I'm now writing the third book in the series and find it tedious to continue a fictional pretense for real Chicago personages and locales. That's the reason for the revised edition of the book you're now perusing. Readers of earlier versions won't find any material changes to the original plot. A few passages have been added to clarify character motivation, and I've corrected some minor proofreading errors. That's all.

Revising *The Fall of White City* and *Shrouded in Thought* spurred me to rethink the series title as well. To call this series "Victorian Chicago" might be useful for SEO purposes, but it doesn't accurately describe the content. Each book is contextually grounded in the excesses and abuses of Gilded Age America, not Victorian England.

Given the fifteen-year interval between books two and three, this seemed an appropriate point for a course correction. I hope my faithful readers will understand and accept my reasoning, especially since I'm far from done telling tales of Gilded Age Chicago.

N. S. Wikarski
Summer 2020

1 – THE HEIRESS AND THE SEAMSTRESS

Lake Bluff, Illinois
October 1893

"Freddie! Freddie! Wake up!" a voice demanded out of the darkness. The words were punctuated by the clatter of stone against glass. A faint drizzle fell as the residents of Lake Bluff slept content. All, that is, except Evangeline LeClair, who was standing on the lawn of Freddie Simpson's house throwing pebbles at a second-story window.

"Freddie! Do wake up," the voice insisted. "Have you gone deaf? Half the village must be up by now!"

Dodging a fresh volley of gravel, the lucky object of all this attention craned his head out of the besieged window. He leaned over the sill, squinting through the mist to identify his attacker. Recognition dawned, since the sun wasn't ready to oblige him. "Engie? Engie, is that you," he gasped. "For God's sake, what are you doing?"

"I'm attempting to raise the dead," the lady replied succinctly from below.

"I won't make the mistake of asking if you know what time it is!" Freddie knew from sad experience that Evangeline's motives for doing anything, like the will of God, were frequently obscure.

"I'm well aware of the time. It's precisely six o'clock in the morning, and I need you to go to the city with me today."

"What on earth—"

Evangeline cut in, "Come to my house at eight. We'll take the late commuter train. It's a very serious matter."

Freddie could barely hear her next words. He could have sworn the wind shaking the treetops distorted the sound.

"We have a funeral to attend. A friend of mine has been murdered." Leaving the young man to collect his wits as best he might, she turned and melted into the fog.

***

In defiance of Evangeline's implied assumption that he needed two hours to get ready, Freddie was washed and combed by quarter to eight. He wore a black suit, a newly starched shirt, and a thoroughly brushed bowler, as he slipped noiselessly out of the back door before his mother could ask where he was going. He darted past street after street of Italianate villas, their barbered hedges exuding propriety. Lake Bluff had become the summer retreat of the wealthy who chose its lake breezes over the swelter of Chicago in July. The village had been described by many as "charming." Freddie thought this description would have been a mystery to anyone who had never used the word "charming" as an adjective to modify "monotony."

When he rounded the corner to Evangeline's house, the young man found she was already waiting for him—umbrella in hand, tapping her foot impatiently on the front porch. Without a word, the two turned down Center Avenue in the direction of the train. The drizzle and fog of early morning hadn't relented. Freddie stole a sideways glance at the tiny woman walking beside him. She stood barely five feet tall, though Freddie always thought she seemed a good deal taller when she was angry. As a débutante, she had been a celebrated beauty. Her dark eyes formed a striking contrast to a complexion just pallid enough to be fashionable. Though still a celebrated beauty, she was now in her mid-thirties, which meant she was past her prime as a great matrimonial prize. It also meant that she would henceforth be described in hushed tones by polite society as "a lady of a certain age."

While Evangeline viewed Freddie as a younger brother, his feelings for her fell into the romantic category. It had been love at first sight. He was seven at the time, and she had run him off her lawn for assaulting sparrows with a slingshot. The eight-year age difference didn't bother him at all, though he doubted that Evangeline would ever seriously consider being chafed by the bonds of matrimony. She had inherited a fortune when her parents passed away. This stroke of good luck had aggravated her already strange notions of female liberty. She seemed content to devote her time to teaching at Hull House, tending her flower garden, corresponding with her friends, attending society functions, entertaining a few remaining suitors, and making Freddie miserable. By her own reckoning, she lived quite a satisfying life. Freddie knew her too well to cherish much hope that she would ever change. Still, he found whatever pretext he could to be near her, even at the price of having rocks thrown at his window in the gray light of dawn.

Since Evangeline continued mute, Freddie broached the topic uppermost in his mind. "Well, are you ready to tell me what this is about?"

At his words, Evangeline's composure seemed to wilt. Her usual bravado was replaced by a look of deep gloom.

"I hardly know any way to discuss it at all, so I'll begin abruptly—a very bad business. It still seems too shocking to be real."

Freddie's concern escalated to alarm. "What do you mean? Is it anyone I know?"

"Not someone you know, but someone I'm sure you've read about."

Freddie's mind began to race. "But if she was murdered, then it would have been in all the papers. I can't recollect... Good Lord, Engie, not the girl at the Palmer House!"

Evangeline's face had drained of color. "As I said, a very bad business, Freddie. She was only twenty. I had just seen her the night before at Hull House. She sat through one of my literature classes. And the next night, dead... To die in such a way, too." Evangeline seemed unable to comprehend the finality of it all. "How much have you heard?"

"Just what I read in the *Tribune* the morning after it happened. Twenty-four-point Roman headline, two-column spread, 'Girl Found Murdered in the Palmer House.'" Even while discussing such a grim topic, Freddie couldn't tear himself away from his enthusiasm for all matters journalistic.

"Bear in mind that you are an attorney, please, and not a reporter as you might wish. What, besides the typestyle, do you remember?"

Freddie looked off into space, thinking back. "Her name was German... Elsa... something beginning with a 'B'... Bremen... Bauhof... Oh yes, now I have it. It was Bauer, Elsa Bauer."

Evangeline nodded.

"It must have created quite a stir for the hotel! With all the rich foreign clientele staying there while the World's Fair is going on, Potter Palmer must be beside himself to have that kind of notoriety for his establishment."

"And Bertha Palmer, too, I expect. You know, in private conversation, she always refers to the hotel as 'our house.' Quite a blow for the first lady of Chicago society."

"Yes, it will be fairly hard for Palmer's palace to live down something like this. A young woman, traveling alone, checks in quietly on the night of October seventh. The next morning when the maid comes in to make up the room, she's found lying on the floor dead."

By this time, the couple had reached the tracks, and their conversation was interrupted by the sound of a whistle as a train rounded the final bend and came into view of the station. The two boarded in the persistent drizzle, Freddie complaining that Evangeline was trying to poke his eye out with the spokes of her umbrella. Their only companions were a few businessmen taking the late train to the city. It wasn't until after the pair claimed their seats and got settled that their discussion of Elsa Bauer continued.

"Did the article mention any details of how she died?" Evangeline spared herself the need to recount the story.

Freddie thought for a moment. "I remember reading that the doctor who examined the body discovered a stab wound in her back. Conveniently for the murderer, no knife was found at the scene of the crime."

Evangeline nodded absently, glancing out the window. "But why was she there at all, Freddie? The Palmer House is the most high-toned hotel in the city. Even the floor of the hotel barbershop is inlaid with silver dollars. Elsa worked as a seamstress in one of the sweatshops on South Ashland Avenue. A room at the hotel would have cost her at least a week's wages—a week's wages she could ill afford to part with. I'm sure her landlady would have been highly displeased not to receive her rent and would, no doubt, have expressed that disapproval by throwing Elsa out into the street."

Freddie cleared his throat nervously, afraid to mention a subject that Evangeline was sure to find offensive. "Well, if she was a pretty girl, there's always the other possibility..."

Evangeline turned from the window to focus her unblinking attention on her friend. "And what possibility would that be?"

Freddie looked down, finding a speck of something on the knee of his pants leg to be intensely interesting. "That she was involved in a private arrangement with some man, and that he paid for the room."

"You needn't worry about distressing my maiden ears with that news, Freddie. Of course, the possibility presented itself to me as well. I find it difficult to credit for several reasons. First, I knew Elsa. She wasn't the sort of girl who would settle for a questionable alliance—far too serious-minded for that. And if the affair was clandestine, why would she have reserved a room at the hotel using her real name? Besides, when and how would she ever have come into contact with a man who could afford an expensive liaison? She and her brother Franz board with an Irish family in the factory district. I once asked her if she had ever gone downtown. She looked at me blankly as if I were referring to a trip to the Orient. It's only ten blocks north of her home, but she's never ventured out of her own neighborhood—only to the Hull House settlement for classes, the factory where she worked, and her church. Now, unless it's become the fashion for well-bred gentlemen to take their evening promenades down Maxwell Street, she would have as much chance of meeting such a person in her neighborhood as she would of becoming Queen of England."

Freddie scratched his head in bewilderment, acknowledging the logic of her argument. "Well, it does seem odd. But once the killer is caught, all these questions can be resolved. I'm sure the Palmers will put pressure on the police to make an arrest quickly."

"I'm sure they will. But I wonder if the need to make a quick arrest will outweigh the need to make the right arrest."

"That's out of your hands, Engie."

"So it would seem, Freddie. So it would seem."

The two sat in silence for some moments before another thought struck Freddie. "Why is this one so important to you that you would commandeer me and travel thirty-five miles for a burial? She was just a student of yours. You must teach twenty just like her in any given class."

"No, not just like her, Freddie." Evangeline's face lightened briefly at the memory. "She was different. She had a fierce determination to make a better life for herself. I admired her spirit. I can still remember the day she came rushing into class after I had lent her my copy of Emerson's essays. She began quoting 'Self-Reliance'—to me, of all people. I saw a glimmer of something like defiance in her eyes when she repeated his words: 'The centuries are conspirators against the sanity and majesty of the soul.' How many seamstresses would have understood what that line meant, much less remembered it?"

"So, she was a test case for your experiment in cultural enrichment?" Freddie observed dryly.

"Not cultural enrichment! The cultural enrichment was only a means to an end. It improved her reading. With that, in turn, she could have applied for a clerical position in an office somewhere. Her pay would have tripled. Materially, her life would have been better. Do you consider it a pointless gesture to have given her a book to read? Books fired her imagination and taught her not to accept her lot in life as inevitable!"

Evangeline stopped abruptly and turned to the window again. Neither one spoke several minutes until Freddie broke the silence. "I wonder if it was those very aspirations that ended up getting her killed."

Without turning towards him, Evangeline smiled grimly. "Yes, I just had the same thought, too."

2 - GRAVE FACES

By the time the couple exited the Kinzie Street train station, Evangeline still hadn't given Freddie a hint as to their ultimate destination.

"We'll take a streetcar from here," she said, marching off in the direction of Clark Street.

The young man trailed in her wake but was so caught up in contemplating Elsa Bauer's fate that he failed to notice a streetcar bearing down on him as he crossed the intersection.

"Freddie! For God's sake, look out!"

The trolley clanged a warning, missing the young man by inches.

He scuttled to the curb as the cable car went careening past. The vehicle, still refusing to slow, narrowly avoided a collision with a fruit peddler who had just nosed his cart out of the next side street.

Evangeline clutched at the young man's arm. "Are you all right?"

"Did you see that? He did it on purpose!" Freddie was outraged.

"I'm sure he did. I've always believed that motormen take a solemn oath to terrorize and, if possible, dismember every pedestrian in their path."

"I hope he derails the deuced thing!" Freddie dusted off his coat and adjusted his hat, trying vainly to regain his dignity.

"Not unlikely. We've had at least three derailments in as many days. The sacred brotherhood must be attempting to set a new record this week."

Evangeline gave Freddie a moment to catch his breath before nudging the young man toward the corner to await the next northbound car. When it arrived about ten minutes later, there were no seats available. The couple was forced to stand on the stairs at the side of the car, grasping the leather straps that were supposed to keep passengers from falling out of the open doors while the vehicle lurched along. Even though the air was bracing, the closed winter cars hadn't yet been put into service.

A few blocks into their journey, Freddie realized their ultimate destination. "I didn't expect she would be buried at Graceland, Engie. How could she have afforded it? It's a private cemetery—not for the likes of the Bauers of Ashland Avenue."

Over the sound of street traffic and the bumpy motion of the cable car, Freddie could barely hear Evangeline's reply.

"She couldn't afford it, Freddie... but I could."

"Well now, isn't this carrying charity a bit far? What possible claim could she have on that much generosity?"

"As I said, she was different, and I had great hopes for her future. If left to the County, she would probably have been buried at the Poor Farm or in some potter's field south of Bubbly Creek." Evangeline was referring to the acid-choked south fork of the Chicago River, which had been used for years as a dumping ground for waste from the stockyards. "It would have been a poor end for a life of such promise."

"And you think the end she made was worthy of anything better?" The young man had trouble keeping a note of surprise out of his voice.

"I think I don't yet know how she came to the end she did and am willing to reserve judgment until I do!"

Freddie was silent for a moment. Not wanting to antagonize Evangeline by casting moral aspersions on her favorite, he turned the conversation in another direction.

"I take it she didn't have any family?"

"Only a brother named Franz—a twin brother at that. They came over together from Germany about four or five years ago. No surviving family there. When they arrived, they both found work. She as a seamstress and he as a furniture maker, though he's since become associated with some German socialist organization and writes for one of their newspapers. When the two of them first came here, they made the unlikely choice of renting rooms from an Irish family rather than a German one because they thought it would help them learn English more quickly."

"I wouldn't think an Irish family would welcome outsiders that easily."

Evangeline smiled thinly. "From what I've heard of their landlady, Mrs. O'Malley, the green of a dollar bill carries far greater weight with her than the green of a shamrock."

"Have you spoken to the girl's brother since the er... er..."

"No, I haven't. I sent word to their house directly after I heard about her death, but the landlady said no one had seen Elsa's brother. No one knew what had become of him. The funeral arrangements were made by my attorney in town. There was to be no wake. The last thing I wanted for Elsa was to find curiosity seekers gawking at her remains. So, we settled on a brief ceremony over a closed casket as the best alternative."

Freddie raised his eyebrows and whistled faintly through his teeth. "Well, that's a bit high-handed even for you, Engie. How do you think her brother will feel about all of these 'arrangements?'"

Evangeline craned her neck to see whether the hapless soul just stepping off the curb in front of their trolley was about to meet an untimely end. After he darted back to the safety of the sidewalk, she replied to her friend's question. "I don't know how he feels about it, Freddie—or her landlady either. Their feelings in the matter are of very little consequence to me. What I do know is that when the police were ready to release the body, no one came forward to claim it or to make arrangements for her burial. I expected better of Franz, but under the circumstances, there was nothing else to be done."

The pair stepped off the streetcar at the corner of Irving Park Road and proceeded on foot through the main gate of the cemetery. The weather hadn't improved. The drizzle and fog continued, though the wind didn't carry the icy edge that it would possess by November. Evangeline walked down the main path, making straight for a gravesite a few hundred yards away where a small group had assembled around a casket. Freddie concluded that this must be their destination. A minister stood patiently waiting to perform the final ceremony. The only other company in attendance appeared to be Elsa's landlady and family.

As Evangeline and Freddie came within shouting range, a red-faced woman whose skin seemed too tight to contain its generous folds of fat trundled toward them. She sniffled and dabbed at her eyes with a handkerchief. "Oh, Miss LeClair! It must be you, for the lawyer said you would come! How can we ever thank you for what you've done!"

As the woman was still fifty yards away, Freddie was impressed by the volume of her voice. Under his breath, he mumbled to Evangeline, "Well, that answers one question about the landlady's attitude."

"Yes, Freddie, it answers the question," Evangeline winced, "but at such a pitch!"

The rotund woman lumbered toward them, dabbing her eyes and professing her gratitude. She was still out of earshot of a normal conversation, which tempted Freddie to continue his running commentary. "Brace yourself, Engie. We're in for it now."

Evangeline kept an absolutely straight face. "Courage, man. I'll protect you. I always carry a derringer in my reticule."

They stopped their conversation abruptly as the female juggernaut bore down upon them. Pausing only long enough to catch her breath, Mrs. O'Malley launched into another round of exclamations and lamentations—each expression of woe being accompanied by a sweep of her arms. "Oh, the poor girl! Poor, poor Elsa! What a world we live in nowadays! To be done to death in such a cruel manner!"

"Yes, yes, Mrs. O'Malley, it's very sad." Evangeline vainly tried to stem the tide as the three walked together to the gravesite.

Her words had no effect whatsoever. The woman continued unchecked until the minister decisively cleared his throat, stopping her in mid-sentence. Recollecting herself, she stammered, "Oh, where are my manners, so caught up as I am in this terrible, terrible tragedy! This is Reverend Schultz, who has kindly come all the way from Elsa's church to perform the burial service." *Sotto voce*, she continued, "them being Lutheran and all."

Mrs. O'Malley allowed herself a brief interlude of lamentation and eye-dabbing. "And here next to me is my husband, Mr. O'Malley." She poked the emaciated man at her right sharply in the ribs. "Patrick, shake hands with the lady and gentleman!"

Rousing himself from whatever daydream he was pursuing, the man quickly pulled off his hat and extended a hand toward Evangeline. "Ma'am" and "Sir" were all he said as he greeted each in turn. Having fulfilled his wife's commands, he stepped back and let her continue.

"And here's my daughter, Patricia." Mrs. O'Malley pushed forward a timid girl of about ten. "Patsy is what we call her. She and Elsa were great friends, weren't you, Patsy?" She gave her daughter a thump on the back to equal the blow that she had dealt her husband. "Greet the lady and gentleman in a proper manner, child! Do you want them to think I didn't raise you right?"

The thump was followed by a shove as further incentive toward the meeting. The girl stepped forward but didn't lift her head to look either Freddie or Evangeline in the eye. "Pleased to make your acquaintance." She bobbed a lopsided curtsy and scuttled aside.

Unruffled by this awkward display, Mrs. O'Malley then propelled forward two boys of about five who had taken refuge behind her skirts to stare up in safety at the strangers. "And these two are my youngest," she said with a glimmer of maternal pride. "Born only a year apart, they were." She nudged the boys forward and bent down to whisper to one of them, "Michael, take your hand out of your mouth, and shake hands with the lady and gentleman."

To Freddie's everlasting gratitude, the child couldn't be made to comply. Eventually, the two boys were allowed to resume their original positions behind their mother's copious skirts.

✳✳✳

The introductions having been completed, Mrs. O'Malley kept still and allowed Reverend Schultz to begin the service. Evangeline chose to ignore the proceedings and scrutinized the O'Malleys instead. Mrs. O'Malley had already impressed her as energetic and overbearing with a strong penchant for personal drama. In contrast, her husband was withdrawn. Evangeline peered sideways under her hat brim to get a better look at him. He didn't exhibit any signs of grief, though it would have been difficult to guess his state of mind under any circumstances. He hardly seemed the sort of person to encourage an emotional confidence from anyone or offer one in return. Elsa had said he occasionally drank. Seeing the man in person, Evangeline was prepared to ignore the word "occasionally." His face hadn't made the acquaintance of a razor for at least two days, and there were dark circles under his eyes. His wife outweighed him by more than 100 pounds, though how she managed to attain such majestic proportions on the meager wages her family and the Bauers brought home was something of a mystery. Elsa had told Evangeline that her landlady didn't work, being content to order the affairs of her household from a seated position in her cramped, dark parlor.

The little boys were of less interest to Evangeline than the young girl who stood to her right. The child was small for her age. Her hair was thin and mouse-colored, and her complexion unnaturally pale. The overall impression was of something so ethereal that Evangeline felt she was standing beside a ghost rather than a girl of flesh and blood. As she looked more closely, she noticed that the child was crying. Since Patsy didn't seem to share her mother's taste for drama, Evangeline could only conclude that her grief was sincere. In a spontaneous gesture of sympathy, Evangeline put her arm around the girl's narrow shoulders. For the first time, Patsy looked directly at her, startled and ready to pull away.

Evangeline exerted a faint, reassuring pressure on the girl's arm and leaned closer. "It's all right. I know how you feel. I'll miss her, too."

Patsy appeared dumbfounded, not quite sure how to react. Eventually, trust must have won out over shyness since she didn't withdraw. She favored Evangeline with a hesitant half-smile through her tears. The two stood together, sharing a melancholy silence for the remainder of the ceremony.

After the casket had been lowered into the ground and the official ban on speech was lifted, Mrs. O'Malley began a new verbal torrent. "How sad a day this is, and a sad day for our house too. To be left destitute, just destitute, Miss LeClair!"

"Oh, surely not destitute, Mrs. O'Malley."

"Yes, destitute, I say again, Miss LeClair. Both Franz and Elsa gone. What will become of us now?"

"There will be other boarders, no doubt, Mrs. O'Malley. You will be able to rent your rooms again." Evangeline tried to reassure the woman and extricate herself at the same time.

"But when, Miss LeClair? I ask you, when? Times are hard. Money is harder still to come by."

Realizing the precedent she had set by paying for the funeral, Evangeline made the offer she knew was expected. "If I were to pay the amount that the pair of them owed you, plus enough to cover the inconvenience you suffered when these unfortunate events transpired, would that suffice?"

Mrs. O'Malley was all graciousness. "Oh, Miss LeClair. You are too kind. Lord love you, such generosity! I never expected you to come forward like this.

But I cannot accept your kind offer. Sure it is, I cannot. My conscience would never allow it."

"Really, Mrs. O'Malley, you must try to overcome your natural diffidence."

The irony was lost on the landlady. "Lord bless you, miss. You are the soul of generosity. The very soul of it, I say."

Evangeline quickened her pace, hoping that Mrs. O'Malley wouldn't be able to keep up with her. The consequence was that the landlady transferred her attentions to Freddie, who had been lagging behind. She bombarded him with questions about who he was, and what he did for a living, and whether he and the lady were engaged. Although Freddie's eyes implored his friend for assistance, Evangeline used the opportunity to walk ahead of the group and talk to the daughter.

Matching her pace to Patsy's, she struck out in the direction of the cemetery gate. "I'm truly sorry," she began.

Patsy's shyness reasserted itself, and the girl looked down at the ground. "Thank you, ma'am."

"Well, that title is formal enough to make me feel like a dowager of seventy." Evangeline smiled. "My friends call me Engie."

"Oh, I could never do that." The girl shook her head vehemently. "You're a lady. You're one of the gentry."

Evangeline's reply was tongue-in-cheek. "I have it on good authority that America is a democracy, albeit a limited one since women don't have the vote yet. Nevertheless, that means the country doesn't have either a king or an aristocracy."

Patsy was silent, confused about what was required of her. Evangeline clarified the issue. "Well, if you won't call me by my first name, then you may call me Miss Engie. That's close enough to being respectful to ease your conscience, isn't it?"

The girl brightened. "Yes, that's fine. I can call you that."

Evangeline paused, at a loss for what to say next. She had deliberately avoided any reference to the events preceding the funeral. She told herself it was to spare everyone's feelings, glossing over the fact that it spared her own as well.

"So, your mother says you and Elsa were great friends."

Patsy looked sad at the memory. "Very great friends, miss. We shared a room. Our house didn't have enough bedrooms for everyone, so I stayed upstairs with Elsa. Franz had the room across from us."

It occurred to Evangeline that Patsy might be the source of valuable information that could lead to Elsa's killer. She began gently so as not to alarm the girl.

"Patsy, I'd like to talk to you some more about Elsa."

The girl's eyes grew wide with alarm. "I don't dare, miss! Ma already told us that Elsa brought shame on our house and that the less we all said about her, the better!"

"Well, I don't think there's any need to distress your mama with this matter." Evangeline's tone was serene as she accented the second syllable in "mama."

"I... I guess I don't understand."

Evangeline linked her arm through Patsy's in a conspiratorial fashion. "We don't have to tell her, do we?"

Patsy blinked as the idea began to sink in. "But how's that possible? Ma keeps a close watch on me."

Evangeline paused to consider the dilemma. "Saturday is a half-day for factory workers, isn't it?"

"Why, yes. That's so. We quit at noon."

"Very good. Then I shall meet you at your factory gates this Saturday at noon."

"It's the Van Ryn Garment Factory on South Ashland," the girl offered doubtfully.

"Never fear, I'll find it."

"But what about ma? What'll I tell her when I don't come home right away?" The girl glanced over her shoulder nervously. Her mother was still deep in conversation with Freddie, leaning on his arm for support. The poor fellow looked as if he were locked in the embrace of a python.

"I'm sure your factory always needs willing souls to work overtime on Saturdays, doesn't it?"

Evangeline paused, allowing Patsy to digest that stratagem for a moment. "Trust me, child. I'll arrange matters so that no harm will come to you."

Evangeline gave the girl's arm a gentle squeeze. "I should be very grateful for your help." They had nearly reached the exit to the cemetery.

Patsy smiled timidly. "I'd like to talk about Elsa some more. It would help. She was the only one who listened to me, and I miss her."

"Yes, she was a very kind person." Evangeline scowled as a new thought struck her. "I always thought she and Franz were just alike. I don't understand why he isn't here!"

Patsy came to a dead stop as if her feet had taken root. "But, Miss Engie. Didn't they tell you?"

Evangeline regarded her young companion with puzzlement. "Tell me what, my dear?"

Patsy showed signs of increasing agitation. "I'm sorry. Ma thought you knew. We all thought you knew."

"Knew what, Patsy?"

"The police came yesterday night. They took Franz away. They say he killed Elsa."

A blast of wind sent a chill through Evangeline's bones. She began to shiver. "But that's impossible!"

The two were standing just inside the cemetery gates. The rest of the group caught up at that moment and, after another round of handshakes and lamentations, went their separate ways.

As Evangeline and Freddie walked back toward the streetcar line, the fog around them seemed to swirl into the core of Evangeline's brain. She could still hear Patsy's last words, and they drowned out the street sounds, the voices, the horses' hooves. She barely heard Freddie when he said through gritted teeth, "I'm placing you on notice. The next funeral we attend together will be yours."

3 – ANARCHY'S RED HAND

The morning following the funeral, Evangeline found herself in an unusual place—staring through the bars of a cell in Cook County Jail. She stood back as a guard unlocked the door and let her step inside. The room was narrow and deep with a double row of cots lining the wall to her right. Only one prisoner occupied the cell: a man in his early twenties with a blond beard that seemed somehow too long and flowing for someone his age. He sat leaning over the edge of the lower cot, clasping his hands and unclasping them, mutely expressing the contradictions battling in his brain. He didn't look up until Evangeline stood directly before him.

Uttering a cry of surprise, he leaped up when he saw her. "*Fräulein! Mein Gott!* What are you doing here? How is it you came to hear about this?"

Looking him full in the face gave Evangeline a shock. Franz and Elsa Bauer were identical twins. Elsa had been no more than medium height. She would have been described as delicate, in form and in face. To see the girl's features and mannerisms, the same green eyes and flax-colored hair in a masculine form, was disturbing. To now link those same features to such unfortunate events— the sister dead and the brother in prison—only increased the uneasiness of the encounter for her. She finally composed herself enough to reply. "Half the city heard about this before I did, Franz."

"And aren't you afraid to be locked in a cell with a dangerous criminal like me!"

"Is that what you are? I would never have thought it possible when you were taking English classes from me at the settlement. Never would have thought it from the way Elsa talked about you with such pride—her brother, the writer on the German newspaper, the *Arbeiter Zeitung*. She always said her brother was going to be known as a great writer someday."

"Her brother is going to be hanged for murdering her, and there is no one in this city who will doubt that he did it!"

"You are hasty in your judgment, my friend. Perhaps there is one person in this city who is disposed to keep an open mind."

Franz Bauer peered into Evangeline's eyes. "You are willing to listen to the truth?"

She half-smiled. "Why else would I have bothered to come here? As you already know, I rarely take other people's opinions as gospel. I prefer to see for myself."

"Yes, yes, you are *Fräulein Klarheit* still. You want to get to the truth of things." Franz used the nickname he had given Evangeline when taking his first English class from her years before—a German variation of her surname.

She settled herself unceremoniously on the cot and looked up at Franz. Her face was expressionless, detached. "Please begin."

He paced toward the opposite end of the narrow cell, his hands now clasped behind his back, head bent once again in concentration. He turned and seemed on the point of speaking several times, but the memories flooding his consciousness overwhelmed him. He sighed and muttered to himself and cursed and paced until Evangeline walked over to where he stood and put her hand on his shoulder.

"Franz!" She shook him. "This does no one any good! Please try to calm yourself."

He threw his head back and took a deep breath. Evangeline could see that his eyes were red from suppressed tears. "You are right, *Fräulein*, I must try. Even though I believe it is useless, I must try to act as if this nightmare will end, and I will somehow wake up from it." He walked her back to the cot and seated her. Still standing and occasionally pacing fretfully, he began.

"I was foolish to think I could prevent anything. I should have known on the night she was killed. Perhaps there is such a thing as fate—*schicksal*—after all."

Evangeline tried to bring him back to the point. "Facts, Franz, we must deal in facts if anything is to be done. What happened the night Elsa died that put you here?"

"*Ja, ja Fräulein, das ist sehr zutreffend,*" he lapsed into German.

"*Sie müssen Englisch sprechen, Herr Bauer. Sie sind nicht in Deutschland jetzt,*" Evangeline cautioned.

"If I was still in Germany, this would not have happened to me."

"That is what we were speaking about, Franz. What did happen?"

He shook his head as if to clear away the multitude of images crowding his brain and to select the one that mattered. "Elsa, she had been acting strange, *merkwürdig,* for many months before. First singing and humming to herself, laughing too easily—too happy. She would disappear in the evenings sometimes. When I would ask where she had been, she would just smile—a secret smile—*geheimnisvoll.* And so, I began to worry.

"I thought she must be seeing a man—someone she would not be proud to have me know about. One evening when she was out, I searched through her room to see if I could find letters, anything. Instead, I found jewelry, a fine linen handkerchief—expensive things—things I knew she could never afford. I was afraid she was throwing herself away on some rich man who would afterward sweep her from him like so much trash swept into the gutter."

Franz had worked himself up to quite a pitch by now. His face had become more feverish with each sentence. Evangeline was about to say something to quiet him. He seemed to guess her intention and waved his hand in irritation. "No, no, *Fräulein*. You must let me finish!"

She sat back down silently and waited.

He continued, "And then her happy moods became less and less. She sighed to herself when she thought no one was looking. When I would ask her what was wrong, she would shake her head and start to cry. I did not know what to do! Finally, I could stand this waiting and watching no longer. I decided to follow her and come face to face with this man, whoever he was.

"Last Saturday, she left quietly in the evening. She did not think I was in the house when she let herself out. It must have been almost nine o'clock, and she was carrying a small valise. I thought she must be planning to stay away for the night. I followed her. She walked north for many blocks until she was near downtown, and then she found a cab. I kept up on foot and saw the driver let her out by one of the fancy hotels on State Street—the one that is called the Palmer House. I saw her go in by a side door."

"You mean the Ladies' Entrance?" Evangeline referred to the side entrance off of Monroe Street, where unaccompanied ladies could check in without being bothered by men in the front lobby.

"Yes, that was where she went. I walked up and down on the street. I wanted to wait until she was in her room, and I could catch her there with the man she came to meet. The more I walked around and around the hotel, the angrier I came to be. How could she do this? How could she throw herself away like this? Who did this man think he was? Was he so rich that he could treat my sister like a... like a... *straßenmädchen!*" Franz seemed to be reliving the rage of that moment.

Evangeline saw his face twisted by fury. Again, she felt the strange sensation of seeing Elsa's face distorted into a grotesque mask. She would never have believed Franz capable of such violent emotion. But she had never seen him provoked by such a set of circumstances either.

He paced back and forth, scarcely aware of her presence as he resumed his story. "So, after some time, I decided to go in. I walked up to the desk clerk and demanded he should tell me what room my sister was in. He looked at me like I was vermin—*ungeziefer*. Something that had crawled across his lobby floor. He was so polite but with so much disgust. 'I am very sorry, sir. We are not in the habit of disclosing information about our guests to unidentified strangers.'

"'Strangers! I am no stranger!' I was furious. He had such contempt for me. 'I am her brother. Tell me where she is at once!'

"The desk clerk said 'Sir, please lower your voice. There are ladies here. They do not wish to be disturbed by the likes of you!' This made me more and more angry. I wanted above all to smash his face in. Instead, I pounded on the desk with my fists and demanded again to see her. But the desk clerk then refused to speak to me anymore. Instead, he rang the bell and had the bellboys throw me out into the street. I tried to come back in, but each time they pushed me back out. Finally, they said they would call the police unless I left for good.

"There was no hope. I knew that I must wait until she came home herself before I could speak to her. I was too angry, *sehr gestört*. I did not think it would be wise to go home. So, I walked, and walked. For hours, it seemed, I walked. When I finally came back to my right mind, I found myself downtown again. I was close to the *Arbeiter Zeitung* office, so I went in and stayed there until I was calm. I could not think of facing Mrs. O'Malley—of her asking questions. It was bad enough that Elsa was gone. How could I explain where I had been or why?"

He paused for breath. His mood seemed to shift. The rage of a moment before was replaced by grief. His eyes began to fill with tears again. "And then in the papers the next day..." he trailed off.

"So, you didn't see her at all that night?" Evangeline tried to keep a steady rein on her own feelings.

"No, I never saw my Elsa alive again." His rage diffused, he slumped against the back wall.

"Try to keep your mind on the facts, Franz," Evangeline counseled as much to herself as to him. "It will help."

"Yes, yes, facts. What are those... those facts? My sister is dead, and I am accused of murdering her."

"Tell me about how you came to be arrested."

Franz sighed again as if a heavy weight had been placed on his chest. He walked forward toward the bars, leaning against them for support as he continued. "All that day I stayed at the *Arbeiter Zeitung* office trying to decide what to do. Do I go to the police to find out what happened? Do I ask them to release her body for burial? Do I go home? Do I go to *Fräulein* Jane or to you so that someone at Hull House knows? *Ich wüste nicht was ich tun sollte.* I still could not make myself think clearly. One of my friends on the paper, Otto Schüler, he told me to come home and stay with him until I was better. And so, I stayed there for two days more. I knew I had to go home sometime. I would have to... to make arrangements... for Elsa...

"Finally, that evening, Tuesday evening, I went back home. When I came there, the police were waiting for me. They had turned my room inside out. Mrs. O'Malley was crying and asking why did I do it? There was no sense in anything. One of the *polizei* showed me a pocket-knife and said he found it in the back of my dresser drawer."

"What?" Evangeline was shocked.

"Yes, a knife." Franz shook his head in disbelief. "I carry no weapons with me. The knife was not mine. How it came to be there, I cannot say, but they insisted it belonged to me just the same."

"Was there any blood on it?" Evangeline was almost afraid of the answer.

"Yes, there was something on the blade. It maybe was dried blood. Again, I cannot say how."

A sense of doubt crept into Evangeline's brain. For the first time in their conversation, she was uncertain. "Franz, you say that you don't remember anything after you were thrown out of the hotel. That you were walking aimlessly."

He turned to her in amazement and then the shock fueled more anger. "*Gott in Himmel, Fräulein, was sagen sie?* What are you saying! That I killed my own sister, *meine liebe* Elsa, and did not know it?" He beat his fists furiously against the bars.

Evangeline stood up and backed toward the opposite end of the cell, ready to call for help if necessary. "Franz, please," she said in the coolest voice she could muster. "You must be calm. I cannot help you if you go on like this."

"Help me? *Bitte erklaren sie mir, Fräulein Klarheit.* How will you help me?"

Evangeline felt herself momentarily overwhelmed by hopelessness. "I don't know yet! I just don't know. But there must be something that can be done."

Franz threw his head back and laughed bitterly. "Even you do not believe me when I say the knife is not mine!"

His listener steadied her nerves and walked directly up to him. "Franz, look at me!" she commanded.

He obeyed.

"Tell me the truth as you know it. Did you kill your sister?"

Franz returned her gaze steadily. He took a deep breath and answered in a surprisingly even voice. "*Fräulein* LeClair, I did not kill my sister."

Evangeline searched his face for a sign of hesitancy or deceit. She did not find it. At least in his own mind, he was telling the truth. Temporarily suppressing her own doubts, she tried to reassure him. "Then I believe you."

At this Franz sighed. "You believe me, and I am glad, but the judge and the jury, they will not also believe me."

"Franz, you mustn't say such things. Not if you're really innocent."

"The martyrs of Haymarket, *Fräulein Klarheit*, were they not innocent? And yet they were hanged just the same."

Evangeline felt a chill creep down her spine at the memory of the infamous Haymarket Riot. At a rally to support striking railroad workers, someone threw a bomb killing several policemen and onlookers. The organizers of the rally were put on trial for murder. None of them had thrown the bomb, but five were condemned to death and two to life imprisonment because their words were considered an incitement to murder.

"Only two months ago Governor Altgeld pardoned the ones who were left—the men sentenced to life in prison," Evangeline offered uncertainly.

"And Governor Altgeld will never be re-elected again. He is hated everywhere for freeing these men who are called anarchists."

Evangeline made no reply. She felt the truth of Franz's comment.

"Look at me, *Fräulein*. What chance do I have? I am German. I am a newspaper writer for the *Arbeiter Zeitung*, a radical paper, and above all, I am a member of the *Sozialistische Arbeiter Partei*, the New Workers' Party. In the eyes of everybody, all these facts make me an anarchist."

Again, Evangeline couldn't contradict his words. A German writer for a red newspaper who was interested in organizing unions would have been automatically branded an anarchist. Such a man causing a disturbance in a public place the evening before a murder could as easily be branded a killer.

"What is the term they use for this thing that is happening to me?" Franz seemed already to know the answer.

"A witch hunt. It's called a witch hunt, Franz."

"Yes, that is what I thought." Franz smiled ruefully at his visitor. "And so, *Fräulein Klarheit*, I ask you now: *Was kann ich tun?*"

"What to do?" Evangeline echoed his words. "I don't know yet, Franz. I truly don't know. But I won't stand by and do nothing."

The prisoner took her hand and kissed it. "I thank you for trying to help, but even so..." He sighed heavily, "*Ich denke das ich bereits tot bin.*"

Evangeline raised a skeptical eyebrow. "*Ist das so, mein freund? Ich denke nicht.* You give up hope too easily. You are not dead yet!"

4 – AIDE-DE-CAMP

It was late Friday afternoon, and Frederick Ulysses Simpson was in a buoyant mood. He fairly danced up the walk to Evangeline's front door and knocked with the air of a man who expected to receive a warm welcome. Delphine, Evangeline's housekeeper, answered the door with the air of a woman confronting a tradesman who had forgotten to use the service entrance.

"*Bonjour*, Delphine," Freddie said jovially. Before the housekeeper could translate her scowl into its verbal equivalent, the young man took a note out of his vest pocket and waved it before her eyes. "Do you know what this is?" He paused for effect. "*Non?* Well then, let me tell you. It's an invitation to tea from Miss LeClair. As she so prettily puts it, the honor of my presence is requested at four o'clock. And as you can hear from that monstrosity in the hall behind you, it's chiming the hour even as we speak." He stopped and waited, silently daring Delphine to contradict a direct order from her mistress.

She hesitated a moment, then shrugged and showed Freddie in. Over her shoulder, she called out to Evangeline, "*Ne te déranges pas, ma chérie. C'est seulement le jeune Monsieur Freddie.*" Her accent on the word "*jeune*" made Freddie wince.

He was painfully aware of just how young he looked. Freddie was tall, and still awkward for a man in his late twenties. He would have struck an observer as all elbows and knees with an Adam's apple thrown in for effect. His boyishness was further emphasized by the humiliating profusion of freckles that decorated his clean-shaven face.

Delphine's eyes held a gleam of malicious delight at the young man's discomfort. She spoke English fluently, reserving her French for those moments when she wanted to appear particularly insufferable to someone—in this case Freddie.

Evangeline had just descended the double staircase into the front hall in time to see him arrive. "Ah, there you are. Quite prompt."

Delphine did not appear at all pleased by Evangeline's cordial greeting to her visitor. She had never given up hope that her darling mistress would marry someone suitable and seemed to believe that Freddie, by monopolizing the lady's time, was keeping away more eligible bachelors. Refusing to comprehend the obvious, she asked pointedly, "*Eh bien, ma chérie,* will the young fellow be staying for tea, *vraiment?*"

Freddie made a mental note that at least this time she was insulting him in English. Evangeline answered with great determination. "Yes, Delphine, and bring him some of the special pastries I know you've got hidden in the pantry. We'll be in the small parlor." Delphine sighed, nodded, and disappeared without further comment.

Given the scale of Evangeline's home, the word "small" seemed inappropriate when applied to any room in the house with the exception of the coal bin. The couple proceeded to the imposing parlor at the front of the house. Despite its heavy draperies and overstuffed upholstery, the room managed to look inviting bathed in the sun's late afternoon rays.

Even Delphine's inhospitable behavior couldn't dampen Freddie's spirits at the invitation. He seated himself comfortably in a purple velvet armchair to one side of the tea table. "I must say, I really feel honored, Engie."

His hostess smiled as she seated herself on the loveseat. Her voice sounded almost apologetic. "It was the least I could do after your ordeal two days ago."

Freddie basked in the glow of her approval. "Only too glad to lend you moral support in your time of need, Engie. I'd do it again in a trice."

"You don't know how glad I am to hear you say that, Freddie." The lady looked at her companion pointedly, a small smile playing about her lips.

Something in her tone alerted the young man to danger, but at that moment Delphine entered carrying a tray. She set down the tea things with a thump and departed, allowing Evangeline to serve as hostess. Because this was a gentleman's tea, the fare consisted of items a bit more substantial than watercress sandwiches. The lady of the house plied her guest with walnut mayonnaise sandwiches and chicken salad. Sweets included ice-cold coffee jelly with whipped cream, seed cake, and lemon gingerbread. While Freddie was busy consuming these delicacies, Evangeline poured tea and chatted amiably about the horrible Mrs. O'Malley.

As Freddie sat digesting, his benign mood undiminished, he commented, "You know, it's funny. The last time you invited me to tea was when you were drumming up money for the Ladies' Charitable Auxiliary, and you wanted me to make a contribution."

"Did I really?" Evangeline's face expressed mock surprise. "How cold-blooded of me to turn a social occasion to such a nefarious purpose." The half-smile played about her lips once more.

Freddie caught his breath abruptly, feeling the same sensation as a man who has just stepped into a bear trap. "Oh no! Not again!"

21

Evangeline laughed demurely. "Freddie, calm down. It's not as bad as all that. I don't want any money from you, but I did want to talk to you about something—something very important."

"Ye gods, what is it this time?"

Her tone shifted abruptly from flirtatious to grave. "It's not only important; it's deadly serious."

Freddie eyed her skeptically.

Evangeline stood up and walked toward the north window. "I went to see Franz Bauer in jail yesterday."

"You did what! You went to see a murderer without telling me? Without telling anyone?"

"I didn't think I was in any danger. I had to see for myself. A man is supposed to be innocent until proven guilty."

"Innocent! Did you read yesterday's paper? They found the murder weapon in his room, with traces of blood on it." The words tumbled out of Freddie's mouth so quickly they tripped over one another.

"He told me the knife wasn't his."

"Well, of course, he'd say that! He'll hang straightaway if he admits it was."

Evangeline turned to gaze directly at her friend. "I don't believe he was lying about the weapon, Freddie. He told me he couldn't remember what happened that night."

Freddie opened his mouth in protest. Evangeline stilled him by raising her hand. "I'm not sure either, Freddie. He's convinced he wandered around the city all night. It's possible he doesn't remember what he did. He was nearly hysterical when I saw him, and that was several days after the murder. He may have been out of his head. I'm sure of his sincerity. I just don't know about his innocence. Either way, finding a weapon in his dresser drawer looks a little too pat to me."

The wind had been taken out of Freddie's sails. He trusted Evangeline's judgment enough at least to consider the matter from a new angle. "What you're saying is that the police planted the weapon."

"Yes, and I can think of at least two reasons why they would. I'm sure there's been pressure from any number of ranking citizens to find the murderer quickly and get this matter out of the papers as soon as possible. And..." she trailed off, shaking her head.

"And?" Freddie sat forward in his chair and craned his neck to follow Evangeline's movements around the room.

"Franz Bauer writes for the *Arbeiter Zeitung*, and he's a member of the *Sozialistische Arbeiter Partei*."

"He's an anarchist!" Freddie spat out the word as if it were a curse.

"There's no proof that he's plotting to plant a bomb in city hall! There's only proof that he's a hot-headed young man who tried to save his sister from ruining her life!"

"Tried to save her life by causing a scene in the hotel right before she died!"

"He says he never got past the lobby."

Freddie stopped short and mentally calculated the odds weighed against Franz. "Well, if what he says is true, then he'll be executed for being the wrong sort of person in the wrong place at the wrong time."

Evangeline was pacing to the far end of the room. Without looking over her shoulder, she said softly, "No matter what doubts you have about him, even the doubts I have about him, someone has to give him a chance. Someone has to look farther afield for an answer. We have to try, Freddie. We have to do something."

The young man stared at her in disbelief. "What are you saying? That you want to go gallivanting around the city collecting clues like some detective for hire. You have no idea how to go about it. Neither do I. What he needs is a good lawyer! Maybe I can get a senior partner from my firm to help."

Evangeline threw back her head and laughed bitterly. "A member of your firm? Oh, that is amusing! With the clientele they usually defend. If Simpson & Austin were to act as legal counsel to a known anarchist, their wealthy patrons would desert them like rats abandoning a sinking ship. Besides," she hesitated for a moment, "did having a good lawyer help Albert Parsons?"

The analogy gave Freddie pause. Parsons had been one of the conspirators executed after the Haymarket Riot.

"The only way we can help Franz is to produce a stronger set of facts pointing to another suspect. And since the police already think they've found the guilty man, they're unlikely to lend us any help."

Evangeline crossed the room to stand directly in front of her friend's chair. "Freddie, don't you see? We're in the best position of all to find out the truth. We can talk to people who would never consider going to the police. At the funeral, I spoke to Patsy O'Malley. I won enough of her confidence that she agreed to meet me on Saturday to talk about Elsa. Do you think she would have uttered so much as a peep if a man in a blue uniform with a billy club came knocking on her door?"

Freddie gazed up at her a moment, considering his reply. "Well, if you're so good at winning trust from the reticent, what do you need me for?"

She sat down on the ottoman next to his chair and took one of his hands in both her own. "Because, my dear friend, you can go places where I can't. If I were to walk into a police station and ask to speak to the officer who first saw the body, do you think something like that would go unnoticed? We need to be discreet and to make ourselves as inconspicuous as possible while we're conducting this investigation."

Freddie recoiled and sat upright in his chair. "First of all, there is no 'we' here. Second, there is no 'investigation.' You're starting to sound like a detective already. If you're looking for employment, you can apply to the Pinkertons. They've been known to hire female agents, though God only knows why!"

Evangeline was undeterred. She gently took Freddie's hand back again. "Do you think I'm doing this just for me?"

"No, of course not." He relented slightly. "I know you care about Elsa and her brother, and you want to see justice done."

"It isn't only that." Evangeline smiled one of her mysterious smiles. "I want to do this because of you, too."

"What?" She had succeeded again in losing him down one of the side passages of her logic.

"Don't you think I know what's more important to you than anything else in the world?"

He was about to reply, "I didn't realize you knew how much you matter to me," but caught himself in time. He didn't want to give her the satisfaction.

She continued, "I know you don't want to be a lawyer. You want to be a reporter."

"Oh, yes, that too." The words were out before he could stop himself.

"What?" For the first time, she looked puzzled herself.

"Never mind," he said hastily. "Go on. I'm listening."

"Well, think about it from this perspective. What would it require for your friends at the Tribune to sit up and take notice of you?"

"Maybe if I died on their doorstep before fetching their lunches for them." He sighed gustily.

"No, Freddie. I'm serious. Do pay attention. What if you were able to bring them an exclusive story?"

Freddie's mental clouds were evaporating quickly. He leaned forward in his chair. "You mean..."

Evangeline smiled. "Exactly! We get all the facts that none of the other papers bothered to ferret out. If Franz didn't do it, then we'll be the only ones able to prove who did. You tell the *Tribune* that you have all the information to provide a front-page story that will beat out all the other papers in town. But the price..." she stopped for effect.

"Yes? Yes?" Freddie was already swept away by the vision.

"The price is that they have to hire you and let you write the story."

Freddie's eyes were dancing with excitement. "Engie, I could kiss you!" Still intoxicated with the vision of his story on the front page of the Tribune, he offered no further resistance to following where she led.

"It seems to me that we have to find some indirect way of learning what the police already know. I mean the part that didn't appear in the papers."

"I suppose I could pick up the trail in the newsroom. The boys there always know far more than ever makes the printed page."

"Excellent! Who will you talk to first?"

"I could start with Bill Mason. He's a friend of mine, and he covered the murder right after it happened. But in order to get anything out of him, I know it's going to mean buying him lunch and probably carrying it back to his desk for him, too!" Freddie found it hard to keep his voice from whining.

"Whatever it takes, Freddie, the effort will be well worth it if we can find anything that may be of use to us." Evangeline was pacing again, her body matching the restless activity of her mind. "While you're following up on that, I need to start making inquiries at Hull House. Maybe some of my students remember something. If I'm very lucky, one of the girls there might even be able to point me in the direction of a suspicious character."

"That is, if you don't frighten her into a fainting fit first." Freddie could imagine Evangeline cutting a swathe through Hull House like Sherman through Atlanta on his march to the sea.

Evangeline wheeled around to face him. "Don't be ridiculous! This calls for tact. I am perfectly able to act with subtlety when I need to. If I weren't capable of finesse, do you think I would have been able to lure you into my parlor? Yet there you sit, only minutes ago blissfully nibbling lemon gingerbread when two days ago you would just as blissfully have paid someone to do me in."

Freddie allowed himself to smile at his own inconsistency. "All right, I concede the point. You're the very mistress of manipulation. The queen of coquetry. Perhaps I find it easy to forget your subtlety since you so rarely practice it on me. Instead, I tend to be the recipient of blunt sarcasm."

"*Mon pauvre petit*, how you have suffered at my hands!" Her voice was dripping with mock sympathy.

"You see, you're doing it again," Freddie squeaked in outrage.

"Calm down, dear boy. You know I reserve bluntness for my friends. I am only courteous to people I care nothing about."

"Using that particular yardstick of intimacy, I must be a tremendous favorite of yours."

Evangeline smiled warmly at him, her eyes twinkling. "You know you are. Stop being dramatic! Can you think of anyone else I would have shared this plan with?"

Freddie could think of nothing clever to say. He was grasping at the emotional straw of being Evangeline's favorite. When he shook himself out of this ephemeral dream, he realized that both her pacing and her talking had started again.

At that moment, the door, which had been left slightly open, seemed to move of its own accord—the hinges creaking slightly. Freddie looked for some explanation other than a supernatural manifestation and saw, near the floor, a mass of fur nudging the door open further. It was the resident god of the hearth, Evangeline's cat.

At the sight of him, the lady clapped her hands together in delight. "*Ah, mon cher petit cœur. Viens ici.*" At the sound of her voice, the cat rubbed his chin happily against the door and then strolled across the room to repeat the same affectionate gesture against his mistress' ankles. Evangeline laughed and picked up the monstrous beast, a huge orange tabby with a head as big as Freddie's fist. She held the cat up so the two were nose to nose. "*Ah, Monsieur Beauvoir, comment va-t-il? Comment va-t-il, mon vieux?*"

Freddie was nauseated by this lavish display of affection. "Look, I'm sure if he understands any language at all, it's English. Is this a domestic conspiracy? First Delphine, and now you. I know that your people came from Quebec, but if you insist on practicing this blatant Francophilia, maybe you all should have stayed there!"

Ignoring the comment, Evangeline seated herself and placed the cat on her lap. She whispered in its ear, "*Je pense qu'il est jaloux, Monsieur Beau.*" The cat meowed softly as if in agreement. By now he was purring and flexing his paws in a state of bliss.

Freddie was confronted by, not one, but two pair of unblinking eyes staring at him simultaneously. Evangeline continued, "My Francophilia notwithstanding, *calme toi-même, mon ami.* I will confine myself to English for the balance of the conversation. Will that appease you?"

Freddie nodded, somewhat mollified. "Anyway, I don't understand what you see in that creature. You treat him better than you treat any man."

Evangeline laughed at Freddie's pique. "Because, unlike all the human members of the male gender with whom I have the misfortune to be acquainted, he doesn't try to tell me what to do or what to think. He is a most sagacious fellow in his way. He doesn't automatically assume that because nature fitted him with a slightly different anatomy from the female sex, she also fitted him with a superior brain."

"Hmmphhh!" was Freddie's eloquent reply. Monsieur Beau, apparently feeling himself vindicated by Evangeline's comment, jumped to the floor and left the room.

The battle of the sexes was cut short when Delphine appeared again at the door. Her face held an unaccountable look of triumph. "*Ma chérie*, there is another gentleman who has come to see you." She moved aside to let the visitor pass. "It is Monsieur Blackthorne."

Jonathan Blackthorne was, with the exception of Freddie, the most tenacious of Evangeline's admirers. He was Delphine's clear favorite in terms of a suitable match for her mistress since he was closer to Evangeline's own age and came from a prominent Lake Forest family. Unlike Freddie, he had managed to succeed at a respectable career with the Merchant's Bank & Trust, one of the city's largest financial institutions.

The man himself also stood in physical contrast to his rival. Both were tall, but there the similarity ended. Jonathan was dark-haired with a saturnine complexion. His eyes had always reminded Freddie of the lake after a January freeze. His features were coarse, but his manners refined enough to win him favor with the ladies. In this regard, Evangeline was no exception. She seemed pleased to see him and held out her hand in welcome.

"Jonathan, what a surprise!"

He strode across the room and bent to kiss her hand, holding it for several seconds before releasing it. "Why should you be surprised, Engie?" His voice was barely above a whisper. "You're always in my thoughts. It was a small matter to convert thought to action."

Evangeline laughed. "I compliment you on your magical powers. I had no idea you could make yourself materialize so easily."

Freddie, who had managed to achieve invisibility during this exchange, cleared his throat in annoyance. Blackthorne turned slowly to acknowledge him. "Hello, Simpson, how are you?" The question carried no hint of warmth. "Shouldn't you be in the city? It is a workday, after all."

"I'm fine." Freddie's tone was equally surly. "I was invited to tea. But while we're on the subject, I might hold you to a similar account of your presence here."

Blackthorne smiled slightly, whether in annoyance or in pleasure because he had flustered Freddie would have been hard to tell. He paused before replying since he was the sort of man who always chose his words carefully and always gave the impression of having suppressed more than half of what he was thinking. "I came up to spend the weekend with Mother and Father, but I wanted to stop in to say hello before going there. Do you object?"

"Why would I object?" Freddie affected a note of carelessness. Unfortunately, he had always been a poor liar.

Delphine, who had been leaning in the doorway, offered, "*Ma chérie*, shall I fetch the young gentleman's hat and coat? It's getting dark, and I'm sure his *maman* must be looking for him by now."

Freddie folded his arms resolutely. "Not just yet, Delphine, if you please. I'll be staying a while."

Evangeline gave her housekeeper a pained look. "That will be all for now, thank you."

Delphine rolled her eyes as if to say, "Well, I tried," and exited the room.

Blackthorne turned to fix his gaze on Evangeline. "My visit also had another object, *ma belle*. I wanted to see if I might persuade you to accompany me to the Columbian Exposition before it closes at the end of the month."

"Ah yes, the World's Fair. The attendance count each day seems to be climbing. It looks as if everyone from the street sweepers to the mayor himself are all making one final attempt to experience the ninth wonder of the world before it disappears forever."

Freddie chimed in. "Be as contemptuous as you like, Engie, but the World's Fair has brought a lot of business to the city—put us on the map, so to speak. Visitors from all over the world now think of Chicago as a cultured metropolis."

Evangeline motioned Blackthorne toward a chair and then stared irritably at Freddie. "You don't find anything ironic in your last statement, do you?"

Freddie gave his best look of serious concentration—a gesture he always used to buy time when he was trying to think of something clever to say after having lost Evangeline's line of reasoning.

Evangeline waited a suitable interval to allow him to redeem himself. Seeing the cause was hopeless, she continued, "I read somewhere that the Exposition took two years to construct at an expense of forty-six million dollars. Presumably, its purpose was to call attention to the refinement of this city. But don't you see just how false that display of refinement is? The buildings are a facade. They're made of some sort of papier-mâché substance, spray-painted white to look like marble. They stand for six months, and then everything is to be torn down because nothing was built to last."

Evangeline paused in her diatribe long enough to pour Blackthorne a cup of tea. He seemed amused at the vehemence of her opinion but took the proffered cup without comment.

"People love spectacle, Engie," Freddie replied. "It's just human nature."

Evangeline smiled slightly, if somewhat bitterly. "In the meantime, children in this city go to work almost before they're old enough to walk. If a man gets sick, he loses his job, and there are fifty others ready to take his place at twenty cents an hour. And those who've profited by this arrangement, the factory owners, are the very men responsible for the Exposition. As what, I'd like to know? A monument to their hypocrisy? The money might have been better spent on wage increases."

"You may be right. But the world's as it is, and most of the fortunes that have been built in this city, your family's as well as mine, have been won at the expense of someone else."

"That doesn't make exploitation right or an appropriate model for emulation," Evangeline shot back primly. "Besides, my father never owned a factory."

Blackthorne shifted uneasily in his chair as the conversation took a more heated turn. He seemed to think it wise to keep his opinion to himself and spent an unusual amount of time stirring sugar into his teacup. The two combatants barely took any notice.

"And aren't you indulging yourself in the belief that building a railroad is somehow exempt from commercial necessity and corruption?" Freddie retorted.

Evangeline was silent. She found herself in the morally tenuous position of having benefited from a set of conditions that she deplored. Now that she had already painted herself into a philosophical corner, she chose the most obvious method to free herself. She equivocated. "I believe that for a man engaged in industry, my father was relatively honest. I also believe that he was willing to settle for being comfortably well-off instead of continuing to accumulate wealth as his sole end in life, no matter who was hurt in the process."

Freddie sighed. "I'm not suggesting your father was a robber baron, Engie. I think he was a good man, too. I'm just pointing out that, carried to an extreme, your plans for social reform may require you to sacrifice this ivy-covered, red-brick mansion of yours, not to mention your townhouse in the city, and move down to Polk Street with the immigrant factory workers."

Evangeline looked away, somewhat abashed by the turn the conversation had taken. "I do what I can to help at Hull House, Freddie. You know I do. It's not so much I mind that fortunes are built, or that inequities exist. I'm fatalistic enough to believe they always will. I just wish there was less pretense in all of it. I just wish the 'whited sepulchers' of this city stopped believing that by covering plaster facades with spray paint, they're also covering a multitude of sins."

She paused a moment, pensively looking off into space. A vague smile began to form as she refocused her attention on the young man seated across from her. "As for selling everything I have and giving it all to the poor... well, everybody knows I'm eccentric, but I'm certainly not that crazy."

Apparently satisfied that the verbal storm had spent itself, Blackthorne ventured to speak at last. "Given your feelings on the subject of the World's Fair, Engie, I withdraw my request. At least promise me the first dance at the Hunt Club Ball next Saturday."

Realizing that her strong opinion about the exposition might have been interpreted as a graceless refusal of his invitation, Evangeline tried to soothe what she presumed were Blackthorne's injured feelings. "Why, of course. How could I say no? Especially since you've asked so charmingly. You may rest assured that yours will be the first name written on my dance card." Freddie was disgusted by her uncharacteristic display of graciousness.

Blackthorne laughed and placed his hand over his heart. "Now, my life is complete."

To Freddie's continued discomfort, Evangeline further tried to make amends. "But where are my manners? I've ignored you shamefully. Why don't you come and sit by me?" She patted the seat next to her invitingly. "Can I offer you another cup of tea?"

Seemingly overcome with pleasure by the honor thus conferred, Blackthorne wasted no time in seating himself on the loveseat beside Evangeline and helping himself to some walnut mayonnaise sandwiches.

The little party remained silent a few seconds before the new arrival tentatively started the conversation in a different direction. "You've been well, then?"

"Yes, fine, thank you." Evangeline offered Blackthorne a plate of seed cake.

"Oh, I thought perhaps with Simpson being here, that you might have been in need of some sort of assistance..."

"No." Evangeline smiled engagingly. "It was nothing like that. I only wanted to thank him for attending a funeral with me."

"A funeral! Good God! No more of your family, I hope!"

"No, no, nothing like that..." Evangeline hesitated. "It was just... just someone I rather considered a friend."

"Please allow me to offer my condolences, Engie. Was it anyone I know?"

"I hardly think so." Freddie cut in from the other side of the tea table. "It was one of Evangeline's students at Hull House. Not the sort of person you'd be likely to meet. It was the girl who was found dead last weekend at the Palmer House."

"Really! The one who was murdered?"

"Do you know of any young girls found dead there last weekend of natural causes?"

Blackthorne ignored the comment. "I had no idea you were on close terms with any of your students, Engie. How well did you know her?"

Freddie cut in again. "She was a particular favorite. Great things were expected of her."

"Great things?" Blackthorne echoed.

"I'm perfectly able to answer questions for myself, Freddie," Evangeline shot back irritably. Freddie knew the danger of antagonizing her when her voice reached that particular pitch, and so he remained still.

"She showed special promise, and I had some hope of moving her into better employment in time."

"I see..." Blackthorne digested that fact for a full minute. "But surely, given the circumstances in which she was found, I would hardly consider her a worthy object for your charity."

Evangeline's temper flared. "And what right have you to judge a girl you've never met? A murdered person is generally considered the victim, not the perpetrator, of a crime."

Looking flustered, Blackthorne tried to repair the damage his words had caused. "Engie, you must forgive me. I didn't mean—"

She cut in recklessly, "And no one has a right to say anything until after we've positively identified the murderer!"

Freddie rolled his eyes and said *sotto voce*, "Well, that's done it, old girl. The cat's completely out of the bag now."

Blackthorne's dark complexion became pallid with shock. He stared at her speechless for several seconds. "I'm afraid I don't understand. Someone's already been arrested for the crime. Her own brother, in fact."

"I'm not convinced that he's the only possible suspect. I went to speak to him to hear his side of things."

Blackthorne's pallor became a shade chalkier. "Did I understand you correctly? You went to visit a man in prison? A man very likely to be indicted for murder?"

"Not to worry, old man. I'm always nearby to protect her from getting into some really awful scrape."

Blackthorne contemplated Freddie as if he were a particularly loathsome insect. "You have no idea how much comfort that thought gives me." He made scant attempt to conceal the sarcasm in his voice. Standing up decisively, he towered over Evangeline. "Forgive me for being so blunt, my dear, but this was an ill-considered thing to do. You gave no thought to what sort of danger you might have been facing by pursuing this mad scheme of yours!"

"On the contrary," Freddie retorted, "you haven't known her as long as I have. You have no idea what she's capable of when she's decided on a really mad scheme. This was one of her tamer plans."

Apparently having ventured into deeper waters than she intended, Evangeline retreated from the topic. "Oh, Jonathan, you mustn't carry on so. No harm was done. I merely needed to satisfy my curiosity." She affected a brittle laugh.

The expression on Blackthorne's face didn't change. "And on the basis of your discussion with this man, you believe him to be innocent?"

Evangeline fell back a bit more. "Well, I'm not sure of that either, but it seems someone ought to look into the matter further."

Blackthorne persisted. "I take it that this 'someone' would be you and Simpson?"

Evangeline's shrug was a calculated gesture of nonchalance. "Well, that is the plan, yes. But at this point, the likelihood of success appears about as promising as finding a needle in a haystack."

"Indeed." Blackthorne never took his eyes away from her face. His own face had become a mask. "You must keep me posted of your progress."

She laughed to break the tension. "This conversation has become entirely too morbid, not at all fit matter for a parlor at teatime. Do sit down here beside me and tell me all the gossip from town instead." She reached up, inviting him to take her hand.

Blackthorne made no move to touch her. "No, I am obliged to you, but I mustn't stay any longer." He turned abruptly toward the door. "It's time I paid my respects at home, anyway." With that, he made a hasty departure and left his rival in possession of the field.

Freddie yawned lazily. "If you keep on at this rate, Engie, the only ones who won't know our plan are the police and your imaginary murderer."

"Oh, fiddlesticks, Freddie! I managed to salvage things just in time, didn't I? Besides, Jonathan is harmless."

5 – THE CAGED SPARROW

The factory whistle shrieked promptly at noon on Saturday. Unlike every other day of the week, on Saturday, noon meant quitting time. The gates of the Van Ryn Garment Factory opened to disgorge an assortment of women and girls all fluttering away like pigeons released from a coop. Evangeline observed them from a carriage across the street. The flock dispersed quickly, unwilling to spend a minute longer than the requisite fifty-five hours per week on company grounds. As the crowd thinned, Evangeline searched the remaining faces for Patsy. She had nearly given up hope of finding her when she noticed one small figure straggling last through the gate.

Unlike her coworkers, Patsy seemed to be dawdling as if she were waiting to meet someone. Evangeline motioned to her driver to walk across the street and collect the girl. Patsy stood near the gate, shifting her weight uncertainly from one leg to the other. She stepped back a few paces when she saw the strange man approaching her.

Evangeline watched the pantomime as it unfolded—Patsy backing away, the man raising his hand, motioning her to wait. When he got closer to her, he bent down to whisper something, probably Evangeline's name because Patsy immediately smiled and nodded. The two walked across the street to the carriage where Evangeline sat.

"Forgive me for not meeting you personally, my dear," Evangeline said as Patsy climbed in and sat opposite her. "But I wanted to be as discreet as possible. That's why I had Jack bring me around in the carriage. In case you haven't been formally introduced, Patsy, the disreputable fellow who just accosted you is Jack. Today he's playing the role of driver, but he's usually the caretaker of my townhouse. Jack, say hello to the young lady."

"Hello, little miss. Pleased to make your acquaintance." Jack tipped his hat to Patsy and flashed a smile that revealed a gold front tooth before he shut the door of the brougham and climbed back up into the driver's seat. Without any further instruction, he turned the horse about in a northerly direction and proceeded up the street.

Evangeline smiled in secret amusement at Patsy's sense of awe. The girl was no doubt agog at the wonder of being seated in a fine carriage with soft leather seats and at having been called "Miss" by someone who was an official caretaker of a townhouse.

"The need for discretion continues, Patsy. That's why I am whisking you away in a covered vehicle to a place where we can talk without fear of discovery."

Patsy looked breathless with excitement at the prospect of a ride to some mysterious destination. She seemed to have momentarily forgotten the consequences of her mother's wrath if her escapade were ever discovered.

"That was very clever of you to come out of the factory last. I had instructed Jack to intercept you if you came out early and to pretend to detain you by asking for directions until all your companions had left. That would have prevented anyone from taking too much notice of your movements."

Patsy smiled broadly. "I told my friends that the forelady wanted to talk to me about overtime, and I sent them on ahead. That way, if Ma hunts one of them down and asks where I'm at, they'll tell her I'm still at work."

"I'm sure your mama would be pleased at the prospect of your working longer hours since she, herself, doesn't contribute to the family income." Evangeline tried to keep an edge of irony out of her voice, but her emphasis on the second syllable of "mama" had become pronounced.

The irony was lost on Patsy whose reply was solemn, "Oh, yes. With Elsa and Franz gone, Ma is really worried about money now. It's just me and Pa and..." Patsy hesitated. "And he doesn't work regular hours much. Just yesterday Ma was wringing her hands and saying she doesn't know what will become of us without those extra paychecks. She said she would be willing to make... to make..." Patsy knit her brows trying to recall her mother's exact words. "'The ultimate sacrifice.' That was it. The 'ultimate sacrifice' was how she put it. She said she'd be willing to go to work herself, but with her being so busy running the affairs of the household and all, she doesn't see how she could do it."

"The affairs to be ordered in your little home must be time-consuming indeed."

Again, the irony of the statement was lost on Patsy. "It must be if Ma says so. Anyway, I tried to think of something to help. I asked her why didn't she just take in washing like Mrs. O'Neal down the street? That way she could stay home and keep an eye on the boys and still bring in some money for the family."

"What a practical suggestion. And what did your mama say to that?"

Patsy's lips drew downward as if she were trying to fathom an extremely complicated puzzle. "Well, at first she couldn't say anything because she lost her breath and she had to keep taking big gulps of air. Then she boxed me on the ear and told me to keep such outlandish notions to myself."

"I see." Evangeline struggled to keep from laughing outright. After she had subdued her rebellious facial muscles, she changed the subject. "Can you guess where we're going, Patsy?"

"Why, no. Indeed, I can't, miss."

"Look out the window."

By now, the scenery had shifted from the feudal strongholds of the factory district to something less grim but equally commercial. The street they were traveling was swarming with carriages, pedestrians, streetcars, delivery wagons, and the cries of newsboys on every corner.

"Do you know where you are now?" Evangeline prompted.

Patsy's eyes were round with wonder. "No, I surely don't, Miss Engie. I've never seen a place like this before."

"Have you never heard of State Street?"

"Oh!" Patsy gasped. "Is that what this place is? I've heard about it, but I never saw it before. It's like a fairy tale!"

Evangeline was amused at Patsy's lyrical description of a place that was less than two miles from the slum where she lived. "Well, it's not the Champs Elysees, but it will do very well for a start."

Patsy was leaning halfway out the carriage, intent on absorbing every passing sight.

Evangeline thought to herself that anyone traveling downtown at midday on a Saturday must either be a fool or have a serious purpose in mind. The congestion of the traffic on the city's busiest street made the carriage's progress painfully slow. Even though the day was sunny, the air was murky from the smoke of the city's coal-burning furnaces. Everyone on the sidewalk, however, seemed to take the noise, smoke, and elbowing as a matter of course. Pedestrians bustled along from store to store, all the while dodging streetcars, horses, and each other.

Patsy's eyes grew even rounder. She bounced from one side of the carriage to the other like an eager spaniel puppy, apparently afraid that if she confined herself to a single side, she might miss something significant on the other. She pointed out mothers with perambulators inching along the overcrowded sidewalk, businessmen nattily dressed in gray flannel and bowler hats, tradesman in shirt sleeves, and the ever-present street sweepers in white uniforms and caps.

"Oh, look at that lady, Miss Engie! Have you ever seen a hat like that before!" The girl gestured toward a woman wearing a creation topped by a monstrous ostrich plume.

Evangeline laughed. "Unfortunately, I have, my dear, and too frequently to suit my taste."

Patsy bounced back to the other window. She presented a running commentary to Evangeline, prefacing every sentence by "Oh, just look at that!"

At the corner of State and Madison, a tangle of traffic stopped Evangeline's carriage. She poked her head out of the window to assess the problem. A policeman was blowing his whistle and trying to redirect traffic around a streetcar that had stalled right in the middle of the intersection.

Evangeline called up to Jack, "Let us out here. We'll walk the rest of the way. Meet us at the back entrance to Field's at two o'clock sharp."

"Yes, miss," the coachman answered wryly. "Though with this mess, it could take me just that long to make the corner of Wabash and Washington."

"I rely on your resourcefulness." Evangeline smiled encouragingly as he helped the two alight.

Jack tipped his hat in a gesture that was half respectful and half playful before climbing back up to his seat.

It was only an additional block to the imposing edifice that was the Field and Leiter Department Store, known as Field's for short. The store took up a full city block and reached a height of six stories. Evangeline frequently shopped at the emporium since it contained everything from a meat market to a beauty parlor with all manner of merchandise in-between. While the store had originally catered to the well-to-do, Messrs. Field and Leiter had wisely established a wholesale market so that the store could lure customers from every class to buy its wares. With the additional attraction of the World's Fair to spur business, Field's had become a landmark that foreign visitors had to see before they could consider their tour of Chicago complete.

Evangeline and Patsy finally arrived at their destination, though Evangeline had to keep a close watch over her young charge to be sure they weren't separated by the press of the crowd gawking at the display windows. With Patsy in tow, Evangeline opened the door to Field's main floor and entered the palace of mercantile delights. Patsy stood dumbly at her side. The effect of so much splendor had rendered her speechless. Evangeline took her by the arm to steer her down to the lower level where the restaurant was located.

Patsy followed along, but her head was turned over her shoulder to absorb the endless aisles of ladies' dresses and hats and jewelry on display.

"Mind the stairs," Evangeline cautioned, fearful that in the girl's rapture she might tumble headlong down to the basement.

Patsy focused her attention on the feat of navigation before her. When they had descended without mishap, she exclaimed, "My heavens, Miss Engie, I didn't think there were so many fine things in all the world, much less all collected in one store!"

"I think you'll find, Patsy, that this is just a small sample of what the stores in this city have to offer. Multiply that by the stores of all the cities in this country and in the world, and the quantity becomes more immense than the imagination can fully encompass."

"Ohhhh!" was Patsy's awestruck reply.

The two proceeded into the store's dining room. They were offered menus by a solicitous waiter dressed in black with a napkin slung over his arm. "And what would the ladies have?"

Evangeline was scanning the menu when she looked up and noticed Patsy blushing furiously. The girl stammered, "Miss... Miss Engie..."

Evangeline said to the waiter, "Give us a few more minutes, please."

"Certainly, madame." He bowed and scurried off to wait on another table.

"What is it, Patsy?"

The girl refused to look up. "I'm sorry, but I can't read." Her voice was filled with embarrassment.

"Ah, I see. It's no great matter. Reading is a skill that can easily be acquired, and for the present moment..." she reached across the table to tilt the girl's chin upward so their eyes met, "I'll order for you."

Patsy smiled shyly, apparently trying to overcome her discomfort.

When the waiter returned, Evangeline took command of the situation. "I'll have the chicken pot pie. The young lady will have a roast beef sandwich with mashed potatoes and gravy. Isn't that what you wanted, Patsy?"

"Roast beef..." the girl exhaled the words reverently. Catching herself, she added, "Oh yes, that's right. I'll have that."

"Very good," said the waiter, "and to drink?"

"I'll have tea, preferably Darjeeling, and the young lady will have a glass of milk."

The waiter hastened back to the kitchen to place the order.

After he left, Evangeline asked in a low voice, "Why didn't you learn to read, Patsy? I'm sure Elsa would have taught you. I know that she taught herself with a little help from Hull House."

"She tried to teach me once." The girl seemed disturbed after she let the words escape. "Ma caught us one night working over the alphabet, and she threw the copybook into the stove. She said she didn't want me ruining my eyes over letters like Elsa had done. She said I should save them for the sewing work because I get paid for that."

"I see." Evangeline sighed dejectedly. "And just how long have you been working in a factory, Patsy?"

"Since I was seven. Before that, I used to do piece work at the kitchen table on the sewing that the neighbor ladies brought home each day. I would pull out the bad stitching, and Ma would get paid for each piece that could be resewed the next day."

"How young were you when that started?"

"I can't remember." Patsy sounded puzzled. "It seems like it was that way from the start, but I think I was about four." She smiled uncertainly. "I guess you can't hold a pair of scissors until you're that old, can you?"

"No, I guess not," Evangeline agreed half-heartedly. "I don't suppose there's any likelihood your mama would allow you to go to school?"

The girl's shoulders drooped. "I don't get paid if I go to school."

"Perhaps there's a way that you could." Evangeline smiled cryptically.

"How?" Patsy's face remained bleak.

Evangeline shook out her napkin and resettled it decisively. "I'll speak to your mother and offer her a greater incentive to send you to school than to keep you at the factory. I can be very persuasive when I need to be. My bank book can be even more so." She tapped her chin thoughtfully. "You may tell your mama I will call on her later in the week to collect Elsa's belongings and to discuss a few other matters of importance."

"But..." Patsy seemed on the verge of asking several more questions when their order arrived. Evangeline took some temporary satisfaction in seeing Patsy devour the sandwich filled with thick slabs of roast beef.

"But Miss Engie, why..." Patsy took another mouthful. "Why did we come here if we were supposed to have a secret meeting?"

Evangeline smiled. "Patsy, look around you."

The girl obeyed, still chewing happily. Her eyes wandered toward the couples and families and society matrons all chattering away at nearby tables. She then gave Evangeline a quizzical look.

"The best place to be private, Patsy, is in public. All the people in this room are preoccupied with their own concerns. Have you seen anyone, aside from the waiter, who has taken any notice of us since we walked in?"

"Well, no. I guess not."

"In this store, all classes of society mingle without anyone commenting about it. If you and I were seen together anyplace else, it might draw some attention, but not here—never here."

"Oh, I see." Patsy glanced down self-consciously at the patched sleeve of her frock. "I guess that makes a deal of sense."

"Of course, it does, my young friend. And now to the matter at hand. What can you tell me about Elsa?"

Patsy had finished eating but was picking up every crumb on her plate, intent on leaving nothing behind. "Well..." she began, "I know she had a gentleman friend."

"Did she, indeed?" Evangeline raised an eyebrow. "And who was this fine fellow?"

"I never knew that, miss." Patsy shook her head emphatically. "She never told me. But, I know she went with him to the World's Fair, because he sent her a flower to wear that day—a red silk rose. She showed it to me, and it was the finest piece of silk work I ever saw... with flowers, I mean."

"But surely, Patsy, she had no time for gentlemen. I know she only went to work, to church, and to Hull House."

"Oh, but that's where she met him, Miss Engie, at Hull House."

"What?" Evangeline gasped. Her voice echoed through the room so loudly that other diners turned to regard her with curiosity. Recovering herself, she moderated her pitch. "What on earth do you mean, Patsy?"

"Just what I said. I never lie. It's a sin to lie. Elsa told me she met a gentleman at Hull House who asked her to go to the Fair with him."

"Was this one of the local people who come for classes?"

"No, miss. I don't think so because she said he was a res... a res..."

"A resident..." Evangeline exhaled the word in amazement. "You mean one of the men who volunteer their time to live and work at the settlement?"

"Yes, that was it! He was a resident."

Evangeline sank into deep concentration. "Well, this is certainly a new turn of events."

"Did I say something wrong, Miss Engie?"

"No, my dear." Evangeline reached over to pat the girl's hand reassuringly. "It's just the last thing I would have expected, that's all. Can you remember anything else? Did Elsa describe the man to you?"

"No." Patsy frowned, trying to recollect. "She said she didn't want to say anymore because it was supposed to be a secret. The gentleman asked Elsa to keep it a secret."

"Well, at least that's no surprise."

"Miss?" Patsy looked for further explanation.

"It's of no consequence." Evangeline smiled consolingly. "Do you remember when this rendezvous at the Fair took place?"

"It was before the summer heat set in. I remember because it was so hot by June that people were sleeping out on the sidewalk. It was before that, maybe right after the Fair opened in May."

"And she never told you anything about the man after her excursion?"

Patsy pondered the question. "No, miss, I'm sorry. That's all Elsa ever told me."

"Never mind, dear. You've done very well, and I'm grateful for your assistance." Evangeline opened her handbag and dug around, searching for something. Finally, she withdrew a silver coin and gave it to Patsy.

"I'm sorry you can't spend this. You must promise to keep it until your next payday and add it to your usual earnings, for your overtime this Saturday. Otherwise, your mama may start to ask questions you won't be able to answer. Will you remember that?"

Patsy nodded solemnly as she took the money.

"Please make sure to put it somewhere your mother won't find it until payday."

The girl thought for a moment, then slipped it into the top of her boot.

"I'll put it under the lining of the sole later when I get home."

Evangeline chuckled. "You are a clever girl, Patsy. And now I'd like to show my appreciation in a less monetary form for the risk you've taken in coming here today."

With a quick gesture, Evangeline beckoned the waiter who had been hovering anxiously out of earshot. She motioned him closer and whispered something in his ear.

"Very good, madame." He smiled and glanced at Patsy before bustling back to the kitchen.

"Unfortunately, any other material expression of gratitude might be discovered by your mother and put you in the way of bodily harm."

Patsy waited, silent.

"Therefore, I think this is the best I can do for the time being. It's a pleasure that your mama won't be able to take away from you."

"Miss?"

"Shhhhh." Evangeline put a finger to her lips. "No more questions."

After a few minutes, the waiter returned bearing an enormous dessert and, with a ceremonial flourish, placed the dish before Patsy.

"Thank you," Evangeline said to the waiter. "I believe that's all we'll require." He bowed and disappeared to calculate the bill.

Patsy eyed the dish with a mixture of longing and suspicion. "Miss Engie," she whispered so as not to proclaim her ignorance to the entire room. "What is it?"

"It's an ice cream parfait, child, and your next alphabet lesson. The word is spelled p-a-r-f-a-i-t. Try it. Most young people your age find it quite delightful."

The girl picked up her spoon hesitantly and tried the concoction. After the first mouthful, there was no holding her back. She didn't raise her head from the dish until the entire mountainous confection had been consumed.

Evangeline watched in silence until this gustatory revel was over. Finally, she asked, "I assume you'll tell your mother you've worked without lunch today?"

"Ohhh," the girl moaned. "I'll have to tell her the truth. That I have a stomachache and don't want any dinner."

Evangeline smiled benevolently. "However you arrange matters with your conscience is no concern of mine."

She rose. "And now, my dear, it's two o'clock, and Jack should have managed to travel the two additional blocks to meet us. Time to drop you back at the gates of the honorable Mr. Van Ryn."

Patsy's eyes were shining. "Thank you, Miss Engie. I'll never forget today. It's the finest thing that ever happened to me."

Evangeline looked down at the girl, smiling a bit sadly. "I shall hope, Patsy, that before long many finer things than this will happen to you. But I'm sorry to say, today's adventure is at an end."

6 – THE HULL HOUSE INQUISITION

"Evening, Martha," Evangeline said pleasantly as she entered the old Hull mansion on Monday evening.

She was greeted in turn by one of the neighborhood girls who presided over the reception desk. "Hello, Miss LeClair."

Evangeline cast a glance around the foyer and found it devoid of its usual chaotic activity of running children and anxious volunteers. "Where is everybody?"

"I think it's just a lull." Martha put down the book she had been reading. "Everything will be back to organized confusion by the time evening classes start. Are you looking for anyone in particular, Miss LeClair?"

"No, not really. I just had a bit more free time than usual before my class begins, and I thought I'd stop by to chat with whoever was around."

Martha consulted the clock on the wall. "Well, by this time I expect most of them have wandered off toward the residents' dining hall. I just saw Miss Starr headed that way. I'm not sure where Miss Addams is. I think she had a late appointment at the mayor's office."

"Oh, never mind about that, Martha. I don't need to find Miss Addams. I'll just go and see who's around. Thank you."

The girl nodded and turned back to her book.

The Hull House settlement was an oddity among Chicago's charities. It was started by two genteel ladies of independent means named Jane Addams and Ellen Gates Starr. They had purchased a moldering mansion in the heart of a slum, moved in, and invited their immigrant neighbors to visit. The mansion soon became the site of meetings and classes that attracted not only the local inhabitants but Chicago's intellectuals as well. Evangeline, equipped with an education many considered excessive for a female, took to the settlement like a swan to water. In addition to attending lectures there, she taught classes in

English and literature. On this particular evening, she came not only to teach but to learn whatever she could about Elsa Bauer's gentleman, a resident at the settlement. She struck off across the courtyard in the direction of the dining hall hoping to find her colleagues there in a talkative mood.

When she walked into the open dining room, she saw two ladies seated at one of the trestle tables that ran down the length of the room. They were both listening to an animated monologue conducted by a middle-aged woman wearing a pince-nez. As Evangeline approached the table, she realized the speaker was Ellen Gates Starr who had founded the settlement along with Jane Addams. While Jane Addams battled for the rights of the poor with quiet determination, Ellen Gates Starr was a more colorful figure. If the former was the strategist, the latter was the field marshal. Her directness of speech sometimes even gave Evangeline pause—a rare occurrence.

"... and so I found the whole approach entirely disgusting," Miss Starr concluded as Evangeline walked up to the table. The speaker looked over her pince-nez at the newcomer. "Evangeline, quite a surprise to see you here. Sit down and join us." The words sounded more like a command than a request.

Evangeline complied, smiling a greeting in the direction of the other two ladies.

Miss Starr returned to her previous train of thought. "As I was just saying, that last newspaper article about Hull House was utterly ridiculous!"

"Oh? I must have missed it."

"Yes, it was an article in the *Daily News* written by that new woman reporter they just hired. It made us all sound like a bunch of vapid creatures who have no more idea of what we are about than... than... a bricklayer in a hen house!"

"Really?" Evangeline laughed. "I suppose we all came off as a dithering group of society ladies determined to help the poor by handing out picture postcards of the Louvre."

Miss Starr folded her arms truculently across her chest. "It was something along those lines—entirely revolting! I can't imagine what it will do to our credibility in this city."

"I shouldn't worry about it too much." Evangeline's tone was uncharacteristically conciliatory. "I'm sure anyone remotely acquainted with the settlement knows better, and those are the people who support our efforts through their wealthy connections."

"That's all very well, but what about the people out of town who subscribe to Chicago papers? In the eyes of the wider world, we'll still appear as foolish do-gooders who are going to waltz off to another more fashionable charity next year. I can't tell you how that sort of misrepresentation sickens me."

"It's just one article, Ellen." Evangeline looked across the table and noticed faint smiles on the faces of the two listeners who shared her view that Miss Starr sometimes defended the public image of Hull House a bit too fiercely.

"What are you doing here anyway?" Miss Starr peered at Evangeline over her lenses.

"Am I not to be allowed the luxury of a harmless social visit before my class starts?" Evangeline countered in mock surprise.

"Why yes, of course." Miss Starr backed away from outright rudeness. "It just seems out of your ordinary routine, that's all."

"Ah, I see. I'm to be held to a standard of consistency. What was it Emerson said about consistency and hobgoblins...?" Evangeline knew the quotation by heart but refrained from being offensive enough to repeat it.

Miss DeWitt from across the table offered helpfully, "I believe it was 'A foolish consistency is the hobgoblin of little minds—'"

"Thank you, dear," Miss Starr cut in sarcastically. "I can remember my Emerson well enough."

"Ohhh," the young lady quavered, belatedly realizing her faux pas.

Miss Starr abruptly stood up to go. "I have matters that require my attention, so I'll leave you ladies to your coffee and quotations."

Evangeline laughed. "Another time perhaps, you and I can brandish Thoreau at one another."

Miss Starr finally allowed one corner of her mouth to tilt upward in a half-smile suggesting that, despite her apparent harshness, she actually liked Evangeline. "In that case, I'd better start reviewing the transcendentalist volumes in the library. Good-bye, all." She nodded to the group and turned to march out of the room.

Miss DeWitt adopted a confidential tone after she was gone. "I don't know what it is about Miss Starr, but I always feel as if I should salute when she enters or leaves a room."

"Your reaction isn't unique, Adele. She has that effect on most people."

"But not on you, Engie."

"Oh, you'd be surprised. You would indeed." Intent on a way to turn the conversation, and at the same time uncover a possible suspect, Evangeline looked around the room. "I see none of the gentlemen have elected to join us."

"There aren't that many on duty this evening," replied Miss Burroughs, the other lady seated at the table, "just Mr. Johnston who's to teach the art class, but he hasn't arrived yet. And then there's Mr. DiStefano who's doing some research in the library. But I think he's taking tea in the study tonight instead."

"Oh, how disappointing. I don't know either gentleman well." Evangeline hoped to lead the discussion to that most favored feminine topic—the dissection of the male psyche.

Miss DeWitt leaped into the trap. "Mr. Johnston is quite the ladies' man, or at least he fancies himself to be."

"Really? And why is that, pray tell?"

"He wears so much hair pomade that one is fairly blinded by the glare when he takes off his hat." Miss DeWitt tittered at the image.

"What a dashing figure he must be," Evangeline encouraged further confidence. "And what about Mr. DiStefano? Does he fall into the same category?"

"I should say not!" exclaimed Miss Burroughs. "He's about as pompous a fellow as I've ever seen—very earnest about his work. That is," she qualified the statement, "as far as I can tell since he hardly ever condescends to speak to anyone about it."

"So, he doesn't join you here often?"

Miss Burroughs laughed. "He comes here about as often as you do, Engie!"

"Oh, I see. Once in a blue moon? But at least when I do decide to show up, I have enough common decency to carry on a conversation."

"The distinction is duly noted. But we only criticize your absence, my dear, because we enjoy your company and miss you when you make yourself so scarce."

"Very elegantly said, Therese. I've never had the knack of turning a potential insult into such a pretty compliment. I'm quite impressed." Miss DeWitt giggled at the retort and indulged in mock applause. Miss Burroughs bowed her head to acknowledge the approbation.

"But on a more serious note, Engie, we're very sorry to hear about Elsa. I know that she was a particular favorite of yours, and I'm sure I speak for both of us when I say how sad we are about it."

Evangeline glanced down briefly at the table. "Yes, it was a great shock. I attended her funeral last Wednesday."

"And to have Franz arrested, too. How could he do such a thing?" Miss DeWitt added timorously.

"It's a little early to make the assumption that he's guilty. But without some solid evidence to point the police in another direction, I'm very much afraid he'll be convicted just the same."

The faces of Miss DeWitt and Miss Burroughs took on a look of gloom.

With a start, Evangeline realized how long she had dallied in the dining hall. She stood abruptly. "I'm sorry to leave you both in such a depressed state, but I had better be getting along to my class now."

The two ladies sent her off with murmurings of condolence. As she retreated toward the end of the room, Evangeline could hear Miss DeWitt heave a tremendous sigh. The young lady summed up the situation with great sincerity, if not great originality. "How very, very sad."

***

Some two hours later when Evangeline dismissed her literature class for the evening, she called out to a girl seated in the back row. "Miss MacGregor, I'd like you to stay. I need to speak to you about something."

The girl nodded nervously. Being singled out at work was usually cause for alarm, and she seemed to apply the same rule to the classroom. Although she was a head taller than Evangeline, she somehow managed to shrink down below her teacher's height as she dawdled her way to the front desk.

"Mary, can I talk to you in confidence about something?"

Still too tense to speak, the girl nodded.

"You must promise not to tell anyone. Is that agreed?"

"Yes, miss." The girl bobbed a curtsy as a sign of assent.

"Very well then, please sit down." Evangeline gestured toward a student desk in the front row facing her chair.

Mary compressed her tall frame into the seat and waited.

Evangeline drew her chair up closer to the girl. "You were a good friend of Elsa's, weren't you?"

"Lord, yes. We were true friends, and that's a fact. I'm going to miss her something terrible now." Mary's eyes filled with tears as she fumbled for a handkerchief in her pocket.

"It's all right, my dear." Evangeline patted her hand. "I was very fond of her myself. That's why I'm trying to find out everything I can about her habits and her acquaintances to see if they can lead to her murderer."

"Good gracious, miss!" Mary's hand flew to her mouth in a gesture that mixed alarm and curiosity. "But they've already arrested Franz. Everybody knows that."

"Just because he's been arrested doesn't mean he's guilty."

"Oh! You think maybe somebody else could have done it? Who do you think it was?"

"Right now, I have no idea." Evangeline chose to conceal her theories for the time being. "But I need to know anything you can tell me about the time she spent here. For instance, who was she friendly with?"

"Miss LeClair! You don't think anyone here had a hand in it, do you?" Mary's eyes, which were abnormally large, flew open wider still. She was breathing very rapidly.

"Mary, please calm down! You needn't distress yourself this way. I'm merely asking the question in order to know who her friends were. Maybe one of them might be able to put me on the trail of something. Do you recall anyone else she was close to?"

Mary took a deep breath, trying to recollect any details. "Well, I've seen her talk to lots of people here, but not in any particular way. Nothing that I thought was odd. She was always quizzing everybody about everything. You know how she was..."

"Curious, you mean."

"Yes, curious—about everything. I used to see her in the nursery room talking to the matrons. I saw her in the workshop looking at how the clay pots get fired in that big kiln they have. She'd talk to the girls at reception and said maybe she'd fancy a job like that, as a volunteer greeting visitors and the like.

One time, I even saw her asking Miss Jane how she put together the daily schedule."

"Yes, she did have a variety of interests, didn't she?" Evangeline tried to assess the potential for Elsa's contact with someone violent. "Did you ever see her with a young man—possibly one of the other students?"

Mary thought for a moment. "No, I can't recollect that. Not anything special anyway. She was shy around boys, you know. I'd put her up to meeting one by dropping a book or some such thing, but she'd have none of it. Always hung back when I'd tease one of the fellows. As a matter of fact, the only one I ever saw her talk to was that Mr. Sidley who does the books."

"You mean the accountant?" Evangeline was puzzled.

"Yes, that's the one. Like you said, she was interested in everything—numbers, too. So, one day she walks past the door of his office and sees him adding up these rows of numbers on a big white sheet of paper and asks him what he was doing and why."

"And how did they get along?"

Mary shrugged. "Oh, fine I expect. She talked to him once in a while, and he always smiled at us when we'd see him in the hallway, but nothing odd about that, is there?"

"No, not really."

"Besides," Mary giggled nervously, "he's not the sort a girl would look at twice, is he?"

An image of the accountant's gawky appearance flashed through Evangeline's mind. With spectacles, a receding hairline and a chin to match, he was hardly any girl's romantic ideal. "Well, maybe I'll talk to him to see what he can tell me about his conversations with Elsa. Is there anything else you can think of?"

Mary concentrated for a moment. "Well, there was just that one time."

"Yes?" Evangeline was all attention.

"I think Mr. Sidley had a special pass for the Fair that he couldn't use, and I'm pretty sure he gave it to Elsa. Yes, I believe she said so. It was sometime way back in the spring."

Evangeline frowned, trying to digest this new bit of information. "Did he accompany her there?"

"I don't know, miss, because Elsa never talked about it again, and after that, I never saw her talking to him again either. I'm sorry, but that's all I remember."

"That's all right. You've been very helpful. One never knows what bit of information might be of use. Perhaps you should be going before it gets too late." Evangeline watched the girl rise to go. "Mary, remember what I said."

"About keeping this a secret?"

"Yes, exactly," Evangeline said in a dramatic whisper. "You must swear it."

The girl looked alarmed again, but Evangeline wanted to gain that reaction. "Yes, miss. I swear it! On my mother's grave, I'll never tell." She put her hand over her heart for further emphasis as her eyes took on the appearance of large, blue glass marbles.

Satisfied with this display, Evangeline smiled and told her to run along home. After the girl left, she sat for a while lost in thought. For the first time in her review of possible suspects, she considered the accountant. Not realizing that she was thinking out loud to the empty classroom, she said, "Sidley? But he's so very common. What an absurd notion!"

As she was collecting her papers to go, she happened to glance down at the volume still lying open on her desk. The class had been studying Edgar Allan Poe's "The Purloined Letter." Her eyes gravitated to the words, "These, like the overlargely lettered signs and placards of the street, escape observation by dint of being excessively obvious; and here the physical oversight is precisely analogous with the moral inapprehension by which the intellect suffers to pass unnoticed those considerations which are too obtrusively and too palpably self-evident."

Evangeline smiled grimly. "Well, Mr. Poe, perhaps I should heed your observation. We shall see if you're right. In due course, we shall see." She closed the book, collected the rest of her papers, and went downstairs to where Jack was waiting with her carriage.

7 – THE ACCOUNTANT'S LAIR

On Tuesday afternoon, Evangeline stood in the doorway of the resident accountant's office. "Ahem!"

Jacob Sidley failed to notice her. He was seated at a desk, huddled over a mound of ledger books. Adding-machine paper littered the desk and snaked its way to the floor, apparently in the hope of eventually making an escape through the door when the list of numbers grew long enough. Sidley seemed to be lost in the mathematical impossibility of reconciling the settlement's funds against its too plentiful expenses. Evangeline heard him muttering to himself. "But that can't be. I told them not to present that bill until next week! Now what's to be done?"

"Ah-hem!" Evangeline coughed again to make her presence known. Sidley jerked his head up and stared at her blankly. His mind was apparently still so focused on debits and credits that he hadn't made the mental connection to the person standing in front of him. After a few more seconds, a look of surprise replaced the scowl on his face. He jumped up from his seat, knocking over a pile of bills in the process.

"Oh, my g... goodness. It's M... Miss LeClair!" Evangeline watched in amusement as the accountant faced a new mathematical problem, that of dividing himself in two. He couldn't seem to decide whether to bend down and scoop up the papers or show her in and tried to do both at the same time. He bobbed back and forth between the two objects of his immediate attention until courtesy won out. Stepping over the debris, he welcomed his guest.

"Here, m... miss, please sit down, w... won't you." He eagerly dragged a chair away from the wall for Evangeline. While she was arranging herself, he attempted to retrieve the evidence of the settlement's debts. In an unexpected move, he dropped down on all fours to peer under the desk.

"So sorry, Miss LeClair. Don't m... mean to be rude, but I don't know if I missed any." He was referring to the bills still scattered about. "It would be a t... terrible thing, wouldn't do at all if one landed under the d... desk and I forgot to pay it. Well, what do you know." He cocked his head to the side and rested it against the floor to spot anything lurking under the desk.

"You see, j... just as I suspected!" He fished around up to his shoulder and emerged with a single piece of paper. "It's the bill for the grocer." He waved the slip under Evangeline's nose for further emphasis. "We couldn't have that now, could we? No f... food deliveries for a week! I'd never hear the end of it from Miss Ellen if this didn't get paid." He pushed his glasses back up to the bridge of his nose in a final emphatic gesture and then resettled himself in his chair behind the desk, mopping his brow with a handkerchief at the same time.

"Well, what a surprise this is! I g... get so few callers and am so often immersed in my work that I forget how enjoyable a break in the routine can be." He smiled nervously, apparently unsure whether his enthusiasm at her presence would be welcome or not. More formally, he added, "In what w... way can I be of service to you, Miss LeClair?"

Attempting to put him at ease, Evangeline flashed her most disarming smile. "Why Mr. Sidley, we needn't so hastily turn to business. While I do have a small matter to discuss, I thought it would be nice to chat awhile first. Both of us seem to spend so little time sharing in the Hull House community that I'm making it a point to get to know my colleagues on a more personal level. Is this an inconvenient time for such a visit?"

Sidley flushed and stammered with pleasure. "N...no, of course not, m... miss... not at all. I welcome such a p... pleasant interruption."

Evangeline paused as if a new thought had just struck her. "But perhaps this isn't the best place. Mightn't we have our little visit elsewhere? Perhaps a stroll would do you good. Fresh air, you know."

At the invitation, Sidley jumped up out of his chair, this time upsetting a ledger book that had been hanging precariously over the edge of the desk. Mumbling, "Clumsy, so clumsy, f... forgive me," he bobbed down on the floor to pick it up. Stepping over the other piles of paper, which surrounded his chair like an encroaching army, he walked over to Evangeline and extended his arm to her. In an inept attempt at courtliness, he said, "Miss LeClair, I am entirely at your d... disposal for however long you choose to hold me c... captive."

Evangeline laughed airily. "Sir, you flatter me and confer a far greater value on my charms than they deserve."

Sidley blushed and shuffled his feet self-consciously. He tried repeatedly to formulate what Evangeline anticipated to be an elaborate compliment, but all he succeeded in mouthing were a series of incoherent syllables. "Miss, I... uh... oh yes, well, I assure you that... uh... I... that is..."

"I think I know what you were about to say, Mr. Sidley," Evangeline intervened smoothly.

"You d... do?" The accountant appeared mystified.

"Why, yes. And a very pretty compliment it is, too. You were about to say that, being an accountant, you spend your whole day calculating values, and you believe you have assessed my attractions at their proper worth." Without giving the poor man time to confirm, or deny, the accuracy of her statement, Evangeline lowered her eyes demurely. "Mr. Sidley, you are too kind." She swept through the door and out of the office.

***

The two walked out of the old mansion and headed east on Polk Street. The air was more than fresh. With a strong wind off Lake Michigan, it was bracing, to say the least. But the sky was sunny, and the season still held a hint of Indian summer.

"I know so little about you, Mr. Sidley. If you don't mind gratifying my curiosity, would you tell me what checkered path has led you to our door at Hull House?"

Sidley seemed to have recovered his composure. He appeared relaxed as he contemplated the question. "Oh, it was a ch... checkered path indeed, Miss LeClair. I am originally from Iowa."

Evangeline noted that Sidley's whispery, hesitant speech was less marred by a stutter when he calmed down. "Well, I would never have guessed. And what could possibly have brought you here?"

"Initially, it was b... better opportunity for employment." Sidley adjusted the rebellious spectacles, which were forever threatening to slip off of his nose. "I had learned the business of accounting at a small bank in Dodgeville. Realizing that the town offered l... little inducement to stay for a young man of ambition, I thought to move to a larger city. Chicago was the nearest and so here I am."

"And so, here you are. But you aren't being paid for the work you do at the settlement. How does that further your ambition?"

Sidley smiled again, the bashful schoolboy being replaced increasingly by the pompous professor. "An astute observation, Miss LeClair. I did not come directly to H... Hull House after arriving here. I was employed for some time in a small downtown concern."

"Really! Which one?"

Sidley hesitated as if trying to remember something that had become only a vague memory. "P... perhaps you've heard of the accounting firm of Hart & Hudson?"

"No, I can't say that I have."

"Well, not many people have. It occupies a rather obscure location on an upper f... floor of one of the State Street office buildings. I was there for three years."

"Fascinating. And what made you leave? Surely, you were under no compulsion to go, were you?"

"N... no, c... certainly not!" Sidley seemed to be disturbed by the question. Evangeline noticed a slight twitch in the corner of his left eye. "Or at least not the k... kind of compulsion you might be suggesting."

"I, suggest?" Evangeline gasped in mock surprise. She didn't want to excite Sidley's nervousness and, perhaps, put him on his guard. "Why, sir, forgive me if I have unwittingly implied anything remotely dishonorable!"

The tension that Evangeline could feel in the accountant's arm gradually relaxed.

"Oh M... Miss LeClair, I do apologize. My words must have sounded unnecessarily defensive. You are right though. There was c... compulsion of a sort in my leaving. It was the compulsion to answer a higher calling."

"Oh?" Evangeline raised her eyebrows quizzically.

"Yes, I had been a selfish man, living only to p... pursue my own advantage. But I had reached a crossroads in my life. Are you a churchgoer, Miss LeClair?"

Taken aback by the abruptness of the question, Evangeline found that it was her turn to stammer. "Well... er... not exactly... that is, I mean..."

Without waiting for her to untangle herself, Sidley continued. "Well, I am. I attend the Third Presbyterian Church regularly. I believe that my t... transformation began the moment I first stepped into the vestibule."

"Really?" Evangeline tried to sound impressed.

Sidley's gaze was directed ahead at something off in the distance. "Yes. Over a period of time, I came to see that my life had no meaning. If I were to die, I would have made no c... contribution to the good of humanity. That is the true measure of one's mark on the world, isn't it?"

"Very true, very true. And that led you to...?"

"That led me to search for an institution where my efforts could benefit the c... community. The minister of my church recommended that I contact Miss Addams and offer my services as a bookkeeper at Hull House. And that is how you find me in the position I currently occupy."

"Fascinating. Quite fascinating how Providence works."

"It is indeed. God works in mysterious ways..."

Evangeline took advantage of this comment to turn the conversation in another, more pointed, direction. "At the moment, I'm consumed by a mystery of another sort."

"Oh?" Sidley looked down at her. "And what m... might that be?"

"Why, the terrible mystery of what happened to Elsa Bauer, of course." Her unexpected words had their calculated effect. Sidley blanched and came to a dead stop in the middle of the street. They were directly in the path of an approaching streetcar and had to scurry to the opposite sidewalk to avoid a collision.

"Wh... what was th... that you s... said?" Sidley quavered. The slight twitch in the corner of his eye became more pronounced every second.

"Elsa Bauer's death. Surely, you were aware she was a student of mine?"

"N... no. No, I wasn't." Sidley's agitation was on the rise. He seemed to have difficulty collecting his thoughts enough to form a coherent sentence. "What... who... no, I m... mean, how long h... had you known her?"

"For two years or more. She had taken a few of my literature classes and became quite a favorite of mine."

"A f... favorite, you say?" Sidley pushed his glasses back up his nose. Evangeline noticed that his hand was shaking.

"Yes, quite. I understand you knew her as well?"

"I... who... that is, er... yes. Yes, I do seem to recall speaking to her."

"Oh, forgive me. I was given to understand that you had more than a passing acquaintance with her."

"Wh... wh... who told you that?"

"Why, it was general knowledge. You were seen conversing together often. As a matter of fact, I seem to recall..." Evangeline tapped her chin as if trying to recollect something lodged at the back of her consciousness. "Oh, what was it now...?"

"What? What?" Sidley's voice was strained and tense. He took out a handkerchief and began wiping his forehead, even though the temperature was barely fifty degrees.

By this time, the two had walked all the way to Lake Michigan. The shore was dotted with small patches of greenery that had been turned into public parks, and they had wandered into one of these. Evangeline spied a bench nearby.

"Mr. Sidley, you appear quite agitated. Perhaps we had better sit down and rest for a few minutes."

"Y... yes, yes. I do need to sit down, just for a few moments, if you don't mind. All this fresh air may be more than my lungs can stand. Ha, ha," he laughed weakly.

"I'm sorry if I've led you to overtax yourself. I'm a great walker myself. When I'm at my home in the suburbs, I can usually be found hiking the bluff along the shore. Unfortunately, I often forget what a strain I place on my companions when I drag them along on an extended promenade such as the one we've just taken."

They sat for a few minutes in silence and watched the procession of steamers and barges that churned across the water. At this time of year, the number of pleasure craft was diminishing as few souls were foolish enough to venture out on the lake for amusement with conditions so unpredictable.

Evangeline waited until Sidley had begun to regain his composure. His breathing had almost returned to normal when she recommenced her inquisition. "Mr. Sidley, you gave me quite a start there. You look almost as if you'd seen a ghost. Was it anything I said?"

"W... well, it's just that talk of m... murder always upsets me. Good Lord, and to think it was someone I knew!"

"Yes, that reminds me again. It's the fact that you knew her. There's something that keeps nagging at the back of my memory. Something to do with you and Elsa. What could it have been?" Evangeline paused and allowed the silence to become deafening, waiting to see if Sidley would leap into the verbal breach.

He didn't but continued to stare off across the water, his hands gripped tightly to the seat of the bench as if he might tumble over forward if he let go.

"Oh, I remember now." Evangeline smiled sweetly. "I understand that you took her to the Columbian Exposition."

"I, wh... what!" Sidley burst out. "Where did you h... hear such a thing!"

"Why, from her landlady." She hedged the complete truth. "Was I mistaken?"

"Well, yes," the accountant paused, "a... and no."

"I see. Thank you for clarifying the matter." Evangeline allowed herself a half-smile at the accountant's distress.

"What I m... mean, Miss LeClair, is that there were plans." He began to rub irritably at the corner of his eye. "Please, p... promise me that this goes no further."

"Sir, you have my word." She waited breathlessly for more.

"It was th... this way. Elsa was a favorite of mine, too. You have seen how isolated my role at Hull House is. I come into contact with so few. There were never many who would stop to visit as you have so kindly done. But one day, Elsa came walking past my door. She said she wanted to ask about h... how the bookkeeping for the settlement was done. I'm sure you know what she was like. She was so curious and w... wanted to learn everything there was to know about everything."

"Yes, I know." Evangeline was saddened by the memory of her young friend's liveliness.

"Well, I found her interest t... touching. I thought her intellectual curiosity deserved a reward. Right after the Fair opened at the beginning of May, a friend of mine gave me two special passes. I'm sure you can guess from the solitary nature of my h... habits that I am not attached to anyone." He glanced down, seemingly embarrassed, before continuing. "A... anyway, there was a spare ticket, and I thought what an incentive it would be for a girl like Elsa, to get a wider glimpse of the world, to see a display of culture such as she'd never known." Sidley appeared calmer now, lost in the reconstruction of the memory. "You must understand, Miss LeClair," he added earnestly, "There was never any romantic design on my part."

"Then what could your motive have been, sir?"

Sidley cleared his throat apprehensively before replying. He seemed to doubt Evangeline would believe what he was about to say. "It was merely as an incentive to a young p... person who deserved better than life had given her."

Evangeline felt a heaviness across her heart as she heard her own sentiments about Elsa echoed by another. "But why all the secrecy then, if your motives were innocent?"

Sidley shrugged unhappily. "That's just it, Miss LeClair. How m... many are there, do you think, who would have believed that my motives were pure? Even though she was hardly more than a child, I can only imagine the vile rumors that would have started had the event become publicly known."

"Yes, I see your point."

"I told Elsa to tell no one about the ticket. I even planned to meet her at the F... Fair, rather than escort her there, so that no one would question our leaving together."

"And did you meet her?"

"N... no, unfortunately, I did not. Some pressing business with the settlement's bank intervened, and I was obligated to attend a meeting instead."

"So, then Elsa went alone?"

"Why yes, as far as I know." He was silent for a moment, catching his breath. Then he asked abruptly, "This landlady who confided in you. Did she tell you anything else?"

"There was one detail that I thought rather bizarre."

"Oh, what was th... that?" Sidley's grip on the bench tightened. His knuckles began to turn white.

"I believe it was something about a silk rose." Evangeline frowned in deep concentration.

"Oh, y... yes, that. I suppose that could be misconstrued as..."

"As a love token?"

"Yes." Sidley sighed. "You see how things can be misinterpreted."

"Then help me to understand the proper meaning of the gesture."

"Well, it was b... because of my eyes."

"Your eyes? Really, sir!" Evangeline couldn't help sounding incredulous since the connection between silk flowers and the accountant's vision was far from obvious.

"Yes, r... really, Miss LeClair. You must believe me. My eyesight is not the best, even with these." The accountant pointed ruefully to his spectacles. "In a crowd of ten thousand people, how could I hope to single her out?"

"Surely, you must have had a prearranged meeting place."

"Of course, we were to meet by the Ferris wheel."

"I don't believe the Ferris wheel opened until sometime in June."

"Y... yes. You're correct. It was still under construction, but it was also the highest object in the fairgrounds."

"Ah, I see. A logical choice."

"That was so Elsa would have no trouble finding the spot."

"And yet..." Evangeline wasn't entirely convinced of Sidley's veracity, "you still thought some additional method of identification would be necessary?"

"I am a very c... careful man, Miss LeClair. I leave nothing to chance. Did your confidante also tell you that I asked Elsa to be specific about the clothes she would be wearing that day?"

Evangeline was genuinely surprised. "Why no. I didn't hear about that."

"Well, the fact is that I asked Elsa to tell me exactly what c... color and style of clothing she would be wearing and also to fasten the red rose to her hat. That way I would be sure to single her out."

"My goodness, you are meticulous with regard to detail, aren't you!"

"I am very careful in everything I do. Did you hear anything else that requires me to defend my character f... further?"

Evangeline commanded her features to remain a mask. "I don't believe so. Is there anything else to be told?"

"N... no, no. I was just wondering. I thought perhaps Elsa herself may have been guilty of some romantic fancy and may have portrayed the rendezvous in that light to her landlady, that's all."

"No, nothing of that sort was said."

"Ah, that's good." The accountant appeared relieved but then began to frown. "Miss LeClair, you know I must r... rely on your discretion in this matter."

"You may rely on it, sir, as a matter of course."

"I d... do thank you, sincerely, for that reassurance." For a few moments, Sidley seemed lost in thought. Then he said, as much to himself as to Evangeline, "Such a shame, such a waste, and such a beautiful girl, too."

"Yes." The two sat silently looking out over the water for a while longer.

Finally, Sidley stood up. He leaned down and offered Evangeline his hand. "It's getting late, and the wind has rather picked up. Don't you think we should be getting back?"

Evangeline squinted in the growing twilight. "Yes, I quite agree. It's getting very late, and it's hard to see anything clearly in this light."

8 – OF BARRISTERS, BARDS, AND BAR ROOMS

Although Freddie had committed himself, in theory, to helping Evangeline, he didn't attack the problem with the same fervor as his friend. He sidled up to the issue, and backed away from it, and sidled up to it again, with the result that he procrastinated a full three days without taking any action whatsoever. By Tuesday, guilt finally outweighed timidity, and he steeled himself to make a contribution to Evangeline's grand cause. He reported to work at his usual time of eight o'clock, intending to sneak out at an opportune moment to hunt for clues.

The law practice of Simpson & Austin had been started by his father and uncle. After his father's death several years earlier, Freddie's uncle had assumed the formidable task of training the young man in the family business. Mr. Horace Simpson was of a sanguine disposition and believed he could achieve the impossible. Freddie, aware of his own limited aptitude for the law, knew his uncle was attempting to refashion a sow's ear.

When Freddie arrived at his desk on this particular morning, he found an unexpected, and unwelcome, note from his uncle requiring a meeting at ten o'clock. Knowing that his uncle only required a *tête-à-tête* when a reprimand was in order, Freddie groaned, sat down at his desk, and shuffled papers until the hour appointed for his execution.

Upon presenting himself at his uncle's office at ten, the young man found the door closed and the elder Mr. Simpson *incommunicado*. As a further guarantee of privacy, the reception area was guarded by Mr. Simpson's secretary, a Miss Louise Russell. Though hiring females in secretarial positions was a recent development in Chicago's business community, Mr. Simpson liked to think he was being progressive by offering the position to a young woman who could type at the phenomenal rate of forty words per minute.

Louise looked up when Freddie approached. The young man raised a quizzical eyebrow. "What's going on in there, Louise? Uncle Horace left a note saying he wanted to see me at ten."

The guardian of the gate laughed. "Don't worry, young master." She liked to use this particular title for Freddie, but whether as a term of respect or insult he could never be sure. "He won't be long. He's in conference with one of Mr. McCormick's attorneys. Why don't you just sit down there." She pointed to the green leather sofas that lined the walls of the reception area.

Freddie sighed and threw himself down on one of the squeaky couches.

Apparently aware of his mood, Louise asked, "Are you about to be called out on the carpet again?"

"By the time he finishes with me, I've no doubt I'll wish I were underneath the carpet."

"What did you do this time? Were you playing hooky with your friends at the paper?"

"Would that I had been. It would have been less painful than what I was actually doing. This time I can use the argument that I was helping an old family friend."

"Use the argument?" Louise echoed in surprise. "You may want to save that one for the courtroom. Besides, young master, you'd better remember that you'll be arguing with one of the finest lawyers in the city. He gets paid a great deal of money because he's very good at arguing with people."

"Thanks, Louise. Your words of comfort have managed to completely alleviate my concern about my fate."

"Oh, Freddie, you're a caution." Louise turned back to her typing and left Freddie to contemplate the epitaph on his tombstone.

After a few moments, the office door swung open, and Mr. Simpson ushered out his colleague. Concluding with a brief exchange at the elevator, the gentlemen parted, leaving Mr. Simpson Senior free to focus his attention on Freddie.

"Nephew," he said curtly by way of greeting.

"Uncle," Freddie offered in return.

"Come in." As Mr. Simpson gestured Freddie through the door, he said to his secretary, "Miss Russell, I'm not to be disturbed during this meeting."

"Yes, sir." The girl shot a sympathetic glance in Freddie's direction.

Mr. Simpson closed the door and motioned his nephew into one of the high-backed Spanish chairs that faced his desk. Before Freddie sat down, he took the precaution of moving the chair back half a foot in case he felt the need to make a speedy exit.

After the older man had settled himself in the seat of judgment, he began. "Nephew, I've heard some unpleasant reports about you lately. Waverly tells me you didn't report to work last Wednesday and that you left early on Friday afternoon."

"I'll have to thank him later," Freddie mumbled under his breath.

"What was that?"

"Nothing. I was just thinking out loud."

"Well, think about this. You are not only a member of this firm, which has a certain reputation for reliability to maintain, but you are a member of the family as well. That means that your behavior ought to be a model to the other young men employed here."

"Yes sir," Freddie assented meekly.

"What were you doing anyway? Gadding about with those newshounds down at the paper? When I think what your father would say if he were alive!" Mr. Simpson raised his eyes heavenward, presumably invoking his dead brother's spirit to witness the proceedings.

"For once, Uncle, I'm not guilty as charged."

"Oh?" Mr. Simpson's bushy white eyebrows drew up at least an inch in surprise.

"I was helping a friend."

"A friend," Mr. Simpson repeated skeptically.

"Yes, a friend of the family as a matter of fact."

"I see. And who might that be?"

"It was Miss Evangeline LeClair. She asked me to attend a funeral in the city with her."

"Hmmm." Mr. Simpson paused, appearing to consider the evidence. Freddie inferred he was really trying to buy time in order to figure out what obscure defense strategy his nephew was using. At any rate, he seemed less confident that he had caught the young man *in flagrante delicto.*

"I didn't think you would want me to be rude to a lady in a state of hysterical grief." Freddie tried to play his hand for all it was worth.

"Hysterical, you say?" His uncle propped his elbows on the desk and leaned forward. "The day Evangeline LeClair exhibits signs of hysteria is the day I expect to see Lake Michigan turn into a desert."

"Well, perhaps I overstated her grief just a bit. But the rest is true. I did attend a funeral with her on Wednesday. Would you have wanted to see her travel to the city alone and unescorted?"

"No, I certainly would not." It was Horace Simpson's turn to look uncomfortable. His old-fashioned notions of protectiveness toward the fair sex made him vulnerable to this particular line of attack, and Freddie knew it.

The younger man pursued his advantage. "What do you take me for, Uncle? Do you think I'm the sort of fellow who would abandon a lady in distress? Here was a young woman of long-standing acquaintance appealing to me for help. I ask you, what would you have done under the circumstances? I didn't think to notify anyone here of my whereabouts. I merely answered the call of duty, and now I see I'm to be treated like a convicted felon for extending a helping hand!" Freddie threw his arms wide in a theatrical gesture of appeal.

"All right, Freddie, that will do. I'm sorry I jumped to conclusions. Whose funeral was it, anyway?"

"It was one of Miss LeClair's students from Hull House who passed away unexpectedly." Freddie neglected to mention the circumstances surrounding Elsa's demise.

"Regrettable," Mr. Simpson tapped a pen contemplatively, "but not entirely unaccountable. That whole neighborhood around Hull House is disease-ridden, and the immigrants who populate it live in filthy conditions. Typhoid, was it?"

"Something equally unexpected."

"I see," the older man replied. Then, to Freddie's delight, he dropped the subject entirely. "Well, I think that's all I wanted to speak to you about today, Freddie. You may return to your office now."

"Thank you, Uncle." He tried to keep all trace of irony out of his voice. "I really appreciate the personal interest you take in my career here." The young man rose to go but turned just before opening the door. "Oh, and Uncle Horace..."

"Yes?" The older man glanced up from the document he had started to examine.

"Perhaps in future, you won't immediately credit all the reports you hear about my bad behavior."

"Agreed, young man, agreed. Now be about your business." Freddie's uncle waved him out of the room.

"Whew!" Freddie closed the door behind him.

"Congratulations." Louise paused in her typing, noting Freddie's expression of relief. "You don't appear to have been flayed alive."

"My dear girl." Freddie leaned impudently over her desk. "My logic was irrefutable, and, in the end, I made him see the error of his ways."

Louise made no comment but held her hands suspended above the typewriter keys, staring skeptically at Freddie as she waited for more.

"And you can tell my uncle that if he should hear any further tattling about my absence from the office for the next few hours, it's because I have to see to some additional arrangements for Miss LeClair."

"Unharmed and with a license to play hooky! You really did come out of this one smelling like a rose."

"Who knows," Freddie said over his shoulder as he left the reception room, "I may make a good lawyer after all."

"I'm sorry, young master, I didn't catch that last part. Did you say 'lawyer' or 'liar?'"

***

Freddie, gleeful at having obtained even an insignificant victory over his uncle, left immediately for the *Tribune* building. He grew more alive with every step he took. Aside from his romantic designs on Evangeline, Freddie's only other object in life was to become a news reporter. This career had been discouraged by every member of his family down to his youngest sister. His mother went so far as to say that journalists were one step below circus sideshow performers. Freddie had been sent to law school for the express purpose of eventually stepping into his father's shoes. His family's assumptions about his destiny were not at all in accord with Freddie's own wishes.

While he reported to work as a junior associate of Simpson & Austin, he spent every available moment hanging around the *Tribune* offices. Being viewed as a mascot was Freddie's curse in life. Not only did Evangeline treat him as one, but his reporter friends sent him on errands as the price of admittance to their inner circle. Rather than chasing down news leads, Freddie spent his time chasing down lunch orders. He bore all of this with the resignation of a man who has never been taken seriously by anyone over the course of his entire life.

The sole bright spot in this bleak personal portrait was that his family shared the popular view of his low potential. This meant that after a decent interval of incompetence at the law firm, he would be left to his own devices. For his own part, Freddie would have been quite content to sacrifice his already tarnished reputation in exchange for one really good feature story. Tracking down Elsa Bauer's murderer was his best hope of ever achieving that dream.

The clock was just striking eleven when he ran up the stairs to the city newsroom. His entrance was heralded by a series of catcalls and howls from the inmates. Comments like "Where in blazes have you been?" and "It's about time!" were followed by a barrage of paperclips and wads of paper aimed in the general vicinity of Freddie's head. Having recently been treated to a similar missile attack from Evangeline, Freddie was becoming adept at dodging injury.

"Greetings, animals! Is it feeding time at the zoo already?"

"What do you mean, already?" a voice demanded from the corner. "When you didn't show up yesterday, one of us had to bring back lunch instead."

"Imagine that. You actually had to exert that much energy on your own behalf? What's the world coming to?"

"Well, now that you're here, you can bring me a corned beef on rye," another voice called out.

"Stop right there, fellows." Freddie held up his hands. "I'm not here to play delivery boy today."

A disappointed rumble arose from the group who had begun to cluster around Freddie. One malcontent even growled, "Well, what are you good for, then?"

Choosing to ignore the insult, Freddie persisted. "I'm here to see Bill. Do any of you fugitives from a public natatorium know where he might be?"

"You could try the print shop," a surly voice answered. "I saw him going that way about fifteen minutes ago to run down some final copy for tomorrow's edition."

"Thanks." Waving his arm above his head, Freddie said to the assembly, "Always a pleasure, gentlemen! You can interpret my use of that term as loosely as you see fit!" Narrowly dodging a copy ruler that came whizzing past his shoulder, he heard "Awww, get lost!" as he ducked out the door.

His exuberance still undiminished, Freddie ran back down the stairwell to the print shop that was located on the ground floor. As he opened the double doors to enter, the roar of the rotary presses pounded his ears like a pair of iron fists. The cylinders were powered by steam engines that could produce twenty-thousand pages of print an hour. The entire building shook from the vibration they made. Freddie edged past one of the monsters, imagining the damage that could be done if a hand accidentally got caught in the mechanism. Eventually, he saw Bill Mason standing against a back window. The reporter was chewing on one of the two-cent cigars he favored and frowning as he read over a galley proof.

"Hello, Freddie boy!" Mason said when he looked up over the rim of his reading glasses and saw Freddie standing in front of him. "Where've you been? I was about to ask the coppers to drag the river for you."

"Personal business, Bill. There's something I need to talk to you about. It's confidential."

Mason's attention had been snagged by the utterance of the magic word "confidential." He crammed his glasses into a vest pocket and took his cigar out of his mouth. He then nudged the brim of his dented, ash-streaked derby farther back on his head. This gesture, Freddie knew from experience, meant that Bill was all ears. "Well, this ought to be good, if it's confidential. Anything fit to print?"

"Since when did you ever cavil over whether a story was fit or not before throwing it on the front page, Bill? In answer to your question, I'm here to get information, not give it."

"What's it worth to you?"

"How about a free lunch at Hennessey's and all you can drink?"

"For a deal like that, Freddie lad, I'd tell you where the mayor keeps his streetcar-concession bribe money!" Unceremoniously handing his galley proof to one of the typesetters standing nearby, Bill sauntered out of the print room with Freddie trailing along behind him.

While great age has sometimes been described by the term "before the flood," Bill Mason was considered an ancient journalist having been a Chicago newsman since "before the fire." Because he had single-mindedly pursued the life of the mind, the life of the body had been sadly neglected. He drank too much, slept too little, and failed to note that his shirt collars were only white on the day he first bought them.

His *deshabille* notwithstanding, Mason was very good at his job. He maintained an intricate network of contacts among Chicago's political community, which had the same membership as its criminal underworld. As a result, he was able to receive information impossible to get through more formal channels of inquiry. For some odd reason, Bill had taken a liking to Freddie—odd, not because Freddie was an unlikable fellow, but because Freddie seemed the last sort of person that a man of Bill's satiric disposition would be expected to like. Even more odd was the fact that Bill actually took Freddie's aspirations as a reporter seriously.

The two left the *Tribune* building and headed down Madison Street to Hennessey's saloon—a nearby tavern frequented by newsmen from one or another of the city's papers. The place was relatively empty but ready for the lunch crowd to arrive; the corner of the bar was piled high with platters of cold cuts, cheese, bread, and pickles. Doc Hennessey, the owner of the establishment, stood presiding with great dignity behind the bar. The hazy light streaming through the tall front windows reflected off his bald head like a cherub's halo. When he saw Bill and Freddie enter, his mild expression turned to a scowl. Spitting expressively on the floor, he said, "I didn't think you'd be showing your ugly mug around here anytime soon, Mason."

"Tut, tut, Doc. Is that any way to treat one of your best customers?"

"My best customers are my paying customers. You're a leech!" Hennessey pointed to the wall behind him. "It's mainly on account of you I put up that sign just yesterday!" In bold Gothic letters, a sign above the bar warned: "NO TRUST!" As if the message might need additional emphasis, another sign flanked it: "Pay TODAY or Thirst TOMORROW!"

Spitting again to emphasize his displeasure, Hennessey leaned forward over the bar, presumably the better to reach Bill's windpipe. Before the dispute could take a physical turn, Freddie intervened. "How much does he owe, Doc?"

"Five bucks and two-bits!" The proprietor was clearly incensed by the enormity of the sum.

"I'll settle his account." Freddie took a ten-dollar bill out of his pocket. "That should cover for today and then some. Fetch us a bottle of whiskey, Doc."

As the proprietor walked out of earshot to bring the requisite item, Bill muttered under his breath, "A whoreson Achitophel! A rascally yea-forsooth knave! To bear a gentleman in hand, and then stand upon security!"

Freddie recollected Bill's penchant for quoting Shakespeare. The reporter had a particular fondness for Falstaff, which surprised Freddie not at all.

"My young friend!" Bill patted Freddie's shoulder. "I am greatly obliged to you. I always knew you had character."

"And I always knew you were a character! How long did you think you could go on like this, Bill?"

"Till payday, my boy, only till payday," Bill responded with aplomb.

"And what will you do when your paycheck isn't enough to cover your tab?"

"I'll hurl myself off that particular precipice, lad, when I arrive there." Bill apparently took note of Freddie's solemn expression. "Good faith, this same young sober-blooded boy doth not love me, nor a man cannot make him laugh; but that's no marvel, he drinks no wine."

This had the effect of making Freddie smile in spite of himself.

"There, that's more like it." Bill's voice expressed satisfaction. "Now let's change the subject. You have bought my time for the next hour or for as long as it takes me to become incoherent from demon whiskey, whichever comes first. Ask your questions."

"All right." Freddie wasn't quite sure his hints on the value of temperance had been persuasive, but he was unready to be lured away from the topic.

At that moment, Doc returned with a bottle and two glasses, placing them on the bar with a loud thud to announce his displeasure at not being able to crack Bill's skull for nonpayment. He growled, "The food's there. Help yourselves," as he stalked back to the other end of the bar to polish some glasses.

Before Freddie had time to pour himself a drink, Bill had already downed his first shot. The reporter then unfolded his handkerchief and meticulously dabbed at the corners of the bushy moustache that completely obscured his upper lip. He nudged his empty glass in Freddie's direction. The young man sighed and poured his friend another drink before filling his own glass. "Let's get something to eat and move off to a table on the side."

"It's your ten-spot." Bill complied with Freddie's request.

When the two were seated, Freddie leaned across the table so as not to be overheard by the few other patrons of the establishment.

"I need some information about the murder you covered over a week ago."

Bill tilted his chair against the wall and fished in a vest pocket for a match, presumably intending to light one of the foul-smelling firesticks he defined as a cigar. Freddie watched the operation, noting silently that the only reason Bill's mouth perpetually drooped at the right corner was because it had been a cigar perch for so many years.

It took three matches before the operation was complete. When Bill had succeeded in igniting the tobacco and creating enough smoke to obscure the air around his head, he picked up the thread of the conversation. "The girl at the Palmer House? That's old news, my boy. A suspect has already been arrested. What's your interest in it?"

"As I told you, it's confidential." Freddie glanced nervously over his shoulder.

"That won't suit, son. You've piqued my curiosity. I smell a story here."

"All right, all right. I'll tell you a few things about it just to shut you up." He took a large bite of his ham sandwich. "Do you know a lady named Evangeline LeClair?"

"The railroad heiress? Don't know her personally, but I've heard a few things about her from the high hats who write the society column. She's said to be a bit odd. Inherited a fortune from her parents. Seems to be sworn off matrimony, though I hear she's still trailed around by a few young fools who keep proposing to her. You wouldn't be one of them, would you, lad?"

Freddie stopped chewing abruptly and gulped down his mouthful of food. "Not exactly. We grew up together. She's a friend of mine."

"I see." Bill puffed on his cigar. The cryptic expression on his face reminded Freddie of Alice's caterpillar. To the young man's relief, he changed his line of questioning. "I'm assuming there's some connection here with the murder at the Palmer House?"

"Yes, there is. Miss LeClair knew the girl who was killed. The lady teaches classes at Hull House, and this was one of her students."

"Oh, ho!" Bill laughed. "An heiress and a blue stocking! That's a deadly combination if ever there was one. So, she's taken a personal interest in this business, has she?"

"Yes."

"And I'm assuming you want to play the hero by finding out for her what she wants to know?"

"Something like that." Freddie gave up the pretense of eating entirely and squirmed in his chair.

Bill eyed him for several moments through the smoky haze without speaking. "All right, my boy. You've satisfied my curiosity. Now I'm ready to satisfy yours. Present your questions."

Freddie was all eagerness now. "Did you get to see the room where the girl was found firsthand?"

Bill snorted derisively. "You ought to know by now, lad, the coppers try to keep us out, but we're usually there before the body hits the floor."

Freddie winced at the image. "What shape was the room in?"

Bill tilted his chair forward before replying. He lifted the corner of his sandwich skeptically to peer underneath the rye bread. He picked up the dill pickle perched on the side of his plate and scrutinized it with the same cold detachment. Apparently not finding anything to whet his appetite, he made no attempt to eat. Instead, he poured himself another shot of whiskey. "It didn't look like anything was out of place. The furniture was all arranged. I asked the chambermaid if anything had been moved. She was scared and shaking, but she said no."

"Did she notice if the door had been forced open?"

"It wasn't. It was just locked from the inside. The maid knocked, and when there was no answer she used her passkey to let herself in and... saw what she saw."

"Hmmm." Freddie thought for a few moments. "Was there a window?"

Bill nodded. "Just one. The window leads out to a fire escape and then down to the alley below. It was a cheaper room at the back of the hotel. I overheard one of the coppers say that the window had been shut, but it wasn't locked."

"What else did you see?"

63

"Only the girl. She was lying face down on the floor. Her head was tilted to one side, almost as if she'd fallen asleep that way."

"Any sign of a struggle?"

"Not that I could see." Bill swallowed the remainder of his drink and poured another. Freddie waved away an offer to refill his own glass. "There was a cut in her back just below the nape of her neck and a trickle of blood. Her left hand was thrown up behind her head as if she'd tried to reach for the spot where she'd been stabbed when she fell. That's all, no bruises—nothing like that—no ripped clothing. But I got the impression she'd been crying."

"How?"

"When I bent down to look closer at the corpse—" Freddie winced again. Bill noted the young man's reaction and corrected himself. "... at the late Miss Bauer, I saw she had a damp handkerchief wadded up in her right hand, and there seemed to be traces of crusted tears around her eyes."

"Hmmm, interesting."

Bill eyed his sandwich suspiciously. He turned the plate clockwise and lifted the opposite corner of the bread, presumably under the impression that the contents had changed since his last inspection. "Anything else you want to know, lad?"

"Yes. I want to know the name of the doctor who examined the body. It wasn't in the article."

"Well, the official examination was performed by one of the medics from the Coroner's Office. But that wasn't good enough for the Palmers. Maybe they were afraid that Jack the Ripper had crossed the pond and started attacking guests at their hotel. For whatever reason, they insisted that one of their cronies in the medical profession check the remains as well."

"Can they do that?" Freddie was shocked.

Bill grinned sardonically. "In this town, they can do anything they want, lad. Their doctor friend is named Doyle. Archibald Doyle. He has a high-toned practice north of the river."

"If I wanted to talk to this Dr. Doyle, where would I find him?"

"Probably at his office during the week. It's on Dearborn Parkway. You can check the address yourself since I don't recall it offhand. You're on your own with that one though. I couldn't get much out of him."

"Nothing? No scrap of information that wasn't mentioned in the news article?"

"Not a thing. For once, what you saw in print was all I knew. Doyle backed up what the Coroner's Office said. She was stabbed, end of discussion." Bill shrugged. "Seeing as how I'm a gentleman of the press, I don't think he told me all that he knew."

"If he won't talk to you, what makes you think he'd speak to me?" Freddie felt worried at the prospect of a dead end to his investigation.

Bill meticulously tapped the ashes from his cigar tip onto the floor. "I don't know, son, but you may be able to get your society friends to back you."

Freddie was silent for a moment, puzzled about how to proceed. Then an idea occurred to him. "Evangeline's part of the golden circle. She gets invited to Mrs. Palmer's parties. Maybe if she were to intervene..."

"It could work," Bill said, puffing away speculatively, his head cocked to one side as he gazed across the table at Freddie. "With enough encouragement from the right quarter, Doyle might open up a bit. After all, it's not as if you were after a news story on this murder—not as if you knew some little fact you aren't sharing with your old friend Bill. That would be a pretty crazy idea, wouldn't it, lad? I mean, you writing a story from a new angle or some such nonsense..." The right corner of his mouth, still clamped around the cigar, lifted in a half-smile.

Freddie laughed, but his voice sounded strained. "Yes, indeed, Bill. Yes, indeed. That would be a pretty crazy idea. Just the fact that you've come up with a notion like that must mean you've already had too much to drink." Freddie reached quickly for the bottle. "Here, why don't we both have another."

9 – HER MAJESTY, THE QUEEN OF CHICAGO

On Wednesday afternoon, Evangeline swept past the doorman and into Chicago's palatial Palmer House. The hotel was built with all the gilding and marble that an architect with a taste for ostentation and an unlimited budget could design. The lobby was a full two stories high and stretched the length of a city block. It was intended to impress and intimidate those who didn't have the wealth that signified their right to be there. Despite the splendor, Evangeline was neither intimidated nor impressed. She had spent her entire life moving about in buildings of titanic dimensions, and the Palmer House lobby was merely one more inlaid marble cavern to be traversed.

Approaching the reception desk, she addressed one of the clerks on duty. "Good afternoon. I'd like to speak to Mrs. Palmer." Her voice sounded hollow as it echoed off the stone counter and walls mingling with the clatter of luggage being moved for a sea of guests that ebbed and flowed like the tide.

The clerk blanched. "Madame, is there anything wrong? Please be assured that we will certainly do everything in our power to make it right."

"You misunderstand me. I'm not currently a guest here. I wish to see Mrs. Palmer on a personal matter." Evangeline presented the clerk with one of her calling cards. "She is expecting me."

"Oh, I'm so sorry. Forgive me." The clerk was obviously relieved. He bowed excessively, then led her through a side door into a walnut-paneled office.

"If you'll just wait in here, Miss LeClair, I'll see if I can locate Mrs. Palmer for you." He seated her in an armchair, hovered solicitously until she was comfortable, and flew out the door to seek his employer's wife.

Evangeline ran her hand appreciatively over the sumptuous upholstery. Her eyes drank in the decorative details of this private space—a marked contrast to the public lobby—Aubusson carpet so thick that no footfall could be heard crossing it. Hand-carved wainscot and wine-colored brocade draperies muted the discordant hubbub from the street. "Only the best for Bertha," she said to herself. Evangeline attributed the elegance of the room to Bertha Palmer's taste rather than that of her husband or the hotel decorator.

Mrs. Palmer was the most formidable woman in a city not lacking in that particular variety of female. She was the acknowledged queen of Chicago society and bore her title with a grace and intelligence that Evangeline rarely associated with *nouveau riche* grand dames. Bertha, when barely out of her teens, had married a man twenty-four years her senior and defied popular expectation by making the union a happy one. Potter Palmer, Chicago's foremost real-estate tycoon, although clearly enamored with Bertha's beauty, had been impressed by her level-headedness as well. He had once told Evangeline that while he had never taken a business partner, the closest approximation of one was his wife, or "Sissie" as he liked to call her.

"Engie, it's good to see you."

Evangeline's reverie was cut short as the connecting door on the other side of the office opened to admit the lady herself.

Bertha Palmer advanced into the room and held her hand out in greeting to Evangeline. "You've been a stranger of late," she said warmly.

Mrs. Palmer had quite a reputation for both her clothing and jewelry collections, but on this day her attire was relatively subdued. She wore a tailored walking suit of mauve wool. It had to be one of Redfern's creations, Evangeline thought approvingly—such understated elegance. The costume was topped by a black velvet hat trimmed with a modicum of feathers. Her only jewelry was a heavy gold brooch flecked with rubies.

Evangeline stood and moved forward to meet her. "I'm deeply indebted to you, Bertha, for seeing me on such short notice. I know how busy you've been with the Board of Lady Managers."

Mrs. Palmer, in addition to other social commitments, was chairwoman of the committee responsible for designing and planning the Women's Building Exhibit at the Fair.

"Yes, that's the reason I had to receive you here rather than at home. I'm on my way to another meeting at the fairgrounds and have a fearfully short period of time at my disposal." Mrs. Palmer motioned for her visitor to sit. "It's been a hectic few months, I assure you. But we've managed to stay the course. Only two more weeks to go."

"You've done a fine job of showing the gentlemen on the board what the ladies can do."

"Thank you, Engie. Given the number of petty disputes that have arisen along the way among the committee members, I'm glad we haven't shown the strain to the rest of the world. But," she added brightly, "the purpose of our chat today isn't for me to air my grievances. Your note said you had an urgent matter you needed to discuss."

"Yes." Evangeline dreaded broaching a topic her hostess would find most unpleasant. "It's about the murder."

"Oh!" Mrs. Palmer gasped. "Of all the possible reasons for your visit, that one never crossed my mind."

Evangeline took off her gloves and began to fidget with them. "You see, the girl who was killed... she was a student of mine... at Hull House."

"Why, I had no idea this matter might affect you personally, Engie. I am truly sorry."

Evangeline bowed her head to acknowledge the effort at condolence.

Mrs. Palmer continued, "If you don't mind my asking, was the young lady of a respectable family?"

"If you're asking whether she was in the habit of forming clandestine attachments to men of questionable character, the answer is an emphatic no."

"I'm relieved to hear that. You can't imagine how relieved." Mrs. Palmer sighed. "After seeing this business exposed so rudely in the press, our clientele doesn't know what to think of the Palmer House. We are the premiere hotel in this city and, with the Exposition drawing an international set, we have worked hard to maintain a cultivated image. This was hardly the sort of thing we wanted the world to see."

"Yes, I understand your concern for the credibility of the hotel, Bertha, but my principal concern is the credibility of Franz Bauer."

"Who?" Mrs. Palmer looked puzzled.

"The young man arrested for the murder, the dead girl's brother."

"Oh, I see." An edge came into Bertha Palmer's voice. "And are you aware of the disturbance he caused here the night she was killed?"

Evangeline adopted a tactful tone. "Yes, unfortunately, I am. Franz's temperament is a bit excitable."

"Apparently excitable enough to drive him to murder."

"It seems a bit premature to assume he's the only possible suspect, Bertha."

"Do you know about his unfortunate choice of political causes?"

"Yes. It's no secret that he's a member of a radical political group, and I'm well acquainted with your views and Mr. Palmer's on the subject of anarchists."

Bertha Palmer began to tap the arm of her chair with her index finger—the only hint of agitation she betrayed. "Then, given these circumstances, what can you possibly say in his defense?"

Evangeline smoothed the creases in her gown as an attempt at nonchalance. "Precious little, I'm afraid. But I have reason to suspect the police planted the murder weapon in his home."

Mrs. Palmer's face registered mild surprise. "That's a very serious charge, my dear. Can you prove it?"

"In order to do that, I need your help." Evangeline felt she had already strained the good will of her listener. She wasn't sure if her next words would elicit a positive response or terminate the interview altogether. "I'd like your cooperation while I conduct a private investigation of my own."

To her credit, Mrs. Palmer didn't react either with shock or anger. She merely raised an eyebrow. "And what would that entail?"

"Your instructions to your staff to candidly answer any questions I might put to them. And a similar set of instructions to Dr. Doyle."

Mrs. Palmer sat back in her chair. She tilted her head to the side and studied her visitor. "And why would I consent to do such a thing?"

Evangeline returned her gaze evenly. "Because I believe you to be a fair-minded person who wouldn't wish to contribute to a miscarriage of justice."

Mrs. Palmer smiled briefly at the observation. Without speaking, she stood up and began to walk around the room in a leisurely fashion—apparently weighing the decision further. At the window, she held the curtain aside to gaze out.

"Engie, come here, please. I'd like you to look at something." Evangeline crossed the room to where Mrs. Palmer stood. "What do you see out there?"

Evangeline looked quizzically at Mrs. Palmer and then turned her attention to the scene outside. "Well, I see carriages, people walking along the sidewalk, a policeman directing traffic at the intersection. Why? What do you see?"

Mrs. Palmer turned away from the view and moved back to her chair. Evangeline followed. "When I look out there, I don't merely see a disconnected set of figures bearing no relationship to one another. I see a society. A well-ordered society that only exists because of a set of commonly agreed-upon principles of conduct."

Mrs. Palmer held up her calling card case. "Why do you suppose we present these? Why do we bow to our acquaintances when we pass them in our carriages? Why are we gracious even to such graceless creatures as the Infanta of Spain?"

"Why, indeed." Evangeline laughed, remembering the insult Mrs. Palmer received from the aristocrat. "A Spanish princess who refused your dinner invitation because, as she put it, you were the wife of her innkeeper!"

Her eyes narrowing at the memory of the slight, the other woman continued. "We choose to overlook rudeness because that is one of the rituals of polite society. All such rituals, as trivial as they might seem, provide a framework for our conduct. They help us to function as a community. Without these, what sort of jungle do you suppose we would inhabit? Your young friend Franz, and those like him, they have a passion to tear down all these rules we live by. And once they have torn down every law and destroyed every fragment of morality, what will be left to stand between them and the devils they've unleashed?" Mrs. Palmer stared at Evangeline as the question hung in the air between them.

"I don't know the answer to that, Bertha. But there is one rule that applies to anarchists and republicans alike. A man is innocent until proven guilty. By law, he is guaranteed a fair trial. If you willfully obstruct my chance to find out the truth, then you have violated one of the most fundamental rules of your well-ordered society. Are you willing to take responsibility for the devils you, yourself, will unleash in consequence?"

Bertha Palmer bowed her head slowly in acquiescence. "*Touché*, my dear." Evangeline held her breath in anticipation. Mrs. Palmer chose her next words with great care. "If I were to consent to assist you in this matter... I say, if... I would require you to conduct your inquiry as inconspicuously as possible."

"Yes, of course."

"There would be no attention drawn to your activities and no public announcement of your progress. If you were to find evidence that might point to another suspect, you would notify me of your findings before the news is made public." Mrs. Palmer paused. "These would be my conditions. Would you be able to accept them?"

"Without reservation."

"If you couldn't fulfill these conditions, I would be required to withdraw my support immediately from you. Do you agree to this?"

Evangeline looked her directly in the eye. "Yes, Bertha, I do."

"Very well, then, I'll arrange matters." Mrs. Palmer rose decisively and opened the front door of the office. She beckoned to the desk clerk to return. "Humphrey, come here. Miss LeClair has some questions to ask you, and you are to give her whatever information she requires."

"Yes, madame, at once." Humphrey clicked his heels and sprang to the door at the first summons.

Mrs. Palmer prepared to leave. She turned to Evangeline and added, "Humphrey was on duty the evening of the unfortunate event. He has already been questioned by the police. I'll send for the chambermaid who discovered the body while you're speaking to him. I'll also telephone Dr. Doyle and let him know how matters stand." She held out her hand to Evangeline. "Forgive my skepticism, my dear. I wish you every success in uncovering the truth. And, more importantly, I hope the truth you uncover will be to your liking."

"Thank you, Bertha. I am most grateful." Evangeline shook Mrs. Palmer's hand energetically. Without further ceremony the queen of Chicago closed the door, leaving Evangeline in the company of the clerk.

10 – IN THE GRAND MANOR

"Humphrey, is it?" Evangeline began tentatively.

"Yes, miss. That's me." The clerk stood at attention and clicked his heels in acknowledgement. There was a military precision about the young man that extended well beyond his method of addressing his employer's clientele—a spit-and-polish shine that traveled from the patent leather sheen of his hair to the gleam of his brass buttons all the way down to his recently buffed boots.

"Have a seat, won't you?" Evangeline indicated the chair next to her own.

"No, thank you, miss. If you don't mind, I'd prefer to stand. Sitting in your presence would make me too nervous."

And would prevent you from bowing and clicking, no doubt, Evangeline thought. "Well then, let's begin. I'm conducting a private inquiry into the death that occurred here the night of October seventh. The unfortunate girl was a student of mine. I understand you were on duty that evening?"

"Yes, miss, indeed. I was at the Ladies' Entrance that evening."

"Can you remember anything noteworthy about the time Miss Bauer came in?"

"Unfortunately, I can't, miss. The police asked me the same thing, but we get so many people checking in and out of an evening. We have seven hundred rooms here, you know. It's hard to keep track of a single person. Except—"

"Yes?"

"Well, that's odd, isn't it," Humphrey said, half to himself. "I didn't remember this until just now when you asked."

"What?" Evangeline had to suppress a desire to pull the words out of him.

"I distinctly recall that she had no luggage with her. Just a small valise that she could carry in one hand. When I rang for the bellhop, she stopped me and said it wouldn't be necessary. And I remember thinking to myself how unusual that was. Then I reasoned that she might have packed a few things in that little

71

bag since it was just an overnight stay, and I thought no more about it. But it's just that ladies usually don't travel that light."

Evangeline smiled to herself at his observation, recalling the trunk she usually ordered packed whenever she was planning even a brief stay in town.

"And there's nothing else you remember about her arrival?"

"Nothing, miss, except that I thought she was deuced pretty, that's all."

"Yes, that was the general opinion about her." Evangeline cut the topic short. "Let's move on to later events. Since she was attacked and killed that night, we can conclude that someone probably came to see her in the evening. She checked in alone, so the visitor must have arrived sometime later. Do you remember anyone inquiring for her, say around nine or ten o'clock? Anyone other than the man who's been arrested, that is."

Humphrey hesitated, then shook his head energetically. "No, miss, I'm sorry, but I can't say that I do."

"Oh," Evangeline replied in a small voice, disappointed to be at another dead end. "I was hoping that you might have seen someone."

Humphrey looked down at his shoes in embarrassment, apparently afraid that he appeared to be uncooperative. "As I said, miss, I'm sorry."

Evangeline persisted. "Is there anyone else you can think of who might have seen something that night or the next morning?"

"Well, that night around ten o'clock, Miss Bauer pressed the call button in her room. All our rooms have electric call buttons, you know. They're silent in the guest rooms, but they ring through to the floor attendant's station. Anyway, she pressed the call button. The floor attendant knocked at her door, thinking she probably wanted her bed turned down, but there was no answer. The door was locked from the inside so the maid assumed she must have changed her mind. She didn't try her pass key because she didn't want to disturb the lady, and so she left."

"For all we know, that might have been an attempt to call for help," Evangeline observed bleakly.

"Yes, that's what the police thought when the night attendant told them."

"So, none of the staff actually went into the room around the time the crime might have occurred?"

"No, the body was found the next morning." Humphrey cleared his throat nervously. "It was found by Sally, one of the chambermaids. The police already talked to her, but you'd better ask her yourself. She's a bit flighty, though. I don't know how much help she'll be."

"That's all right. One never knows what will emerge, Humphrey. Thank you for your candor." Evangeline extended her hand to the clerk. He bowed over it, clicked his heels thunderously one last time, and left to fetch Sally.

A few minutes later, a plump girl with frizzled blond hair was propelled into the room, probably with the assistance of a nudge from behind. She stood near the door after it was closed and eyed Evangeline curiously.

Evangeline began simply, trying to put the girl at ease. "Hello, Sally, my name is Miss LeClair, and I have some questions to ask about the night Miss Bauer died here."

As Evangeline soon discovered, shyness was not in Sally's nature. The maid's eyes immediately began traveling around the office, taking note of the pictures, books, and rich draperies. "I never been in this room before. It's nicer'n some of the guest rooms."

Evangeline laughed. "Perhaps the hotel ought to rent it out to increase profit."

"That's what I'd do if I was them." Sally showed an amazing amount of assurance for one of such humble station.

The girl walked boldly up to Evangeline's chair and put her hand forward. "Pleased to meet ya, miss."

"And I, you." Evangeline was taken slightly aback by the girl's brazenness as they shook hands. Quite a contrast to Humphrey, who surely outranked her. "Why don't you sit down here." Evangeline indicated the chair next to her own.

Sally, needing no urging, quickly flopped down into it. "Lordy, my feet are so tired from going up 'n' down, up 'n' down."

"Then, why not put them up on that footstool." Evangeline gestured to the item in the corner.

It took Sally little additional time to make herself completely at ease. Breathing a long sigh of relaxation as she sank deeper into the chair, she closed her eyes dreamily for a moment.

"This is sure enough the life. A big, comfy chair where I could give orders an' have somebody else fetch 'n' carry for me the livelong day 'stead of the other way around. Right now, I feel like a regular queen."

Stifling a smile, Evangeline forged ahead. "I'm glad you're so relaxed, Sally, but I have some serious questions to ask you about the young lady you found dead in her room."

Sally opened her eyes slowly, showing no trace of alarm at the question. "Oh, that was somethin', wasn't it? Gave me quite a turn when I walked in an' found her that way."

"Tell me about it."

Sally sat up a bit in the chair. "Well, I started my rounds makin' up the rooms around nine that morning. I knocked before I tried the pass key to get in, like usual. Well, there's no answer, so I figure whoever's stayin' in the room must've already checked out. Anyhow, I let myself in an' I seen her lyin' there on the floor. At first, I figured maybe she was just passed out, so I go over to see if I can maybe wake her up. I take her by the wrist to shake her, but her arm is stiff an' cold as marble. I dropped it pretty fast after that, I can tell you. When I hopped up on my feet, all of a sudden, I seen the blood on the back of her gown. That's when I figured she wasn't just dead; she's been murdered. I threw down the towels I was carryin' an' ran down the hall yellin' for help at the top of my lungs. I didn't want no part of stayin' there by myself longer than I had to." Sally was out of breath from the drama of her narrative.

"And then the police arrived?"

"That's so, and they dragged me back in the room again to describe what I seen when I came in, and I told 'em just what I'm tellin' you now."

"Is there anything else that you remembered afterward? After the police left?"

Sally knit her brows together in concentration. "No, not a blessed thing. But I been havin' quite a time of it since then, I can tell you."

"Oh, why's that?" Evangeline wished to draw out every scrap of information that she could.

"Because everybody I know who works in the hotel wanted to see the murder room, which is what they're all callin' it now. So, I'd just use my pass key and show 'em around and tell 'em the story. It got to be so much trouble that I started chargin'."

"Really!" Evangeline laughed. "I must compliment you on your entrepreneurial spirit."

"On my what?" Sally wasn't sure whether to be offended or not.

"On your ability to turn a bad situation to your advantage."

"Oh, that!" The chambermaid relaxed. "Well, business has died down some now, but while it was goin' strong, it was enough for me to buy myself a pair of red silk stockings." She raised the hem of her skirt above her boot tops to reveal some lurid scarlet leggings. "See?"

"Quite impressive." Evangeline's face registered a variety of emotions which she hoped the girl would interpret as admiration. "Sally, how much do you charge for a tour?"

"Ten cents. But Humphrey told me to do whatever you want anyway." She appeared glum. "So, I guess if you want a tour it's gonna be for free."

Evangeline reached for her purse. "Nonsense, he doesn't need to know that I'm paying the going rate, and with the tip I intend to give you, maybe you'll be able to save up enough to buy matching garters."

"Oh, I'd cut a dash in them for sure." Sally's eyes gleamed as she took the money. "Step right this way, miss, an' I'll give you the grand tour."

Humphrey looked quizzically at the two as they emerged from the office, but when Evangeline explained they were going upstairs to look at the room he merely nodded.

"Sally, what if someone's occupying the room? Won't that be a problem?"

The maid waved her arm dismissively. "No need to bother yerself about that, miss. Nobody's been stayin' in that room since the night of the murder. What with the coppers traipsin' through, an' Mr. an' Mrs. Palmer so jumpy about the 'reputation of the establishment' as they're callin' it, it's gonna be a long time before it gets used again."

"Oh, I see." Evangeline was secretly pleased that she would have the opportunity to inspect the scene at her leisure.

The two took the elevator up to the fourth floor and turned down to the end of a long corridor. When they came to the door of Room 402, Sally used her pass key to enter. "These are all the cheap rooms at the back. That's 'cause they got no view."

Evangeline took a deep breath before entering. Until that moment, her pursuit of a murderer had been little more than a fascinating intellectual exercise. Now she was about to confront the reality of the place where her young friend had died.

The room was small by the standards of the Palmer House. It had little in the way of opulent amenities to recommend it. A brass bed, a marble-topped dresser, a carved oak chevalier mirror, and a chaise longue were all it contained. Evangeline paced back and forth, lost in thought. Sally stood watching her.

Finally, she turned to the girl. "Where was she when you found her?"

"Over there," Sally pointed toward the window. "She was layin' with her face pressed against the floor over there."

"Ah." Evangeline stepped forward and examined the sash for signs of forced entry but found none. Over her shoulder, she asked, "The window, was it locked or open when you came in?"

"It was shut. I didn't look to see if it was locked, but the copper said afterward it wasn't."

Evangeline continued her inspection. Despite the lack of a pleasant view to frame, the window was large. The bottom pane reached up to Evangeline's eye level, which made it close to five feet above the floor. She grasped the handles to see if it would raise and it slid noiselessly upward on its track. She leaned out over the sash and saw a fire escape leading down from the window and criss-crossing each subsequent level until it reached the alley below. The building directly across from the room where she stood had no windows at all fronting the alley. "How convenient for the murderer," Evangeline murmured under her breath. "No witnesses."

She pulled her head back into the room and shut the window. Turning to Sally, she asked, "Is there anything else you can recall? Something you forgot to tell the police?"

"Like I said before, miss, nothin' I can think of. But since you been so nice to me, there is somethin' somebody else saw that maybe you should know about."

"Really!" Evangeline was all attention.

"I didn't say it to the coppers because I didn't know it till afterwards, and the party who did see it wants to be kept out of it. He hates the law 'cause they ran his brother in on some trumped-up pickpocket charge."

"And this is someone you work with here?"

"He's a porter. I'll tell you that much. And the day after all this happened, a bunch of us was chit-chatting about it and this party I was tellin' you about, he takes me aside and says he seen somethin', too."

"But he didn't want to come forward?"

"Not likely. He says if I tell the coppers, he'll swear he didn't see nothin' at all."

"Then why do you suppose he told you about it?"

"Because he had to tell somebody or he'd bust, that's why! Men 're bigger gossips than women about some things. I can tell you that." Sally giggled. "So anyways, this party was carryin' luggage that night. He tells me he forgot to lock up one of the rooms here, so he runs back up the stairs and doesn't wait for the elevator. Just between you an' me, I think the real reason he came back up here was that he's got a bottle of gin stashed in the broom closet on this very floor. He prob'ly came back up for a nip is what I'm thinking. Anyway, as he comes round the corner, what do you think he sees?" Sally was clearly enjoying the suspense she was creating.

"What?" Evangeline felt breathless with anticipation.

"Why, there's a man standin' in the hallway outside this very room. But he didn't just knock and go in. From what my party says, he looked to be worked up about somethin'. He just kept walkin' up 'n' down the carpet in a brown study. The man in the hall didn't see my party 'cause he ducked back around the corner."

"Did your friend get a good look at him? Did he describe him to you?"

"Well, he says the man was tall, maybe six feet or so, and that he was dressed expensive, like a gen'lman."

"That's rather vague." Evangeline was disappointed at the lack of detail. "Anything else?"

Sally frowned in concentration. "Well, my party says the gent had his hat off, so it was easy to see he had dark hair, maybe black, maybe dark brown."

Evangeline made one last attempt to connect Sidley to the murder. "Was he wearing glasses? A moustache or beard, perhaps?"

Sally shook her head. "No, I remember my party says the gent was shaved clean. He didn't say nothin' about glasses, but I expect he would've if the gent was wearing some 'cause that's the kind of a thing anybody'd notice right off."

Although the description hardly fit Sidley, an unknown man with distinguishing characteristics was beginning to emerge. "Do you think your friend would know this man if he ever saw him again?"

"Prob'ly. My party said he saw the man turn full around and walk the other direction, just pacin' back 'n' forth in front of that room."

"What else did your friend see him do?"

"Well, after he'd wore out the hall carpet for a bit, he finally stops an' knocks. Never says nothin' but just taps on the door—real light, like he don't want nobody else on the floor to hear him. When the door opens, my party hears a lady's voice from inside. 'Come in,' she says, 'I've been expecting you.' My party just hits the stairs after that. He figures what's goin' on in that room is none of his business anyhow."

"Did he remember what time this happened?"

"He said it was around five 'til ten. He remembers 'cause he was due for his dinner break at ten and he wanted to finish up before he went."

Evangeline, highly satisfied with the information she had received, reached in her purse and produced a silver dollar. "Sally, you've been a great deal of help to me. Here's something for your trouble. It should be enough for the garters and a hat, too. Someday I may have to prevail on you to speak to your very observant friend, but don't say anything to him about this in the meantime."

"I won't, miss. You can count on me."

The two made their way back down to the lobby where Evangeline thanked Humphrey once more for his cooperation, handed him a tip, and departed.

As she began walking up State Street at a leisurely pace, a contented smile began to form. She entertained herself with visions of catching a killer.

11 – MEMENTO MORI

On Friday morning, Evangeline climbed into her carriage for a trip to the shabby section of town where working people lived. She wanted to collect Elsa's belongings and see if she could talk Mrs. O'Malley into sending Patsy to school, in return for a slight monetary incentive, of course.

The genteel mansions of Astor Street receded abruptly before the two-flats and tenements of the near west side. The very thought of her destination would have given the vapors to most of her society friends. The neighborhood surrounding Hull House, while not the poorest or most crime-ridden slum in the city, was scarcely a place where the well-to-do chose to be seen. In common parlance, the west side was known as the port of entry. Immigrants fresh off the boat came here and took whatever wretched accommodations they could find and whatever equally wretched work was offered. Once they had learned the language, found better jobs, and scrimped together enough money, they usually moved out. Considering that the O'Malleys had been in the city for some time, it was odd that they hadn't tried to flee the area as well.

Evangeline was jolted out of her reverie when the carriage lurched to one side and then righted itself. She poked her head out of the window to see what the problem was. It appeared that the pavement in this part of town was badly in need of repair. There were gaping holes in the street where rain had flooded and washed away the cedar paving blocks. The carriage wheels churned through the stagnant water and unmentionable debris that had collected in the craters that remained. Evangeline quickly put a handkerchief to her nose and pulled her head inside the window. She noticed a woman standing in front of a six-flat building shaking out a dust mop. The woman gaped as the vehicle moved sedately past.

Farther down the block, Jack reined in the horse before a decrepit workingman's cottage. He opened the door to hand Evangeline out.

"Do you want me to go in with you, Miss Engie?" He eyed the building suspiciously.

Evangeline stood on the curb contemplating the neighborhood. Several boys were playing stickball in the middle of the street. Most of them were about Patsy's age or younger. While it was a wonder that all the children in the neighborhood hadn't been put to work in factories, it was less than wonderful that none of them were in school either. At the moment, two of the boys were engaged in a screaming match that was likely to end in a scuffle. A terrier ran around them in a circle, offering his opinion by barking emphatically. The rest of the urchins diverted their attention from the prospect of the impending fistfight to the fine carriage with brass fittings and gleaming harness leather that had just driven into their domain.

Evangeline smiled wryly. "I think you'd better wait here, Jack. I'd like to find the carriage in the same spot, and in the same condition, when I come out."

Jack chuckled and tipped the corner of his hat. "Right you are, Miss Engie. They're a dangerous-looking lot, to be sure."

Eyeing Jack's height and girth, the diminutive desperados approached the carriage warily. Jack struck up a lazy conversation with the leader while Evangeline made for the O'Malley residence.

The cottage was constructed of red brick, though the brickwork sagged in places where the mortar had crumbled. A sparrow cheeped at Evangeline from a chink below the eaves. The building was two stories tall with a raised basement. Five warped stairs surmounted by a rusted railing led to the front door. As she climbed them, Evangeline noticed an open door below the sidewalk and opposite the basement door. It led to a water closet. Despite the lack of a convenient lavatory, the building was a sight better than many of the surrounding tenements that probably had no running water or plumbing. The O'Malleys must have been the most well-to-do family on the block since they had managed to put money down on their own ramshackle cottage and, according to Elsa, met the mortgage payments by taking in boarders.

She rapped decisively at the front door but could hear neither voices nor movement within. She knocked a second time and waited. After a few moments, she tried the doorknob. It turned. The tiny foyer was dim after the bright outdoor light. She walked in and called, "Hello. Is anyone home?" Her voice echoed off the walls but met with no reply.

It was strange that no one was about. Elsa had told her Mrs. O'Malley rarely moved from a sitting position, preferring that the world should come to her if it had a mind to. How very annoying—a wasted trip. Evangeline debated what to do. She had never been the sort of person to allow good manners to stand in the way of common sense. Freddie had often used the vulgar expression "high-handed" to describe her approach. She resolved to gather whatever she could find of Elsa's belongings rather than call a second time in as many days. She would deal with the matter of Patsy's schooling another time.

A staircase leading to the upper floor was directly in front of her. Evangeline knew that Elsa's room was in the attic because the girl had complained frequently of the summer heat in the stifling upstairs quarters she shared with Patsy. Evangeline ascended and found the stairs ended abruptly in the midst of a bedroom. The air was musty and close even on a chilly October day. From the masculine attire that hung on a wall peg, Evangeline assumed this had been Franz's room. It was surprisingly neat considering the police had rifled through it so recently looking for blood-stained daggers. She attributed its current tidiness to Patsy. Evangeline advanced across the room in a straight line because it was only safe to stand upright in the center. The steep pitch of the roof on either side would have required her to go about in a crouched position if she wanted to poke around in the corners.

Not wishing to receive a nasty bump on the head in the process, she moved forward and opened a door at the far end of the room, which led into the chamber that Elsa and Patsy shared. It was larger than the first but just as sparsely furnished, containing a double bed, a pine dresser, a cracked mirror, and a cedar chest pushed back against the rafters. There was very little place to store, much less hide, anything.

Patsy must have anticipated Evangeline's visit because a box of clothing sat on the dresser. Evangeline immediately recognized the shirtwaist folded on top to be one Elsa had worn. She rummaged through the drawers and cedar chest, but all the remaining clothing appeared to belong to a child. Picking up the box, she made her way downstairs.

When she peeked out the front door, she saw that Jack had made friends with the dog and was telling his ragamuffin audience the best way to train a terrier to catch rats. They appeared to be much impressed with his extensive knowledge of the subject. Seeing that he had matters well in hand, Evangeline chose to use this singular opportunity to examine the rest of the house unobserved. Perhaps she might stumble across something relevant to her investigation.

The first room off the foyer was a cramped parlor. Judging from its size, Evangeline doubted that the entire O'Malley clan could fit into the room all at the same time. The few sticks of furniture it contained were drawn close to the cast iron stove in one corner. A poker and several dry logs sat in a box next to it. Evangeline shivered slightly when she guessed that this was the single heat source for the house, other than the kitchen cook stove—hardly a sufficient protection against Chicago's blustery winters.

A horsehair settee on one side of the stove was dwarfed by an armchair of royal proportions on the other side. When Evangeline noticed that the seat cushion had lost some of its stuffing and a metal coil was working its way through the material, she was fairly certain who the chair's usual occupant was. The settee wasn't robust enough to hold Mrs. O'Malley's weight.

Evangeline was struck by the gloominess of the room even on a day when the sun shone brightly outdoors. It took her a few moments to comprehend that there was only one grimy window and that its lace curtains held enough soot and cobwebs to smother even the hardiest rays. Scant heat and less light made a disturbing contrast to her own warm, well-lit abode.

Off the parlor on the left was a small bedroom. It would barely have qualified as a closet in Evangeline's boudoir. She guessed this was the room the two little boys occupied. She could see another bedroom beyond it. An archway at the back of the parlor led her into the kitchen.

As she turned her attention away from the cold-water sink stacked with dirty dishes, Evangeline realized with a start that she wasn't alone. A figure was seated at the table, or rather half-sprawled across it. Evangeline recognized the vague man she had met at the funeral. It was Mr. Patrick O'Malley who sat slumped over in his shirt sleeves, a three-day stubble on his chin, his left cheek resting on the table, and his hat still partially perched on his head. As she drew near him, Evangeline became aware of the stench of alcohol. She saw a gin bottle on the table close to his left hand while an empty glass was still clutched in his right. He made no movement. Evangeline couldn't tell whether he was breathing or not. She tried to shake him gently by the shoulder.

"Mr. O'Malley?" She nudged him again. "Are you all right?"

He sat up with a snort. His hat went spinning to the floor. Jerking his arms up in surprise, he nearly clipped Evangeline on the ear. She leaped back out of range.

O'Malley turned toward her, startled and disoriented. His glazed eyes held a fearful expression. "Who are you?" he quavered, groping protectively for the nearly empty bottle.

Evangeline stood perfectly still. She replied in a calm voice. "I'm Evangeline LeClair, Mr. O'Malley. So sorry to have startled you. We've met before."

"What do you want? What are you doing sneaking up on a body like that?" He unsteadily poured the last of the gin into his glass.

She held forward the box of Elsa's clothing. "I came to collect these. I assumed your wife would be here."

"She's gone to Maxwell Street with the boys." He offered no details as to the reason for his wife's errand. Furtively glancing at the bundle, he asked, "What's that?"

Evangeline sighed and tried again. "It's Elsa's. I came by to collect her belongings."

He seemed not to hear the entire sentence. His comprehension hung on one word. "Elsa?"

"Yes, Elsa. You remember. We met at her funeral."

"Elsa." He rubbed his hands across his face as if the gesture would clear his mental stupor. "Elsa," he repeated this time in bewilderment. "She's gone, you know, all gone." He began to croon her name as if it were a lullaby. "Elsa. Pretty little Elsa. Poor little Elsa. Gone now. All gone." His face contorted and he began to sob, slumping back over the table.

Evangeline was stunned by his response. The man she met at the funeral seemed incapable of any feeling at all, much less such a mawkishly sentimental display. For the second time in a week, Evangeline found herself at a loss to account for human behavior—first Franz's violent outburst and now this!

"Mr. O'Malley, you must try to get a grip." She disliked the idea of touching him again but gently shook him by the shoulder. He shrank away from her touch.

"Go away! Leave me alone," he muttered petulantly. "What does it matter now anyway. She didn't love me." He sat up and guzzled the last of the gin. Turning his bloodshot eyes to glance up at her, he added, "What did she need me for when she had some rich man buying her things? I wasn't good enough!" He shook the bottle irritably when he realized it was empty.

"How do you know she received presents from a rich man?" Evangeline tried to sound only mildly interested, but her heart was racing.

He chuckled as if pleased with some private joke. The sound was like a death rattle. "I know about everything. More than her brother knew. More than she ever wanted me to know. More than I'll ever tell." He sniffled and rubbed his shirt sleeve distractedly across his runny nose.

Evangeline probed further, trying to ignore her own feelings of disgust. "You were in love with her, weren't you?"

The haunted expression in his eyes turned to a dull resentment. "Much good it did me! I wasn't fine enough for her! But things are fixed now so she can't love anybody anymore." He smiled maliciously at the thought. "There's a deal of comfort in that! If I can't have her, nobody else can either!" He tried to chuckle again, but the sound stuck in his throat and emerged instead as a series of fractured sobs. He rubbed his knuckles impatiently across his tear-streaked face.

Evangeline hesitated briefly before asking her next question. "Did you kill her?"

The question knocked the breath out of him. He gasped in panic, "I... I... Get out!" Without warning, he threw the empty gin bottle. It came hurtling through the air, sailed past Evangeline's ear and smashed against the wall behind her.

"Get out! Get out! Get ooooooouuuuuut!" O'Malley half rose from his chair, weaving unsteadily.

Evangeline prided herself on remaining cool in a crisis. She barely flinched at the sound of shattering glass while her eyes quickly scanned the room for a weapon to defend herself. She remembered the fire poker in the parlor. Surely, she could reach it before he caught up with her. It took all her self-control, but she stood her ground long enough to take the measure of the man. She guessed that he was too much of a coward to attack.

He tried to stare her down, but his gaze slid away. The effort of his outburst had cost him. He sagged back into his chair. "Leave me alone," he whined and sunk his head into his hands. "Stop bothering me. I don't want to think about her anymore."

Evangeline backed out of the kitchen cautiously, keeping her face toward him until she reached the front door. As she closed it behind her, she could hear him wailing Elsa's name like a funeral dirge.

During the bumpy carriage ride back to her own well-heeled neighborhood, Evangeline enumerated her suspects. The list had just grown longer by one.

12 – FREDDIE'S MALADY

It wasn't until late on Friday morning that Freddie was able to disentangle himself from the tentacles of Simpson & Austin to visit the physician who had examined Elsa's body. After his extended absence on Tuesday afternoon, Freddie could feel his uncle's benevolent mood evaporating. Getting a chance to interview Dr. Doyle would be a tricky matter since the doctor didn't keep evening office hours. Without any idea how to fabricate a new excuse so soon after his last disappearance, Freddie decided to use his basic maneuver of sneaking out when no one was watching and then apologize afterward.

Unfortunately, his uncle had taken the precaution of setting a watchdog on Freddie in the person of Aloysius Waverly. Like Freddie, Waverly was a junior associate in the firm, but not possessing Freddie's advantage of having been born into the right family, Aloysius chose to rise through the ranks by toadying for a senior partner.

As Freddie was about to run down the stairs to the front lobby and make his escape, Aloysius caught up with him. Trying to make his interest sound as casual as possible he inquired, "So where are you off to?"

"I thought I'd get a breath of air and, for your information, it is almost lunchtime."

"A breath of air?" Waverly was incredulous. "It's pouring outside!"

"Thanks, old man. I forgot my umbrella." Freddie offered no further information. Instead, he stamped back down the corridor to his office to retrieve it.

Trailing behind him, Aloysius grumbled, "But what will I tell Mr. Simpson if he should ask where you are?"

Freddie wheeled about suddenly, nearly causing a collision with his colleague. "And why, pray tell, would my uncle apply to you for that information in the first place?"

"Well, aaah, I suppose..." Waverly fumbled for words. His nose had a habit of twitching for no particular reason, which reminded Freddie of a rabbit. The resemblance to a rabbit extended to Aloysius' ears which were large, pointed, and, Freddie inferred, could pick up sounds inaudible to other humans.

"Don't bother to think up a good excuse. You could strain a part of your brain that might be needed to hatch a new scheme to stab me in the back."

"Why, Simpson, I'm appalled you would think that about me." Waverly displayed as much injured dignity as he could summon on such short notice, his nose twitching violently all the while.

Freddie stared at him impassively. "Aloysius, just how dumb do I look?"

"Well, there are times when you can be——"

"It was a rhetorical question, for God's sake!" Freddie cut in before he heard anything too unflattering about the level of his intelligence.

Waverly just stood there in silence, waiting for Freddie to do something significant that could be reported.

"Aloysius, how much would it cost for you to develop a temporary case of amnesia?"

"A what?" Waverly was aghast at the question.

"I'm speaking of a business proposition here. Something to compensate you for your silence in a matter that doesn't concern you anyway."

"Well, I don't know..."

"How does twenty dollars sound?"

"It sounds like a great deal of money." Aloysius appeared awestruck.

"And so it is. That's at least two days' pay to you, isn't it?"

"A bit more than that."

"Well, here you are." Freddie counted the bills out of his pocket. "And you didn't see me leave, and you have no idea where I am, is that clear?"

"Oh, yes, indeed. Quite clear." Waverly grabbed the money eagerly, rubbing his nose to quiet its vibrations.

Freddie waited until the bills had changed hands before saying, "And if my whereabouts today should somehow, accidentally, be reported to my uncle, you can rest assured that he will also hear that you accepted a bribe from me. Is that equally clear?"

Waverly blanched at the realization that he had stepped into a trap. "Agreed. You've bought my silence for the day. But it really is a pity." He paused to contemplate Freddie for a second. "You would have made a fine attorney after all."

"That's the limit! I've just heard the last insult I'm prepared to accept from you today!" Freddie reversed direction and marched toward the stairwell.

Sadly, Aloysius' prediction about the weather had been correct. It was pouring when Freddie left the building, and he had never gotten all the way back to his office for the umbrella. Rather than walk the twelve blocks to the doctor's address, he jumped into the first available cab. The driver let him off in the middle of a quiet street of residential greystone buildings. There was a plaque on the door of one indicating that the building contained a physician's office. In brass letters, it proclaimed: "Dr. A. C. Doyle—Consulting Physician."

"I wonder if the consultation ever involves a cure," Freddie asked himself as he ran up the stairs two at a time. He rapped on the door authoritatively. A young man with a pencil-thin mustache answered the summons.

Freddie announced himself. "Hello, my name is Frederick Simpson, and I'm here to see Dr. Doyle."

"Certainly, sir." The young man was unctuously polite. "What time is your appointment?"

"Well, that's just it." Freddie scraped his feet a bit. "I don't have one."

The attendant sized him up and down to determine if the cut of his clothing suggested a person to whom he could afford to be rude. The fact that Freddie was drenched didn't make him an imposing figure. "Oh my, that is unfortunate."

"Young man." Freddie took great pleasure in using that title which had so frequently been applied to him of late. "Young man, you may tell him that I have been recommended to his notice by a friend of Mrs. Potter Palmer and that I have come to discuss a matter which requires a certain degree of tact."

"Oh, I see." The attendant's tone immediately changed to one of deference. "And if I tell him this, he will understand your message?"

"Perfectly." Freddie spoke with far more confidence than he felt, but he was determined to get past the door before being thrown out on his ear.

"Come in, sir." The attendant bowed slightly and gestured toward the front parlor, which was used as a waiting room. The curtains were partially drawn even though the sky was almost black outside. Freddie sat down at one end of the room, near the bay window. The only other occupant was an elderly female with a formidable hat seated at the opposite end.

Freddie had learned through sad experience that ladies who wore formidable hats generally possessed temperaments to match their chapeaux. In consequence, he tried to avoid looking her directly in the eye. The lady was not to be so easily dissuaded. Even though he kept his head turned toward the opposite wall, Freddie could feel her staring at him. From the corner of his eye, he could see the ostrich plume perched on top of her head bobbing and swaying in the draughty air currents like some feathered cobra. When he couldn't stand the scrutiny any longer, he turned to gaze in her direction.

The woman used this as a signal to speak. "You're all wet!"

"Thank you, madame, for that bit of news. It is, after all, raining quite hard outside."

"Well, why didn't you just get a cab?"

"I did, but if I might direct your attention to the window, you'll notice that there's a veritable downpour going on."

Glancing imperiously out the window, the grand dame declined to comment further on the state of the weather. She changed the subject. "What are you here for?"

"Madame, that's rather a personal question!" Freddie was shocked at her impertinence until he realized that the woman was less interested in the details of his malady than in a segue to a discussion of her own.

She didn't wait for a further response before forging ahead. "I'm here for my weak nerves."

"Nerves?" Freddie was aghast. To himself, he mumbled, "I wouldn't have thought your nerves needed fortifying!"

"Yes, that's it. Nerves. The doctor gives me a tonic that does the trick every time."

"Alcohol, I'll bet," Freddie muttered, again under his breath.

"What was that? Speak up, young man. I can't hear you mumbling over there in the corner."

"I said..." Freddie tried to think quickly but his mental faculties, like his clothing, had been rendered soggy by the weather. "I said, all that rain is a threat."

"What!" The woman apparently didn't understand his meaning.

"Yes, well, you know. A threat to livestock carried away by flooding, that sort of thing," Freddie ended lamely.

The grand dame stared at him a long time before pronouncing judgment. "You are a very strange young man. Here for weakened mental faculties, aren't you?"

"Yes, that's right." Freddie surrendered completely. "How astute of you to notice."

Before he was subjected to any further humiliation, the door to the office opened, and the doctor emerged.

"Mrs. Parker, please come in." He glanced anxiously at Freddie. "I'll be with you shortly if you'd be good enough to wait."

"Certainly." Freddie felt a fair amount of surprise. The mention of the Palmer name carried more weight than he would have imagined.

The young man passed the time by studying the pictures that were hung around the waiting room. These consisted of tableaux of the great moments in medicine—from prehistoric times to modern. One that particularly intrigued him was a picture of a Greek physician performing surgery on the cranium of a patient who was seated in an upright position and appeared to be smiling euphorically through the whole procedure.

Each succeeding picture presented more outrageous inspiration for someone with a macabre sense of humor, but Freddie's contemplation of the artwork was cut short when Dr. Doyle returned.

"Won't you step in." Dr. Doyle was an impressive figure. In his mid-fifties, his temples just beginning to gray, he possessed an air of graceful self-assurance that must have been quite soothing to his clientele. Freddie inferred that the doctor's practice consisted mainly of middle-aged women complaining of nervous disorders. The doctor was dressed in a black frock coat and a pristine white shirt. A diamond-and-gold stick pin set off his black silk cravat. When Freddie approached to return the doctor's handshake, he noted that the older man's nails had been recently manicured and that his clothing exuded a faint hint of sandalwood. It occurred to Freddie that "ladies' man" wouldn't have been an inappropriate term to apply.

"Welcome, Mr. Simpson. I've been expecting you."

"You have? I wasn't aware that you even knew my name."

The doctor smiled slightly. "Mrs. Palmer and Miss LeClair both called a few days ago to offer an explanation."

"Oh, do you know Miss LeClair?"

"I knew her father, Armand LeClair, quite well. Met him soon after he first came to this city. He referred several of his wealthy friends to me as patients. Helped me build my practice. I doubt if I'd be as successful today without his assistance."

"It would appear that intervening in other people's business is a LeClair family trait."

"So it would seem." Doyle laughed good-naturedly. "But only with the best intentions, I'm sure." He gestured toward a chair. "And now, Mr. Simpson, having made one another's acquaintance, I invite you to have a seat and tell me what I can do for you today."

Freddie sat down as instructed and began. "As you already know, it's about the murdered girl who was found at the Palmer House over a week ago. I understand that the Palmers asked you to perform an independent examination of the body?"

"Yes. It's out of my usual line but, given the delicate nature of the situation, I became involved as a personal favor to the Palmers. What is it specifically that you wish to know?"

"To begin with, the papers all reported that there was a stab wound in the girl's back, but they reported very little else. Can you give me any more details of what you found?"

Doyle seemed uncomfortable and hesitated before replying. "This is rather a tricky matter, Mr. Simpson. Truth is such a complex notion, after all. Rather than being all of a piece, it can only be peeled back, layer by layer, like an onion."

"Meaning?"

"Meaning that, technically speaking, Miss Bauer was murdered, and the immediate cause of death was a knife wound in her back. This is the cause of death reported by the coroner. These are the facts that were released to the press."

"Shall we start peeling onions now, doctor?" Freddie asked pointedly.

"Yes, I suppose so. In my opinion, she died of respiratory collapse and heart failure."

"What?" Freddie sat bolt upright in his chair, all attention.

"As I said, a tricky matter. Was she attacked with intent to kill? Of that, I have no doubt. Was she stabbed? No question. But here is where I part ways with the coroner. His medical examiner believes the knife wound was sufficiently deep to cause death. I don't."

"Well, then what are you saying?"

"That I was required to delve deeper into the matter to determine the real cause. Superficially, she appeared to have been quite healthy. I doubted she had a weak heart or weak nerves. Fortunately, a small hobby of mine proved helpful in determining the true cause."

"A hobby?" Freddie was skeptical.

"Yes, you could call it that." Dr. Doyle smiled wryly. "I dabble a bit in poisons."

"What?" Freddie looked at the doctor in disbelief. "Exactly what do you mean by 'dabble?'"

Dr. Doyle chuckled at the consternation he had created. "Perhaps that was a poor choice of words on my part. Call it a professional interest, if you will, but I have an extensive knowledge of the subject. There are several poisons that could produce the symptoms exhibited by Miss Bauer."

"Really?" Freddie felt his own sense of morbid curiosity beginning to grow despite himself.

"Yes, I found a substance coating the fabric and skin around the wound that didn't appear to be dried blood. I scraped off a small sample that looked to be a sticky, brownish residue of some kind. Since some poisons are only effective if injected into the bloodstream, this seemed the most likely way of introducing the unknown substance."

"Did you find anything?"

"I conducted a few tests on the sample I had collected and was able to isolate the poison in question."

"Cyanide?" Freddie's own knowledge of poisons was hardly as extensive as the doctor's.

"Nothing quite as common as that. Cyanide is administered by ingestion, and none of the other signs associated with cyanide poisoning were present. I assumed I was looking for something that would kill in a matter of minutes. This, of course, would rule out snake venom as a possibility since that takes a while longer to work, and the victim might have had time to call for help before she died. Of the toxic substances which I knew would act quickly, I decided to test for *strychnos toxifera*, and my suspicions were confirmed."

"So, it was strychnine?"

"Only a distant cousin. The Latin name has thrown you off. I'm referring to a substance known under the name of 'curare.' It's a poison extracted from the bark and juice of trees in the Amazon jungle. Natives there have used it for centuries to coat the tips of arrows."

"Well, I suppose that would improve their chances of killing their prey even if their aim wasn't too good to begin with."

"Yes, I should think so. Ironically, curare is harmless when swallowed. It must be injected into the blood stream in order for its poisonous properties to be activated. Its chief advantage, if you can call it that, is that it can be administered in minute quantities through an abrasion in the skin, and it will kill almost instantaneously by causing respiratory paralysis and heart failure."

"I see. Then it might have been possible to coat the tip of the murder weapon with this substance and poison her that way?"

"Yes, absolutely. A knife dipped in the substance and then used to stab a person would have done the trick."

Warming to the subject, Freddie asked, "How would the blow have been delivered?"

"As nearly as I can approximate, it would have been inflicted from above. I would also judge that the attack didn't come from behind. The angle of approach suggested a murderer who was standing face-to-face with the victim and was several inches taller than she was as well."

Freddie pictured an image in his mind. "You mean, someone who was on close terms with her, someone she trusted?"

"Yes, that's the most probable scene."

The young man shook the unpleasant picture out of his head. "At what time would her death have occurred?"

"The coroner's office has estimated it to have been between ten o'clock and two in the morning."

Freddie thought about the knife in Franz Bauer's room. "What about the murder weapon the cops say they found? Did anybody test to see if it contained traces of poison on the blade?"

Doyle shook his head. "Since the coroner's office believes the cause of death was a stab wound, it's unlikely the police will pursue the poison angle. The matter will be for the courts to decide."

"I see." Freddie could guess the most likely verdict for Elsa's brother, whether guilty or not. "And was there anything else you noticed about the condition of the body?"

The doctor thought back for a moment. "No, that's all I can recall—no other evidence of a struggle, no bruising."

Freddie sat silent, wrapped in thought.

"I did, however, discover that she was more than four months pregnant."

"What!"

"Yes, that fact was kept out of the newspapers as well. There was no point in opening up another avenue of scandal for the hotel."

"The Palmers must have a great deal of respect for your discretion." Freddie rose to go. "Thank you, Doctor. This has been most helpful."

"Give my regards to Mr. LeClair's daughter and tell her she may call on me for any assistance she requires in this matter." Doyle ushered Freddie to the door.

By this time the rain had stopped, and Freddie decided to walk back to the office. "Well, Engie," he said, carrying on a mental conversation with his absent friend, "I think we've found a new motive for murder. I just hope you're sitting down when I tell you what it is!"

13 – THE FABRIC OF TRUTH

By Friday evening, Freddie was straining at the leash to have a long talk with Evangeline. They had only managed to communicate by hurried notes and telephone calls since the beginning of the week. He took the early commuter train back to Lake Bluff and didn't bother to stop at home first. As he walked down Center Avenue in the purple dusk, he could see several lights burning in the windows of Evangeline's house. Knowing Delphine's thrifty rules of domestic management, he concluded that she would have kept only one room lit if her mistress were away. Therefore, the lights must mean that the lady of the house had returned to the country. He was grateful for this since telephone service had only been installed in the city and not as far north as Lake Bluff. Keeping in contact with Evangeline during their investigation had become a challenge as she moved about from one place to another.

Freddie dashed up the stairs and rapped on the front door. After a few minutes, he saw a shadow behind the curtains of the side window and knew that Delphine was staring at him. When the door still didn't open, he renewed his attack. He raised his voice loud enough to disturb the entire street. "It's no good pretending you didn't see me, Delphine. You may as well let me in, or I'll continue to knock until I rouse either the dead or your next-door neighbors!"

He could hear her muttering, "*Mon Dieu! Quelle sottise!*" as she undid the lock and swung the door open.

"*Bienvenue,* Monsieur Freddie," she said caustically as the door opened.

"Same to you," Freddie replied without cordiality. "Where's Evangeline?"

"Mademoiselle is resting. She has just come back from the city, and she is very tired."

"I still want to see her!" Freddie barked. "Tell her it's important."

Delphine tilted her chin up defiantly but motioned him to follow her down the hall. When the housekeeper opened the door to the library, Freddie could see Evangeline leaning back in one of the wing chairs with her eyes closed and her feet resting on a tapestry-covered ottoman. The massive ball of fur and inertia she called a cat was curled up in her lap asleep.

"Pardon, ma chérie. Tu dois ouvrir les yeux. Ton chiot est revenu."

Freddie's French vocabulary didn't extend far enough to include Delphine's latest insult. Evangeline scowled, her eyes still shut. "Delphine, *je suis très fatiguée, et je n'ai pas de chiot!"* When she opened her eyes and saw Freddie standing in front of her, she gave Delphine a long-suffering look. *"Très amusant."*

Delphine whirled around and, without a word, closed the door behind her.

"What did she call me this time?" Freddie's tone was resigned.

"She referred to you as 'my puppy.'"

"Well, I suppose it could have been worse. Her allusion to the canine species might have extended to a rude reference to my mother."

He sighed and drew up the wing chair next to Evangeline, who by this time was sitting forward trying to shake off her drowsiness. Monsieur Beauvoir, disturbed by all the human racket interrupting his nap, had jumped down on the floor to wash his face and make himself presentable to company.

Freddie was about to launch into a colorful narration of his visit to Doctor Doyle when he noticed the solemn expression on Evangeline's face. The story died on his lips. "What is it, old girl? You look as if you'd just returned from another funeral."

"It feels something like that." She rubbed her hand across her brow. "This morning, I went to the O'Malley house to collect Elsa's effects."

"So that's what put you in this bleak mood."

Evangeline grimaced. "I wish that were the only reason." She then told her friend about her encounter with the very drunken Mr. O'Malley and his less than paternal feelings toward Elsa.

"Good Lord!" Freddie exclaimed. "Maybe he did it!"

Evangeline nodded. "It seems he had a motive at least as strong as Franz did."

"He might even have hidden the knife in her brother's room!"

"That thought also occurred to me. If Franz really is telling the truth, and if the police didn't plant the weapon, then O'Malley is the most likely person to have done so."

Freddie scratched his head. "Well, this is becoming a fine kettle of fish!"

Evangeline rested her chin in her hands and stared off into space. "I have more fish to add to the kettle, my lad. Both Franz and O'Malley were outraged at Elsa's involvement with a mysterious gentleman. They both said he bought her expensive gifts. I may have just found one of those gifts."

"What?" Freddie sat bolt upright.

"Follow me." Evangeline walked across to the desk and opened a cardboard box that had been placed there. "These were Elsa's things. Patsy packed them for me before I arrived. Inside, I found a separate parcel sent back by the police.

It contained everything they didn't want to keep as evidence. Have a look at this."

Freddie sauntered over to the desk and stood watching over Evangeline's shoulder. She held up a gold object that flashed and sparkled in the firelight.

Freddie whistled through his teeth. "That must have cost a pretty penny. What is it?"

Evangeline held the object out for him to examine. It was a lady's hair ornament, about four inches long and shaped like a cross. The face of the ornament was encrusted with sapphires and rubies. Combs were soldered to the ornament, and these would have held the jeweled object pressed against the back of the wearer's head.

"How would somebody wear a contraption like this?" Freddie was mystified.

"Like this." Evangeline demonstrated. "You see, the hair would have to be swept up toward the crown of the head in a topknot or a pompadour and secured by pins. Then the combs on this ornament would fit against the back of the head."

Freddie studied the effect. It reminded him of the elaborate combs that Spanish ladies wore with their mantillas.

Evangeline removed the ornament from her hair and gave it back to him for further inspection.

"Do you think the stones are real, Engie?"

"I'd say so. I know expensive jewelry when I see it."

"How did this slip by Mrs. O'Malley?"

"I don't believe she ever opened the bundle from the police station. Otherwise, I'm sure this would have ended up in a pawn shop, and Mrs. O'Malley's financial circumstances would have improved considerably. No doubt this was a gift from Elsa's mysterious admirer."

Evangeline rummaged around in the packing box once more. "There's something else here you should see."

Producing a crumpled piece of fabric, she spread it out on the desk to smooth out the wrinkles.

"A handkerchief!" Freddie almost danced with excitement. "That must be the one Bill told me about—the one he saw clutched in Elsa's hand after they found her."

"Yes, but it's odd just the same. This doesn't appear to be a lady's handkerchief. The dimensions are too large. The weight of the fabric is too heavy. There's no lace trim."

"And look at the embroidery." Freddie traced the pattern with his finger. The design was stitched with heavy black thread. It appeared to be a single flower with vines trailing out from either side. Below it were two rows of alternating black and white squares. "What are these?" Freddie pointed to sharp knots of embroidery that sprouted from the vines.

"I'm not sure. The whole design is so stylized, almost like a woodcut. It's hard to tell. Leaves, I suppose." She studied the item again. "This must have belonged to the man Elsa met that night. It's an expensive piece of work, no doubt custom-made, and the owner probably ordered a full dozen just like it. At least this confirms what both Franz and O'Malley suspected. She was involved with a gentleman of means."

Evangeline was pensive for a few moments. "But where did she meet him? She never left her own neighborhood. How could she possibly have crossed paths with a man who could afford something like this?" She gestured toward the hair ornament.

Freddie pondered the question awhile. "Well, did the Bauer girl know that Jacob Sidley wasn't going to meet her at the Fair?"

Evangeline thought back. "Why, no. As a matter of fact, she didn't. Mr. Sidley told me he was called into a meeting at the last minute. There would have been no way for him to get word to her in time."

"Then let's imagine poor little Elsa Bauer standing alone and forlorn, waiting for her companion who never shows up."

"Yes, and...?"

"Let's further imagine a wealthy gentleman strolling through the Fair. He's unaccompanied. It's a fine day, and he has some time to kill. Forgive the unfortunate choice of words. He sees this striking young lady standing by herself. Maybe he waits. Maybe he makes several rounds past that same point to see if she's still standing there. Perhaps fifteen minutes go by during which he sees her growing more and more dejected and more and more uncertain about what to do. Clearly, her companion has abandoned her. It seems the perfect opportunity, doesn't it?"

"Oh, I see. Yes, that would explain the initial contact."

"And what if he then strikes up a conversation and offers to show her the sights?" Freddie continued with his hypothesis. "No doubt, since he's wealthy and bored, he's been to the Exposition at least once before and knows all the principal things to see. She's grateful that he's taken charge of the situation. She allows herself to be led by him."

"Down any number of paths, one of which leads to the garden, I daresay." Evangeline's voice was tinged with sarcasm.

"Yes, but you see how it could have come about, don't you? It would have been a simple matter for him to pursue the acquaintance after that— prearranged meetings in out-of-the-way places."

"Unfortunately, I believe you're right, Freddie. That's probably exactly how it unfolded. Poor Mr. Sidley. If he'd only known his absence that day might have made the difference between life and death." Evangeline lapsed into silence. She focused her attention on the pattern of the handkerchief again, staring at it with great fixity. "There's something familiar about this. I think I've seen this design before, but for the life of me, I can't remember where."

"Of all times for your memory to fail you."

"No, I mean, it was the sort of thing you see out of the corner of your eye. Not quite aware of it. Something in the background, lurking somewhere." Evangeline scowled as she tried to recall the context.

"Well, let it go for now, Engie. Maybe it'll come back to you later. Besides, I haven't told you about the doctor yet."

"My goodness! With all the other information that's been uncovered, I completely forgot about that."

"Then listen," Freddie began sententiously, "and you shall learn." The young man launched into a description of his conversation with Dr. Doyle, expounding at great length on the nature of the poison. As he reached the end of his narrative, he hesitated a moment. "But that's not the worst of it."

"Good Lord, how much worse could it be than seduction followed by murder!"

Freddie led his listener back to her chair and sat down beside her. He took a deep breath. "She was expecting a child."

Evangeline's face registered shock. She exhaled a long, slow sigh. "I suppose it was inevitable. I just kept hoping that her death wouldn't have such sordid implications."

"It raises an even more sordid implication than illegitimacy."

"Yes?" Evangeline looked at him and waited.

"Have you considered the possibility that she might have been trying to blackmail her seducer? That she arranged the meeting at the hotel to collect payment but that her plan misfired?"

Evangeline rubbed her temples wearily. "I suppose in light of all this new evidence, anything is possible, but I just can't believe I was that mistaken in her character. I knew her during the course of two years, Freddie. Two years. People have a tendency to reveal their true colors over time, but I never saw her do anything remotely underhanded."

"Well, we can't prove that one way or another. There's still so much we don't know."

"One thing I do know. Even if we assume the worst, her hypothetical crime of blackmail is far less serious than murder. There is still a man out there somewhere who is responsible. We now have three suspects to consider. I'm less concerned about the first two because we know who they are and where they are. Franz is safely locked away in jail. Mr. O'Malley, without money, friends, or influence, could be locked up just as easily on the basis of my testimony alone. If he remains in his usual state of inebriation, I don't expect him to have the sense to flee. We know where to find him if the need arises. It seems to me we should devote all our attention to uncovering the identity of Elsa's mysterious gentleman friend. He may prove to be the most elusive because he has the wherewithal to cover his tracks."

"Well and good, but where do we start?"

Evangeline stood up and began to pace. Monsieur Beauvoir, who had been a witness to this entire exchange, sat motionless on the floor, only his eyes moving from side to side as he tracked Evangeline from one end of the room to the other.

"We have one solid bit of evidence to begin with. We know he is probably rich and is the owner of handkerchiefs with a most distinctive pattern. The fact that I have a nagging memory about the pattern leads me to believe that I've crossed paths with this person before. Obviously, we'll have to start tomorrow night at the Hunt Club Ball."

While Freddie had followed her logic up to the final sentence, she succeeded in losing him at the very end. He stared at her in surprise. "What do you mean? Why the Hunt Club Ball?"

"It's the beginning of the North Shore winter season. Everybody we know in Chicago society will be at the ball. You and I can take our time and survey all the guests until we find the person we're looking for. Thanks to a very observant porter at the Palmer House, I know that this mysterious gentleman is tall, clean-shaven, and has hair that is either dark brown or black. He is probably in his late twenties and probably does not wear glasses. Furthermore, we can hope he will have occasion to use a pocket handkerchief over the course of the evening. You will keep an eagle eye on all the guests in search of such a man with such a handkerchief."

"But Engie! That description could fit two dozen fellows I know. Don't you think I'll look like an idiot staring at so many pockets in one evening?"

"Freddie dear," the lady sighed, "I've often thought you looked like an idiot for far less reason than that."

14 – PAS DE DEUX

The evening of the long-awaited Hunt Club Ball finally arrived. As Freddie came up the front walk of the LeClair house, the young man noticed a shadowy figure in the side yard leading one of the horses over to the carriage trace.

"So, she's dragged you up from the city to drive her to the gala, has she, Jack?"

Squinting in the feeble light provided by the carriage lantern, the caretaker asked, "Is that you, Mister Freddie?"

"The same." Freddie sauntered up the stairs. "We'll be out as soon as Milady is ready."

"With the way Delphine's been fussing over her get-up for the past hour, that might not be as soon as you're expecting."

Freddie just chuckled and continued through the vestibule unannounced. When he walked into the front hall, he saw Delphine still putting the finishing touches to Evangeline's costume.

"*Ça suffit*, Delphine! Stop flitting around me. I don't need a fairy godmother!" Evangeline stamped her foot as the housekeeper adjusted the train of her gown for what must have been the fiftieth time that evening.

Delphine sniffed self-righteously. "You know, *ma chérie*, this would not be the style in Paris or even New York. There is no Monsieur Worth, no Monsieur Doucet. No, not even Madame Paquin! I just do what I can to make you look in fashion. *Mon Dieu*, these American couturiers. They are all... all..." she searched for the right English word, and not finding it, finally spat out, "*dégoûtant!*"

Evangeline walked over to the hall mirror. "We're not in Paris now, Delphine, so we'll just have to make do. Besides..." she said as she tilted her head up to show off her sapphire necklace to better advantage, "I think I look very well, very well indeed." She turned around with an arch expression to regard her visitor for the first time. "What do you think, Freddie?"

The young man swept his eyes admiringly over her blue silk gown. A small cluster of peacock feathers was pinned to her coiffure, and turquoise satin opera-length gloves completed the picture. "Stop fishing for compliments, Engie. You know you look swell."

The lady moved toward him, leaned in close, and adjusted his bow tie. "And so do you, my boy, so do you."

Freddie felt himself blushing and stepped back a pace or two to regain his dignity. He hated the fact that his feelings were an open book to her. "Well, if you're through trifling with me, I think we can go," he said stiffly.

Delphine, in wordless protest, handed Evangeline her shawl and fan, watching morosely as the couple made their way down to the carriage. "*Dégoûtant!*" she huffed one more time for emphasis before she closed the door.

***

It was a fine, dry evening with only a slight bit of autumn chill in the air. The Onwentsia Club was a flood of amber light through the trees as Jack rounded the turn off of Green Bay Road into the main drive. Several liveried attendants were waiting to open carriage doors and help the passengers out. Another servant in uniform stood at the door surveying the arrivals. Upon seeing Evangeline, he bowed and let the couple pass. After the lady was fussed over for a few more minutes by a maid in the cloakroom, the pair descended into the club ballroom. Even though it was barely nine o'clock, the room was already crowded with onlookers chattering away and dancers forming the intricate patterns of a quadrille.

Freddie nudged his friend's elbow. "There's something called too much of a good thing. How do you ever expect to find a clue in all this crowd?"

Evangeline examined the assembly. She noted the stifling air in the room, the roar of conversation, and the blur of multi-colored silk and flashing jewelry that was the dancers in motion. "I'm trusting to luck at this point." She tried to keep a note of dismay out of her voice.

"Why, Engie, look who's here." Freddie motioned to the far side of the dance floor. "It's the police superintendent and your father's old friend Judge Franklin. Maybe they'll have some new information about Franz Bauer."

"Over the course of this evening, I certainly intend to find out."

"Just try to be civil, will you?"

"I will be quite a model of self-possession." Evangeline fanned herself vigorously. "Unless one of them says something ridiculous, of course!"

"You have a very low tolerance for the ridiculous in anyone except yourself. Try to give them more latitude than that or you'll have picked a fight even before they can finish saying 'good evening.'"

"Very well, I promise to behave, if you promise to start checking pocket handkerchiefs."

"Yes, yes, I know. The pocket handkerchiefs, my own personal *ignis fatuus* for the evening." Freddie sighed. "Well, I'd best be about it then."

"So you should, for I fear I'm about to be claimed for a dance." Evangeline motioned with her head, and Freddie looked up to see Jonathan Blackthorne making his way slowly, but with great determination, through the crowd—his eyes locked on Evangeline.

When he finally reached the pair, Blackthorne said, "Engie, I've been waiting for your arrival all evening. I hope Simpson here hasn't preempted me and had the honor of dancing with you first?"

"Never fear, Jonathan," Evangeline laughed gaily. "I gave you my word a week ago, didn't I?"

"A lady who doesn't change her mind from one day to the next. What an admirable creature you are." Blackthorne bent over Evangeline's hand to kiss it. Freddie walked away in disgust and muttered something about needing some fresh air.

With an expectant look, Blackthorne led Evangeline onto the dance floor as the band began playing a Viennese waltz. Despite the fact that the two were mismatched in height as dance partners, they made a passable couple once they began to glide along in time to the music.

"You look quite radiant this evening, *ma chérie*." Blackthorne's eyes sparkled with admiration.

"Thank you, Jonathan." Evangeline felt more than a bit flustered. She was accustomed to meaningless compliments, but something in Blackthorne's manner of delivery made it seem as if he'd never spoken so warmly to a woman in his entire life. Evangeline wondered why this particular man had succeeded in intriguing her when so many others had failed. She thought briefly of Freddie—so innocent, so honest, so easy to read. Jonathan Blackthorne's face was anything but an open book. She could sense undercurrents in the man but had never succeeded in plumbing their depths. The attempt always implied the possibility of drowning. She chalked it up to her own perversity that her interest increased in proportion to the danger.

"I was concerned when I saw you with Simpson. Is he your escort for the evening?" Blackthorne's question broke into her reverie.

"Hmmmm? What was that? Escort? Only in the loosest possible sense. You should know by now that we're just friends."

"Ah yes, friends. The last time I saw you two together you were conspiring to catch the man who murdered your unfortunate protégé at the Palmer House. I read in the paper that her brother has been indicted. Has his trial date been set?"

"I haven't heard." Evangeline tried to sound nonchalant to keep Jonathan from noticing her agitation at the mention of the topic. She glanced sideways, thinking her heel had caught the train of her gown. When she turned her attention back to her partner, her eyes focused for the first time on

Blackthorne's waistcoat. What she saw froze her in place, almost causing Jonathan to trip over her as he took his next dance step.

She could feel all the blood draining from her face. Her hands went numb. Her feet seemed rooted to the floor.

Recovering his balance, Blackthorne asked anxiously, "Engie, are you all right?"

She laughed, somewhat feebly. "Oh, how clumsy of me. I must have lost my balance in that last turn. Why, it almost seems as if the room is spinning."

"Perhaps you'd better sit down." Blackthorne hovered solicitously. "Let me fetch you a glass of water."

"No, Jonathan, don't be silly." Evangeline laughed again in a strained manner. "I'm fine. Please, let's just continue dancing."

"As you wish, my dear." Blackthorne stared intently at her face, apparently not convinced she was well. The couple continued to waltz, Evangeline fighting to recover her composure step by step. Jonathan's next words did little to relieve the awkwardness of the moment since he renewed the topic of their previous conversation. "But to continue, I asked if Franz Bauer's trial date had been set."

"Oh, yes that." Evangeline thought quickly. "I saw the police superintendent across the room and asked Freddie to check with him to find out where things stood for Franz."

At that moment, the dance ended, and Freddie walked up to the couple. "There you are, old girl. No sign of it—" Before her friend could finish, Evangeline shifted all her weight to one heel and stepped squarely on Freddie's instep.

"Ye gods, Engie! Watch where you're going!" Freddie crumpled to the ground in pain.

Evangeline bent down and whispered urgently in his ear, "Freddie, not a word about pocket handkerchiefs! Be quiet and just follow my lead!" He looked up at her intently but remained silent.

"Here, let me help you up," she said aloud, still bending over him. "So sorry. That's twice in one evening that I've almost caused a gentleman physical injury."

"What do you mean, almost?" Freddie rubbed his injured foot ruefully.

"Why don't we sit down over in the corner there? I see that a couch is free." Taking Freddie by the arm, and with Blackthorne still tagging along, she continued. "Yes, Freddie, I already told Jonathan that I had you chasing down Superintendent Flint to find out if there was any new information about Franz Bauer's trial."

"Wha—," Freddie couldn't finish the word before Evangeline cut in again.

"I'm assuming there's nothing to tell or the papers would have reported it. That's what I've told Jonathan. Isn't that what you think, too?" She dug her fingers into his forearm.

"Oh, uh... yes, well, ahemm... I guess that's right." Freddie tried to keep up the bluff. "I couldn't find him though. Maybe we'll bump into him later."

"Why, he's right there," Blackthorne said in bewilderment. He pointed to a man standing no more than five feet from the couch where the three had decided to sit. The superintendent, a man of ponderous weight and even more ponderous opinions, was still deep in conversation with Judge Franklin.

"Affording us a perfect opportunity to speak to him now." Evangeline's tone was tense.

"What's your rush? I can't even walk without limping," Freddie whined.

"Then you sit still. Jonathan can accompany me while I go and question him."

Apparently not trusting that Evangeline could keep her temper in check, Freddie brushed personal injury aside in order to act as an intermediary. "No, wait a minute, Engie, I'll take you to him." He stood up, wincing.

Not to be left behind, Blackthorne spoke up. "I'm coming along just the same if you don't mind. I'd be curious to hear what he has to say."

Evangeline made no comment but moved forward with the two men trailing behind her.

"Good evening. Superintendent, Judge." She held out her hand to each in turn.

"Hello, Miss LeClair, gentlemen," the superintendent acknowledged the party. The judge nodded a greeting as well.

"And how are you enjoying the revels so far?" the lady asked.

"Oh, well enough, well enough." The judge was in an amiable mood. "Superintendent Flint and I were just discussing the sad state that Chicago has come to when one of our best hotels can become tinged with scandal."

"How apropos." Evangeline smiled archly. "I assume you're referring to the killing that occurred recently at the Palmer House?"

"Yes, quite so. From what I gather, the girl worked in a factory. In my opinion, she had no business in a room at one of our best hotels, except possibly as a chambermaid sent in to clean it!"

The superintendent laughed appreciatively.

Freddie, apparently noting that a vein on Evangeline's forehead had begun to throb, tried to intercede. "Engie, count to ten!" he exclaimed under his breath.

She snapped her fan open and began to wave it energetically. "And what would you gentlemen suggest as a counter measure?" She forced a brittle smile. "Compulsory disclosure of one's family tree before checking into the hotel? Or perhaps a statement of account from one's bank would be sufficient? What else? Letters of reference?"

The two older men appeared discomfited by her remark. Freddie jumped in to try to repair the damage. "What she means is—"

Evangeline cut him short. "What I mean is what I have said! Since when does social rank determine one's right to occupy a public hotel?"

"When murder is involved, Miss LeClair. That's when," the superintendent retorted. "The judge is simply suggesting that if we didn't have riffraff putting on airs and thinking they can go anywhere, then we wouldn't have a crime like this occurring in a reputable establishment. She would have been killed in a back alley where she belonged, and it never would have made the papers at all. Instead, we've got a local scandal on our hands."

"My, how unfortunate for you." Evangeline's voice dripped acid.

"It's just a shame this had to be blown out of proportion by the newspapers," Judge Franklin added. "It made her sound like an injured innocent, which I'm sure she wasn't."

"I wasn't aware you knew her personally and could presume to formulate an opinion of her character." Evangeline's tone held a dangerous challenge.

"God forbid! I didn't know her personally," Judge Franklin exclaimed.

"Well, I did!" Evangeline made little attempt to conceal her anger. "I see no point in standing by and hearing either one of you malign the character of an unfortunate young woman you never knew and would never have taken the pains to protect while she was alive! I'm sorry her murder has proven to be such an inconvenience to you! Good evening..." she glanced scornfully from one to the other, "... gentlemen!" Turning on her heel, she marched out of the room.

***

The four men stood together, silent and somewhat chastened. The judge finally shrugged. "Ah, the ladies! Who can understand them? When they take up a cause, they make up in sentiment what they lack in reason." The others laughed uneasily.

Freddie looked nervously toward her retreating figure. "I'd better go after her and calm her down."

As he headed toward the buffet room to find Evangeline, Blackthorne followed him. Turning about, Freddie said, "Look, old man, I don't mean to be rude, but you'd better let me speak to her alone before you try to see her again. She's pretty upset."

"Well, you know her better than I do." Jonathan sounded skeptical.

"Unfortunately, I do."

"Under the circumstances, I won't intrude myself any further on her notice this evening, but when you find her, please tell her I'll call tomorrow afternoon." Blackthorne paused. "You will tell her that, won't you?"

"I'll give her your message. You needn't worry." Freddie waved him away distractedly.

The young man eventually found Evangeline, not by the buffet table, but standing near the entrance where she was in the process of summoning her carriage. "Oh, there you are, Freddie! I think it's time to go."

"Well, this has been an unusually short party. I've never known you to run from a fight before. What's going on?"

"I need time to think. I just need time to understand this." Evangeline seemed agitated.

"And what about that assault on me?"

"Shhhh! Not now! Wait until we get into the carriage. I'll tell you then."

Luckily, Jack arrived at the front steps at that moment to drive them home. When they were settled inside, Freddie broached the topic again. "All right, this had better be good!"

Evangeline was silent, apparently collecting her thoughts. When she spoke, her voice was tight with nervous tension. "You went off inspecting handkerchiefs?"

"Yes, you know I did."

"Find anything?"

"No, nothing. Not a clue."

"I don't suppose you noticed Jonathan's waistcoat?"

"Why would I? He was with you, and besides, he's a friend of yours..." Freddie trailed off, realizing the implication of her question. "Oh my God, Engie. You don't mean..."

"Yes, I do, Freddie. Indeed, I do. I couldn't believe my eyes when I saw it. In his waistcoat pocket, I caught a glimpse of a handkerchief. A handkerchief with the same embroidered pattern as Elsa's. When I started to think about it, everything made horrible sense."

"How?" Freddie was lost.

"The flower on Elsa's handkerchief. The same flower on his handkerchief. What sort of flower do you think it was?"

Freddie knit his brows in concentration. "How should I know? You're the horticulturist."

"Yes, but I would imagine that even you would recognize a rose when you saw one. More specifically, it was a black rose, Freddie. Don't you find that significant?"

"Should I?"

"Of course, you should. Elsa's handkerchief showed flowers, vines, leaves, and notches that we couldn't identify—all stitched in black thread. If the flower is a rose, what do you imagine the notches to be?"

"Thorns, I suppose." He caught his breath with a hiss as the full force of the answer struck him. In a far-off voice he whispered, "Yes, I see. Black thorns. Blackthorne."

15 – OF ROSES AND THORNS

"It's impossible! He couldn't have done it." Sunday afternoon found Evangeline no less shaken than the night before. In an attempt to quell the debate raging inside her head, she had retreated to the conservatory to tend her plants. Unfortunately, physical activity did little to calm her mental distress.

"I've known him for years. It's almost as absurd as thinking that Freddie might kill someone!" Evangeline's mind refused to accept the possibility that a man she knew could be capable of cold-blooded seduction, much less murder. Her world, so safely enclosed by the ordinary—theater matinees, lawn parties, and charity auctions—couldn't contain knives and blood. It simply couldn't. No matter that her bravura displays of independence suggested a woman who had no difficulty embracing life's stranger elements. Those stranger elements had never included poisoned corpses or libertines seated at her own tea table.

Evangeline sighed and watered an African violet. She glanced at the listless bougainvillea and rusted ferns struggling for life beneath the cloudy autumn afternoon. A weak beam of sunlight shivered down through bare-branched trees past the glass ceiling panels and touched her shoulder. Outside, bone-dry leaves rattled across the lawn driven by a chill north wind. So little time before the snows came and laid waste to everything.

Her mind drifted to a picture she had seen of Lizzie Borden, a woman who, just the year before in Fall River, Massachusetts, had been accused of hacking her father and step-mother to death with a hatchet—thirty blows with a hatchet to be precise. The crime was so dreadful that it even made news half a country away. The Tribune, the *Inter-Ocean*, and all the other local papers had carried sketches of the infamous spinster. Evangeline felt a morbid fascination for the story, and she had studied the woman's face over and over, looking for some trace of viciousness—some hint of a demon capable of such brutality. The eyes of Lizzie Borden didn't betray a crazed murderer. They suggested cool streams and tranquil shade. Evangeline tried, but never found a way to reconcile the contradiction—to combine the mundane with the monstrous.

She turned her attention back to the task at hand—a tea rose badly in need of pruning. She set to work cutting away the dead undergrowth with feverish intensity. The paradox bedeviled her. Lizzie Borden looked harmless. Jonathan Blackthorne looked harmless as well. He was certainly not the sort of man to go lurking about in hotel hallways. But she could hardly ignore the description given by the chambermaid's friend—a tall, clean-shaven, dark-haired gentleman. It fit too well. "Maybe he only went to see her that night. Maybe she was killed by one of the others," she thought. But this possibility still implied some connection to the murdered girl—a connection that cried out for an explanation.

Evangeline paused to contemplate the plant she was holding, now free of its misshapen twigs, its yellowed leaves. She brushed the delicate coral petals with her fingertips. Her mind drifted back to all the dinner parties she had attended at the Blackthorne home; the first time Jonathan had sent her a bouquet of camellias; his first, almost timid request to pay his addresses to her. Mysterious he might be, but there was nothing in his manner, nothing in his voice to suggest the beast who had certainly seduced and possibly killed Elsa.

"How can this be? I know him. I know him!"

Lost in her mental struggle, she didn't hear the door open. Nor did she realize that someone had quietly walked up behind her until she saw a shadow cast over her shoulder. She gave a start and wheeled around to see Blackthorne smiling down at her.

"Good afternoon, *ma belle*."

Evangeline backed away a few paces when she saw who her visitor was and clutched convulsively at the plant she was still holding.

He caught his breath sharply, taking her hand. "Why, Engie, you're bleeding. Let me attend to this."

She tried to laugh. "Oh, it's nothing. I'll never learn. That's what comes of handling roses without gloves." She took out a handkerchief to stanch the blood. "Never mind, Jonathan. Please don't make a fuss." To cover her trembling, she turned around to resume her work.

"Forgive me, my dear. Delphine told me you were here and suggested that I surprise you. I'm sorry if that surprise turned to alarm."

Evangeline distractedly twisted the blood-stained handkerchief between her fingers. "You needn't be concerned. I'm very happy to see you. Very happy. I just wasn't expecting you today, that's all."

"Oh, I see." Blackthorne's tone was icy. "Then Simpson must have forgotten to convey my message of last evening."

"What message?" Evangeline asked over her shoulder in puzzlement.

"I was quite concerned about you yesterday night. When you left the ball, you seemed very distressed. I wanted to follow to make sure you were well. Unfortunately, your young friend discouraged me from doing so."

"Oh." Evangeline paused in embarrassment. "I'm sorry about that little scene. It was rather awkward."

"Under other circumstances, I would have found it amusing." Blackthorne smiled as he toyed with a pair of pruning shears lying on the table. "If only you'd seen the faces of the judge and the superintendent when you walked out. I believe it was a new experience for either of them to be at a loss for words."

"I wish I had seen it. There are a great many things I wish I'd seen." She crumpled the stained handkerchief into a ball and tossed it into an empty clay pot.

"Engie, I believe this business of the murder has unnerved you. You seem shaken, and I've never known you to act squeamish before. All this morbid talk about corpses must be upsetting you. Don't you see the futility of dwelling on it?"

Jonathan was standing directly beside her, his jacket brushing her sleeve. He had tilted her chin up so he could look directly at her while he was speaking. Evangeline looked into his eyes for a long time, trying to read something there. She hoped to see some glint of remorse, or guilt, or even fear, but his face revealed nothing more than a disconcerting tenderness. "Perhaps I'm imagining things," she thought. Finally, turning away from the potting table, she gestured toward the wrought-iron chairs in the corner. He took her hand and led her gently to sit down next to him.

"Maybe you're right, Jonathan. Maybe I should just stop thinking about it." She appeared to relent.

"The police are clearly unwilling to pursue another suspect now that Franz Bauer has been indicted. Isn't that so?"

"Yes, that much is obvious."

"And since I've heard nothing to the contrary, should I infer that your own investigation has been unsuccessful?"

She hesitated a long while before answering. "Yes!" she exhaled in the attitude of one unwilling to admit defeat. She could scarcely tell him how much she had uncovered.

His tension eased, and he smiled sadly. "Sometimes it can be hard to let go of the past. Especially if it means the loss of those we care about. It's even harder to admit we've been mistaken in the character of those we trust. I'd advise you to put the whole business behind you. Let it go, Engie. There's nothing you can do."

"I suppose not."

Her visitor nodded briefly and continued. "But it isn't the past that concerns me today. I came to speak about the future."

"Oh?" Evangeline pulled herself back to attention.

Blackthorne stroked the top of her hand gently with his thumb. "It must be obvious to you what my feelings are."

Evangeline was speechless.

"I wanted to bring the topic up last night, but circumstances prevented me."

"Jonathan, before you go any further..." she tried to intercept him.

"No, please, my dear." His manner was soothing. "You must hear me out this once. I've been looking for an opportunity time after time, but you were always engaged with other company. So, it's now or never. I must know if my affections are returned."

"You place me in a very awkward situation." Evangeline's heart was hammering like a bird trying to escape a cage. "You've been courting me for such a brief time."

"What does time mean to the heart?" Blackthorne searched her eyes in appeal. "One loves, or one does not."

"One may grow to love in time."

"Such slow-growing affection makes a poor substitute for passion in full bloom," Jonathan said glumly.

Evangeline affected a light tone to break the tension. "Every gardener knows a rose must bud before it blooms."

Blackthorne's hand tightened over her own. "Your words give me hope."

"I'm afraid I can give you no more than that at the moment." Evangeline tried to put the right note of regret in her voice.

"I'll feast on that crumb for the present. If you hadn't given me at least that much of a hint of your inclination, I was prepared to do something desperate."

"Desperate?"

"I was thinking of leaving the city—even more, leaving this area of the country and settling in the east."

"Why, Jonathan, you shock me!" This time, Evangeline didn't need to falsify her response. "All that simply because of unrequited love?"

"*Ma chérie*, once you've aspired to love an ideal and have seen that love rejected, what else remains? The fall from such a height is terrible indeed."

Evangeline gazed at him fixedly, but his face was still unreadable. His eyes were cast toward the ground. When he looked up again, she fancied she saw tears in them.

"All this because of me?"

"All this because of you, *ma belle*." His voice had become a silken whisper. "Surely my suffering deserves some recompense."

To hide her distress, Evangeline stood up and walked back toward the potting table. Over her shoulder, she said, "I'm sorry. I can't reward you with any better answer than I've already given. You must be patient with me."

Blackthorne came to stand behind her. She could feel him placing his hands on her shoulders. He bent down to murmur in her ear. "Then take as much time as you need. I'll watch, and I'll wait."

Evangeline drew her breath in sharply. She could feel him running the tips of his fingers gently down the back of her neck. Without her knowing quite how he managed it, he had turned her about to face him. "I'll only beg this one last favor before I take my leave, Engie." He bent down closer and kissed her softly on the lips.

Shuddering inwardly, she put her arms around him and returned the kiss. His lips felt very, very cold. Without another word, he released her and walked out of the room.

Evangeline stepped over to the windows. She felt dizzy—the same dizziness she'd felt the night before on the dance floor. She stood a long time looking out over the brown lawn, anxiously rubbing the cut on her finger.

16 – THE EDGE OF THE BLUFF

Two hours later, Evangeline was still haunted by her unsettling encounter with Blackthorne. Since her usual method of calming herself had been the occasion of her most recent upset, she resorted to another source of distraction. Changing into a sturdier pair of shoes, she started for the lake. She felt that a walk along the beach would help restore her nerve or, at the very least, exhaust her enough to allow her to sleep that night.

Evangeline's house stood only three blocks from the edge of the precipice for which the town of Lake Bluff was named. From there it was a hundred-foot drop to the shores of Lake Michigan. The Baptists who had originally claimed the village's picturesque setting for their summer revival meetings had carved a series of trails down the bluff to the water. Even though the sun was making its final descent and the shadows were lengthening every minute, Evangeline managed to pick out a sandy trail as she clambered down the steep slope.

When she was about half-way down, she stopped. She imagined she heard a rustling in the bushes below her. "Probably a squirrel," she muttered. She squinted off toward the horizon. The wind had shifted to the northeast, and the waves were frothy with whitecaps. She continued to navigate her way down the narrow, sandy path.

She came to a dead stop when she heard the rustling again. This time it was off to the right of where she stood. She tried to still her breathing so she could hear any movement, no matter how small. "Is anybody there?" she called out. But only the waves and wind answered her.

She was about to continue down the slope when she heard a crashing through the undergrowth. Closer this time and directly behind her. She spun around to locate the source and saw, or rather felt, the presence of a figure blotting out the sunset. His face was in shadow, but the sight of an unexpected human shape was enough to startle her into losing her balance. She slid down

110

the trail, tree branches snapping as she vainly tried to grasp at anything to slow her fall. She tumbled head over heels the rest of the way down to the base of the bluff. When she landed, her forehead struck an outcropping of rock. That was all she remembered before the world went black.

***

"Engie! Can you hear me? Are you all right?"

She felt someone shaking her.

"Engie, answer me!" The voice was urgent and full of fear. She thought it belonged to Freddie, but she couldn't be sure. When she was able to blink her eyes open, she confirmed that it was, indeed, Freddie, but there seemed to be two of him. She became aware of a throbbing mass of pain at the front of her head. The pulse points at each temple pounded insistently until they collided in the middle of her skull, triggering a wave of nausea and dizziness.

"Oh!" She sat up, trying to touch the bump on her forehead. When she drew back her hand, she noticed it was coated with a sticky, red substance.

"Thank God, you're alive!" Freddie cried in relief. His arms were around her. "Can you stand up?"

He tried to draw her upward, but her legs refused to follow the command her brain was sending. She crumpled back to the ground.

"Wait," she managed to whisper through the roaring pain in her head. "Wait a bit. I think I'll be all right in a minute."

Freddie sat down beside her and drew out a handkerchief to dab at the blood on her forehead. "Well, thank God, it only appears to be a shallow cut. What happened to your hat?"

Evangeline touched the top of her head and realized she was bareheaded. "It must have been knocked off when I tumbled down." She winced as she moved her arm to feel the back of her head. The muscles in her neck and shoulders ached.

"Here, put your hands down and let's have a look." Freddie tried to part the masses of hair at the back of her head in an effort to find any other injuries to her scalp.

"Owww! Stop that!"

"Well, it doesn't appear that the skin is broken anywhere else. There's just that nasty bump on your forehead. How in the world did you manage to tumble down the trail? I always thought you could hike it with your eyes closed."

While the pain refused to subside, her vision was beginning to return to normal. "I had a little help."

"What! Do you mean someone pushed you?"

"Not exactly. I heard a rustling in the bushes. Someone came rushing up behind me and startled me so that I lost my balance."

"Could you see who it was?"

She shook her head, wincing again at the flood of pain that the movement cost her. "No, the sun was at his back, and he was half-covered by trees."

"It's lucky for you there's so much undergrowth on the way down. That must have slowed your tumble a bit."

"Maybe, but it wasn't so lucky that my head found the only rock sticking out of the sand to bump itself on."

"Still, it could have been far worse," Freddie's tone was ominous. He looked up at the bluff appraisingly. Only a few of the maples had completely shed their leaves even though it was late in the season. Plenty of places for someone to lurk in the dense undergrowth. "You must have tumbled along the trail for about fifty feet. You'd think if it was just someone out walking, and he'd startled you by accident, he would have run to your assistance to see if you were hurt."

Evangeline, now able to focus her eyes clearly, looked back up at the bluff with a slight shiver. "Maybe he wasn't just someone out walking. Maybe he'd been following me. Perhaps he wanted to push me down the cliff, but I saved him the trouble."

"But who?"

"I don't know. I just don't know. Maybe it's just my imagination. Maybe it was nothing more than a silly accident. Everything is so confused now!"

Freddie was up on his feet in a flash. "We have to get you out of here."

"No, not yet. Let me see if I can walk on a level surface first before we start climbing any more hills."

The young man held out his hand to steady her as she tried to rise.

"So far, so good. Give me your arm to lean on."

He complied and began to lead her slowly along the beach.

After a few tottering steps, Evangeline seemed to regain her balance. "It hurts damnably, but I don't believe there's any serious injury." She took a deep breath to clear her head further. "Yes, I do believe I'll live." Recollecting the odd circumstances of her rescue, she asked, "What are you doing here, anyway?"

"After I got back from escorting my mother on her interminable round of calls, I went to your house. Since we didn't spend any time planning a strategy after I brought you home last night, I thought perhaps you'd be ready to talk now. I had to pry the information out of Delphine, but she said I could find you down here. That you'd only left about ten minutes before I arrived." He looked up at the ever-darkening sky, the waves crashing on the sand. "Trust you to come out here only when the weather is unfit for man or beast!"

Evangeline stared at her companion. Lost in her own dazed thoughts, she only half heard his words. "It won't do. It just won't do at all, Freddie!"

"What won't do, old girl?"

"Nothing fits anymore. What we've discovered the past two days changes everything."

"Engie, it's getting dark. Maybe we'd better go back." Freddie eyed the shadows anxiously. "You need to see a doctor."

"I don't need a doctor! I'm not hurt that badly. This event only compounds what's already happened today. I can't sit still and try to sort this out. I need to walk." Evangeline reversed direction and headed south down the beach.

"How much could have happened? I saw you only last night."

"For one thing, Jonathan paid me a visit this afternoon."

"Oh, I forgot." Freddie sounded guilty.

"So it would seem. He was quite put out that you didn't convey his message. Was that deliberate?"

"Of course not! I just forgot, though I can't say I'm sorry if I managed to inconvenience your gentleman caller."

"Well, whatever the case may be, he very nearly proposed."

What!" Freddie came to a dead stop and grabbed Evangeline by the shoulders. "He what!"

"Yes, you heard me correctly. He hinted, at the very least. But there's more." The rushing of the waves made her voice almost imperceptible. "He kissed me before he left, and the fearful part about it is that I kissed him back."

Freddie stopped dead in his tracks for the second time. "Engie, if you're trying to kill me, why don't you just get it over with in one blow! What do you mean, you kissed him back?"

Evangeline shook her head vehemently to clear the image from her head, but this only made her wince. A dull thud in her temple reminded her that abrupt physical action was still inadvisable. "Oww!" she moaned. "What was I supposed to do, Freddie? What was I supposed to do?" A note of desperation crept into her voice. "I've been wrestling with that dilemma ever since this afternoon. If I discourage him too strongly, he'll become suspicious, and I need to keep him under close observation, especially now."

Freddie covered Evangeline's hand with his own to lead her forward. "Let's keep moving. It's the only way you'll be able to stay warm."

The couple paced onward in silence for several moments before Evangeline spoke. "I feel as if I'm walking a tightrope. I hate deception! You of all people should know how much I do! Now, I have to pretend an interest in a man who may very well be a murderer. In order to buy time, I have to allow him to make advances toward me. And as he gets closer, I have to maintain such command of my responses that I never let him know I suspect him of anything! If I fail to convince him, my own life may be at risk." Her voice had become ragged with strain. "If I withdraw from him too quickly, he'll sense he's in danger, and there's no telling what he might do." She looked worriedly up at the cliff. "What he already may have tried to do in an effort to silence me forever."

Freddie followed her gaze nervously but remained silent, not sure what consolation to offer. After a few minutes, he smiled weakly. "Don't worry, old girl. Now that I'm on my guard, I'll watch him like a hawk for you. Besides, you're a terrific actress."

"No one's that good an actress, Freddie!" Evangeline rubbed her head distractedly, ignoring the pain. "No one!"

Freddie stood gazing out over the darkening water. He took Evangeline's hands, chafing them between his own to warm them. "You'll just have to try to be, Engie. You'll have to pretend to be. You're the bravest person I know— even if you are a woman." He ignored the scowl on her face and continued. "It's too late for us to retreat now. Whether it was Blackthorne or one of the others who killed Elsa, the only way out is for us to bring the murderer to justice. If you run away in fear, we're lost."

Evangeline watched the gulls skimming the horizon for a few moments before she answered. "Wouldn't you be afraid, Freddie, if you thought you'd just unmasked the devil?"

To this, her friend made no reply. He merely put his arm around her shoulder and steered her gently in the opposite direction. "We'd better be getting back. It's almost dark, and if we wait any longer, we'll lose the trail."

17 – MEN OF VISION

Evangeline awoke with a nasty headache on Monday morning. Ignoring the pain, she attempted to conceal the bruised cut on her forehead by applying a thick layer of face powder and rearranging her hair. At all costs, she wanted to avoid the scolding and clucking that would ensue if Delphine discovered what had happened. Evangeline hoped to avert a scene by absenting the house as early as possible. She intended to pay a visit to Franz Bauer in jail. Perhaps he might recall his exact whereabouts the night of Elsa's death. He might also unknowingly reveal some information about his sister's secret admirers— O'Malley and Blackthorne.

As she was getting ready to leave for the mid-morning train, Delphine poked her head into the dressing room. "*Ma chérie*, there is a Monsieur Humphrey to see you."

"I don't know anyone by that name, Delphine."

"He says he works at the Palmer House."

"Oh, that one." Evangeline remembered the desk clerk with the propensity for clicking his heels at the least provocation. "Show him into the reception room. I'll be downstairs shortly." She set aside her immediate plan to leave for the city and, with one final worried glance in the mirror, hurried down to meet her guest instead.

When she opened the door to the reception room, she noted that Humphrey had already taken a chair, though he had chosen to balance precariously on the edge of his seat. His hat was balanced even more precariously on his knees. When he saw Evangeline enter, he sprang to his feet, upsetting his hat, which fell unceremoniously to the floor and rolled across the carpet before he could scramble to retrieve it. Flustered, but still on his best behavior, Humphrey recovered himself and snapped to attention as his hostess gave him her hand.

115

"Mr. Humphrey, please be seated." Evangeline gestured for him to return to his chair.

"Just Humphrey, miss, that's what I'm usually called."

"Very well then, Humphrey. I must say I'm quite surprised to see you here." Evangeline took the chair opposite him.

Humphrey sat down and stared at the floor. At the hotel, he had struck Evangeline as the high-strung sort; now, he was exhibiting a degree of nervousness that was beyond high-strung. He rolled his hat brim around and around in his hands, apparently searching for a way to begin.

Evangeline decided to help the process along. She smiled, trying to put him at ease. "Since it's a long train ride from Chicago to Lake Bluff, I'm assuming you have something important you wish to discuss with me. Would I be correct in making that assumption, Humphrey?"

The desk clerk sighed. "It's my conscience, miss. It's been kicking up a ruckus with me ever since we last talked."

"Indeed?" Evangeline raised her eyebrows in surprise.

"There was something I should have told you, but I didn't. I... I... was afraid I'd lose my position."

"Humphrey, I assure you, whatever you tell me will remain in strictest confidence."

He sighed again, looking only moderately relieved. "It doesn't sit well with me to tell a lie, and of all nights for something like that to happen."

"What happened?" Evangeline tried to maintain a soothing tone of voice even though she wanted to jump out of her chair and shake the information out of the desk clerk. She knew she was on the brink of something significant.

Humphrey was quiet for a moment. "Well, you see, when I told you no one else came that night inquiring after Miss Bauer, I wasn't exactly telling the truth. There was someone. I didn't mention it to the police. It happened a little while before the other fellow came by—the crazy one. A man walked in around nine-thirty and stood looking around the lobby. I asked if I could help him. He said he had come to see Miss Bauer and asked what room she was in."

"Did you get a good look at him?" Evangeline had difficulty containing her excitement.

"Nothing about him was unusual. His clothing was a bit rumpled, but not shabby. He talked like a gentleman; sandy brown hair, thinning on the top; medium height, maybe five-foot-seven or so; but plain somehow."

"No facial characteristics that you remember?" Evangeline hoped for more detail. "Did he wear glasses? Did he have a beard?"

Humphrey thought a moment. "No, no glasses. I don't remember about the beard, but I think he was clean-shaven. Nothing I recall about his face that was out of the ordinary—blue eyes, maybe, but I'm not sure."

"Did you give him Miss Bauer's room number?"

Humphrey looked down at his brightly polished shoes again. "That's where the problem came in, you see. We're not supposed to tell the room numbers of our unescorted lady guests. That's why they don't sign the front register to begin with, to protect their privacy."

Evangeline studied him for a moment. "Despite what is customary, I'm assuming you did give him her room number?"

Humphrey continued to hang his head in embarrassment. "Well, yes. But he looked like he meant no harm. He said he was her cousin and that he only wanted to surprise her by calling the following morning, and he gave me a generous tip besides. I watched closely; you can be sure. He never went up to the room that night."

"Are you sure of that? You may have been away from the desk for a few moments and—"

"I assure you, miss, I never left my post for the rest of that evening. My shift didn't end until two in the morning, and I never saw him go up. The doctor who examined the body said the girl had died before two, so it's pretty unlikely he would have tried to sneak upstairs after that time anyway."

"I see."

"Of all nights for me to do a thing like that! Who would ever imagine a girl would be murdered, and it would be the same one whose room number I gave out. But it's just that he appeared so...so...harmless."

Evangeline sat up with a start. Something in the description triggered an association in her mind with the Hull House accountant, Jacob Sidley. "Harmless, you say?"

Humphrey looked surprised at the intensity in her voice. "Yes, miss. An awkward sort of fellow. Not somebody I'd worry about."

"Think again, Humphrey. Are you sure the man you saw wasn't wearing glasses? Did he stammer when he spoke?"

The clerk shook his head vigorously. "No, miss. He was a well-spoken sort of fellow—no glasses either, of that I'm sure."

Evangeline relented. "Well, never mind. I seem intent on proving a case against an innocent man." She became lost in thought, pondering the new evidence presented to her—weighing Jonathan's involvement in the murder against that of the sandy-haired gentleman.

"Miss?" Humphrey tried tentatively to draw her attention back.

"Oh, I am sorry." Evangeline belatedly recalled her visitor.

"Unless it becomes absolutely necessary, you'll say nothing about this? It could mean my job."

"Oh, of course, I won't." Evangeline smiled reassuringly. "And if it ever comes time to speak of this, I'll make sure no action is taken against you. After all, you may have given me a vital clue to clearing up this matter. It would be a poor show of gratitude on my part if you were to lose your position because of it."

"Thank you, miss. Thank you indeed!"

"May I offer you some refreshment?" Evangeline reached for the bell to summon Delphine.

"No, no thank you, miss. I really need to get back to the city. I shouldn't have come at all, but I couldn't stand it any longer." Humphrey stood to go, shaking Evangeline's hand energetically. The tension had finally left his face altogether. "But I think my conscience is finally clear."

Evangeline waited for the inevitable click of his heels as she showed him to the door. She was not to be disappointed.

***

Although she had missed the morning train to the city, Evangeline could still see Franz if she left by mid-afternoon. She told Delphine she would be staying in town overnight and departed. On her ride into the city, Evangeline contemplated the best way to question Elsa's brother without arousing his suspicions. Given his unstable temperament, this would be no easy matter. She resolved to begin by telling him about the legal defense fund that Hull House was raising on his behalf. She hoped this news would be sufficient to divert his attention away from her real motive for the visit.

By four o'clock she was once more standing before the bars of a cell in Cook County Jail. When the guard admitted her, she was surprised to see that Franz already had another visitor with him. The two men rose at her arrival.

Evangeline was struck by the prisoner's woebegone condition. His face looked pinched, as if he hadn't eaten in weeks. His rumpled, threadbare clothing probably hadn't been changed since the last time they'd met. Given his wasted physical state, his mood was unaccountably elated. A feverish intensity glowed in his eyes.

"*Fräulein*, it is good to see you again!" Franz exclaimed with great feeling. "It is good I have friends who do not forget me now!"

"That's hardly been the case, Franz. Everyone at Hull House has been quite busy on your behalf."

Before she could give him any further news, Franz interrupted. "Please, let me introduce to you my very good friend, who comes to see me almost every day. *Fräulein* LeClair, this is *Herr* Otto Schuler."

The visitor stepped forward to shake her hand. He was a short, barrel-shaped man in his mid-forties. He wore a sack suit of brown tweed that looked as if the cuffs had been turned at least three times. While the hair on his head was sparse, the quantity on his upper lip was flourishing so admirably that it obscured the lower half of his face.

"I am very pleased to meet you, Miss LeClair." Evangeline noted that he had the bearing of a man overburdened by the weight of his own importance. Unlike Franz, Otto Schuler spoke English without the slightest trace of a German accent.

"How do you do, Mr. Schuler. I'm sorry to intrude, but I had no idea Franz would be entertaining another visitor today."

"Otto is my friend from the newspaper," Franz offered. "I stayed with him after my poor Elsa was murdered. He helped me to see things clearer." Franz regarded his friend solemnly for a moment. "He is always helping me see things clearer."

Otto Schuler waved away the compliment. "You would do the same for me. After all, we must band together at a time like this, for who else is there to help us?"

Evangeline was surprised by Schuler's interpretation of events. "I hardly think Franz is so bereft of resources as all that."

"Miss LeClair, perhaps you are not aware of certain economic realities. A crime has been committed—but not the one of which Franz is accused. It is the crime most typical of our present social system, where wealth and privilege conspire to crush the working man."

"Mr. Schuler, I really think you're overstating—"

"You are deluding yourself, miss, if you think Franz will get a fair trial in this city. Nay, in any major city in the country, for that matter. Those in power would never allow it!"

"We can but try, sir! We have a few weeks to prepare. I inquired and found his first court appearance isn't until November 4th."

Schuler waved his hand airily. "You can try all you like, miss. By all means, organize a committee, stage a rally. Franz will be convicted as a criminal and hanged just the same."

"Are these the words of a friend, Mr. Schuler?" Evangeline was aghast. No matter how ambivalent her own feelings toward Franz might be, she found Schuler's behavior appalling. "Is this the only comfort you can offer to a man in prison?"

Schuler smiled mysteriously. "I have other words of comfort for Franz's ear alone." He cleared his throat importantly. "One may die an ignominious death as a felon, or one may live forever in the memory of the people as a hero. All men must die, Miss LeClair." Schuler looked sadly at Franz. "Some of us sooner than others, but each man has a choice of how he will be remembered. If he dies for the sake of a good cause, then he has not died in vain."

"What are you suggesting?" Evangeline was afraid she understood the implication only too well.

The little man puffed out his chest as if he were about to launch into an oration. "It has become increasingly clear to me, as it has now become clear to Franz, that the time for talk is over."

"Over?" Evangeline noted that Schuler seemed addicted to cryptic allusions and half-finished thoughts.

"This injustice must be brought to the eyes of the world by a more direct method." He squared his shoulders as if expecting resistance.

119

Franz had said nothing during this interchange. He merely nodded his head in assent as Schuler spoke.

"Franz?" Evangeline appealed to the prisoner helplessly. "Are you in agreement with this?"

Franz smiled quietly. He did not appear at all distressed by the turn the conversation had taken. "Otto has spent many hours with me here, and we have talked and talked. He has convinced me that there is only one way for me now."

Evangeline turned angrily from Franz to Schuler. "Sir, I fear that in your passion for grand gestures, you will create a martyr to your cause."

"We are not afraid, Miss LeClair. We are prepared for that!" Schuler waved away the objection as if he were brushing at a fly.

"Mr. Schuler, you are very free in sacrificing a life that is not your own to give!"

Schuler drew himself up to his full height, such as it was. "Forgive me. I was under the impression you wanted to help Franz. I was clearly mistaken." He abruptly put on his hat to leave. With a curt "Good day to you, miss," he called for the guard to let him out. Once on the other side of the bars, he turned to his friend. "Don't worry, Franz. I won't forget you. We'll talk again."

Evangeline stood very still, too shocked by the turn the conversation had taken to move. She stared through the bars to the spot where Schuler had been standing only a moment before. To herself, she said, "Whether Franz is guilty or not, if I don't find a way out of this soon, that man is going to get him killed!"

***

After a fruitless attempt to convince Franz that his chances weren't as bleak as Schuler suggested, Evangeline finally gave up. She also gave up all hope of gathering any other useful information from him that day. Rather than proceeding directly to her townhouse for the evening, she made a quick change of plan. She decided to go to Hull House to discuss Schuler's influence over Franz with Jane Addams or Ellen Gates Starr. They might be able to undo the damage by visiting the prisoner to tell him about the money they had raised for his legal defense. Evangeline decided not to share with them her own doubts about Franz's innocence. His willingness to consider suicide might be owing less to political fanaticism than to the belated prompting of a guilty conscience. If so, he ought to be made to stand trial before he had the chance to act as his own executioner.

Only after she had hailed a cab and was en route to the Hull mansion did Evangeline recollect that her chances of speaking to either of the settlement's founders, on this day of all days, was virtually nil. An event of great significance to them was to transpire that evening. They were to receive a visit from an august personage—none other than Canon Burnett, whose Toynbee Hall in England had been the inspiration for Hull House. He had come to Chicago as a guest of the settlement and would give a lecture on social reform at eight o'clock in the auditorium. A reception in his honor was scheduled to be held at the residents' dining hall prior to his speech so that those who wanted to speak directly to the great man might do so. Evangeline's only recourse was to attend the reception and hope that she could get a few minutes' conversation with one of the founders.

The weather didn't provide an auspicious start for such a significant occasion. The moon was obscured by fast-moving clouds that carried a hint of rain. After alighting from her cab, Evangeline made straight for the dining hall to get out of the night chill. When she walked in the door, she could feel her face begin to thaw thanks to a blast of warm air coming from inside.

She was not entirely surprised to see how popular an event this had proven to be. At least two hundred people were wedged into the residents' dining hall—a room that usually held no more than fifty. Those who couldn't find chairs were content to line the walls and carry on animated conversations at the very top of their voices.

Evangeline stood hesitating in the vestibule, not quite sure where to find either Miss Addams or Miss Starr when a new arrival caught her attention. Shivering and rubbing his hands together for warmth was Mr. Sidley. He looked at the woman standing next to him in the doorway and blinked when he realized who it was.

"Miss LeClair, w... we meet again. What a delight!"

"Oh hello, Mr. Sidley. Very nice to see you, too." Evangeline smiled. "Have you come to meet our foreign dignitary as well?"

"Of c..course, of course. Even my reclusive habits were no match for the persistence of Miss Starr. She declared that this event would improve my mind."

Evangeline laughed. "That's Miss Starr for you, an opinion on every topic. Just for the record, I don't share her view that your mental faculties require any improvement."

"Oh, Miss LeClair," Sidley murmured and shuffled his feet. "You n... needn't defend me so."

"And why not, sir? I fear I've done you a great injustice." Evangeline took his arm as the two advanced into the dining hall.

"In what w... way, miss? You've taken a greater interest in me than anyone else here."

"Oh, let's just say I misjudged your character." She was unwilling to confide the full extent of her suspicions that he was involved in Elsa's death.

Apparently, Sidley's mind had made the connection to their previous conversation as well. "No harm done. Let's speak no more about it."

"That's very Christian of you, sir."

"And now, if I may be so b... bold," Sidley began with a hesitancy that belied his choice of words, "I see you have no companion for the evening. Might I accompany you to the lecture?"

Evangeline smiled graciously. "Mr. Sidley, I would be honored, but you must give me ten minutes first to find Miss Addams or Miss Starr. I have a pressing matter I need to discuss with one of them." Evangeline squinted in the dim light the room afforded. "I usually don't have this much trouble finding someone I'm looking for. For the life of me, I can't seem to locate either of them."

Sidley, having a small advantage of height over his companion, cast his eyes around the room as well. "Why that's Miss Starr, over there." He pointed off into the distance.

Evangeline followed the direction he indicated with no luck. "I'm sorry, Mr. Sidley, but I don't see her. Where specifically?"

"Why there, in the far corner. See, in the shadow by the fireplace. She's sitting down."

Evangeline looked again and finally spotted the co-founder of the settlement. Because Ellen Gates Starr was as diminutive as Evangeline herself, she would have been hard to see even if she were standing up. This difficulty was compounded by the fact that she wore an inconspicuous blue gown and was seated among a group of six or seven others in an obscure corner across a room occupied by a small army of visitors. Evangeline began to feel a vague uneasiness steal over her as she moved forward to Miss Starr's table. Sidley followed her there.

"Good evening, all," Evangeline began as she forced her way through a final knot of onlookers.

Ellen Starr stared up at the newcomers over the lenses of her ever-present pince-nez. "Evangeline, good evening to you. I see you've got Mr. Sidley in tow. Good. I'm glad to see he's decided to abandon his cloister for once."

Evangeline smiled consolingly at the awkward man who stood beside her. He was obviously not comfortable in Miss Starr's presence. His discomfort was augmented by the founder's determination to hold forth on the topic of his character. She turned to a gray-haired gentleman seated at her right.

"This is our accountant. He's a very unusual fellow. Shy, I suppose. Keeps to himself most of the time. For the life of me, I can't understand such anti-social behavior from the inhabitant of a social reform settlement. Mr. Sidley, since you're an accountant, how can you account for your behavior?"

The others at the table chuckled at Miss Starr's attempt at wit.

Sidley cleared his throat self-consciously. "Ahem... ah... I'm s... sorry to offend, Miss Starr, but your q... question puts me at a l... loss."

"You see." The founder gestured emphatically. "Loss! All he can think about are debits and credits!"

The group laughed appreciatively until Evangeline intervened.

"Ellen, if you're through baiting Mr. Sidley, I have something urgent to discuss with you."

The founder surveyed Evangeline for a moment without replying, clearly displeased at having her vivisection of the accountant interrupted. "Yes, all right. We may as well go to my office for a few moments. The noise in this place is ridiculous." She rose. As an afterthought, perhaps as a belated gesture of apology, she said, "Sidley, you may have my chair!"

Taking her suggestion as a command, the gentleman obediently sat.

***

At five minutes before the hour, having convinced Miss Starr to visit Franz and counteract the damage caused by Otto Schuler, Evangeline came back to collect Sidley for the lecture. The dining hall, by this time, was nearly empty as most of those invited had already adjourned to the auditorium. However, Sidley, now alone at the table, kept his vigil faithfully.

"I'm sorry that took so long, Mr. Sidley."

"Oh, I... ahem... would have waited a great deal longer still for you, Miss LeClair."

"Sir, you are far too quick to compliment me."

"No, miss, really. You don't know what it means to have a friend, especially a lady friend." Sidley stood up and offered Evangeline his arm as the two walked to the auditorium together. "I've never been very comfortable—with the l... ladies, that is."

"On the contrary. From the first time we met, you seem to have done just fine with me."

"Yes, but you're different," Sidley insisted. "You p... put a fellow at ease."

"Not always. My friend Freddie could disabuse you of that notion quickly enough."

"Well, at least you've put me at ease, and that's saying a great deal, for I'm never at ease. Miss Starr positively terrifies me."

"As she intends to. I believe it to be her main object in life to terrify the world in general. It's her method of command. You needn't be self-conscious about that."

"Just the same. Th... thank you, Miss LeClair."

Evangeline studied her companion's face thoughtfully. "You're very welcome, Mr. Sidley."

By now the couple had entered the auditorium, the largest room in the settlement complex. The two hundred who had attended the reception only represented a fraction of the audience who had arrived to hear Canon Burnett speak. Luckily, there were still a few chairs left at the back of the hall, and the pair claimed these.

Evangeline was silent for several minutes, wrestling with a contradiction that had begun to nag at her. She decided to put the matter to a test and resolve it once and for all. She turned Sidley's attention to the speaker's podium, which, given the immensity of the room, seemed a quarter mile away. "Oh look, there's a banner in our speaker's honor, but the lettering is so small when you're seated at the back. I can barely make out what it says. 'Welcome Canon Burnett. Har... har...'" She strained to make out the rest of the sign.

"'Harbinger of social reform,'" Sidley answered readily. "And look! They've decorated the rafters with t... tiny emblems of the Union Jack. I suppose that's a compliment to his heritage since he's English."

"Yes, I would imagine so," Evangeline said vacantly. In her mind's eye, she watched as the contradiction grew.

18 – SECOND SIGHT

Freddie didn't arrive in Lake Bluff on Tuesday evening until long after sunset. Still worried about Evangeline's frame of mind, he decided to call at her house first before going home. As he came up the gravel walk, he saw Delphine standing on the porch, holding a kerosene lantern in one hand and clutching her shawl around her neck with the other. "*Qui est là?*" She peered into the darkness. "*Ma chérie*, is it you?"

"It's Monsieur Freddie, Delphine."

"Where is *ma petite?*"

Freddie was totally mystified. "I haven't got her. Can't you keep track of her any better than that?"

Delphine muttered to herself as she descended the stairs, apparently ready to go in search of her mistress. Freddie was about to follow her when a dark shape rounded the corner of the house.

"Engie?" Freddie squinted in the lantern shadow.

"Yes, Freddie, it's me," a voice replied wearily. "I've been out walking."

Upon hearing her lady's voice, Delphine rushed to her, draping her own shawl around the young woman's shoulders and launching into a bilingual harangue on the dangers of hiking on the cliff after dark.

"*Pourquoi, ma chérie, tu fais comme ça?* What do you think you are doing? And this one," she jerked her head in Freddie's direction, "he is no help. *À quoi pensais-tu? Mon Dieu!* You come inside now," she said to Evangeline. "You go home!" she commanded Freddie.

Evangeline tried to control her chattering teeth. "No, Delphine. I need to talk to Monsieur Freddie awhile. Put on some tea, please. I'm so cold that I could drink it boiling."

Freddie silently followed the two indoors. Delphine continued to cluck and scold and remonstrate and cast evil looks in the young man's direction, but

Evangeline made straight for the library to warm herself in front of the fire. Freddie sat and waited until she had thawed sufficiently to speak.

"Engie, do you really think it was wise to go down there so soon after—"

"I had to go. I had to sort things out. Just when I thought matters couldn't get any more complicated." She launched into a summary of her encounter with Humphrey and her distressing visit with Franz.

Freddie didn't interrupt until she was finished. "There's something else, isn't there?"

"Yes, Freddie. Something quite ugly if I'm not mistaken." Evangeline's composure began to return as the blue tinge left her lips.

"About Franz?"

"No, about Sidley."

"But I thought you dismissed him as a suspect."

"And so I did, Freddie. So I did. But something happened yesterday evening to make me change my mind. When I got to Hull House, I remembered there was a guest lecturer from England. All the residents showed up to meet him. One of them was Sidley. He became my escort for the evening."

Freddie shrugged, seeing no heinous offense in that.

"But an accident occurred—one of those small events to which one pays no attention but which, in retrospect, changes everything."

"You found him pocketing money from the admission receipts." Freddie adopted a teasing tone in an effort to lighten his friend's mood.

Evangeline smiled weakly. "No, nothing quite that obvious." She sat forward in her chair. "Freddie, do you remember what I told you about his eyesight?"

"Well, it's rather hard to forget when you describe someone as being blind as a bat even with spectacles."

"That's just it. I discovered he isn't. The residents' dining hall was crowded with people, and I was trying to locate Miss Addams or Miss Starr, but to no avail. He managed to pick out Miss Starr seated at the opposite side of the room. Seated in shadow, Freddie, and wearing a dark gown. He was able to find her in a matter of seconds."

"Interesting. But it's possible that he was just looking off in the right direction at the time."

"That's what I thought, so I put the matter to a further test. We were seated at the back of the auditorium. You've been there. You know the size of that hall."

Freddie nodded his assent.

"I directed his attention to a small banner directly over the speaker's podium. I had to strain to see the lettering and could just barely make it out, but I wanted to know if he could see as well, so I pretended not to be able to read the entire inscription."

"And?"

"And he rambled off the whole motto with ease. As a matter of fact, he pointed out some decorative detail that I could barely see."

"Hmmm," was Freddie's considered response.

At that moment, Delphine entered carrying a tray. She set it down on the small table beside Evangeline's chair. "I have not brought you tea, *ma petite. Voilà, du chocolat chaud.* It will warm you better."

Evangeline looked down at the tray and then back up at Delphine with a pained expression. "Delphine, there is only one cup on this tray."

"Hmmph! I did not think this one," meaning Freddie, "would be bothering you so long." Then, as if the hint were not broad enough, she turned to stare directly at the young man. "I did not think he would be so *outrageux* as to sit here half the night when you are cold and tired and need your rest!"

Freddie smiled placidly. "Oh, I'm quite that *outrageux*, Delphine. Probably far worse even."

Before Delphine could pick up the lone tea cup and hurl its contents at Freddie, Evangeline intervened. "*Bien! C'est assez,* Delphine! What I have to say to Monsieur Freddie is very important. Please bring another cup. Now!"

Delphine backed away at the sharpness in Evangeline's tone. "*Oui, madame,*" she said and left the room. The two sat and waited in silence until she returned with the second cup and finally closed the door to leave them in privacy.

The interlude had given Freddie time to formulate a few more questions. He settled back into his easy chair and sipped his hot chocolate with great satisfaction. "Well, I don't see why this is troubling you so much, Engie. The man in the hotel lobby was most likely Blackthorne."

"Humphrey said the man was sandy-haired, not dark."

Freddie shrugged. "He might have been mistaken."

"I don't think so." Evangeline's voice was ominous. "The desk clerk says medium coloring, medium height. The porter says dark-haired and tall. What if they're both right?"

"I can tell from your tone that you've drawn a whole string of conclusions about this—conclusions that I apparently don't grasp. Would you care to share them with me?"

The lady stood up and walked closer to the fireplace, spreading her fingers to warm them in the glow. "It's not the business in the hotel lobby so much that I'm concerned about. It's what happened at the Fair."

"How do you mean?"

"When I first interrogated Sidley, he confirmed what Patsy O'Malley, the landlady's daughter, had told me—that he'd requested Elsa to wear a red silk rose in her hat."

"Yes," Freddie agreed cautiously.

"Furthermore, he requested that she tell him what sort of apparel she would be wearing that day."

"And the reason he gave you, as I recall, was that he feared his eyesight wasn't good enough to pick her out in all that crowd." The young man whistled through his teeth. "Well, what do you know!"

"Yes, Freddie. Now you see." She smiled fully for the first time that evening. "Forgive the wordplay."

"All right, Engie, you've established that he's a liar. But why?"

"I retract my previous observation." Evangeline smiled again, this time wryly. "I guess you don't see."

The young man waited in martyred silence.

Evangeline returned to her chair. "The reason why he lied may be the grimmest part of this whole business. Do you remember your hypothetical scenario in which Elsa met a gentleman at the fair?"

"Not a gentleman," Freddie corrected her, "we can be fairly certain that the man she met was Blackthorne."

"And on that point, I agree, but in your hypothesis, the encounter was purely by chance."

Freddie felt himself turn pale as the implication of her words struck him. "My God, Engie! Do you know what you're suggesting?"

"Yes, Freddie. I'm afraid I do. I'm suggesting that Elsa had been targeted for the encounter before it ever occurred. The thought gives me chills. She never stood a chance."

"Of course. Why else would he take such care to know what she was wearing ahead of time, if not to describe her to someone who'd never seen her before."

"And the rose?"

"To make her as conspicuous as possible in the event the rest of the description failed to bring her to Blackthorne's attention."

"Exactly."

"But Engie, I don't understand the motive for this!"

"Neither do I. But that's only one of any number of things I don't understand about this business, Freddie. Now, do you comprehend my agitation? When confronted with such a dizzying array of unanswered questions, I had no idea where to start." Evangeline stood up again and returned to the fire. Freddie watched her in silence as she stirred a log.

She continued speaking while brandishing a poker. "I suppose we can only begin with the facts that have been established. We know that Jonathan is somehow connected to Elsa, and Sidley is most probably responsible for arranging their initial contact. My principal concern at the moment is to understand the connection between these two men."

"Was Blackthorne ever a visitor at the settlement?"

"Not to my knowledge. And even if he were, the chances that he would encounter Sidley during a visit are fairly remote."

"Well, what do you know about Sidley, then?"

"Not nearly enough. And that's where I think we must begin. Wait here." Without another word, Evangeline put down the poker and flew out of the room.

Freddie listened as her footsteps retreated down the hall. He poured himself another cup of hot chocolate, by this time lukewarm. He swirled the dark liquid contemplatively for a few moments, pondering the new scenario Evangeline had suggested. His ruminations were cut short as his friend came bursting through the door, out of breath.

"Here." She handed him a photograph.

"Who are these people?"

"It's a group photograph of the residents at Hull House. This was taken about six months ago. You'll oblige me by noting the gentleman in the second row, third from the left."

"Is that Sidley?"

"Yes."

"Not particularly distinguished looking, is he? What do you want me to do with that bit of knowledge?"

"I would like you to call on his former employer and find out as much as you can about his tenure in that job."

"And where would that employer be found?" Freddie's interest was sparked, his latent news-reporter ambitions beginning to take control.

Evangeline noted the transformation in her friend. "At this moment you remind me of nothing so much as a racehorse put out to pasture who has just heard the starting gun."

Freddie smiled self-consciously. "Yes, I suppose. But all this sitting around and waiting has gotten very depressing."

"Then despair no more, young Frederick. Your waiting is at an end. Tomorrow morning you must pay a call on Messieurs Hart & Hudson. I'm told they conduct an accounting practice on one of the upper floors of a building on State Street. I trust to your resourcefulness to discover the rest."

Freddie, in a mock chivalric gesture, went down on one knee. "Fear not, dear lady. I shall not fail."

Evangeline took the picture, rolled it up, and tapped Freddie on each shoulder with it. She returned the item to him with a flourish. "Your weapon. Rise, Sir Freddie, and God go with you!"

"Lady, I take my leave." Freddie bowed deeply as he stood in the doorway.

Delphine had walked down the hall just in time to hear him utter his parting words. "*Bon!*" the housekeeper muttered, "And it is high time, too!"

19 – EXCHANGES

The following day, Freddie set out with high hopes of learning something useful about Sidley's past. Since State Street was only a few blocks from his office, the young man ducked out during his lunch hour and assumed he could wrap up his investigation without being missed.

He managed to find the building where Hart & Hudson was located, only to be confronted by a shaded window and a locked office door. He was informed by the building manager that no one had rented that particular office for the past decade. The only significant clue Freddie derived from this wild goose chase was that Sidley had lied about his previous place of employment.

He then reasoned that if he couldn't trace Sidley to Blackthorne, maybe he could trace Blackthorne to Sidley. With that purpose in mind, he sauntered off to the Merchant's Bank & Trust where Blackthorne worked, to see if Sidley had ever been employed there as well. After being informed by the personnel manager that no one named Sidley had ever worked there, Freddie was running out of ideas.

"Some reporter I turned out to be!" he said to himself. "Chasing down leads that end up being blind alleys. Following hunches that don't pay off! I can't go back to Engie with this. She's counting on me to find something, and right now I feel like a complete fool!"

He walked out of the bank in a dismal mood. By now it was 1:30, and he had been away from the office for over two hours. He had no desire to return and had no idea what to do next, so he headed for Lake Park and found a shady bench where he could sit and indulge his misery. He sat motionless in an attitude of despair for so long that the park pigeons began to flock around him. Whether they came looking for food or because they mistook him for a new, oddly shaped statue would have been hard to tell.

Freddie's eyes were still fixed on the ground when he noticed a shadow obscuring the patch of sunlight he had been focusing on. He looked up to find his own figurative shadow standing beside him.

"Aloysius, what in God's name are you doing here! I didn't think my day could have gotten any worse!"

"Simpson, do you know what time it is?" the company spy asked anxiously. "Your uncle will be asking me where you are and why you aren't at work."

"I know the hour is late, my friend. And getting later. You may tell my uncle that I have decided to commit suicide by sacrificing myself to the park pigeons. You will find my bones picked clean by tomorrow morning."

"Simpson, what's wrong with you? Do you really want me to tell your uncle that?"

"Aloysius, does the word 'hyperbole' have any meaning whatsoever to you?"

"Of course it does, but I find it a useless bit of nonsense just the same." Waverly's nose twitched in disapproval. "Really, what shall I tell your uncle?"

"Whatever you like, whatever the hell you like!"

Waverly sat down beside him. "Look, I'm trying to help you. Don't you see?"

Freddie studied him contemptuously for a few moments. "I'm sure you expect some recompense for the trouble you're taking on my behalf?"

Aloysius looked down at his shoes. "Well, you were rather generous last time."

"As my desire to live diminishes so does my fear of reprisal. I'll give you five dollars to tell my uncle I went home sick. Not a penny more."

Waverly hesitated, apparently realizing that Freddie's present mood made bargaining a waste of time. "Very well."

Freddie opened his billfold, counted out the money, and gave it to Waverly. "Aloysius, the five dollars is also to buy some privacy. I don't expect to see or hear you again for the remainder of the day."

Waverly stood up and nodded. "I was never here." The company spy walked away to fabricate a plausible lie.

Freddie sighed. A pigeon standing on the ground by his left foot gurgled sympathetically. The young man put his head in his hands and said to himself, "Engie, old girl, if there ever was a time when I needed to speak to you, this is it."

Freddie tried to imagine what his friend would say if she were there. The image took such control of him that he could see her pacing the sidewalk in front of him, dressed in purple silk, hands clasped behind her back. Finally, she wheeled to face him, eyes flashing. "Think, man, think! For God's sake use your head for something other than a hat rack!"

Freddie chuckled at the image he had conjured. "Well, that sounds like Engie, all right."

"Freddie, what do Blackthorne and Sidley both have in common?"

"Well, they're both connected to Elsa Bauer somehow."

"Yes, we know that!" The manifestation stamped her foot impatiently. "But what about their past? What do they share in their history?"

Freddie racked his brain and could come up with nothing.

"What do they do for a living?"

"One's a banker, and one's an accountant," Freddie said, half-aloud. "They both have a background in finance."

"Quite so."

"But Engie," Freddie defended himself. "I've already tried tracing Sidley to Blackthorne's bank, and it didn't pan out."

"Maybe, maybe not. Perhaps he used an alias."

"But the clerk didn't recognize his picture either."

"It's a big bank, and Sidley may have left there three years ago."

"You know, you really aren't helping me!" Freddie said out loud in exasperation. Evangeline's image smiled and sat down beside him.

"Maybe we just need to go a little farther back in time..." She trailed off and then evaporated.

Freddie cocked his head to one side, evaluating the idea. "Well, it's worth a try. I'd be no worse off than I am now. Hmmm." He stood up abruptly, causing pigeons to flutter in all directions. Dusting feathers off his coat with great resolution, Freddie marched westward once more to the Merchant's Bank. He intended to find out the name of Jonathan Blackthorne's previous employer.

***

A half hour later, Freddie stood before an imposing edifice known as the Board of Trade. This was the building where all of Chicago's commodities were traded. Architecturally, it resembled a Gothic cathedral—a cathedral dedicated to the worship of fatted calves and pigs. Blackthorne's former employer was Dresden & Company, a brokerage firm located on the fourth floor. As Freddie turned the door handle to the company's office, he was sent spinning by a messenger rushing down to the trading floor.

"Sorry, sir, are you all right?" The boy helped Freddie regain his balance. "Have to run. I have to get this trade downstairs right away!" With that, the boy flew out the door leaving the young man to collect himself.

Dazed by this encounter, Freddie wandered into the waiting room, where a small multitude of the firm's clients were checking quotations being updated on a chalk board suspended from the wall. All around him, he heard a sea of turbulent voices muttering angrily. The muttering increased to a collective shout of rage with the appearance of an innocent-looking number newly chalked in the column for May wheat. Though Freddie didn't dabble in commodities trading, he could smell financial ruin in the air and guessed that someone had just tried to corner the market in wheat futures.

To his horror, he saw one of the spectators pull a gun out of his coat pocket and point it at his own head. Before the man could pull the trigger, two others tried to wrestle the gun away from him. A shot fired and whizzed into the wall above Freddie's shoulder. The battle for control of the gun continued as a dozen other bystanders ran for cover. Another shot tore through the air.

Freddie ducked low to the ground, frantically searching for somewhere to hide. Spying an unmarked door at the back of the waiting room, he crawled to it for cover and shut it behind him. His head was still spinning as he uttered a silent prayer of thanks that his father had been a lawyer instead of a broker.

The serenity of the inner room was shocking in contrast to the donnybrook going on outside. A middle-aged, balding man sat at a desk immediately before him. He looked up and said mildly, "May I help you?"

It was all Freddie could do to bleat, "Personnel?"

The man at the desk smiled reassuringly. "You've found it, sir. I'm Mr. Wallace, the personnel director. In what way can I be of assistance?"

"I'll let you know as soon as I regain my hearing." Freddie noticed a dizziness along with the ringing in his ears.

"Yes, it can be a bit much out there, can't it? You picked an unfortunate time to arrive. The market is just about to close, and it's been an unusually active day of trading."

"But... but..." Freddie stammered, "I just saw a man try to shoot himself!"

Wallace sighed. "Yes, that does happen from time to time. Very unfortunate. Well, what can I do for you?"

Freddie looked askance at the man's composure. "But shouldn't you do something? Call someone for help?"

Wallace smiled, unruffled. "Don't worry. The security guards will be up soon. They're accustomed to handling situations like this."

"Oh," Freddie trailed off in a small voice, trying hard to assimilate the meaning of business-as-usual in the world of stockbrokers. Realizing that Wallace was still looking at him quizzically, he attempted to state the reason for his visit. "Well... you see, Mr. Wallace. Well... ahem... My name is Frederick Simpson, and I represent the firm of Simpson & Austin."

At first tentatively, and then by degrees more confidently, Freddie launched into a story about how his law firm needed some background information on Jonathan Blackthorne. The personnel director, apparently used to far stranger scenes than a lone attorney asking for information, nodded and went in search of the employment file. Freddie managed to calm himself as he waited for the man to locate it in the back room. His attention was drawn to a group photograph hanging on the wall behind the personnel director's desk. "These things seem to be all the rage now," Freddie said to himself. He walked behind the desk to get a closer look.

When Wallace returned, he noticed Freddie's interest. "That's a photograph of all the members of our firm, about fifty of us."

Freddie scanned the faces and located Blackthorne standing in the top row, looking serious and financially responsible. He pointed to the face and turned to look at the personnel director for confirmation.

"Yes, that would be the man you've inquired about. That's Jonathan Blackthorne. I remember him well. A very quiet young fellow, as I recall."

On an impulse, Freddie pulled out the Hull House picture. "I wonder if you might recognize another gentleman in this photograph I have. I'm not at all sure he ever worked here. His name is Jacob Sidley."

Wallace looked at it for only a second. "Oh yes, I remember him too. But his name isn't Sidley, it's Kingston. Jacob Kingston. That's him right here." Wallace pointed to one of the figures in the group portrait on the wall, standing in the row below Blackthorne. Freddie could make out a face that exactly matched the one in his own photograph. In the Dresden picture, however, Sidley was sporting muttonchop whiskers, which made the resemblance more difficult to see at first glance.

"Good Lord, it's him!" Freddie exclaimed. It's really him!" He looked at the date in the lower right corner of the picture. "This was taken in 1889?"

"Yes, I realize it's a bit out of date. But there seemed no reason to have it redone since only two men have left the firm in the interim."

"Let me guess which two." Freddie began to feel a sudden chill.

"Yes, now that you mention it, you're right. If my memory serves me correctly, Kingston left early in the winter of 1890 and Blackthorne in the fall of the same year. How odd."

Freddie's pulse began to race. "I would consider it a great favor if you could give me the exact dates when these two men left and also the previous employer of Mr. Sidley, that is, Mr. Kingston."

Wallace, appearing somewhat taken aback by the feverish intensity in Freddie's voice, nodded and went into the file room to retrieve the Kingston file. He returned quickly, studying a page in the manila folder he was holding. "It says here that Mr. Kingston's previous employer was a bank in Iowa."

"The exact name, please!" Freddie reached in his pocket for a notebook and pencil.

"It was in Dodgeville. The First Dodgeville Savings Bank is the name of the institution. He was a bookkeeper there. That was also the position he occupied here. He came to us in 1889 and left on January 21, 1890."

"Would you happen to have the name of the person who wrote his letter of introduction?"

Wallace examined the application file further. "The letter is signed by Harcourt Smythe, a vice president of the bank."

"One final question. Can you give me the same information regarding Mr. Blackthorne?" Freddie turned another page in his notebook.

"Of course." Wallace picked up the other folder on his desk. "It would seem Mr. Blackthorne came to us straight out of college. His letter of introduction is from one of his professors at Northwestern University. He started at the firm in 1885 and left on September 10, 1890."

Freddie wrote an additional note to himself and then shook the older man's hand enthusiastically. "You have no idea how much you have helped me, Mr. Wallace! If there's ever anything I can do to repay you, please don't hesitate to call on me."

Wallace appeared flustered by this outburst of gratitude. He cleared his throat self-consciously. "Very well, Mr. Simpson, very well. No need to make such a fuss. All in a day's work, I'm sure—" Before he could finish the last sentence, Freddie had already bolted out the door.

20 – A CHAT WITH MOTHER

Evangeline sat in a box seat at the Acropolis Theater watching Jonathan Blackthorne's mother arrange herself. Unfortunately, she had committed herself to attending this social event long before Elsa's death. The Ladies' Charitable Auxiliary was staging a benefit theatrical performance to raise funds for the Chicago Children's Hospital. Many of the ladies of Lake Bluff and Lake Forest were active members of the society. Evangeline was no exception, and neither was Mrs. Blackthorne.

Evangeline feared that an evening spent with her mother-in-law elect might provide an opportunity to discuss an extremely unpleasant topic—Jonathan's veiled proposal. However, Mrs. Blackthorne appeared to have other things on her mind as she greeted acquaintances from the heights of her private box. She was a plump little woman with skin like rose petals that had just begun to wilt. The pleasure she derived from displaying her social status was equal to, if not greater than, the pleasure she derived from Shakespeare.

"I will never understand why on earth the planning committee chose this play to present." The older lady adjusted her silk shawl and took her opera glasses out of their Moroccan leather case.

"I think *Measure for Measure* was an interesting choice and not nearly as well-known as Shakespeare's other comedies. It possesses some intriguing, dark elements. 'Some rise by sin, and some by virtue fall,'" Evangeline intoned ominously.

Mrs. Blackthorne paused in the midst of refurbishing herself to give Evangeline a puzzled look. "That line has always been a mystery to me. I hear it quoted often enough, but what in the world is one to make of it?"

"I think it's about hypocrisy. Those who offer a model of public behavior are often the greatest villains at heart, while those who are publicly condemned for some act of indiscretion are often the most innocent."

Mrs. Blackthorne's attention was temporarily diverted as she nodded to a lady in an adjoining box.

Evangeline forged ahead. "I also think the line offers a warning. Those who think themselves above the reach of the law are eventually brought to justice. Those who have been wrongly condemned are, in the end, acquitted."

Mrs. Blackthorne waved her lace fan distractedly. "What a moral dilemma that presents. How is one to know what is good and what is bad, if the voice of authority itself is called into question? How is one to know who can be trusted? Who can be believed?"

"That's just my point. One never knows."

The older lady sighed and patted her companion's hand. "My dear, you think entirely too much."

"So I've been told, Mrs. Blackthorne. So I've been told." Evangeline sighed. "But given my present state of mind, I should have preferred to see *Titus Andronicus* instead of *Measure for Measure.*"

Mrs. Blackthorne turned pale at the mention of the name. "That awful tragedy! That bloodbath! Why, whatever for?"

Evangeline smiled bitterly. "Let's just say the character of Lavinia interests me at present."

"My dear, you shock me! A character who is ravished by two men and then has her tongue cut out and her hands hacked off so she can't reveal the guilty parties! What sort of morbid thinking is this?"

"Mrs. Blackthorne, I had no idea you were so conversant in your Shakespeare, even the awful plays. Despite all the atrocities committed against her, Lavinia still manages to write the names of the guilty men in the sand, holding a stick between the stumps that were once her hands. One can't help but admire such grim tenacity of purpose."

By this time, Mrs. Blackthorne's complexion had taken on a faint greenish tinge. "Really, my dear, you must stop. You're making me quite ill with your description."

"I am sorry, Mrs. Blackthorne. I truly am, but such things happen in the world."

"Such things happen only in fiction! I can't imagine encountering in my own life such a devilish business or people capable of such brutality."

"Oh, madame," Evangeline's tone was grave. "You must have a care and look about you more closely. You may know someone quite well who is capable of it."

Mrs. Blackthorne shivered slightly. "The thought is preposterous. Such people do not... cannot exist! Let us speak no more about it."

Evangeline complied and gave up the topic.

The two women lapsed into silence as they surveyed the new arrivals entering at the back of the theater. Mrs. Blackthorne edged forward in her seat to see over the railing. "Oh, look my dear. It's Mr. and Mrs. Fenton just walking in. Did you know that he has just purchased one of those horrible horseless carriages?"

"Indeed, I didn't. I had no idea he was that progressive."

"Progressive? Progressive, you say?" Mrs. Blackthorne seemed astonished. "He has frightened the entire town half out of its wits with that foul-smelling, noisy contraption. And that just accounts for the general population, not to mention how it's upset the horses."

"Really?" Evangeline leaned farther over the railing for a better look at the malefactor. "It's hard to believe that one motor car could cause all that commotion."

"But it has, my dear, it has." Mrs. Blackthorne placed her hand solemnly on Evangeline's arm. "It became such a crisis that we had to organize a committee!"

"You did what?"

"We organized a ladies' committee for the public welfare and went to call on Mrs. Fenton."

"On Mrs. Fenton?" Evangeline failed to grasp the connection. "Not Mr. Fenton?"

"Well, we thought it would be more tactful if we appealed to her first. The committee went all around Lake Forest and got up a petition. Two hundred signatures. An overwhelming response! And we presented it to Mrs. Fenton."

Evangeline was having a difficult time forcing her features to assume the solemn look that the subject required. "And what were you petitioning for?"

"Nothing unreasonable. We merely wanted advance notice for those days when Mr. Fenton was planning on driving his mechanical horse around town."

"Advance notice, how?"

Mrs. Blackthorne looked exasperated at her companion's dullness of wit. "We requested that Mrs. Fenton fly a black flag on those days so that the whole town could be alerted to keep clear. I mean, think of the consequences otherwise. Careening down the street at twenty miles an hour! Have you ever heard the like? Twenty miles an hour! This is a great danger to us all, and we deserve appropriate warning. Considering the gravity of the situation, Mr. Fenton should have been relieved we asked no more of him than that!"

"And was he relieved?" Evangeline could guess the reply.

"He certainly was not! And he was most uncivil in his response, too! He happened to walk into the drawing room while we were in conference with his wife. After she handed him the petition, he tore it up and said he would... he would..." Mrs. Blackthorne fanned herself vigorously at the thought of what her lips were about to utter. Steeling herself, she continued. "He said he would drive his motor car around town whenever he deuced well pleased, and we could make of it what we liked! And 'deuced' wasn't the exact word he used!"

Evangeline snapped her own fan open quickly to cover the lower half of her face. By this time, she was shaking with suppressed laughter. Luckily, before her convulsions became obvious, the electric lights began to flicker as a signal the performance was about to start. She closed her eyes in relief when Duke Vincentio and his attendants walked on stage.

***

When the house lights rose again for intermission, a few of the august dames of Lake Forest walked around to pay a visit to Mrs. Blackthorne. The topic of conversation continued to be the recalcitrant Mr. Fenton and his infernal machine. While the controversy over what to do next raged behind her, Evangeline glanced absently across the theater to the boxes on the other side. To her amazement, she saw Freddie, looking quite the martyr, surrounded by his own brigade of female relatives. He must have seen Evangeline at the same moment she spied him because he broke into a relieved grin and motioned with his head that he was coming around to see her.

To avoid having their conversation overheard, Evangeline decided to meet him in the hall. She stood waiting, tapping her foot impatiently until he arrived, even though Freddie managed to squeeze his way through the crowd in record time. Without a word, he took Evangeline by the elbow and steered her away from the box-seat doors, toward the stairwell.

"I had no idea you'd be here!" she exclaimed.

"I called the townhouse only to be told you were out. When I got home, I was presented with an ultimatum. Either attend this, or a church bazaar on Saturday afternoon, and you know how I hate those." Freddie rolled his eyes.

Evangeline smiled in mock sympathy. "Poor Frederick. What a sad life you lead."

"Oh, stop it, Engie! We don't have much time, and I have such news!" Pulling her farther down the stairs so they wouldn't be seen, Freddie launched into an extended narrative of his investigation that afternoon—playing up his own ingenuity and perseverance.

"So, Sidley, or Kingston, or whoever he is, was lying all along."

"He must have something to hide. But what?"

"Unfortunately, we don't know just yet." Evangeline scowled and concentrated. "It's a disturbing coincidence that he and Jonathan left Dresden together over three years ago. Three years! Why come together again now?"

"Yes, I was wondering the same thing. We can be fairly certain that they left at close to the same time for a reason. But if they were both implicated in something sordid, why didn't Blackthorne conceal his identity as well?"

Evangeline pondered Freddie's question. "Maybe because Jonathan wasn't implicated in the crime, whatever it was. Maybe he discovered it."

"And perhaps he's been blackmailing Sidley with that discovery ever since."

"Yes, but Sidley isn't a rich man now and probably never was."

"Maybe..." Freddie suggested, "maybe the payment Blackthorne's exacting isn't in currency."

"You mean Jonathan is using Sidley to perform a service for him, such as arranging the meeting at the Fair with Elsa?"

"Yes, something like that."

Evangeline stared off into space. "But why wait three years to call in a debt? Especially for a girl that he'd never even seen before. Unless—"

"Listen, Engie, we can't stay here much longer. They'll be starting again any minute. Now isn't the time to get all dreamy-eyed and obscure."

Evangeline barely heard him. Her attention was focused on the idea forming in her mind. "What if this wasn't the first time! What if they've been doing this all along, and this is the first time they got caught at it!"

"My God! If that's true, it's almost too horrible to consider. The cold-blooded calculation of it. It's... it's..." Freddie struggled to find an adjective strong enough to describe such a level of depravity. "It's beastly! It's beyond beastly! It's monstrous!"

"Steady on, young Frederick." Evangeline tried to pull him away from the image she had provoked. "We don't know that for certain yet. But I know a way we can find out."

"How?" The echo of fewer and fewer voices on the steps above signaled that intermission was nearly over.

From above stairs, Evangeline could hear the door of Mrs. Blackthorne's box open and her own name being called. "We know Sidley's been at Hull House for three years, so I'm going to find out if any girls have gone missing during that time." Almost as an afterthought, she said hurriedly, "Oh, yes, and it's clear you must go to Iowa."

Freddie, who had been nodding in agreement up to that point, balked like a mule being led to harness. "What do you mean I have to go to Iowa? Why can't I just send a telegram? How in God's name am I going to explain a little junket like that to Uncle Horace?"

As ushers began the final call for patrons to return to their seats, Evangeline patted him reassuringly on the cheek. "I have every confidence in you, dear boy. Use some of that newfound ingenuity you just bragged about to me. It's imperative that you see this Harcourt Smythe in person. A written reply can conceal too much. I really must go." With that, she ran up the stairs to rejoin Mrs. Blackthorne, leaving Freddie to scramble back to his seat before the theater went dark.

***

Evangeline didn't see Freddie as the crowd swarmed out after the performance. As a gesture of gratitude for the invitation, Evangeline had offered the use of her carriage so that Mrs. Blackthorne might be spared the unspeakable horrors of crude public transportation. The ride would be a short one since the older woman was staying with friends in town. When the two were settled, Mrs. Blackthorne said cozily, "Well, here we are."

"Yes, here we are." Evangeline tried to keep her voice from sounding too wary.

"There's something that's been weighing on my mind all evening, my dear, but I haven't had the nerve to broach the subject until now."

"Oh, and what might that be?" Evangeline looked out the carriage window for distraction but found only darkness around her.

Mrs. Blackthorne laughed deprecatingly. "Surely, my dear, you must know what I'm referring to. I keep a watchful eye on my son, after all."

"Madame?" The younger woman hoped her voice conveyed genuine puzzlement.

"Come now, Evangeline. I've known you all your life. Your mother was my friend since first she and your papa moved to this part of the country. I never thought of you as one of those giddy young women who indulge in meaningless flirtations merely to gratify their vanity."

"You're right on that count, Mrs. Blackthorne. But I don't know what you're referring to."

The older woman frowned in perplexity. "Do you mean to deny that my son proposed to you on Sunday?"

Evangeline tried to appear perplexed herself as she equivocated. "I'm sorry, but you're mistaken. While it's true that Jonathan bought up the subject of his personal feelings, he merely hinted at his inclination toward me."

"Jonathan can be a bit too subtle for his own good at times. I'll have to speak to him about it." Mrs. Blackthorne tapped her fan against her chin while she considered what to say next. "Well, it appears the cat's out of the bag, even if the news comes from his mother. Do you intend to accept him when he does get around to formulating the proper question?"

Evangeline resisted the urge to open the door and fly away into the night. "I... I don't know what to say. You've placed me in a very awkward position, Mrs. Blackthorne."

The older woman patted her hand reassuringly. "Forgive me, my dear. I really didn't mean to force you into a decision this very moment. It's just that I'm terribly worried about what he might do if you turn him down."

Evangeline toyed nervously with the beads on her evening bag. "I seem to recall he mentioned something about moving away."

Mrs. Blackthorne nodded sadly. "Yes, I believe he would do that. Jonathan is quite sensitive, and I doubt he could stand to be rejected. If you won't have him, I'm quite sure he will make good on that promise to leave."

Trying to sound light-hearted, Evangeline laughed. "Surely he wasn't serious about that."

"Oh, my son is a very serious young fellow. If he says he's going to do a thing, he does it, and that's that."

Evangeline began to breathe rapidly. The stays of her corset constricted her ribcage. Her agitation rose as she considered her own worst fears about what

Jonathan might do. "Oh, please, madame, can't you convince him to wait a while?"

No doubt attributing her reaction to an entirely different emotion, Mrs. Blackthorne smiled and patted her hand again. "It's all right, my dear. It's all right. I see where your heart is. You're just being delicate. No need to say anymore at this time. I'll have a talk with my boy. I'll tell him he needs to be a bit more patient."

Evangeline breathed a sigh of relief, which also was misconstrued by the mother who smiled benevolently at her. "Love, when it strikes an independent young woman such as yourself, must be a very alarming sensation indeed."

"Oh, quite alarming, I assure you." Evangeline was thinking of a different subject altogether.

Mrs. Blackthorne leaned back in the carriage, seemingly content that she had nudged her son's romance one step closer to marriage. Evangeline waited a few moments and then made a request that she had wanted to make all evening—knowing full well that her motive would again be misinterpreted.

"Mrs. Blackthorne?"

"Yes?" The matron's eyelids were half-closed as the rocking motion of the carriage began to lull her to sleep.

"I wonder if you might have a small picture of your son that you would be willing to give me."

Mrs. Blackthorne perked up immediately. "You young people. All so sly. You're just like my Jonathan, never telling me what he's about and leaving me to guess. Fortunately, I'm a shrewd judge of character, so I know what you're up to, and what he's up to as well. Of course, you might have a picture of him. You might have a dozen if you like. I'll have several sent round to your house tomorrow!"

"Just one will do," Evangeline murmured dryly. "And please don't tell him. I don't want him to know what's in my heart just yet. Can this be a secret kept between us?"

"Of course, my dear, of course." By this time, Mrs. Blackthorne was glowing. "It will be our little secret until you say otherwise."

21 – SAINT JANE

"Engie, dear, how nice to see you. Come in and sit down." Jane Addams held out a hand in welcome.

Evangeline smiled and came forward to return the greeting. She stood in the office of a personage who had achieved sainthood in the eyes of Chicago's poor—none other than the founder of Hull House herself.

Jane Addams was a tall woman who favored shirtwaist blouses and drab skirts. Her liking for order extended to her personal attire. She insisted on so much starch and bluing in her white blouses that her guest was rendered nearly snow-blind by the sight of the one she wore now.

Evangeline's dislike for Ellen Starr didn't extend to Jane, whom she regarded with a mixture of admiration and bewilderment. While Jane was as independent and idealistic as Evangeline, the similarity ended there. Jane Addams was a plain woman, in appearance and in speech, whose only true need in life was to be needed. In contrast, Evangeline had little desire to be needed by anyone and heartily wished her fellow man to the devil if he thwarted her own need for freedom.

Jane was wise enough to accept Evangeline's contribution to the settlement on its own terms—never insisting, as Ellen might have done, that she make Hull House her one consuming passion in life. In consequence, Evangeline and Jane got along well together, mutually tolerant of what each regarded as the other's eccentricities.

Evangeline's eyes swept over the clutter in the office. Jane's rolltop desk was piled high with books that threatened to topple and crush their owner if one more were added to the stack. Jane sighed as she regarded the bibliographic mountain before her. "There's so much to wade through. We've gotten our first set of statistics back on the neighborhoods, but I never imagined there would be so much paper!"

"What do you intend to do with it?"

"We're compiling a map for the mayor's office showing where each immigrant community is located and how many people live in each neighborhood. This is the first time any city has attempted a study of this magnitude."

Evangeline eyed the desk warily. "You have my congratulations and my condolences as well."

"I don't suppose you'd have time..." Jane was hesitant, as always, to ask for assistance.

"At any other time I would, Jane, but I have a little matter that's occupying a great deal of my attention just now."

"Of course, I understand." Jane cleared her throat self-consciously. "I'm sorry, I didn't mean to presume." As a distraction from embarrassment, she took her glasses off to clean them. Like Ellen Starr, Jane Addams was near-sighted but rather than a pince-nez she wore spectacles. The lenses were of such small dimensions and pressed so close to her face that they gave the impression of propping her eyelids open. She polished the spectacles for a full minute which, considering the surface to be cleaned, was far in excess of what was required.

Evangeline watched her with a faint smile, amused by so much effort expended to so little purpose. She tried to ease Jane's unfounded discomfort. "It seems very generous of you to go to such trouble for the mayor. I hope he appreciates it."

Jane readjusted her spectacles. "Well, this time I had an ulterior motive."

Evangeline said teasingly, "You? I don't believe it! Jane Addams does not possess a calculating bone in her body. That is, if bones may be said to calculate. What can you be after?"

Jane sat back down at her desk and replied significantly, "Well, it's the garbage, you know."

Her visitor sat as well. "Ah, I see. The garbage. Well, that explains everything, doesn't it?" Evangeline knew that she was being teased in turn. "Please elucidate, Miss Addams, or I shall be forced to conclude that you are being deliberately enigmatic to addle my poor, weak brains."

Jane smiled, half to herself. "Engie, your brains are about as weak as a bear trap."

The two women looked at each other and laughed.

"Seriously, what are you after?"

"Seriously, I'm after the garbage. City contracts were awarded for garbage collection in the Nineteenth Ward, and as far as I'm concerned, the men who received those contracts are nothing but a pack of boodlers!"

"Well, that's a strong charge coming from you, Jane, since you never criticize anybody. I take it they've been pocketing the money and leaving the garbage to rot in the alleys?"

"Exactly." Jane spoke in her characteristically quiet voice, but a grim look had come into her eyes. "No one at City Hall may take the spread of disease in this neighborhood seriously, but I do."

"I pity the gentlemen of the city council if you've decided to adopt this cause as your own. You have the persistence of water dripping on granite. It may take you several thousand years, but you will eventually crack the most obdurate stone just the same." She looked at her listener appraisingly before continuing. "But I believe it would be easy to underestimate someone like you— so soft-spoken and mild-tempered."

"Oh, bother, Engie, am I really that much of a shrinking violet?"

"Only to those who've made the fatal error of superficial judgment. Such creatures will get what they deserve."

"And what might they deserve?"

"A painful lesson in never judging a book by its cover."

Jane tilted her head to the side and smiled again, almost shyly. "Yes, I suppose I've taught that lesson more than a few times over."

"Well, it's not something you need to be embarrassed about, Jane. It's hardly your fault that the elected officials of this city are dolts."

"Not all of them, Engie. Not quite all."

"Then you have a few friends at City Hall?"

"Yes, enough to carry my point if need be. But in return, I've offered to undertake this study of the neighborhoods as a gesture of cooperation."

"Oh, I see. Remind me never to call you ingenuous again."

"How could I be, Engie?" The champion of the poor sighed. "We live in one of the most corrupt cities in the country. If we ever hope to accomplish any good here then—"

"Then, to paraphrase from scripture," Evangeline completed the thought. "The doves must be as wise as serpents."

"Yes, quite.

"I always thought you were a rare bird indeed, Miss Addams." Evangeline's eyes twinkled with mischief. "Now, I know it's literally true."

"That's funny. People keep telling me the same thing about you." Jane laughed demurely. "But enough of our silliness. What is it you wanted to see me about?"

Before Evangeline could begin, the door opened, and one of the girls who managed the reception desk came in bearing a tea tray.

"My goodness, look at the time! Is it so late already? Rachel, would you be kind enough to fetch a cup for Miss LeClair as well?"

Taking the mild request as an edict, the girl flew from the room and returned bearing a table setting for the great lady's guest.

As the brief refreshment ceremony began, Evangeline broached the subject uppermost in her mind. "Jane, you know I've adopted a crusade of my own lately."

"Oh, what is that?" Jane stirred her tea.

"I'm looking into the cause of Elsa Bauer's death."

"Yes, I thought you might be. It's hard to believe something as shocking as that could have happened to one of our own."

"Even more shocking to consider that her brother might have been responsible. No doubt Ellen has filled you in on the details?"

Jane nodded gravely. "Yes, I've heard all about it and about Mr. Schuler's unfortunate influence over poor Franz."

Evangeline balked at Jane's choice of adjective. She wasn't sure whether Franz deserved to be pitied or not. Suppressing her own ambivalent opinion of Franz's innocence, she forged ahead. "Schuler's influence worries me more than anything else. I must solve this little mystery before he talks Franz into some fatal gesture of defiance."

"Do you have any evidence that might cast suspicion in another direction?"

Evangeline laughed ruefully. "Suspicion, yes. Evidence, no. There are at least three other persons who could be implicated in Elsa's death but no evidence that would stand up in a court of law. However, I am on the trail of something promising. That's why I need your help. I have a theory that Elsa's murder may not have been an isolated incident."

Jane looked up from her teacup in surprise. "What on earth do you mean, Engie?"

"I mean that the man who killed Elsa may have done the same before and that his target may have been another girl who came here."

"Good heavens! Surely not here!"

"I know how you feel, Jane. Hull House was meant to be a refuge for the poor. The one place they could come and be treated as human beings."

"And you have reason to think..." Jane's eyes entreated a denial.

"Yes, I have strong reason to believe that at least a few girls here have been preyed upon, perhaps murdered by a creature I can scarcely define as human!" Evangeline was becoming unsettled. She put down her cup, stood up, and began to pace back and forth. "At first, the possibility seemed so absurd that even I couldn't believe it. But each day, I grow more convinced that a pattern exists and that it can be traced here."

She wheeled about, her hands gripping the desk urgently. "Jane, you must help me! Think back. You've always kept a close watch on everything that touches Hull House. You know nearly everyone who comes through the front door by name."

Jane shook her head in distress. "But there have been so many... so many. Like falling leaves. I can't begin to guess."

"Please, you must try! Another life could well depend on your answer. I'll narrow the field for you. Over the past three years, can you think of any young women who left without an explanation? Any bad news you heard about them afterward? Please think!"

Jane set down her own cup and walked over to the window, lost in thought. She looked out over the street for several minutes without saying a word. Finally, she turned back to Evangeline. "I can only think of two who struck me as particularly unfortunate cases during the time you mention."

"Yes?" Evangeline sat down on the edge of her chair.

"Well, there was poor Janet Stewart. But that happened quite a while back. It may have been very soon after we began the settlement here."

"Janet Stewart? I don't think I remember hearing anything about her."

"Oh, it would have been well before your time, my dear. She was one of the very first young girls to visit us."

"What happened to her?" Evangeline dreaded to know.

Jane sighed deeply. "It was a suicide. She hanged herself in the attic of her tenement building."

"Are you sure it was suicide?"

Jane looked puzzled. "Well, it certainly appeared to be. That was what the police concluded."

"But did she leave a note?"

"I don't remember hearing about it if she did."

Evangeline was not convinced. "Why would she have wanted to do away with herself?"

"I'm not at all sure, though I do remember her family said it had something to do with a failed romance. There was apparently a mysterious gentleman she had been seeing. He may have abandoned her." Jane waved her hand distractedly. "But that was all speculation. I don't believe a satisfactory answer was ever found."

Evangeline tried another approach. "Do any of her family still live around here?"

"I'm sorry. I don't think so. Her mother passed on soon afterward. Her brother, being a tradesman, was able to find work elsewhere. Cleveland, I think, and so he moved away."

"Oh." Evangeline felt disappointed. "I suppose that means there's no one left that I could speak to. But you said there was a second incident?"

Jane walked back from the window and sat down again. She shook her head sadly. "In some ways, I think it was the more unfortunate case of the two. Do you remember Rosa Grandinetti?"

"No, should I?"

"Perhaps not. This happened about a year and a half ago after you had joined our little band, but I don't think Rosa ever took any of your classes. Her primary interest was in crafts—weaving and pottery mainly."

Evangeline waited for more without interrupting.

"Anyway, for no accountable reason, she stopped coming to classes here. Since she had been such a regular student, I wondered what had happened and went to pay her mother a visit. When I asked Mrs. Grandinetti about her daughter, she told me that she had no daughter."

"She couldn't have meant that literally."

"No, figuratively. Rosa had turned to prostitution to make her living."

Evangeline registered surprise. "Was her family in such dire straits that she had no alternative?"

"Not at all. She had three brothers and a father—all of whom were working at the time. That's what made the business so unaccountable. I couldn't let the matter rest. Like you, I suppose I wanted to explain an event that made no sense to me. So, I traced her whereabouts and went to see her. I began to ask her questions, but she wouldn't speak to me. Just hid her face in her hands and started crying. It was most distressing to see her that way. Most distressing. She showed such promise, too."

Evangeline felt a chill run down her spine as she heard her own words about Elsa repeated back to her. On a hunch, she asked, "Was she unusually pretty?"

"Oh, my yes. Shy though. Not the sort one would ever expect to take to the streets."

"Did you hear anything about a romance that ended badly in connection with her?"

"No. I couldn't get anyone in her family to talk about her at all. I was fortunate that they even told me where to find her."

"Perhaps she still lives in the same neighborhood." Evangeline had already begun planning her next move.

"I'm sure she does." Jane's voice held a note of strain. "It's one of the houses of prostitution on Clark Street. I can give you the address if you really feel the need to speak to her."

"That would be a great help to me, Jane. As it is, I'm grasping at straws."

The other lady nodded and wrote an address on a slip of paper. As she handed it to Evangeline, she asked, "Engie, you don't seriously believe there's a connection here, do you? If that were true, then somehow I can't help thinking we may all be at fault."

Evangeline was troubled by the thought. "Well, that would be a hard truth to face, wouldn't it? By creating an island of trust here, we may have opened the door to a murderer masquerading as a benefactor." She stopped short. "No, I won't have it! The work you do here, the work all of us do here is good. It may have been put to an evil use, but how could we have known it would be? All we can do now—all I can do—is to make certain the wolf who has been preying on your little flock never has the opportunity to do it again."

Evangeline folded the paper decisively, placed it in her handbag, and left. She fancied that the worried look on Jane's face wouldn't depart until long after she had gone.

22 – THE NEW JERUSALEM

"Good morning, Jonathan," Evangeline whispered playfully.

The junior banker looked up from his paperwork in surprise. "Engie!" he exclaimed when he realized who stood before his desk. "This is certainly a welcome diversion! I hope it will be the first of many such visits."

Evangeline assumed her most pleasing manner. "I've come to see if I can persuade you to be derelict in your duty."

Blackthorne frowned. "I'm afraid I don't understand, *ma belle.*"

She sat down in one of the wooden chairs facing his desk and leaned forward conspiratorially. "*Carpe diem,* dear man. The Exposition will be closing next week."

"Yes," Blackthorne agreed warily.

"I've had time to reconsider my rather abrupt refusal of your invitation a few weeks ago. It would be grand to see the Fair one last time, don't you think?"

"Yes, I suppose that it would. But today?"

"Jonathan, don't tell me you would be so ungallant as to disoblige a lady?"

Blackthorne appeared to be impaled on the horns of a dilemma.

"It's such a beautiful autumn day. There won't be many more of them before winter. Do say you'll come with me! I would be inconsolable if you were to fail me now!" To complete a convincing gesture of appeal, she extended her hand across the desk toward him, waiting for him to take it.

Blackthorne glanced around him apprehensively. He sighed and looked down at his appointment calendar. After wrestling for a few more moments with his sense of duty, he took the lady's hand in his own. "Of course, my dear, of course. I have nothing pressing today, and I would hate to disappoint you. Who knows, second thoughts about one proposal might lead to second thoughts about another." He stood up, put on his hat, and offered his arm to Evangeline. "Shall we?"

She approximated a giggle of delight and took his arm. Outside, Jack was waiting at the curb in the driver's seat of Evangeline's brougham. "I thought we might take my carriage rather than braving *la canaille* on the Illinois Central line," she said as Blackthorne helped her inside.

He laughed. "Why, Engie, what an undemocratic sentiment to come from you. However, I'm delighted you share my view of the rabble."

He swung in beside her and closed the door. Jack steered them as best he could through the traffic-choked downtown streets until they were well south of the business district. Skyscrapers gave way to the genteel dwellings of Chicago's wealthy citizens along Prairie Avenue. This elegant scenery, in turn, gave way to a flat weedy plain containing a marvel that some observers had called the "New Jerusalem."

For there on the shores of Lake Michigan, in what had formerly been the swampy and undistinguished mud hole of Jackson Park, the world's most noted architects had fashioned a city of dreams—the great White City of the Columbian Exposition. The fairgrounds ran two miles in length and like the Grand Canyon, that other wonder of the new world, had the effect of exceeding the capacity of imagination to comprehend what the eyes beheld. With endless lagoons and fountains, statuary of Greek gods and goddesses, and exhibition buildings more immense than the great pyramid at Giza, it was no surprise that spectators required the relief of the Midway to bring them back to earth.

The Midway Plaisance was an offshoot of the Exposition and stretched about a mile from Stony Island Avenue on the east to Cottage Grove Avenue on the west. It contained a series of exotic and lurid attractions, which the planners of the fair acknowledged only to the extent that they boosted revenues. Here a polyglot of nations was represented. Here stood the Street of Cairo where Little Egypt danced. Here stood Hagenbeck's Animal Show and the Dahomey Village where a primitive tribe had been imported for the inspection and amazement of the civilized world. Here, too, the great Ferris wheel pushed the limits of the sky itself. At its apex, the wheel lifted the spectator two hundred and sixty-six feet in the air—commanding a godlike view of the city skyline seven miles to the north, the blue gem of Lake Michigan to the east, and the Midway to the west. A thirty-minute ride on the wheel, costing fifty cents, was as expensive as an admission ticket to the Exposition itself.

Evangeline instructed Jack to drive to the entrance at Fifty-Seventh Street and Stoney Island, where she and Blackthorne alighted. As the two entered the fairgrounds, Evangeline asked, "Can you guess how many tickets have been sold to this event, Jonathan?"

Blackthorne surveyed the milling crowd of foreigners, rustics, and city dwellers before him. "Judging from today's attendance alone, I should say several million."

"Over twenty-four million, to be precise. I've been reading up on the latest news from the Fair."

"Well, I'm just grateful they aren't all here today," he muttered.

"Jonathan, you seem unhappy to be here. Have I upset you by dragging you along with me?"

"Not at all, *ma belle*. Not at all." He took her hand and folded her arm under his own. "I'm just disappointed that I have to share your company with so many others." He fixed her with a slow smile. "My sole intention today is to please you. Where do you wish to begin?"

She affected a casual air that she hoped would disguise the purpose she had in mind. "I should like very much to start at the Palace of Fine Arts if you please."

"I am your servant, *ma chérie*." Blackthorne raised her fingers to his lips before he let go of her arm. He then walked over to a concession stand to purchase a guidebook to the exhibits.

After the two had located their destination on the map, Evangeline said decisively, "Well, let's be off then. The Fine Arts Building is that way." She gestured with her parasol toward the far end of the fairgrounds.

The couple skirted the North Pond, one of the endless shallow pools complete with gondolas that made Jackson Park more reminiscent of Venice than Chicago. Eventually, they arrived at the colossal bleached building that housed a temporary collection of the world's art treasures. These were on loan from the royal houses of Europe, primarily through the efforts of Bertha Palmer. Evangeline held her hand up to shade her eyes.

"How bright the glare is from these white buildings. A shame none of them will withstand the blast of one frigid Chicago winter." She looked up at the immense stone maidens supporting each side portico of the building by bearing the massive weight of the roof on their equally massive heads. She secretly felt herself as overburdened as they at the moment. The couple climbed the steps and reached the shady protection of the main entrance.

"Well, it says here that this one will." Blackthorne consulted the description of the Palace of Fine Arts in the guidebook.

"Really?"

"Yes, it seems that the construction was made sturdier and more fireproof at the insistence of the governments that loaned so many of their national treasures to the Exposition."

Evangeline laughed. "You mean they weren't willing to trust that Chicago had learned its lesson after the last blaze?"

"Apparently not." Blackthorne squinted up at the front pillars. "This building is to be converted to a permanent museum after the Fair is over."

"Well, that's something at least! Jonathan, doesn't it bother you that all this splendor was created out of nothing more substantial than painted burlap and plaster?"

"Should it bother me?"

"Doesn't it seem a form of trumpery to you? To invite the world to come and marvel at our accomplishments when all that we've created for their inspection are a series of stage sets, and neoclassical ones at that."

Blackthorne squeezed her hand. "My dear, you think too much."

Evangeline raised an eyebrow. "How odd. Your mother told me the same thing. It must be a Blackthorne family trait."

"But if you just consider the matter, Engie, don't you see that everything in life is a facade? Civilization is nothing more than a veneer that only thinly coats the savage within."

Evangeline chose not to contradict him. She didn't want him to become suspicious of her motives for bringing him here. Her plan was to lead him through the exhibits at random and tire him out. When his guard was down, she would make her move.

***

They spent the next several hours touring not only the Art Palace but the exposition buildings devoted to fisheries, horticulture, manufacturing, electricity, mining, and transportation. Evangeline was particularly interested in viewing the Women's Building designed by a female architect. Finally, as a much-needed diversion from all these educational exhibits, Evangeline proposed that they go to the Midway to see Little Egypt dance.

Blackthorne scowled at her daring suggestion. "Do you really think that's an appropriate place for you to be seen, Engie?"

"Oh, nonsense, Jonathan, it's a fair, not a bordello. I certainly don't expect to have my morals corrupted by the sight."

"It's not your morals that are at risk, my dear, but you are in very real danger of having your purse stolen."

She smiled up at him impishly. "I'm quite sure you'll protect me if it comes to that."

Blackthorne sighed. "As you wish, though I find the entire Midway distasteful."

"How so?" Evangeline led him on.

"It's vulgar and cheap. The Exposition is debased by its proximity to something so common."

"You don't much care for the common man, do you, Jonathan?"

Blackthorne gave a contemptuous grimace. "I have very little reason to. The city is overrun with foreigners, who seem to do nothing but push and shove their way through the streets and knife one another in alleys. Every time I open a newspaper, I expect to see a list of casualties suggesting that this city is in the midst of a war."

"Perhaps it is a war. A war between the way of life that you and I know, and theirs."

Blackthorne looked at her gravely. "God help us all, if you're right, Engie. I think it was a great mistake to allow them into our country in the first place—with their disease and their violence. At times, I feel as if they should all be exterminated like the vermin they attract."

"They're human beings, Jonathan. Just as you and I are." Evangeline could barely conceal the shock she felt at his words.

"Are they, Engie? Are they?" Blackthorne came to a full stop as they neared the entrance to the Midway. He pointed toward two dirt-encrusted urchins standing outside the gate. He reached into his pocket and casually flipped a nickel in their direction. The boys dove to the ground for the coin, kicking and gouging one another until the victor ripped it away from his mate and took to his heels before a counterattack began. The loser screamed curses in some foreign language and ran after him.

Blackthorne cocked an eyebrow as he looked down at his companion. "Human, you said. Are you quite sure of that?"

Evangeline made no direct reply to the question, but she shivered as a cloud blew across the sun. The couple walked in silence through the entrance to the Plaisance. As they proceeded down the central path that led them to Evangeline's chosen destination, the walls echoed with a barrage of carnival sounds. At close range, the music of a German band contended with North African drums. The odor of food from a variety of countries, French and Turkish, Irish and Moroccan, Dutch and Chinese, assaulted them as they made their way toward the Street of Cairo exhibit.

They entered the crowded lane, which was swarming with a visual polyglot to match the aromas and sounds they had already encountered. They saw Americans and Arabs, Soudanese and Nubians, camels and donkeys, all crowded together as the couple searched for the theater where sword dancers and ladies who performed *la danse du ventre* could be found.

Evangeline knew they had arrived when she saw that the crowd milling around waiting for the next show was primarily male. They were all eager to see the foreign girl who had started such a flurry among Chicago's more straitlaced residents. She was a Syrian dancer named Fareeda Mahzar, and she did what was known in local papers as the "hootchy-kootchy." Although her costume as described in the press contained more material than a lady's bathing suit, the force of imagination had weighed so heavily that there were those willing to swear they had seen her dance wearing nothing more substantial than a diamond garter. Evangeline was curious to test the accuracy of such reports but, as she was about to press forward through the doorway to the theater, Jonathan gripped her hard by the arm. She wheeled about in surprise.

"No!" he said urgently. "I cannot allow this! You don't belong here, Engie."

"Jonathan—" she began to protest, but he roughly pulled her away from the entrance.

His voice carried an undertone of menace that she had never heard before. "I will not have you polluted by contact with anything this vile! Come away, Engie! I don't wish to be seen here, nor should you!"

Under normal circumstances, Evangeline would have done as she pleased, but she was too stunned by the raw outrage that Blackthorne was exhibiting. He hadn't released his grip on her arm, and she believed he would have dragged her away if she resisted.

"Very well, Jonathan," she murmured in a small voice. "As you wish. I'll go along peaceably."

She allowed herself to be led back to the central path. Blackthorne said nothing the whole time. His composure didn't return until the beating drums and wailing music from the theater in the Street of Cairo were well behind them. Evangeline wasn't quite sure what reaction she had expected to provoke, but the one she received was far beyond anything she anticipated.

Affecting a sweet smile, she steered him in another direction. "Perhaps you're right, Jonathan. Perhaps we should confine ourselves to more dignified pursuits." She linked her arm through his.

He seemed to relax by degrees as the couple strolled further down the Midway. As if on impulse, Evangeline came to a dead stop in the middle of the Plaisance. "I know what we should do next!"

Blackthorne looked at her quizzically.

"Let's take a ride on the Ferris wheel!"

She watched him closely to judge his reaction. She could have sworn his swarthy complexion had turned pale. He tried to sound unruffled, but she was attuned to a certain nervous tone in his voice. "Why whatever for, Engie? You must have been on that ride before."

"Of course I've been, Jonathan." She added, almost as an afterthought, "I have little doubt that you must have been there too, but the view is so spectacular I can't resist."

Blackthorne seemed to hover on the brink of refusal, but he finally relented. "As you wish. I've already disappointed you once. I have no wish to do so again. Lead on, my dear, lead on."

They traveled the short distance to the base of the gigantic wheel that dominated the fairground. A fence had been constructed around the ride so that only paying customers could ascend the stairs that would lead them to even more Olympian heights. Evangeline happened to notice a young woman standing alone near the ticket booth, obviously waiting for someone.

With reckless bravado, she exclaimed, "Oh, what a shame! To be left all alone at the Fair."

Blackthorne followed her gaze but said nothing.

"I wonder if some kind gentleman will take pity on her and show her the sights. Wouldn't that be a fine thing for her, Jonathan?"

"Yes, a fine thing, I'm sure." His voice was noncommittal, but his foot had begun to tap.

Evangeline paused, seeming to be in a quandary. "And yet, there are so many tricksters and confidence men around the fairgrounds. One never knows whom an innocent girl might meet here."

Blackthorne turned to face her directly. He regarded her intently for several seconds. "An innocent girl," he echoed skeptically. "Innocence is nothing more than a sham virtue, an attempt to manipulate a response of pity out of one's fellow man."

Evangeline tried to match his slow, smooth tone. "Then, I take it, you don't pretend to be your sister's keeper?"

He laughed lightly. "I feel no moral obligation to support hypocrisy no matter what guise it assumes, whether female or male, sister or brother!"

With a languid movement, he reached his hand out to touch her cheek. His hand moved down until it came to rest on her neck. She could feel his thumb pressing ever so slightly against the side of her throat. In a low voice, he said, "But since you're so concerned about her welfare, perhaps you should warn her." He paused. "Yes. Perhaps you should warn her of the wolves lurking in the shadows all around, the wolves that prey on innocence."

A shock of electricity traveled through Evangeline's spine at his words. She tried to laugh but failed. She stepped back to take herself out of his reach. "What nonsense you talk, Jonathan. I don't see any wolves lurking around here."

"Don't you, Engie?" Blackthorne's eyes had grown cold. A thin smile formed on his lips. "Forgive me. I must have been mistaken."

The silence that followed opened like a chasm between them. After what seemed like several hours, Blackthorne finally asked, "Shall we go up?" He held out his hand to help his companion ascend the stairs to the ride. Evangeline wordlessly complied as he sent her to the loading platform while he went to the ticket booth to pay for their admission.

While she waited, she studied the construction of the wonder to end all wonders. The immense wheel had thirty-six wooden cars suspended from it. Each one looked like a cable car turned sideways. In total, the observation cars could hold over two thousand passengers at a time. Blackthorne returned to escort her inside. The minute the car door was secure, the giant wheel lurched into life.

Evangeline looked around in surprise at the dozens of empty seats and the ground receding below them. "Jonathan, we're all alone. Where are all the other passengers?"

Her companion chuckled. "I thought it would be a delightful diversion that in this White City of thousands, we should have an island to ourselves at the top of the world."

Evangeline was too shocked to speak. She continued to stare at Blackthorne in amazement until he added, "I bought all the seats in this car. It's surprising how much solitude twenty dollars can buy."

"But the conductor," Evangeline protested. "The last time I rode the Ferris wheel, the car had a conductor who locked the door from the inside."

Blackthorne seemed highly amused at some private joke. "I gave ours a slight monetary incentive to rest his feet for a while. He did argue with me about safety. I simply asked if he thought I appeared to be the sort of fellow who would take chances. He said he didn't think so." Blackthorne paused before adding, "Do you think I would, Engie?"

Evangeline glanced nervously around her. "I think you aren't the sort of man to put yourself in jeopardy, Jonathan."

She walked toward the window at the front of the car. It was covered with a thin screen of wire mesh to prevent anyone from jumping or falling out. She relaxed slightly after reassuring herself that there were no gaps in the mesh.

Although she stood perfectly still, she could see the ground receding below her just the same. The ride stopped at six different points to allow patrons to savor the view from different elevations. At its second stop, when the wheel paused midway in its ascent, Evangeline sighed. "Wouldn't it be wonderful to have this perspective all the time? Look at how much one can see in a single glance."

"There are some things not worth seeing, Engie. Take that, for instance." Blackthorne pointed toward the sooty haze that overshadowed Chicago to the north—the contribution of the city's innumerable factory smokestacks.

Evangeline gazed off into the distance. "I suppose you'd prefer to look there instead." She gestured to the sterile purity of the White City directly ahead of them.

"Yes, I find that particular prospect most pleasing."

"But it's not real, is it? The only reality is that brown mass of burning coal and rotting garbage and slum flats seven miles to the north of us."

Blackthorne came to stand behind her to see the view from her perspective. He rested his hands on the window frame—pinning her within the span of his arms. He leaned down to match her eye level, his lips near her ear. He said softly, "The White City is a dream come to life. Of all man's aspirations, it is the crowning achievement."

"And the brown city is the substance of man's achievements, in spite of his aspirations." The soft tone of her voice belied the harshness of the sentiment.

Blackthorne didn't stir. "For shame, Engie. I thought you were the idealist, not me."

Evangeline continued to look at the city skyline. She answered sadly, "You mistake me. I am painfully idealistic. The money that built this Exposition might have been better spent on wage increases."

She could feel his breath against her cheek as he whispered, "It must be lonely to be so much of an idealist."

"On the contrary, I am never lonely." She made the statement with far more certainty than she felt. Turning her eyes away from the real city, she looked out at the lake instead. Blackthorne remained motionless. He offered no comment.

When the giant wheel had paused once more, and they were at the apex of their ascent, Blackthorne walked over to the door of the observation car. Without warning, he opened it and stepped forward to peer over the edge. Evangeline expected him every moment to invite her over to join him. He didn't. Her natural curiosity couldn't stand the strain any longer. Perfectly aware of the risk she was taking, she stepped toward the door.

"What do you see?"

He glanced casually over his shoulder at her. "What God must have seen on the seventh day, once his creation was complete." He stood back from the open doorway, his eyes silently challenging her to join him at the edge of the world.

It wouldn't have been in her nature to resist the dare. She expected he knew that. Stepping forward two paces more she stood with the tips of her boots protruding over the edge of the platform. Her left hand firmly grasped the door jamb as she peeked over the edge. There was no glass, no wire mesh separating her from thin air. She knew what a bird must feel like to breathe the intoxicating breeze that floated just above the reach of gravity.

"Look there!" Blackthorne swept his arm wide to point at something in the distance. He bumped her shoulder as his arm shot forward, knocking her off balance. Knocking her through the open doorway into the void.

Evangeline shrieked. Her left hand still held fast to the door jamb as her right clawed at the outside frame of the observation car. The only word she could manage to gasp was "h...elp!"

"Engie!" he cried. He seemed paralyzed by shock.

To her horror, she saw the Austrian village directly below her—no net, no platform intervening between her dangling toes and 266 feet of open air. She grew dizzy as she struggled to pull herself back into the car. She could see a crowd of people gathering on the ground below, pointing upward, pointing at her. With a sick sense of dread, she realized a hand had grasped her elbow. She waited, scarcely breathing, through the endless second it took to determine whether that hand meant to help her up or push her the rest of the way down.

The verdict came when Blackthorne grasped her by the waist and swung her back into the car. "God in heaven! My darling!"

She fell to her knees, too much in shock to stand.

"Are you all right?" His hands cupped her face. He was on his knees beside her, the portrait of solicitude.

Drawing a deep breath, she took several seconds before replying. "Yes, quite." She drew herself back up to her feet. He rushed to assist her.

"What a fright you gave me! I'm so sorry. How stupid of me! How careless!" He appeared seriously shaken.

As shaken as she herself was.

Smiling ruefully, she said, "As a child, I always wished I could fly. Little did I know I'd so nearly have the opportunity."

Blackthorne slammed the door decisively. "I'm a careless fool! I'll never forgive myself for this! Never!"

Evangeline dusted off her sleeves in what she hoped was a show of nonchalance. "No harm done, Jonathan. Freddie always says that I have reflexes as quick as any cat. Fortunately for both of us, he was right. You mustn't carry on so."

Blackthorne looked at her worriedly. "It's kind of you to make light of this, but I can't."

Evangeline inclined her head. "Take it as you wish. For my part, I don't want to waste another minute of this glorious scenery that I so nearly became a part of." She walked back to the window and stood resolutely contemplating the view. In part, it was to hide the fact that her hands were still shaking, and she had to bite her lower lip to keep it from trembling with the aftereffects of shock.

The wheel began to spin again ever so slowly so that the couple was unaware of the motion as it occurred. Neither one spoke again until the final jolt of gravity signaled that the ride was at an end. They escaped from the platform before the operators of the Ferris wheel were alerted to the fact that one of their riders had found a new and more thrilling vantage point for viewing the fairgrounds.

At a loss for any other strategy, Evangeline allowed herself to be led back to more seemly amusements, but her brush with disaster ended any possibility of savoring the rest of the sights of the Fair. Mirroring her distress, Blackthorne didn't press her to wait for the sun to set in order to see the Exposition grounds ablaze with its 120,000 incandescent bulbs. Instead, by four o'clock the couple made their way back to the entrance where they'd begun and found Jack waiting to take them home.

After climbing into the carriage, they sat in silence for some time. As they neared downtown, Evangeline steeled herself for one final maneuver.

"Jonathan, your mother has hinted that you have a particular inclination toward me."

Blackthorne gave her a searching look and then smiled knowingly. He took her hand between his own. "You've heard the same hint from my own lips. I can only attribute your statement to feminine delicacy if you're suggesting that it required my mother's intervention to clarify my intentions toward you, Engie."

Evangeline offered no response. She merely gazed out the carriage window.

"Have you had time to consider matters since our last conversation on the subject?" He toyed with the needlepoint rosettes embroidered on her glove.

"To what specifically are you referring?"

"You are far too clever a woman to mistake my meaning. Therefore, I must assume you wish to make this as difficult as possible for me." He took a deep breath. "To be blunt, I'm referring to my proposal of marriage."

"Oh, I see. You never actually came out and asked me, you know."

"It didn't occur to me that you could fail to recognize the implied question. I stand corrected. I'll speak more plainly now, *ma chérie*. Will you marry me?"

Evangeline closed her eyes briefly. She felt an odd sense of triumph adulterated with dread. He had taken the bait. Summoning her most gracious smile, she said, "I hadn't expected quite so direct a statement of your intentions when I broached the topic, Jonathan."

Blackthorne laughed ruefully. "I see. I'm to be abused no matter what course of action I take."

"Not exactly. I merely meant that such an important question requires serious consideration before a reply is given." Evangeline began to fidget. "I... I don't know what to say just now."

Blackthorne pressed his hands more closely around hers to quiet her restlessness. "You'll have to say something. Believe me, it would be far kinder to hear an honest 'no' than more equivocation."

"I'm afraid you'll have to bear with my equivocation a bit longer. It's just too much to ask of me during a mid-afternoon carriage ride. As I said, this decision requires forethought."

"How much forethought?"

"You may expect my answer a week from today. Will that do?"

"I'm afraid it will have to." Blackthorne was silent for several minutes. In an unexpected move, he leaned over and brushed his lips against hers. His voice was so quiet that she felt, rather than heard, his words. "Engie, don't you realize how alike we are? Who else could ever match you as well?"

She turned her face away from him to look out the window. She could hardly tell him the truth—that only days before she might have agreed with him. Perhaps it was a distortion in the glass, but her vision had become unaccountably blurred.

Blackthorne was about to speak again when the carriage stopped abruptly. They had arrived at the train station where he was to catch the commuter line back to Lake Forest. As he got out of the carriage, he said quietly, "Deny it if you must, Engie. I believe you love me, at least a little."

He took her hand and bent down to kiss it. Evangeline allowed him to do so without remark. She found herself wondering what it was, if anything, that Jonathan Blackthorne himself actually loved.

23 – OF SWAN BOATS AND VICE

"Freddie, I'm glad you called. We can talk about your trip when you get here. I must see you today!" The voice on the other end of the line sounded urgent. "Meet me at the brownstone as soon as you can." Then she hung up.

Freddie, valise in tow from his trip to Iowa, walked out of the train station to find a cab. Once he saw the congestion of the midday crowd, he decided to forgo the cab and travel on foot. When he rang the doorbell of the Astor Street palace that Evangeline offhandedly called the "townhouse," she met him herself at the door. She was wearing her hat and coat in anticipation of leaving.

"Where have you been!" She was clearly upset about something. "You called over an hour ago."

"Engie, don't be a shrew. I called less than twenty minutes ago and had to walk."

"Well, it doesn't matter." She waved her hand dismissively. "Let's go. I have something to show you."

Freddie opened and closed his mouth like a fish gasping for air before he could formulate a proper question. "Wha... wha... Why? What's wrong with right here?"

"Because I can't think properly! So much has happened! I need some air to clear my head. I've had Jack pack us a picnic lunch."

"But I'll never get the train back to Lake Bluff in time! My mother is sure to send out a search party for me, and I'll have to dream up some new excuse to explain where I've been." Freddie rambled on for several more moments but eventually allowed himself to be led around the back of the house where Jack sat in the driver's seat of the carriage.

"Good day, Mister Freddie." The coachman touched the brim of his hat in greeting.

"Same to you, Jack. Do you know where she's dragging us to?"

"Where else but Lincoln Park? It's a fine day for a drive."

"You're in much better humor about it than I am." Freddie remained surly. "I still don't see why we can't talk right here and now!" Evangeline poked his arm as an indication to help her into the carriage. He complied grudgingly, and they were off.

Jack was able to move the horses up Lake Shore Drive at a steady trot, and they reached their destination just as the sun touched the top branches of the trees along the western boundary of the park. The two alighted and walked across the broad expanse of green lawn toward the lagoon. Evangeline maintained a taut silence until they reached the water. Because it was so late in the season, there were few people about. A knot of fishermen and a solitary cyclist were their only company. Wanting to ease Evangeline's tension, if only with small talk, Freddie pointed to the swan-shaped gondolas that could be rented if one was inclined to paddle about the inlets. Most of them had been removed from the water in anticipation of winter, which might claim Chicago any day.

"You'll never believe the story Bill told me about those boats."

"What?" Evangeline apparently had decided to humor him.

"Well, it seems the City Council wanted to subsidize the cost of six more of them for the park. An alderman, who shall remain nameless for the purposes of this conversation, in a burst of civic duty felt it was an unnecessary waste of taxpayers' money. I was told he said, 'Why not purchase two swan boats and just let nature take its course.'"

Evangeline burst out laughing and shook her head. "I'm surprised that there weren't at least ten other men on the council ready to second his motion."

"Oh twenty, at least." Freddie chuckled. "That one will never make the papers, so I tell you knowing I can rely on your discretion..."

"... to repeat it at every social gathering I attend for the rest of the season."

"I knew I could depend on you. Now let's get down to business. Just wait till I tell you what I discovered in Iowa!"

"A great deal of corn, I should think." Evangeline looked about her distractedly. "Wait, let's get one of those." She gestured toward the small rowboats still anchored in the lagoon. A rheumatic attendant in a derby sat on duty lest anyone try to make off with any of his charges.

"Now?" Freddie was aghast.

"Now, Freddie. We'll have more privacy that way." Evangeline stood firm. Her companion sighed and walked over to the old man. "How much?"

The man pointed laconically to the sign behind him that indicated rates and rental times. "I'm sorry to ask so late in the season." Freddie dug into his pocket for the requisite amount. "But the lady—," gesturing with his head toward Evangeline who stood farther back by the water, "has taken an odd notion that she'd like to go boating."

The old man looked from Freddie to Evangeline and back again. "If I was you, son, I'd be grateful of the opportunity and wouldn't question how I came by it." He took a long puff on his cigar. "Take as long as you like. Just bring the boat up on the grass when you're done. I'm on my lunch break." With that, the old man picked up his stool and placard and retreated to some secret recess of his own for a surreptitious nap.

"Well, come on then," Freddie called to Evangeline. She had become intrigued with the collection of waterfowl circling the shore in search of food. Seeing that Freddie had secured a boat for them to use, she marched up to it, climbed in, and waited for the young man to push off.

When he had rowed to the center of the lagoon, Evangeline finally spoke. "All right. Now tell me all the news from the wilds of Iowa."

Freddie launched into his story with far more eagerness than he had launched their vessel. He told her about his interview with the illustrious Mr. Smythe who had been promoted to president of the bank, and a far more useful interview with a banker named Jeremiah Sidley.

Evangeline registered astonishment. "You mean our Jacob Kingston had the nerve to use the last name of someone he knew back in Dodgeville as his alias?"

"Not just someone he knew, someone who hates his guts. Mr. Jeremiah Sidley discovered that our friend had been embezzling funds. When Jeremiah told Harcourt Smythe about it, he was ordered to keep his mouth shut or lose his job. Kingston was allowed to get away scot free."

"You mean Vice President Smythe wanted to cover up the matter?"

"Exactly. Smythe stood in a fair way of being appointed president at that time, and the last thing he wanted was a run on the bank by panicked farmers."

"Does your Mr. Jeremiah Sidley have proof of fraud?" Evangeline asked doubtfully.

Freddie beamed. "He kept the ledger sheets showing the discrepancies. His grudge is personal since he lost some of his own money through Kingston's scheme. When I told him the alias Kingston was using in Chicago, he offered to come here and horsewhip him personally."

Evangeline's tense expression disappeared. A broad smile spread over her face. "Well done, Sir Frederick. Well done indeed! I can't tell you how relieved I am. We finally have something to force Sidley to talk. At least he'll be able to tell us what part he played in relation to Jonathan." She added worriedly, "We have to run the murderer to ground soon. We're almost out of time."

"Oh, come now, Engie, what are you so concerned about? Franz is in jail. O'Malley is probably still drunk. Blackthorne doesn't think we're after him. Neither does Sidley. We can take all the time we need."

Evangeline knit her brows. "There's the small matter of Franz's upcoming trial, not to mention what happened this morning. I went back to the O'Malley house to arrange for Patsy's schooling and to see what else I might pry out of Mr. O'Malley."

"Judging from your face, things didn't go as planned."

"Things went quite well—up to a point. Mrs. O'Malley agreed to allow Patsy to go if I could find a school to take her and compensate the family for her loss of income."

"Then why so serious?"

"Because Mr. O'Malley has disappeared."

"He what!" Freddie sat bolt upright, causing the boat to rock precariously. "How could this happen? You said he was usually too drunk to move."

Evangeline braced her hands against the sides of the boat to steady herself. "Apparently, I underestimated his resolve."

"Running away is a clear admission of guilt!" Freddie grabbed the oars and began to row energetically, albeit aimlessly. "We have to find him! You must have put him on his guard when you started asking questions last time."

"Perhaps, perhaps not. Mrs. O'Malley says he does this quite frequently. She didn't seem at all alarmed about it."

"Maybe this time is different," Freddie muttered darkly, churning water in every direction.

Evangeline shook off the spray from Freddie's vigorous oarsmanship. "You might be right, but it's equally possible he's gone on a drinking binge and will return when he sobers up."

Freddie paused in mid-stroke to stare at his friend. "You're taking this far too calmly." He brought the dripping oars back into the boat.

"That's because we have something more urgent to ponder than Mr. O'Malley's disappearance."

Freddie raised a skeptical eyebrow.

"Do you know where I was yesterday?"

"Based on your past record, I'd guess it was a place called 'out.'"

"I was at the White City—"

Freddie cut in, "A fine time for you to go on holiday when we're trying to hunt down a murderer."

"With Jonathan." She finished the sentence and Freddie abruptly fell silent.

"That wasn't a very smart thing to do, Engie. You don't know what he's capable of if you alarm him."

"I had hoped to alarm him, Freddie, but instead he alarmed me." Evangeline looked uncomfortable. She recounted her misadventure on the Ferris wheel.

Freddie felt himself grow pale with shock. "My God, Engie! Do you really believe it was an accident? He must have meant to kill you."

Evangeline seemed disturbed, even in the retelling. "I can't be sure. It might have just been a horrible bit of clumsiness on his part. But if it was an attempt to dispose of me, and it failed because too many people were watching, then he's bound to try again. I had to find a way to keep him at bay for a while."

"I take it we're coming to the part where time has become of the essence?"

"Yes. On the carriage ride back, I broached the subject of marriage. With very little prompting, he came right out and popped the question."

Freddie heaved a huge sigh. "Somehow, it doesn't seem quite so shocking to hear it the second time around. Why did you start him off in that direction? You couldn't have said yes?" He looked to Evangeline worriedly, imploring a denial.

"All I wanted was a stay of execution. If he really is guilty, his offer of marriage is nothing but a cat's paw to see whether I suspect him. I could only hope to throw him off guard by promising to consider his proposal and give him an answer by a set date."

"How much time do we have?"

"One week."

"One week!" Freddie exclaimed loud enough to cause a gull floating nearby to flap away in alarm.

"Yes, I told him I'd give him an answer by this coming Friday."

"I don't know if we can come up with anything by then. All we have to go on is the fact that Sidley—that is, Kingston—embezzled money from a bank in Iowa and probably did the same at Dresden & Company." Freddie now sat slumped over the oars, letting the boat drift on the placid water.

"Cheer up, my boy. That may not be quite all we have." Evangeline related her conversation with Jane Addams and the prospect that a former victim might still be alive.

Freddie smiled wanly. "Well, that helps a bit. What's our next move?"

"That's where you come in," Evangeline replied with too much alacrity.

Freddie came to apprehensive attention and instinctively leaned backward in the boat, away from his companion. "Engie, you've got that devilish gleam in your eyes. It's the same look that sent me bouncing all the way to Dodgeville. What fresh hell have you got in store for me now?"

Without saying a word, she dug into her coat pocket and brought out two pieces of paper. She handed them to Freddie.

"What's this?"

"The first is a picture of Jonathan. I'm sure it's a good enough likeness for even you to recognize."

"How did you get it?"

"I wheedled it out of his mother on false pretenses." She laughed mischievously.

"I can't imagine you playing the love-struck damsel convincingly enough to make her believe you would pine away without a picture of her son."

"It's amazing what nonsense mothers will believe where their sons are concerned."

The other piece of paper contained a name and address. Freddie read it aloud: "'Rosa Grandinetti, Mother Connelly's, 480 South Clark Street.' I take it this is the girl who left Hull House so unexpectedly?"

"Yes, that's right. Jane was kind enough to write down her current address for me."

"The young lady's current address," Freddie grinned wickedly, "is in the Levee District. Do you know what Mother Connelly's establishment is?"

"Of course, I do, Freddie. I wasn't born yesterday. It's a brothel."

"Not just a brothel. According to what I've heard about this place, it's one of the most unsavory houses of ill repute in a city that grants a great deal of latitude in judging the depravity of such establishments. I've heard that Mother Connelly herself boasted that there is no act so disgusting or degraded that one of her girls would be unwilling to perform it."

Evangeline raised an eyebrow. "Well, that sort of advertising must really bring them through the door in droves. And how is it, young man, that you come to know so much about these things?"

"Call it a prurient interest that lingers from the days when I was just a callow youth."

"By my reckoning, you're still a callow youth. And forgive me if I doubt that you acquired this information first-hand."

Freddie laughed in embarrassment. "You've found me out. I'm not the man about town you think me to be."

"Ha!" Evangeline barked by way of a reply.

"In all seriousness, Engie, this isn't the sort of place you ought to be visiting."

"Oh, I have no intention of visiting Mother Connelly's myself." She fixed Freddie with a steady gaze.

He rolled his eyes. "Why do I never see it coming? Why, in all the years I've known you, do I always walk into the traps you set for me? Fool that I am!"

Evangeline continued to stare at him impassively. "You said yourself that I can't go there. They'd think I was a social reformer out to pray over the girls or make them give up smoking or some such thing. I'd never get through the front door."

"Or worse yet, you'd get through the front door, and they'd never let you get back out again."

"Yes, there is also that possibility." Evangeline shuddered.

"I've never been to a place like that before. What will I say?"

"You'll part your hair down the center in a most unattractive fashion and say you are a clerk from Peoria come to the big city to see the Fair and a few other sights as well."

"Yes, I suppose I could do that," Freddie agreed half-heartedly.

"Look, all you have to say is that a friend of a friend referred you to Rosa. I don't think anyone will question that. Once you're in a room alone with her—"

"Oh, God!" Freddie's distress increased at the thought.

"Just tell her you want to talk. I'm sure she's had stranger requests than that before." Evangeline trailed her fingers through the chilly water.

"Yes, I suppose."

"Show her Jonathan's picture and see if she recognizes him. Find out whatever you can about her past and why she left Hull House."

Freddie sighed deeply at the prospect of the humiliating trial before him.

Evangeline reached over and squeezed his hand. A look of appeal had entered her eyes. "Please, Freddie, it's the best hope we have left. And we really are running out of time."

Freddie patted her hand reassuringly in turn. "I know, Engie. I know. But it's the longest of long shots."

Evangeline smiled slightly. "If this doesn't work, I suppose I'll just have to marry Jonathan, or be murdered by him—perhaps both."

"Say no more! You've convinced me. I'll do it."

"There's a good lad. Now, row us back to shore and let's sample whatever Jack packed in that picnic hamper for us."

24 – CLOCKWORKS IN THE LEVEE

On Saturday afternoon, Freddie contemplated the visit he was supposed to pay to Mother Connolly's, but like a man dipping a toe into the icy waters of Lake Michigan, he couldn't quite bring himself to jump in. He procrastinated by pretending that he needed time to plan a strategy.

The only relevant action he took was a trip to a theatrical supply shop in the Loop before he caught the train back to the North Shore. Here he purchased a false set of sideburns and mustachios, along with enough spirit gum to fasten the whiskers to his own clean-shaven face. He told the proprietor that he was part of an amateur drama group staging a revival of *Our American Cousin*. The owner didn't appear suspicious about the purchase, though he did say that the choice of play was in poor taste.

Since Freddie's own overwrought imagination convinced him that everybody suspected him of something, his precautions became not only elaborate but silly as well. He went home that night and locked himself in his bedroom despite repeated calls from his mother to come downstairs and join the family for dinner. Instead, he tried on his disguise and postured in front of the mirror in what he hoped was the attitude of a clerk on holiday.

Late Monday morning, having finally locked onto a glimmer of resolution cowering somewhere at the back of his mind, Freddie marched out of the offices of Simpson & Austin. He said he was going to call on a client but instead skipped around the corner to the nearest public lavatory where he could apply his whiskers. He prayed for the thousandth time that Aloysius hadn't seen him leave. For once, his heightened sensitivities didn't detect any reason for alarm. After checking that the coast was clear, Freddie ducked out of the restroom and headed south on Clark Street in search of the infamous address.

The would-be reporter had pondered the best time to pay his visit to Mother Connelly's. He decided that there was less likelihood of being caught in a raid or of being recognized by anyone he knew if he arrived in broad daylight before the vice district came alive at sundown. Unfortunately, this also meant that, if he were found out, his family disgrace would be complete and everlasting. The idea of a young man of good family visiting a bordello would have been mildly disturbing to female relations. This was nothing compared with the outrage of his male relatives at the idea of a young man of good family visiting a bordello of the lowest moral order during his lunch hour on a workday.

Freddie took a deep breath and stepped across the Rubicon separating the business district from the vice district. He knew that despite the efforts of reformers for at least two decades, Chicago's purveyors of illicit pleasure had maintained an indestructible presence in an area called the Levee. It spanned a four-block radius from Clark to Dearborn Streets on the west and from Polk to Harrison Streets on the south. The houses that lined the thoroughfares were mainly brothels with a few cheap rooming houses and saloons thrown in for variety. Although Chicago mayor Long John Wentworth had personally burned down the original vice district in the late 1850s, his successors in City Hall found it more lucrative to let the Levee remain. Vice raids occurred infrequently and were usually directed at madams who hadn't made timely protection payments to their local police. While the Columbian Exposition had brought a flood of tourist money into the city to purchase legal commodities, the purchase of vice was thriving as well.

During the time of day that Freddie wove his timid way down Clark Street, there were few pedestrians. Most of the brothels on the street didn't actively seek business until sometime around noon. This would make Freddie one of the first prospective customers of the day. The ladies in the houses that lined either side of the street certainly viewed him that way. It had become a common practice for watchful madams to station a girl as a lookout in one of their upstairs windows. The girl would tap on the glass and attract the notice of pedestrians—an inexpensive form of advertising. When Freddie heard what sounded like fingernails tapping gently on a windowpane, he looked up and was greeted by an impish smile from a girl who couldn't have been more than fourteen. She waved at him and gestured for him to come into the parlor, adding a few other gestures more apropos to the purpose of his visit, which modesty declines to mention. Freddie was blushing to the roots of his hair and stared resolutely at the sidewalk as he marched on despite many further taps beckoning him to look skyward. Glancing sideways under his hat brim, he tried to count down the addresses until he arrived at the one he was seeking.

He finally braved a peep upward when he arrived at his destination. He verified the numbers on the building and also noted the ever-present second-floor sentinel, but Mother Connelly had improved on the methods of her competitors. Instead of stationing a live girl in the window, who would have to be relieved sooner or later, she had posted what appeared to be a mechanical woman. Freddie couldn't be quite sure how she operated, but some hidden clockwork caused her to strike the pane of glass at regular intervals. While the automaton wasn't as inviting as a real girl, she was effective in gaining Freddie's attention. He stood gawking in awe, wondering how she managed to avoid breaking the window each time as her hand struck it with such force.

He was startled out of his scientific observation when a woman of flesh and blood opened the door of the establishment. "Well," she said, "are you going to come in, sweetie, or just stand and stare all day?"

Freddie looked around nervously to see if anyone else saw him. The street was empty, but he still scuttled up the steps to the front door as fast as he could. The woman who stood there was dressed rather loosely in a kimono, which she hadn't bothered to wrap around her ample endowments. She linked her arm through Freddie's and drew him through the door. He stood in the foyer like a man just waking up from a bad dream and having difficulty recognizing where he was. He stared at the ceiling, and he stared at the walls but said nothing by way of introduction.

Finally, he stammered, "Are you... uh... are you... that is... the lady... um... who runs this establishment?"

The woman at his side laughed. "Nope, honey, I ain't. I'd be a damned sight richer if I was, though. Ma Connelly's gone to the bank with last night's receipts. Left me to keep an eye on things. My name's Sadie. But you don't have to tell me yours. I can see you're a shy one. You look like you're from out of town, ain't you?" Then, turning to face the upstairs balcony, she bawled at the top of her lungs, "Gentleman in the house! One of you lazy sluts get down here!"

This shocked Freddie into trying to clarify the reason for his visit. "No, uh... miss... uh... that is madam... no, I mean..."

The woman patted him reassuringly on the arm. "That's all right sweetie, don't you worry. We'll take good care of you here. It's your first time, ain't it?"

"Uh, yes... that is..." Freddie stopped when he realized what she meant, and he reasserted his masculinity with an outraged denial. "I mean, NO! Of course, it isn't. It's just the first time I've been in this particular house. That's what I meant."

The woman looked him over appraisingly. "Uh huh. Well, then mister, since you been around some, what's your pleasure?"

By this time, Sadie had led him into a shadowy front parlor where another woman sat smoking a cigarette. She appeared to be dressed in some sort of satin jockey costume, but the top showed far more décolletage than jockeys usually display on the racecourse. Freddie squinted to make out the details of the costume in the dim light. Mistaking his interest, the woman with the cigarette took a long drag and blew several smoke rings before saying, "Forget it, honey, I just woke up. I'm what you might call an early riser around here. Besides, I haven't had my breakfast yet." She held up a tumbler which Freddie assumed contained a large quantity of gin. "I don't work on an empty stomach, you know. There's plenty of others upstairs. Take your pick of them, and just let me be."

"Oh, no, you misunderstand me." Freddie was stammering again. The woman on the sofa regarded him impassively. He turned to Sadie to explain. "That is, I mean, I had someone particular in mind."

At this, the madam pro tempore smiled broadly. "Well, now we're getting someplace. There's a nice new girl, we just got in last week, hardly been broke in yet. She's about twelve."

"Twelve!" Freddie squeaked.

The woman frowned as she refastened a hairpin. "Yeah, or it might be eleven, I forget. Anyway, the sweetest little thing you ever did see—"

Before she could finish, Freddie cut in. "No, no! I mean there's a particular girl I have in mind."

"Oh?" Sadie was intrigued. "Considering you ain't ever been to this house before, how might that be?"

Freddie tried to assume his role. He leaned over confidentially. "Well, a friend of a friend of mine said if I was ever in Chicago, I should come to Mother Connelly's and ask for Rosa." He nudged Sadie for effect. "He said she'd take care of me."

The woman put her arms on her hips. "Well, well. Rosa! Who'd of thought it. She's never been a real big hit with anybody before. She's kinda on the quiet side. Just does her job and minds her own business. Drinks way too much. Still, I guess there ain't no accounting for taste."

She turned her head suddenly and screamed up the stairs in a grating voice, "Rosa! You, Rosa! Drag your sorry rump down here! There's a gentleman asking for you."

When there was no response, Sadie smiled unctuously in Freddie's direction and walked closer to the stairs to lure her young charge down with further blandishments of affection. "I mean now, Rosa! Or so help me God, I'll come up there and drag you down here by the hair!"

A moan could be heard echoing down the upstairs hall. Then a door slammed. A far-off voice called, "I'm coming, Sadie, I'm coming. Keep your corset on!"

Freddie looked up the stairwell and saw a dark-haired girl emerge from the shadows and dawdle her way down the stairs. She appeared to be in her late teens. Her hair was black and hung in a tangled mass over her face. When she pushed it aside, he could see that her eyes were very large and very dark. She was dressed, or rather undressed, in a camisole and pantaloons covered by a thin wrap of some gauzy material. She seemed disoriented and still flushed from sleep. Her complexion was mottled, and her breathing seemed labored when she finally reached the bottom of the stairs. As she drew within a few feet of him, Freddie detected the reek of alcohol.

Attempting to focus her glazed eyes on him, she said vaguely, "You asked for me? I don't know you."

Sadie, without warning, slapped her hard across the face. "Of course, you don't, you silly whore. It's a friend of his sent him."

"Oh." Rosa rubbed her cheek where a red imprint remained. The blow hardly seemed to faze her. She held out her hand to Freddie to lead him upstairs. "Come on, then," she said simply, still yawning.

Freddie trailed along after her like a man sleepwalking. From behind him, he could hear Sadie growling, "Now you treat him nice, or you'll have me to answer to. You hear me? You, Rosa! Answer me!"

Without a backward glance, Rosa sighed wearily. "I hear you, Sadie. I hear you."

She led Freddie up the stairs and down a long, drab hallway. The uncarpeted floorboards creaked under their steps. There were no other sounds in the house. Apparently, all the inmates were still asleep. Rosa's room was the third from the end of the hall. When she opened the door, Freddie was overwhelmed by the staleness of the air. The window was shut, and the shade pulled down low, but a reflection of afternoon sunlight managed to radiate through the shade, giving the room a dark yellow glow.

Mother Connelly's establishment hardly fit into the luxury category. Rosa's room was furnished with a dresser, washstand, and narrow, metal-frame bed. A collection of bottles—whiskey, gin, and other spirits—stood on the dresser as well as a few unwashed glasses. Some dirty water remained in the bottom of the wash basin, along with a dead fly. The bed was rumpled and still warm since Rosa had so recently been pulled from it by her unexpected gentleman caller. She pointed to a chair standing in the corner. "You can put your clothes there." She began to remove her dressing gown.

"No!" Freddie said in a panic, so loudly he was sure Sadie heard him all the way downstairs.

Rosa stopped and looked at him strangely. "What did you say?" Her mind was apparently still numb from sleep or drink, or both. She seemed to think she had misunderstood his command.

"I just want to talk!" He was frantic. By this time, Freddie was sweating profusely, and one corner of his false mustache had come unglued. He put a finger to his upper lip to hold it in place, hoping Rosa wouldn't notice.

The girl was having difficulty bringing her eyes into focus, so she stared at him for half a minute before repeating in disbelief, "You just want to... talk?"

"Yes." Freddie giggled nervously. "Is that so strange?"

Rosa laughed bitterly. "Well, it's sure a new one on me."

"How much do you charge for your time?" Freddie tried to frame the question as delicately as possible.

"The house collects five bucks for a trick."

"And," Freddie cleared his throat self-consciously, "how would that translate into time?"

Rosa shrugged. "Depends on the trick. Anywhere from five minutes to an hour."

"All right then. Say I double that and give you ten dollars for an hour of your time. Is that fair?"

The girl slipped her wrapper back on. "Well, it'll give me a rest, and Sadie won't care what goes on so long as you pay afterward." She walked over to the dresser. "You want a drink?"

"No, thank you, nothing," Freddie responded as primly if he had just been offered a cup of tea in Evangeline's parlor.

He watched as Rosa selected a green bottle from her collection and poured herself a shot glass of absinthe—straight.

"Good God! I'm no temperance advocate, but if you drink enough of that concoction, it could kill you!"

She downed the first shot in one gulp and poured a second. "The sooner, the better. So long as I don't feel it coming."

Freddie watched the absinthe take effect. Her speech, which had been slurred before, became even thicker and slower. She sat down heavily on the bed. Rather than sit beside her in what he considered a compromising position, Freddie drew up the chair.

When he was seated, she began. "So, you want to talk. What about?"

"Actually, it's the man who sent me to you. He wanted me to show you this to see if you remember him." Freddie dug in his coat pocket for the picture of Blackthorne that Evangeline had given him.

Rosa threw her head back and laughed scornfully. "To see if I remember him? I don't even remember my own name most of the time, and it's just as well I don't, mister. If I did, I'd go crazy!"

By now Freddie had located the picture, and he handed it to Rosa. First, she glanced at it uncomprehendingly. Then, as the image registered in her brain, it seemed to send an electric shock through her body. Her face went white, and she started to tremble. The picture fell to the floor as she put her face in her hands. She began to wail, rocking back and forth like a child in need of comfort.

Freddie didn't know what to do. He stood up and paced around in front of the window, hoping her crying would subside if he ignored the situation. It didn't. Finally, not knowing what other measure to take, he sat down on the bed and put his arm gingerly around her. She clung to him, burying her face against his shoulder, and sobbed for several minutes more. Freddie awkwardly patted her hair and murmured what he hoped were comforting sounds. Eventually, her emotional storm began to dissipate.

"He didn't forget me," she finally whispered through her tears. "After what I did to him, he still didn't forget me." When she looked up into Freddie's eyes, her own were red and swollen from crying. "Oh, mister, you have to tell him for me how sorry I am! Tell him that for me, please!"

"Sorry?" Freddie repeated the inexplicable word. "Sorry for what?"

"Then he didn't tell you about me?"

"No, not a word. Just gave me the picture to show you." Freddie had no idea what turn the conversation had taken but decided to follow wherever Rosa led.

The girl slumped down farther. Her head still rested dejectedly on his shoulder. She sniffled to clear her nose and wiped the tears away with the back of her sleeve. "Oh, it's a long story, and it happened a long time ago. But seeing his picture. It brings it all back to me. I've never told a living soul except Mr. Sidley till now."

At the mention of the name, Freddie's spine stiffened, but he said nothing.

"You say you're a friend of his?" Her face had taken on the innocent expectancy of a child on Christmas morning. "How did you come to know him?"

Freddie fended off the question. "That's not important right now. Let's just say I've been commissioned to take a personal interest in this matter."

"But you do know him well, don't you?"

"Yes." Freddie managed to force the word out between clenched teeth. "Yes, I know him very well. You can trust me. I'll make sure that matters are put to rights."

"Oh, if only they could be." She sighed and sat up straighter. "But it's a long, long story.

25 – DEJA VU

"I guess I first set eyes on Mr. DeVille—"

"Mr. DeVille?" Freddie interrupted.

"Yes, Mr. Jonathan DeVille... your friend...," Rosa looked at him doubtfully, "the man in the picture?"

"Oh yes, how stupid of me." Freddie laughed. "I always think of him by his nickname, and so it startles me when I hear him called something else."

"Oh," Rosa replied, without curiosity as to the specific alias and without noting the sigh of relief Freddie had just exhaled.

"Anyway, as I was saying, I guess I first met him at the union dance, and it was just by accident."

Freddie returned to his chair so he could face Rosa while she spoke. "Go on. I'm listening. How was it by accident?"

"Well, of all things, I was supposed to be there with somebody else—Mr. Sidley, as a matter of fact." Rosa pushed her hair back off her face. The shock of seeing Blackthorne's picture had apparently sobered her up. She looked at Freddie in embarrassment. "Oh, I'm sorry. You probably don't know who Mister Sidley is, do you?"

Without that lucky prompt, Freddie had almost put his neck in the noose again. "No. Never heard of him. Who is he?"

Rosa looked down at the floor and surprisingly, given her occupation, began to blush. "Well, I think he was sweet on me at one time. I wasn't always the way I am now." She sighed and her eyes filled with tears. She looked at the ceiling to blink them back before continuing. "I used to work in a book bindery. I even wanted to join the trade union, and I took classes at Hull House. You've heard of that place, haven't you?"

"Oh, yes." Freddie assumed his clerk-on-holiday persona in time. "Even in Peoria, we get the news from the big city. I hear Hull House has helped many people."

"Yes, it has. Miss Jane is a living, breathing saint if ever there was one. Well, anyway, Mr. Sidley volunteered his time there as the bookkeeper. We became friends, and one day he said someone had given him tickets to the Printers' Union Dance, and he asked if I'd like to come with him, seeing as I was interested in joining the union."

"I see." Freddie was beginning to trace an unfortunate pattern. Rosa's next words came as no surprise.

"But the funniest thing happened. Mr. Sidley and I arranged to meet at the dance because he said he had to stay late at Hull House and couldn't escort me there himself. So, he gave me my ticket ahead of time. What a funny man he was." For the first time, Freddie saw Rosa indulge in a brief smile.

"How so?"

"Well, he was very particular to know what I was going to wear. He even asked me to pin a red rose to my hat so he could be sure to spot me in the crowd. Doesn't that beat everything?" She shook her head. "But he was like that. Always wanted to plan things out in advance."

"He sounds like a very careful planner indeed. And did he manage to find you in the crowd with your red rose?"

Rosa frowned. "That's the odd part. He never came. I found out afterward that he was called in by Miss Ellen because she wanted some bills paid right away, so he couldn't be there at all."

"And I take it, that's when you met Mr... uh... Mr. DeVille?"

"Yes." Rosa nodded. "That was the first time I ever laid eyes on him. I think maybe I even fell in love with him right then and there."

Freddie stared at her as if she had lost her mind. "He had such an immediate effect on you?" He tried to keep from sounding too skeptical.

"Oh, yes. He did." Rosa smiled wistfully at the memory. "He wasn't like any of the other fellows I knew. He was a gentleman. He knew how to talk to a girl and make her feel like she was a queen."

She stood up and walked over to the window. Unexpectedly, she pulled up the shade and let in a burst of afternoon light. "It's stuffy in here, isn't it?" She turned to Freddie for confirmation before lifting the sash and letting in a cool lake breeze. The threadbare lace curtains began to float delicately on the air current. Rosa resumed her seat on the bed.

"So anyway, there I was in the dancehall, standing in the corner and looking for Mr. Sidley to come in. I must have been standing there half an hour, and I'd just about decided to go back home when he walked up to me."

"He, being Mr. DeVille?"

"Yes. He was so polite. 'Excuse me, miss,' he says. 'I couldn't help noticing that you were looking for someone. Is there anything I can do to assist you in locating your companion?' That was just how he said it. So genteel. I knew right then that he wasn't one of those fellows you have to watch out for."

"I'm sure he always acted the part of the gentleman."

Rosa took his observation at face value. "Oh, yes. Always. So, he asked me to describe Mr. Sidley and told me that he'd go around and look for him and that I should wait right there. But before he left, he found me a chair and fetched me a glass of punch, too. 'So that you'll be comfortable while you wait' was what he said. After about fifteen minutes, he came back looking very down-in-the-mouth. 'I'm sorry, dear lady'—you can be sure nobody ever called me that before. Anyway, he says, 'I'm sorry, dear lady, but your gentleman friend seems to have deserted you. I've made several inquiries, and no one matching that description has arrived.'"

"What did you do then?"

"Well, I was about to get my wrap and go home when Mr. DeVille says, 'May I escort you, miss? It may not be entirely safe for you to go home alone. I wouldn't feel right about abandoning you.' He was so very kind to me. So very kind, and to think the way I repaid that kindness." She looked as if she were about to burst into tears again.

Freddie tried to forestall another outburst by distracting her. "Well, did he walk you home?"

Rosa caught herself and focused again. "As it turned out, we had just about gone out the door when an idea occurred to him."

"Just like that, on the spur of the moment?"

"Yes, he says to me, 'But, dear lady, perhaps I'm rushing you home without consulting your wishes in the matter.' Wasn't that a nice way of putting it?" Rosa's eyes sparkled at the memory. "I can't remember anybody ever consulting my wishes about anything at all before that night."

"Oh yes, that was most thoughtful of him."

"Anyway, he asked if I wanted to stay at the dance, and he offered to be my escort."

"And I take it you decided to stay?"

"Oh, my yes. It was still early, and everyone was so jolly that I didn't want to miss the fun. We had such a time." She smiled in disbelief that there could be that much pleasure in the world. "Such a time."

"And afterward?" Freddie saw that Rosa had become tangled in the memory and was unwilling to return to the present.

"Well, afterward, he escorted me home and asked if he might see me again sometime."

"And you said, 'yes?'"

"I did," Rosa confirmed with a smile.

"And what about Mr. Sidley? He mustn't have liked the way things turned out."

Rosa grew embarrassed. "Well, you have to understand. Mr. Sidley and I were just friends. I never cared for him that way. He was clumsy and awkward, and he stuttered whenever he got nervous which was most of the time. A very nice man but..." she trailed off, leaving the rest of Sidley's oddities unspoken.

"But didn't he care for you?"

"Oh, I suppose. But when I explained things to him, he understood. We remained friends. Sometimes I think after all that happened, he was my only real friend."

Freddie decided to let that remark pass for the moment. He focused back on Blackthorne instead. "So, in any case, you continued to meet with Mr... Bl... that is, DeVille?"

"Yes, but there was a complication." Rosa grew hesitant. "You see, Mama always watched me like a hawk. She was scared that I'd turn out to be... to be..." She stopped, and her face contorted with bitterness.

"It's all right. I understand." Freddie intercepted the explanation, fearing that it might upset her to continue.

Rosa laughed unpleasantly. "All my friends who went out in the evening with young men, she called them whores. But they weren't doing anything wrong—just innocent fun. I don't know what she wanted from me—to stay home and pray the rosary with her, I suppose. Maybe she thought there would be an arranged marriage for me someday like there was for her and Papa in the old country. But things are different here. Girls don't get shut up in houses until they're married. They work in factories, and they go out in the evening. When I'd come home late, even from Hull House, she'd call me a slut. She'd say if I didn't go to confession and tell the priest all the wicked things I'd done, then I'd burn in hell. Isn't that funny? What she was most afraid of, that's just what happened." The twisted smile remained on her face.

Freddie tried to distract her once again. "So, you agreed to meet Mr. DeVille somewhere other than your own front porch?"

Rosa drew her wrapper more closely around her shoulders. "It had to be that way. Mama would have beat me half to death if she knew I had a gentleman friend. So, we'd meet at different places in the city. Places where I was sure no one would tattle on me."

"Such as?"

"Well, we'd go to different beer gardens on the North Side. They were respectable places and families would go there. There would be orchestras so it was noisy, with plenty of people so you wouldn't get noticed. And he didn't want to get noticed either."

"Oh, why was that?"

"Well, from what he told me, he came from a rich family. And the turn things took between us..."

Freddie was confused. "I don't understand."

Rosa smiled wistfully. "Well, we got more and more attached to each other, so one evening, he said he wanted to marry me."

"Really? That's a surprise!" Freddie tried to fit the pieces together.

"Yes, it would have been quite a shock to his family. He said he was afraid they would disinherit him if they found out about it in the wrong way. I told him I didn't care if he didn't have a penny, as long as we could be together. But he just smiled and said, 'No, my darling, I want to be able to treat you like a queen.'"

Rosa was luminous at the memory. "Can you imagine? I never expected anybody to say that to me my whole life. Yet, there he was saying something that wonderful. 'I want to dress you in silks, and I want to have enough money to give you servants and a fine house, and you'll never have to lift a finger to work ever again.' That was what he wanted for me."

"Quite a generous man. There seems to be no limit to what he's capable of."

"It was wonderful! Like a beautiful dream, and I was floating on a pink cloud somewhere up in the sky. He gave me a china rose pendant to wear around my neck. He said that it was a pledge of true love, that I should wear it until he made good on his promise, and that on our wedding day he would exchange it for a gold ring. He said that if I ever parted with it, he'd know I didn't love him."

Dreading the answer to his next question, Freddie asked anyway. "And what happened then?"

Rosa shook her head as if she couldn't reconcile the contradiction. "It all went wrong. Terrible things began to happen—terrible. One night, when we parted, he said he was going to break the news to his family about me. We arranged to meet the following Thursday at a beer garden we used to go to. But when I went there, he didn't come."

"Oh?" Freddie was puzzled. "Did he try to get a message to you?"

"No." Rosa's face grew troubled. "I waited and waited, but there was still no word. So, I went back there every night for a week, hoping I could see him."

"But didn't you try to contact him?"

"I never knew where he lived. It was somewhere north of the city. I'd never known anybody in high society before. I didn't know where to start. I got more and more downhearted. I still kept up with my classes, but my blue mood must have shown through because one night Mr. Sidley came by as I was leaving and asked me what was wrong."

"And what did you tell him?"

"We went to his office, and I just blurted out the whole awful story—how I couldn't reach Jonathan, how I didn't know if he'd forgotten me. I even showed Mr. Sidley the rose pendant."

Rosa stood up and walked to the window. She leaned out for a breath of fresh air. Freddie got up and came to stand beside her. "I'm sorry this is so painful for you to tell me." He felt genuinely concerned.

She looked up at him and smiled slightly. "The way I recollect things, it's so strange. After two years, you'd think it wouldn't matter to me at all, wouldn't you?"

Freddie regarded her sadly. "I think memory can have a way of making you feel as if the past is happening right now. All the misery of it can feel just the same."

"You're a very kind man, mister." Rosa looked at him pensively. "But you asked, and I won't quit until I've told you the whole story." She took a deep breath of fresh air and returned to her seat on the bed.

"So anyway, Mr. Sidley said he knew some people who might be able to tell what had happened. He told me not to give up hope until he could find out the truth. In the meantime, I still went to the beer garden every night, but Jonathan was never there. And every night when I came home late, Mama would spit on the floor and call me a whore."

Freddie remained at the window, looking down at the street. He saw a man, obviously a tourist dressed in his Sunday-best checkered suit, wandering up and down Clark Street trying to decide which brothel to visit. Freddie turned away and sat down next to Rosa. "What did you do then?" he asked distractedly.

"I might have gone on doing the same thing 'til doomsday, except one night at about ten o'clock I was sitting at a table alone when who should walk up to me but Mr. Sidley."

"What a small world."

"Oh, it was no accident, mister. He had followed me there."

"Why?"

"Well, as I told you, he was a true friend to me. He knew I went there every night, and he wanted to tell me as soon as he found out anything about Jonathan. From the look on his face when he walked up to the table, I knew it wasn't good. 'I'm sorry, Rosa,' he says to me, 'but it's bad news about your gentleman.' I remember my heart was pounding so hard I thought it would burst. Mr. Sidley told me he found out Jonathan was engaged to marry some society lady and that it was announced in one of the suburban papers."

"Hmmm." Freddie was still trying to make sense of Sidley's role in the charade.

"I was so upset by this time that I nearly fainted from the shock. Mr. Sidley jumped up and said he was going to get me something to revive me. He came back with a glass of brandy."

"That's rather a strong drink for a young girl."

"Yes, that was the first time I ever drank it. Awful-tasting stuff. So bitter it makes absinthe taste like honey."

"Bitter, you say?"

"Yes, I'll never forget the taste of it, and I've never been able to bring myself to drink it again since that night because it would remind me..." she trailed off, distracted.

Freddie had to prod her to continue. "Did Sidley offer to take you home then?"

"Well, what happened next was strange. I stood up to go, but the room was spinning. I could hardly walk, and he had to help me out the door. When we got outside, I still was doing poorly from the shock, so he said to me, 'Rosa, you're not well. You can't go home in this condition.' And didn't I know it. Mama would have beat the daylights out of me and then prayed over me a month after. So, I asked him what I should do.

"'Come with me,' he says. 'I know a boarding house nearby. It's one I used to live in when I first came to Chicago. The lady who owns it will let you stay the night, no questions asked. You can tell your mother tomorrow that you stayed overnight at Hull House in one of the guest rooms.' Then, we walked about three blocks to the house he mentioned. All the while I kept thinking to myself, how could Jonathan do this to me? How could he say he wanted to marry me and then turn around and marry somebody else? I remember I felt dizzy and weak and sick to my stomach. Mr. Sidley said he thought it was the shock and that I shouldn't distress myself any further about it."

As the memory of the night came flooding back, Rosa grew more agitated. She stood up and began pacing back and forth in front of the window. Freddie merely watched her without interrupting.

"When we got to the boarding house, the lady who owned it opened the door. She recognized Mr. Sidley because she called him by name. He told her I was ill and needed a place to stay for the night. He even offered to pay for the room since I only had enough money with me for carfare. So, Mrs. Hatch, that was the owner's name, she led us to a room on the first floor, at the back of the house. She told us to keep quiet because all the other boarders were asleep. By this time, it must have been almost midnight. I just kept feeling sicker and sicker, and when we got to the room, it was spinning. Mr. Sidley asked her if she had anything to quiet my nerves and she said yes there was a special cordial she kept for just such purposes. He was so kind to me. Sat there with me and waited until she came back. He insisted that I finish every drop of the cordial, though I thought it tasted just as bad as the brandy. It's funny how your feelings can affect your senses that way."

"Yes, funny." Freddie wasn't laughing.

"So then Mr. Sidley and Mrs. Hatch sat with me awhile, but I seemed to be feeling worse instead of better. Finally, at about one in the morning, Mr. Sidley got up to leave. He said I needed my rest, so Mrs. Hatch let him out the back door because there was a separate entrance right off the room where I was staying. He said he'd come back for me in the morning to see if I was well enough to go back home."

"Very solicitous." Freddie still wasn't sure what game Sidley had been playing, but he was unwilling to risk a question that might arouse the girl's suspicions. Finally, he asked, "Did you sleep well?"

Rosa shook her head. "No, not at all. I kept having terrible dreams. I felt like I'd been locked in the room and there was a man there with me. I couldn't get out. Every time I thought I called for help, I couldn't hear the sound of my own voice. It was like drowning in a nightmare, and the man in the dream— his face kept changing. First, it was Jonathan. Then he seemed to look like Mr. Sidley. It was all so jumbled up and confusing. But then, when I woke up, I realized it hadn't been a dream at all."

"What?"

"When I woke up, I felt numb all over. My head was pounding so hard I felt it would split in two. My clothes were lying all over the room, but I wasn't wearing anything. When I went to pick my shirtwaist up off the floor, I saw that it had been torn, but I couldn't remember how. I reached around my neck for the pendant, but it was gone. I felt as if I had lost my mind. I started searching everywhere. But then Mrs. Hatch burst into the room, and she was furious. She had Mr. Sidley with her. I scrambled to put on some clothes, but she tried to drag me out of the room before I was dressed. Mr. Sidley stopped her, though."

"What on earth had happened?"

"I didn't know it at the time, but it came out in bits and pieces. Mrs. Hatch was in a rage. She turns to Mr. Sidley and says, 'I run a respectable house, Mr. Sidley. I welcome your friend into my home, and this is how she repays an act of kindness!'

"Well, I can tell you I didn't know what to say or think. Mr. Sidley looked just as shocked as I did. 'Why, what's wrong, Mrs. Hatch?' he says to her.

"'Just this,' she says, still in a rage, 'after you left, she went out like a common streetwalker because she brought a man back to this room—into my house, sir! What can you say to that!'

"Mr. Sidley, he just stood there, and then he looks at me like I had played him for a fool. 'Is this true, Rosa?' he says. My head felt as if it was being squeezed in a metal vise, and I couldn't think. I couldn't remember. Yet, somehow, I knew there had been a man there. I just couldn't remember how he came to be there in the first place. 'I don't remember,' I said. 'Please stop asking me. I don't know!'"

Rosa was in a frenzy by now, reliving the episode. She was still pacing, and Freddie stood up to catch her in mid-stride. "Rosa, you must calm down. It happened a long time ago. Here sit down by me. Take a deep breath and try to relax."

His words helped to pull her out of the memory, but still, she had begun to cry. "I couldn't remember anything, and yet something inside of me said that it was true. My body ached everywhere. There were bruises on my arms, and I don't remember how I got them. So, it had to be true."

She wept for a few minutes, and Freddie didn't attempt to push her forward in her story until she was ready. Finally, she continued. "Well, Mrs. Hatch didn't believe me, and as soon as I was dressed, she pitched the both of us out the back door. She told Mr. Sidley never to come back, and she said if she ever saw me anywhere near her place, she'd report me to the police for soliciting."

"But how did she know you'd brought a man back to your room?"

"She said she saw him sneaking out the back as she came down the stairs to prepare breakfast. She called him out, and he told her he had been with me— that I had invited him in to spend the night. That I said something about needing to pay somebody back for something he did to me."

"Do you remember that part of it?"

"No, not at all," Rosa said desperately. "I've gone over it a thousand times in my mind, and it's as if my memory has been erased. And then there was what happened to the pendant."

"What happened to it?"

"Well, after Mrs. Hatch threw us out, I was still upset, and I told Mr. Sidley I had lost the pendant, and he says, 'Rosa, don't you remember what you did with it?'

"'No,' I said. 'Not a bit.' Well, he looked really surprised, and he said, 'Why, you smashed it in the gutter before we came up to the house.' 'But I couldn't have done that!' I said. 'I never would have done such a thing!'

"He just stared at me as if I had gone crazy. 'Look I'll show you,' he said. Then he led me around to the front of the house. There in the gutter, I found the chain and bits of smashed porcelain in the street. He told me that before we got to Mrs. Hatch's, I was carrying on and talking pretty wild about how I'd get my revenge on Jonathan for what he did to me. He told me that I stopped in the street and ripped the chain off my neck. 'I'll start with this,' was what I said, and I threw it down and smashed the china rose against the curb. And sure enough, there it was lying in the street. I bent down and picked up the chain to keep."

"Did he know anything about the man you were with?"

Rosa shrugged. "No, just what Mrs. Hatch told him. It must have been a stranger." She laughed again bitterly. "Just the first of many strangers."

"Rosa, don't talk like that!"

The girl looked cynically in his direction. "If I could betray somebody who loved me, there's nothing I couldn't sink to."

"But you're forgetting. He betrayed you."

She began to cry again—not violently, but tears ran silently down her cheeks. "No, he didn't. That was the worst part of it. He never betrayed me at all. Mr. Sidley was wrong."

Freddie sat open-mouthed in astonishment at the twists her story had taken. Knowing Blackthorne's character as he did, he couldn't believe his ears. "What do you mean Sidley was wrong?"

"He had gotten bad information from somebody. There was an engagement, but Jonathan never intended to go through with the marriage. That was just to buy some time. He had come to meet me that very same night—the night Mr. Sidley showed up. When he saw the two of us together, he didn't know what to think. He couldn't afford to be seen by anyone else, so he waited outside until we came out and he followed us. He saw everything."

"What do you mean, he saw everything?"

"I mean he was outside there the whole night and saw everything I did."

"But how do you know that?"

Rosa got up and wordlessly walked over to the dresser. She opened the top drawer and took out a creased, stained envelope, which she handed to Freddie. "A week after everything happened, I got this letter in the mail."

The envelope bore no return address. The note inside was only a page long but quite effective in destroying Rosa's hopes. Freddie read:

Rosa,

It pains me beyond belief to have to write these words to you. I was being watched too closely to reach you any sooner, and when I managed to break away, I found you in our usual spot with another man. Because I had no desire to be recognized, I determined to wait outside until I could speak to you privately. Instead of going home, I saw you go with your new friend to a house where I can only presume you had a rendezvous. I saw you call for revenge as you smashed the rose necklace that I had given you. Still, I waited, thinking that I might be able to see you alone after the man left in order to explain myself. To my surprise, I saw you invite the attentions of a stranger and bring him back to what I now can only assume was a house of ill repute. Apparently, I was as much mistaken in your love as I was in your virtue. You failed to wait for word from me. You had no faith that I would make good on my promise. Instead, you chose to betray me with the first man you could find. No matter how great my love for you once was, such a breach of trust is unforgivable. Do not try to explain because I would have difficulty believing whatever you might have to say. I cannot bear to see you again. Do not attempt ever to find me.

Farewell,

Jonathan

Freddie put the letter back in its envelope. All he could think to say was, "You must have been shocked to receive this."

"I think a part of me died that day. I couldn't plead my case with him. I didn't know where to find him. Besides, he confirmed what Mrs. Hatch and Mr. Sidley had already told me I had done. It seemed as if I didn't know myself at all till then. Didn't know just how evil I could be."

"No, Rosa, not evil. Don't say that."

"Yes, evil! I betrayed the only man who ever loved me, don't you see? What could be worse than that? Mama was right about me all along. I never told her about this, but I just packed up and left home that day."

"Where did you go?"

"Here," she swept her arm around the room, "where somebody like me belongs."

"And you've been punishing yourself ever since," the young man observed in a soft voice.

"Punishing myself?" Rosa echoed in disbelief. "Not just punishing myself. I've been trying to kill myself! One day at a time."

Freddie was silent.

She looked at him expectantly. "But if he sent you, maybe it's because there's still a chance?"

Without replying directly to the question, Freddie took a piece of paper out of his pocket and wrote an address on it. "Rosa, I'd like you to see a lady friend of mine. She knows Jonathan even better than I do. I'd like you to talk to her. She may be able to do something to help."

"Do you really think so?" Rosa was overwhelmed at the prospect.

"Can you get away to see her tomorrow?"

"I think so. They won't worry if I leave for a while." She laughed coldly. "They know I've got no place else to go, and I'll always come back."

"Well, I'll tell the lady to expect you. We'll see what we can do about finding someplace else for you to come back to."

Rosa said nothing, but her face took on an expression it hadn't shown for over a year and a half. She looked hopeful.

26 – RSVP

After Freddie left Mother Connelly's, he fairly flew back to the office, both because he had been gone an inordinate amount of time and also because he wanted to call Evangeline to let her know the news. In his haste, he almost forgot to remove his disguise. About a block before he reached the offices of Simpson & Austin, he realized his error and started tearing off his false whiskers. A lone female pedestrian walking toward him froze in her tracks as she saw him apparently trying to rip the skin from his face. He merely tipped his hat to her and wished her good day before she ran to the other side of the street. He managed to remove most of the glue before he entered his office.

"Afternoon, Aloysius." He brazened it out as he passed the company spy in the hallway.

"Afternoon, Simpson, what happened to your hair?"

Freddie immediately tried to muss up the top of his head to remove the slick center part and the thick layer of pomade he had applied to keep it in place. "Oh, nothing. Nothing. Just went to a new barber, that's all."

"Are you sure he wasn't a butcher instead of a barber?" Aloysius's nose had begun to twitch ever so slightly with suspicion.

"Ha! Ha!" Freddie enunciated the laugh with sarcastic precision before retreating to his office and shutting the door. His heart was hammering by the time he called Evangeline's townhouse. His enthusiasm was dampened the minute Jack's voice emerged from the other end of the line and informed him that the lady had gone back to the country house. Cursing the lack of telephone service to the North Shore, Freddie was forced to wait until he got back to Lake Bluff that evening to deliver his report in person.

While making a pretense of examining the stack of documents on his desk, he marked the clock at five-minute intervals until quitting time. The second the

185

pendulum gave him permission, he ran out of his office with hat and briefcase, nearly knocking Waverly over on his way out.

"Watch out, Simpson. You almost trampled me," the spy complained.

"Well, what are you doing skulking outside my door?"

"I wasn't skulking! I was merely passing by."

"Then pass by some other time," Freddie said over his shoulder as he darted out the exit. "I have a train to catch."

Waverly stood looking after him and shaking his head in disapproval. "Nepotism!" he muttered under his breath. "That's the way the world is. The spoils go to the unworthy every time. If anyone deserves to have an uncle who owns a law firm, it's me!" He wandered off to present his inconclusive report to Uncle Horace.

Freddie was able to catch the 5:15, which made all local stops as far as Waukegan. Every time the wheels ground to a halt at another station, Freddie ground his teeth in frustration. More than an hour later he exited the train and hurried down Center Avenue to the LeClair house. By this time, it was pitch dark, and the gas lamps that lined the street twinkled like fireflies against the overarching night. He loped up the porch stairs and pounded authoritatively on Evangeline's front door. Knowing that he would have to face interference first, he was prepared.

When Delphine came to the door muttering, "*Mon Dieu, qui est là?*" Freddie merely pressed himself through the narrow opening she had made in the doorway. "Not now, Delphine. Any other time I'd be happy to trade insulting remarks with you in the language of your choice, but not tonight. I need to speak to your mistress immediately."

When she hesitated, he summoned his meager knowledge of French and thundered, "*Maintenant!*" Then added only somewhat less aggressively, "*S'il vous plaît!*"

Looking at the young man as if he were a dangerous madman, Delphine merely said, "*Oui.*" She motioned him to follow her to the drawing room. Over her shoulder, she said, "Mademoiselle is with a guest."

"Well, it doesn't matter. I don't care if it's Blackthorne. I need to see her!"

Freddie could have sworn a malicious smile crossed Delphine's face. "*Mais non, jeune monsieur. C'est* Mademoiselle Henrietta Burke."

Freddie turned pale at the name. Henrietta Burke bore the dubious distinction of being the only female he knew under the age of thirty-five who didn't interest him romantically. Unfortunately, she found him irresistible and used every excuse to throw herself in his way. Nature hadn't favored Henrietta with a pleasing appearance unless one defined beauty in exclusively equine terms. However, it had compensated by giving her an overabundance of tenacity.

"Ye gods!" Freddie muttered under his breath. "Why now!"

"Pardon?" Delphine turned to him with exaggerated politeness. "I did not hear your words."

"Nothing, Delphine. Never mind." He sighed dejectedly.

The housekeeper smirked as she opened the door of the drawing room to announce the visitor. *"Mesdemoiselles,* a gentleman has just arrived. It is Monsieur Simpson." She quickly stepped out of the doorway, exposing Freddie to the attack that he believed was imminent.

Evangeline and her guest were seated together on the sofa, going over some papers. Evangeline nodded a greeting when Freddie was announced, but Henrietta sprang from her seat as if ejected from a cannon.

"Frederick! Frederick Simpson! Why how positively felicitous to see you!" She rushed over, extending her hand for him to kiss. "It's been an age at least since last we encountered one another." Freddie recollected that Henrietta was addicted to romance novels. He knew that she adopted an elevated style of diction whenever she was speaking to some poor fool that she'd set her cap for.

Freddie took her hand and gave a limp handshake in return. He cleared his throat nervously. "Very sorry to intrude, but I have some important business I need to discuss with Evangeline."

"Oh, what creatures you men are! All you can contemplate with any degree of enthusiasm is business." Henrietta rolled her eyes in a languishing manner.

Freddie thought she looked like a cow in its final death throes. Alarmed by the sight, he stepped back a few paces—almost out the room in fact—when Evangeline intervened. The mistress of the house stepped between Freddie and his captor.

"Well, are you coming in, or aren't you?" Evangeline took his arm and pulled him toward the sofa. He noted gratefully that she seated him next to her. Unfortunately, she had miscalculated the available space and allowed about a foot to remain free between Freddie and the arm of the couch—just enough room for Henrietta to wedge her sturdy frame in the gap.

"Well, this is cozy, isn't it?" The latter pressed herself close to Freddie and batted her eyelashes.

He turned desperately toward Evangeline and whispered, "For God's sake, move over before she crushes me to death!"

Despite the fact that Evangeline was having a great deal of fun watching the scene unfold, she took compassion on her friend and slid all the way to the opposite end of the couch, leaving about four feet open in the middle. Freddie claimed this space immediately, defying even Henrietta to commit the unthinkable breach of decorum of moving over to press up against him.

Instead, Miss Burke only readjusted herself so that all of her bulk fit on the couch. She contented herself with looking upon Freddie dotingly from that vantage point. "Well, Frederick! What can be so excessively important that you come bursting in here to confabulate with Evangeline the minute you get off the train?"

It was one of the sad ironies of Freddie's existence that he had always longed to be called Frederick by someone as a sign that he had grown to adulthood. But the only person who ever called him that was Henrietta.

"Sorry, Henrietta, but it's rather personal."

"Personal, is it?" Henrietta raised her eyebrows in mock surprise. "You'd better have a care, Mr. Simpson, or there will be gossip about wedding bells for you and Miss LeClair."

"Don't I wish," Freddie muttered *sotto voce*.

"What was that?" Henrietta asked. "I didn't catch what you said."

"I said that's a nice dish." He nervously pointed to a crystal candy dish on the table in front of the couch.

"Indeed," Evangeline retorted archly. "You've only seen it a thousand times before today without remark."

"You seem to have forgotten my question," Henrietta intruded. She was apparently intent on establishing if Evangeline was a rival for Freddie's affections.

Evangeline placated her with a laugh. "Don't worry, Henrietta. Freddie and I aren't attached."

"Says you," Freddie growled to himself again.

Evangeline looked at him irritably. "Freddie, if you don't stop muttering to yourself like an escaped lunatic, I'll send you home this instant."

The young man sighed and lapsed into a martyred silence.

"Oh, spare him I beg you, dear Evangeline," Henrietta gushed. "He's a thinker, and thinkers are always musing out loud. You shouldn't interrupt his ineffable cogitations. I'm sure he's thinking something brilliant even as we speak."

Evangeline seemed to be having difficulty commanding her facial muscles to keep still. "Is that what you were doing Freddie? Thinking brilliant thoughts?"

"You have no idea some of the things I've been thinking," he said with acid dripping from his voice.

Henrietta seemed oblivious to the undercurrent and finally moved on to another topic.

"Before you arrived, Frederick, Evangeline and I were perusing the menu for the next event the Ladies' Charitable Auxiliary is planning. Would you like to see?"

"Who are you trying to save this time?" Freddie asked sarcastically. "Vagabond polo players?"

Henrietta laughed violently for an undue amount of time to demonstrate the delight she took in Freddie's repartee. "Oh, Frederick! You're so clever and erudite. I do so enjoy your eruptions of wit."

"And I enjoy it a great deal more when he adopts the soul of wit rather than its form."

Freddie rolled his eyes, knowing the direction in which his friend was going. "The soul of wit?" Henrietta repeated, looking lost. "What might that be?"

"Brevity. There's been precious little of it in this conversation."

"Oh, my." Henrietta took the rebuke personally.

"Henrietta is staying for dinner, Freddie. Would you care to join us?" Evangeline asked in a pointed tone.

At these words, the young man was panic stricken. He sprang off the couch, and words began to tumble out of his mouth about "... late..." and "... home..." and "... family..." and "... must be going..." and "... let myself out..."

Before the two ladies could collect themselves enough to bid farewell, he had dashed out of the room and run from the house.

Henrietta heaved a melodramatic sigh, "That Frederick—so *je-ne-sais-quoi*. So unusual." Then she added sententiously, "You know I've heard it said that eccentricity is a sign of true genius."

Evangeline stared at her in perplexity a long time before replying. "There's a fine line between genius and insanity, Henrietta."

"What do you mean by that?"

Evangeline rose and rang the bell as a signal that dinner should be served. "I mean that most of the time it's difficult to tell which side of the line Freddie is on."

"Oh, I see. Still, I suppose an insane genius is quite as good to have as a normal one."

"I'm sure you two will be very happy together," Evangeline commented laconically. "Shall we go into the dining room now?"

***

By nine o'clock Evangeline stood on the front porch waving goodnight to her guest. After Henrietta had walked down the street and out of sight, Evangeline noticed a rustling sound in the hedges below the verandah. "Oh, the devil take them! It's those raccoons again."

A choked whisper emerged from a hydrangea bush. "It's not the raccoons; it's me."

"What on earth!"

"Is she gone yet?" the bush asked.

"Yes, she's gone, and what do you mean by wearing my shrubbery in that manner?"

Freddie stood up with a groan, pressing his hand tentatively into his backbone. "Thank God! Do you have any idea how long I've been crouched in those bushes waiting for her to go?"

"However long it was, I hope your back aches tomorrow for it. You're an incredible coward, Freddie!"

189

The young man limped up the stairs to join her. "Until you've been hunted by Henrietta Burke you have no right to talk. Anyway, let's go in. What I have to tell you can't wait until tomorrow."

"Very well." Evangeline relented at the mention of the investigation. "Let's go into the library."

***

A half hour later, Freddie had finished recounting Rosa Grandinetti's sad story. He paused for effect, expecting Evangeline to applaud his skill as a detective. Instead, she sat motionless, hands clasped, staring at the floor.

Finally, to break her out of her mood, he asked tentatively, "Well, old girl, what do you think?"

She looked up. Her face seemed careworn in the dim light. "I have never had a high opinion of my fellow man, Freddie, but what you've told me is almost incomprehensible. Such calculated wickedness is beyond the scope of what I might ever have believed possible."

"I know. I felt very sorry for Rosa. It was painful to listen to her and not break out and tell her the truth."

"They were so careful, the two of them. How elaborately they must have planned these little scenarios. Their stories always tallied, but they were never seen together. She wouldn't have had the slightest reason to connect them."

"What do you think of her dream?"

"That it wasn't a dream at all. I'm sure they drugged whatever she was drinking, but apparently not enough to render her completely unconscious."

"Then the nameless stranger never accosted her at all?"

"Oh, he had a name all right, and I'm sure it was Blackthorne. But I doubt that she went out in search of him. He let himself into her room instead."

"Well, if she didn't go out and invite the attentions of a stranger, then that means—"

Evangeline finished the thought, "That Mrs. Hatch was in their confidence too and fabricated the story about a stranger in her house."

"Maybe the boarding house wasn't a boarding house after all. Maybe it was a brothel."

"No, I don't think so. Mrs. Hatch lives in a respectable neighborhood. A brothel would have been too obvious, too hard to disguise. It might have aroused the suspicions of even someone as naive as Rosa."

"And the pendant?"

"Probably smashed by one of them to make their story of her betrayal more plausible." Evangeline rubbed her forehead wearily. "It's incredible, isn't it? After all this time, she still thinks she's the one to blame."

"Are you going to tell her about Blackthorne when she comes to see you tomorrow?"

"No, not just yet, Freddie. If I were in her position and found out the truth, I'd probably contemplate murdering the men responsible for ruining my life.

190

She's been through enough without a charge of well-justified homicide being laid at her door. Anyway, a vengeance killing would be too quick and easy. You can be sure I want those two scoundrels to suffer the pains of the damned before I'm through with them."

Freddie drew back in surprise at the cold fury he saw in his friend's eyes.

Evangeline continued to think out loud, unaware of Freddie's reaction. "Poor Rosa! She never found out Jonathan's true identity. In fact, she never suspected him of anything. He was able to walk away clean—" Evangeline stopped short. Her eyes flew open wide in shock. "My god, I've been so stupid!"

"What?"

She stood up and began pacing. "All this time I never made the connection. I can't believe it! What an utter fool I am!"

Freddie jumped to his feet and took her by the shoulders to shake her out of her soliloquy. "What is it?"

Evangeline looked at him and smiled bitterly. "Do you know how Elsa found out Jonathan's real name?"

"Of course, I don't!"

"I was the one who told her." She sat back down, shaking her head in disbelief.

"You what?"

"It never occurred to me. The event had little significance at the time. Now in retrospect, it seems so clear."

Freddie sat back down beside her. "Then please elucidate. I've spent the better part of the evening under cover of darkness. I don't want to experience the mental equivalent of that condition any longer."

Evangeline sighed. "Sometime at the end of the summer, I began to notice a change in Elsa's attitude. When she came to class, she was listless and didn't seem to care about anything. It was so unlike her. I thought an outing to the theater might cheer her up. One of the downtown theaters was performing Sheridan's *The Rivals*. Thinking that a comedy might be just the thing, I arranged an excursion for her and several of her classmates. The evening started off well enough, and she actually seemed to enjoy the play—at least as much as her general despondency would allow.

"During intermission, I saw her glancing around the theater, looking at the faces of the other patrons. Given the size of my group, we weren't in the box seats but in the first balcony. She asked me if I knew anyone at the theater that evening. She specifically asked about society people—the ones in the box seats lining the walls below us. I pointed out several people I knew, and then I happened to notice Jonathan seated with his family. I don't believe he saw us since we were seated above him and out of his range of vision. Anyway, I mentioned his name, and she repeated it almost as if she were trying to memorize it. I remember because she commented on what a distinguished fellow he was and asked whether I had known him long and if he lived near me. I attached no importance to the questions. She had always exhibited a great deal of curiosity, and I took it as a sign that her spirits were reviving. A little while later, she pleaded a bad headache and said she had to go home immediately. Because there were so many others in my group, I couldn't leave with her. I sent her home in a cab and stayed to watch the rest of the play."

"And nothing triggered your suspicions?"

"No. Elsa had been acting strangely for some time, and I attributed it to a physical ailment. But now I realize that by telling her Jonathan's name, I must have made her realize he'd been lying to her. She probably put enough of the facts together to understand what had happened. She may have contacted him and threatened exposure. That was probably the reason they met on the night of her death."

"Well, where do we go from here?"

Evangeline leaned back in her chair and stared at the ceiling for a few moments to collect her thoughts. "It's clear to me that these two are devoid of conscience and morality. Their behavior with respect to Rosa proves that."

"Yes, and?"

"If there's such a thing as honor among criminals, I don't believe it applies to these two. Up until now, they've been held together by mutual selfish interest."

"Each one deriving some sordid benefit from the association."

"Exactly. I'm convinced that if the two of them remain united in their silence, we'll never know who was responsible for Elsa's death."

Freddie looked at her despondently. "Thank you for that ray of hope."

"But there is hope!" Evangeline smiled triumphantly. "What if we were able to drive a wedge between them, break asunder their unholy alliance?"

"And just how do you propose to accomplish that?"

"I think something dramatic and unforeseen is required," Evangeline said pensively.

"Like having them arrested together and dragged downtown for questioning?" Freddie waited expectantly.

Evangeline looked at her companion as if she had lost all hope that he would ever amount to anything as a detective. "No, I was thinking of something more effective than that." She tapped her chin. "More along the lines of a dinner party."

"A what?"

"Yes, a dinner party will do quite nicely, I think." Evangeline strode over to her desk, sat down, and began writing. "So much to do before Friday and so little time. You'll be good enough to return to me the photographs of Sidley and Jonathan. I'll be needing them tomorrow. Oh yes, and I'll also have to contact the butcher, the baker, and the candlestick maker, not to mention the tailor, the jeweler, the doctor, and the innkeeper's wife."

Freddie followed her to the other side of the room, protesting. "Have you completely lost your mind? We're talking about two dangerous suspects who need to be handcuffed and locked away in a cell. And all you can do is plan a party?"

Evangeline smiled up at him serenely. "Exactly so. But before you cast judgment on my methods..." She handed him the paper on which she had been scribbling. "Just have a look at the guest list."

27 – PARLOR GAMES

At promptly eight o'clock on Friday evening, Freddie and Bill Mason stood on the steps of Evangeline's townhouse. Bill had paused just long enough to light up a cigar before Freddie rang the doorbell. Jack answered the summons.

"Evening, Jack. Are we the first to arrive?" Freddie asked.

Jack smiled, briefly flashing his gold tooth, and nodded conspiratorially. "Evening, Mr. Freddie. The first as planned."

He ushered the two into the drawing room where Evangeline sat waiting to receive her guests. The newspaperman eyed the expensive French tapestries that hung from the walls. He also noted the oil paintings, most of them from that avant-garde school for myopic painters known as Impressionists. He catalogued the marble floors and oriental carpets, the walnut paneling and antique Chinese vases on the mantelpiece, and finally the lady herself who owned all of it. He could see why Freddie was jumping through hoops for her. Blue stockings weren't usually so good looking.

He realized, with a start, that while he had been taking inventory, so had she. Evangeline watched him silently, a slight smile on her face. She rose to greet him, holding out her hand as she said, "You mustn't judge me too harshly for these decorative embellishments, Mr. Mason. I am the humble recipient of the objects you see about you, not their collector."

Bill, usually not at a loss for words, was taken aback by both her vocabulary and her directness. He merely mumbled, "Miss," and shook her hand like a schoolboy being introduced to his first-grade teacher.

Freddie stood back, grinning at his friend's discomfort. "I told you she was a terror, Bill. Now you can see for yourself."

Belatedly recovering his usual aplomb, Mason retorted, "I'd hardly call the lady a terror, my boy. Formidable might be a better word." He ground out his cigar in an ashtray, not quite sure why he felt the need to be on his best behavior.

"You are a quick study, Mr. Mason. I can see why Freddie enjoys your company so much." Evangeline seemed amused by Mason's crusty manner. She gestured toward the sofa as she spoke, indicating that the three should sit down together. "How much has our young friend told you about the little scenario we've planned for this evening?"

Mason replied, "Not much, other than something is going to happen that will make a terrific front-page story."

"Only if I'm right in my assessment of the situation, Mr. Mason," Evangeline qualified. "But if I am correct, and your paper gets an exclusive on something that's worth printing, I must exact a promise from you in return."

"Name it, miss, and it's yours," Mason said cavalierly.

"That's the rub, Mr. Mason. I will not name my price. You'll have to trust me for a while. But I will give you the opportunity to judge the quality of the product I'm offering for sale."

"Well, you wouldn't be asking me to cut off my arm, or take a temperance vow, or anything like that, would you?"

Evangeline laughed. "No, nothing quite that extreme. I merely require your word as a gentleman of the press that you will comply with my wishes in regard to how this matter is to be handled journalistically. Consenting to my terms will do you no personal harm."

"Even though I may have just bought myself a pig in a poke, you have my word." Mason held out his hand. "Let's shake on it."

"Agreed." Evangeline shook his hand. "And to seal the bargain," she turned to Jack who had been standing near the door, "bring the gentlemen some whiskey."

Mason could feel his eyes assuming a luminous glow at the mention of spirits. "Freddie, you didn't tell me your lady friend was such a good hostess."

"She usually isn't," the young man said curtly. "It must be a full moon or something."

"Freddie, I distinctly remember inviting you to tea and lavishing you with delicacies no less than a month ago," Evangeline retorted.

Freddie took the glass of whiskey Jack offered. "And given the high price you exacted for those delicacies, the very thought of them ruins my digestion even now."

Evangeline regarded Freddie with a skeptical eye. She turned to Mason to remark, "You are doubtless already familiar with his penchant for exaggeration whenever it suits his purpose?"

Mason eagerly received the glass Jack held out to him. He took a delicate sip of whiskey and rolled it around on his tongue. Smacking his lips appreciatively, he swallowed it. "No, Miss LeClair, I wasn't. But I'll be on notice henceforth."

"Well, now that we've settled matters between us, I expect our next guests to arrive any moment."

***

Almost as if prompted, the doorbell rang. The three in the drawing room waited expectantly. Instead of Jack, the door was opened by a young fellow in livery, presumably the doorman for the evening, who announced, "Mrs. Palmer has just arrived, miss."

"By all means show her in, Humphrey."

The doorman almost doubled himself in two as he bowed the grand dame into the room.

Smiling graciously at Freddie and Bill, Bertha Palmer walked over to greet Evangeline.

The lady of the house warmly embraced her guest. "I'm so grateful for your presence here tonight, Bertha."

"I wouldn't have missed it for the world," Mrs. Palmer replied archly. She was dressed in a white satin evening gown whose train swept half the room as she crossed it. Her pearl choker was surmounted by a diamond as large as a robin's egg.

"Gad, Mrs. Palmer. Your get-up is too flash for us. That diamond alone must be worth a king's ransom," Mason offered impishly.

Freddie jabbed Bill in the ribs. He apparently felt that the newsman's attempt at charm left a bit to be desired.

Ignoring the awkwardness of the comment, Mrs. Palmer favored Mason with a wink. "Yes, the diamond did set Mr. Palmer back a few pennies. It's one of my favorite pieces."

Evangeline took Bertha's arm and led her to a chair where the two ladies held a conspiratorial *tête-a-tête*. Freddie continued to lecture Bill in an agitated undertone until the doorman announced, "Police Superintendent Flint is here, miss."

"You may show the gentleman in, Humphrey."

The newcomer entered the drawing room warily. When he saw Bill Mason, he glared.

"What's the meaning of inviting *him* here, Miss LeClair?" Flint spat out the pronoun with contempt.

Evangeline replied with aplomb. "Politics and a number of other crimes sometimes make for strange bedfellows, Superintendent. I told you that you would hear something to your advantage if you attended my little *soirée* this evening, and so you shall. So you shall."

"Maybe I should have asked to see the guest list ahead of time," Flint mumbled. "A boy still wet behind the ears and an alcoholic newshound are hardly what I would consider good company."

Bill Mason stood up defiantly. "Sir, I must protest. I'm quite sure Freddie dried his ears before he arrived here this evening!"

Flint glowered and, after paying his respects to the ladies, took a seat in the far corner of the room.

Jack moved around unobtrusively, dispensing refreshments. About five minutes later, the doorman reappeared to announce, "Mr. Sidley, miss."

"Send him in then." Evangeline stood up and walked toward the door. Humphrey clicked his heels and drew back to allow the gentleman to enter.

The near-sighted accountant bowed his way into the room and, in his most self-effacing manner, greeted the assembled guests. Comments like "what an honor" and "I never expected to m... meet anyone so important" flowed haltingly from his lips.

Mason, who dismissed Sidley as of no interest, walked over and began to badger the police superintendent good-naturedly. In the meantime, Bertha Palmer and Freddie carried on a whispered conversation regarding the deplorable state of law enforcement in the Levee District—a conversation not meant for the ears of the superintendent. Ignored by the others, Sidley commandeered Evangeline's attention, presumably to establish her motive for the gathering.

"Miss LeClair, I was so overwhelmed with g... gratitude to receive your invitation. Quite taken by surprise, and by joy, I might add. To th... think that you would include me in so distinguished a party for one of your elegant suppers."

Evangeline half-smiled. "Oh, I'd hardly call a party that includes Freddie a distinguished one. But thank you for the compliment all the same."

"And who else might w... we be expecting this evening?" Sidley hesitated. "Forgive me if the question appears impertinent, but I want to prepare myself m... mentally in case I am introduced to any more eminent people of your acquaintance. I'm quite overcome as it is."

"Calm yourself, Mr. Sidley." Evangeline's voice held cool detachment. "Only a few old friends, that's all."

"Oh, I see."

Evangeline could guess that he wanted to ask specifically whose old friends they were but ultimately decided not to press the matter.

A lull had just developed in the conversation when the doorman returned again to say, "Mr. Blackthorne has arrived."

"Oh yes, by all means, show him in."

Humphrey stood aside to allow the newest guest to pass. Blackthorne appeared apprehensive as he cast his eyes around the room and saw the number of people it contained. Evangeline was well aware this was the evening on which she was to give him a final answer to his proposal. No doubt, he hadn't anticipated so many witnesses to that scene. Nor was he aware that the response she had planned didn't fall within the range of possible alternatives he had imagined. The muscles in his face seemed to twitch ever so slightly when he saw Sidley, but Evangeline thought perhaps her imagination was playing tricks on her.

She walked toward him, wreathed in smiles and held out both hands to him in greeting. "Jonathan, how lovely to see you. I believe you know almost everyone here."

Blackthorne looked disturbed. "I assumed your invitation to dinner would be just the two of us, Engie. We have matters to discuss." He took the lady's hands uncertainly and allowed her to lead him to the center of the room.

"Yes, there are important matters to be discussed—matters of life or death, as a matter of fact. But all will be revealed in time." Linking her arm through his, she began a round of introductions. Sidley, she noted, had stepped back into the corner as far as he could, presumably trying to be mistaken for a potted fern.

Blackthorne acknowledged the introductions and then turned toward Sidley. "I don't believe I know that gentleman over there."

"Don't you?" Evangeline gasped theatrically in surprise. "Oh, do forgive me. For some strange reason, I thought the two of you were acquainted. Quite extraordinary." She shook her head in disbelief. "So, you mean to tell me you've never set eyes on this man before in your life?" She stared directly at Jonathan, a challenge in her eyes.

He returned her stare. "No, never. But if you'd be good enough to introduce us now, we might form an acquaintance."

"Quite so." Evangeline walked over to Sidley, who had been nervously shredding a palm frond while the foregoing interchange was being concluded. She separated him from the greenery and dragged him forward.

"Jonathan, may I introduce you to Mr. Jacob King—," she broke off in seeming alarm. "My goodness, what a silly goose I am! I almost said Mr. Jacob Kingston. Now, why do you imagine I would have done a thing like that?" She turned from Blackthorne to Sidley in helpless appeal for an explanation.

Sidley, by this time, looked like a bird caught in a trap. His mouth had flown open, and he was inhaling huge gulps of air.

Evangeline waved her hand dismissively. "No matter. The name I should have said was Mr. Jacob Sidley. Mr. Sidley, this is Mr. Blackthorne."

The two men shook hands politely as Evangeline watched. Blackthorne's face was unreadable. Sidley removed his glasses and began to polish his foggy lenses most energetically.

From the corner, a voice interrupted, "Are there to be no other ladies, Miss LeClair?" It was Superintendent Flint.

Mrs. Palmer laughed airily. "Really, sir, how ungallant a sentiment. Not content with the scintillating presence of Miss LeClair and myself, you long for other female companionship? I hardly know what to think."

The Superintendent blushed to his sparse hair roots when he realized his faux pas.

Evangeline allowed him to squirm and stammer for a sufficient interval before relieving his distress. "This was primarily intended to be a business gathering, and I have provided as many members of the fair sex as propriety demands. But, as it happens, there will be another lady to indulge your need for feminine variety. Since I fear she's been detained, we may as well all go into the dining room. We can discuss the reason for this assembly after a full meal."

When the party had regrouped in the dining room, Evangeline directed their seating. "Jonathan, you're at the opposite end of the table, with Mr. Sidley on your right. The seat on your left is to remain vacant. It will be for the lady. Freddie, you're at my right with Superintendent Flint next to you. On my left will be Mr. Mason with Mrs. Palmer next to him. There, I think that covers everyone." Evangeline looked around with satisfaction at her guests and at the table covered with a brilliant profusion of orchids, lilies, Limoges, and Baccarat.

She rang a silver bell that had been placed next to her plate. A white-gloved attendant entered the room.

"Briggs, you may serve the first course now."

"Yes, miss. Very good." The servant disappeared toward the kitchen.

The party indulged in idle conversation as one course followed another. Even Superintendent Flint lost his grumpiness after a very good lobster bisque and some escalloped oysters. The only event that marred the perfection of the dinner was Briggs's clumsiness when pouring the wine. He was in the process of refilling Jonathan's glass when he tipped the bottle at an unfortunate angle, staining the tablecloth and nearly hitting the banker's coat sleeve in the process. Blackthorne glared at the man in annoyance at the prospect of his expensive suit being ruined.

"Clumsy fool!" he muttered.

Rather than rebuking the servant, Evangeline smiled inexplicably. "Very good, Briggs." She appraised Blackthorne's person. "Well, it appears no harm has befallen you, Jonathan. So sorry. Please do have a little more stewed terrapin."

After this episode, the dinner proceeded without a ripple. They had just begun on the boned quail in jelly when a knock was heard on the dining room door. Jack poked his head in. "Sorry, Miss Engie, but there's a gentleman at the door who insists he has to see you on some urgent business. Says it can't wait. I tried to make him go away, but he wouldn't."

"Why not invite him in here, Jack? We can always make a place for him." The caretaker nodded and disappeared. A rumble of speculative conversation began around the table. Jonathan stared at Evangeline quizzically, looking for some hint regarding the unknown visitor. The lady merely shrugged and said, *"Qui sait?"* before taking another forkful of quail.

Jack opened the dining room door again and scratched his head in puzzlement. "Excuse me, Miss Engie, but the gentleman wants me to announce him as Mr. Sidley. Don't we already have one of those here tonight?"

Blackthorne looked at the Sidley who was seated next to him. The banker was obviously mystified by the turn events had taken, but he was exhibiting no signs of alarm. Sidley, on the other hand, had begun to loosen his collar and complain of the stuffiness in the room.

Evangeline watched in amusement. "I believe, Jack, our new visitor is a Mr. Sidley lately arrived from Dodgeville, Iowa. Freddie, perhaps you'd like to do the honors?"

Freddie dabbed his mouth with his napkin and stood up importantly. A blond man walked into the room, hat in hand. He was in his late-thirties and sported a thin moustache on which he used a sparing amount of wax. Freddie announced, "Ladies and gentlemen, may I present to you Mr. Jeremiah Sidley, a banker I met a while back in Iowa. I believe he's here tonight to renew an old acquaintance."

Mr. Jeremiah Sidley looked around at a half-dozen pairs of eyes staring back at him inquisitively. He remained sheepish until his gaze settled on the gentleman to Blackthorne's right. Then his expression changed to that of the wrathful prophet who was his namesake. Without so much as a hello, he pointed a finger and said, "That's him. Glasses or no glasses, I'd recognize that lying, thieving swindler anywhere, anytime! It's Jacob Kingston, all right!"

The accountant had pulled out a handkerchief and begun to mop his brow. "I don't k... now what you m... mean. Is the fellow m... mad? My name is J... Jacob Sidley."

The visitor thundered in reply, "Your name is Jacob Kingston, and you robbed me and my bank of one-hundred-thousand dollars! Deny it, if you can! I'll testify in court that it's what you did. You can lie about it, but I've got proof."

Blackthorne had begun nervously tapping on the table. He was becoming unsettled by the confrontation and tried to interpose. "Surely, Engie, this isn't the time for accusations such as this. It's a matter for the police."

"For once, I quite agree with you, Jonathan. It is a matter for the police. That's why I invited Superintendent Flint. And there are several more accusations to be heard before this dinner ends."

"I hardly think this problem falls within the jurisdiction of the Chicago Police Department," Flint said.

"Perhaps not," the lady relented, "but I should think that embezzlement from a Chicago brokerage firm would."

Blackthorne gasped at Evangeline's words. It appeared as if Sidley had stopped breathing altogether.

"I also think a murder committed in a Chicago hotel would fall within your jurisdiction, wouldn't you?" she asked the superintendent pointedly.

Bill Mason rubbed his hands together with glee. "Oh boy, do I smell a story here!"

Mrs. Palmer was drinking in every word. She fixed her eyes on the superintendent as if silently daring him to answer in the negative.

Instead, Flint agreed. "Well, yes, I suppose both those crimes would be handled by my force. But these are serious charges, Miss LeClair. You'd better be able to substantiate what you're suggesting."

"Oh, I intend to." Evangeline rose from the table and whispered for Jack to take Mr. Jeremiah Sidley to the library so that he could calm down in private. She then walked over to the end of the table where Sidley and Blackthorne were seated. Placing her hands on the back of the banker's chair, she directed her comments over his head to the superintendent.

"Sir, I have serious reason to believe that these two were involved in an embezzlement scheme at Dresden & Company. They worked there together for over two years, but strangely enough, the two of them seem to have lost all memory of their former association. Perhaps they had reason to forget so sordid a shared past. I'm convinced Mr. Sidley actually embezzled the funds while Mr. Blackthorne covered up the crime in order to blackmail Mr. Sidley."

"That's absurd." Blackthorne's voice was chill with contempt.

Sidley shook his head violently and seemed to be mouthing the word "no," but no sound emerged.

Flint's response was characteristically patronizing. "Well, that makes no sense, Miss LeClair. We all know Mr. Blackthorne comes from a wealthy and distinguished family. He wouldn't need to blackmail anyone for money."

Evangeline smiled thinly. "One may blackmail for a variety of reasons other than money, Superintendent. In this case, I believe that what Mr. Blackthorne required was an accomplice in seducing innocent girls."

Evangeline couldn't see Blackthorne's face when she said the words, but she could feel the physical shock wave that traveled through his body as she held onto the back of his chair.

"What!" the superintendent gasped. The others were equally shocked but said nothing. Everyone looked tensely at the two seated at the end of the table.

Blackthorne's voice, dangerously low and controlled, broke the silence. "I hope, my dear, you have a great deal of proof to back up an accusation like that."

Evangeline returned to her own chair. "What I have found are an enormous number of coincidences. Such a number that they defy the laws of probability. Odd bits of information that, taken together, present a most damning case against you both." She looked at the two men with contempt. "Regrettably, rape and abandonment are not capital offenses. However, it gives me great satisfaction to point out that one of you committed another crime that is — murder!" She quickly rang the little silver bell again.

As if they had been waiting for the signal, Evangeline's two servants entered the room. She acknowledged their presence and then addressed the group. "As my guests this evening, you have all made the informal acquaintance of these two worthy fellows. You'll recall that one opened the door for you, and the other waited at table. What you may not know is that neither one is regularly employed by me. One is a reception clerk at the Palmer House, while the other is a porter there. They have come here tonight with the blessing of Mrs. Palmer to see if they could identify anyone in connection with a murder that occurred at their hotel over a month ago."

"Oh yes, that German seamstress who was killed there," Superintendent Flint said offhandedly.

"Her name," Evangeline corrected, "was Elsa Bauer, and she was a student of mine."

"That was quite a sh... shocking business," Sidley chimed in nervously. "But the police apprehended the killer, didn't they?"

"They apprehended a suspect. There were a few other equally suspicious characters they overlooked. In their haste to solve the case, they may even have planted evidence in order to justify the arrest."

A howl of protest rose from the superintendent. Blackthorne grumbled at the absurdity of the accusation. Sidley made a superhuman effort to keep breathing. Bill Mason and Freddie traded significant looks, while Mrs. Palmer serenely fanned herself.

"But do not despair, Superintendent," Evangeline continued. "Freddie and I have done your work for you so your department will have no need to falsify evidence in order to gain a conviction. Lo and behold, we've uncovered eyewitnesses who can point you in the right direction."

She wheeled about and addressed the two servants. "Humphrey, you said you saw a man who asked for Elsa Bauer's room number shortly before the murder occurred. Is he in the room this evening?"

Humphrey sprang forward. "Yes, miss. No question. It's the man near the other end of the table. I clicked my heels as a signal to you when I announced him earlier."

"Do you mean Mr. Kingston, or rather Mr. Sidley as he likes to be called now? Just so there'll be no doubt."

"Yes, Mr. Sidley. He wasn't wearing glasses when I saw him at the hotel, though."

"Quite. I have ascertained to my own satisfaction that Mr. Sidley doesn't really need his spectacles. But at any rate, you're sure it's the same man?"

Humphrey nodded energetically. Sidley looked at Blackthorne in a panic, his eyes imploring some sort of escape plan. Blackthorne merely gazed back at him coolly, promising nothing.

Evangeline continued. "There was also a witness who saw a man loitering about in the hall outside Elsa Bauer's room. A far more suspicious place to be seen, wouldn't you agree?" She asked the question of the assembled group. All, with the exception of the two suspects, nodded in assent.

"Briggs." She addressed the other servant. "Perhaps you'd be good enough to point out the man you saw there."

"Yes, ma'am," the porter answered readily. "It's the one I spilled wine over on purpose."

"Mr. Blackthorne? This man?" She walked over to the banker's chair and placed her hand on his shoulder. He flinched at the contact but made no further movement.

"That's him, sure enough. I got a good look at him," the porter added. "I'd just popped out of the stairwell, but I saw him clear enough. He seemed like he was in a trance. Just walking back and forth outside the door for a few minutes. And when he knocked, the lady opened the door and told him to come in because she was expecting him."

The tension in the room was at the breaking point. Everyone nearly jumped out of their chairs when Jack quietly opened the door to the dining room and said, "The lady has arrived." Turning to Evangeline, he asked significantly, "Shall I show her in?"

"Yes, please do, Jack. And stand by, will you?"

The caretaker nodded. He stepped aside and announced, "Miss Rosa Grandinetti."

At the sound of the name, Sidley sprang from his chair in terror and backed away from the table.

The girl entered the room, shy and a bit disoriented. It would have been hard to tell her profession judging from the modest way in which she was dressed for the occasion. She turned first to Evangeline. "Miss Engie? Who are all these people?"

"Friends, Rosa. Mostly, that is."

"You said he would be here." She searched around for a face she recognized. Barely glancing at Freddie, her gaze rested on Sidley. "Mr. Sidley, is it really you?"

Sidley backed even farther against the wall. "Rosa, I... I'm sorry, I never meant for this to happen. It wasn't my idea, you see. I wasn't really to blame."

She said nothing more, like a dreamer who doesn't question the absurd presence of the figures who populate her sleep. She continued to cast her eyes vaguely around the room until she finally saw the face she'd been looking for.

"Jonathan?" she began tentatively. She took a step forward. Blackthorne regarded her apprehensively.

"Do I know you?" His face, which had registered nothing more than contempt through the entire meal, took on a haunted expression.

"Jonathan, please! They said you'd forgiven me. Don't do this now! My heart will break instead of the china rose if you turn me away again."

Blackthorne looked tensely at the assembled party. "Really, I don't know her. She's clearly mistaken me for someone else."

Evangeline came to stand behind Rosa, putting her hands on the girl's shoulders. "Never mind what he says, Rosa. Do you know this man?"

"Yes, of course, I do."

"What's his name then?"

"Why, it's Jonathan. Jonathan DeVille."

"That's what he told you his name was?"

Rosa turned to look at her in surprise. "Why, of course. How else should I know his name if he didn't tell me what it was?"

"Rosa, did he make any promises to you of a personal nature?"

"He said he loved me. He told me he wanted to marry me." Her voice grew increasingly troubled. "Then he said I betrayed him, but I can't remember how. So, he told me he didn't care for me anymore, and he took all the love back." She whispered to herself, "All the love I'd ever had in the world, and he took it back again."

At this, Rosa began to sob. She fell to her knees in a knot of misery at Jonathan's feet. Blackthorne turned his head away.

Evangeline knelt down beside her to whisper, "Everything will be all right. I promise you." She motioned for the two servants to assist in getting Rosa on her feet again. "Please take her into the kitchen. Delphine is there. She'll know what to do."

The girl wept as she was being led from the room. "How can you be this cruel, Jonathan? I have thought of no one but you for two years. Two years! Haven't I paid enough?"

A deathlike silence settled over the room after she left. In amazement, Bill Mason asked, "Who was that?"

"One of their former victims, who had the misfortune to live," replied Evangeline. "She can tell you a great deal about their method of operation in these matters, as can a certain boarding-house owner by the name of Mrs. Hatch."

The mention of the name was apparently the equivalent of the proverbial straw because Sidley finally lost control. With nary a pause or a stutter, he shouted at Blackthorne, "I won't take the blame for this!"

"Jacob, sit down and be quiet!" Blackthorne ordered authoritatively.

Sidley was too near hysteria to comply. "You said no one would ever connect us! Well, you were wrong! God knows I've gone outside the law at your bidding, but murder was never part of our bargain. All I did was find out for you which room Elsa was in. I didn't kill her. You did! I know you did! And now you want me to be quiet so you can pin the blame on me! I won't hang for you, Jonathan!"

Without warning, Sidley attempted to bolt from the room. Jack, who had apparently been prepared for just such an eventuality, pulled a revolver out of his coat pocket and pointed it directly at Sidley's chest. The latter froze in his tracks.

"Really, Mr. Sidley, enough of this nonsense. Do sit down." Evangeline folded her napkin neatly at the side of her plate. "Jack is quite a good marksman, and I think he would be most irritated at the person responsible for leaving bloodstains on the carpet."

Sidley cowered back down into his chair.

Blackthorne's composure had begun to crack. "This is all wild accusation! A case of mistaken identity. You can't prove I was in that hotel room at all!"

"You're quite wrong." Evangeline walked over to his chair and reached into his coat pocket. She casually drew out his handkerchief. "A handkerchief matching this one in every detail was found clutched in Elsa Bauer's hand. A few days ago, I contacted your tailor. He says the pattern is a design of your own. Quite as distinctive as a signature, wouldn't you say?"

At these words, Blackthorne's composure shattered altogether. "What! But that can't be! I never gave Elsa—" He stopped short.

"What an unfortunate choice of words, Jonathan. Not at all what one would expect from an innocent man. Better to have said, 'I never knew her, I never met her, I was never there,' rather than what you were about to say: 'I never gave Elsa a handkerchief.'" Evangeline paused for effect. "Oh, but there's more proof you were there that night—and quite a bit more damning than a handkerchief."

The lady leaned over the table to reach the centerpiece and extract a golden object that had been hidden among the flowers. It glittered and flashed in the candlelight.

"Do you recognize this, Jonathan?"

The blood drained from his face when he saw it.

"It's quite a pretty hair ornament, and expensive too. Elsa was wearing it at the time she died. I had a little difficulty finding the jeweler who made it, but his records indicate the commission was given by one Jonathan Blackthorne."

She walked around the perimeter of the table, holding the object in her hand for the other guests to see. Then she held it up toward the chandelier. "The piece was reworked by another jeweler at a later date to give it a most curious property. If you press this ruby at the top, something interesting happens." Evangeline demonstrated by pushing down on the gem with her thumb. The stone, which had appeared to be raised above the surface of the hair ornament, remained depressed. With a quick motion of her hand, Evangeline pressed down on the vertical bar of the cross.

To everyone's amazement, a knife blade shot out from the hollow bottom of the ornament. When Evangeline released her hold, it just as quickly shot back into place. The red stone had popped back up above the surface of the ornament as well.

"I'll do that again slowly," Evangeline said. This time when she released the knife, she kept pressure on the bar preventing the weapon from slipping back into its hiding place. She held the object forward for the guests to see. The end of the knife contained a brownish coating. Superintendent Flint was about to touch the blade when Evangeline cautioned, "I wouldn't do that if I were you."

He looked up at her in surprise.

"It still contains traces of curare mixed in with the blood stains you see there. Dr. Doyle very kindly analyzed a small quantity of the substance for me yesterday. It's the same poison that killed Elsa. Administered by the man who presented her with this gracious gift."

Blackthorne cast his eyes about the room, looking for someone to support him, but all he saw were looks of judgment. "I will make no comment until I've spoken to my attorney." He then retreated into a stony silence.

Evangeline turned to Flint and suggested delicately, "Superintendent, I believe this would be an opportune moment for you to use the telephone to call the nearest police station house. You might want to tell them that you've apprehended two dangerous criminals who need to be held on a charge of suspicion of murder."

"I?... Oh... ahem... yes... I guess I should. A very good suggestion. Thank you, Miss LeClair." The superintendent collected his wits and made straight for the telephone in the hall.

When he left the room, Evangeline turned her attention to Mrs. Palmer. "Bertha, I trust that if any of the facts that were brought to light this evening should go astray in police files, or if this case were never brought to trial, say perhaps because of some unforeseen political influence exerted on the murderer's behalf, that you would hold the matter to strictest account?"

"As a member of the Civic Federation, I'm sure I could apply the necessary pressure to see that nothing untoward occurs." Nodding to the other guests, Mrs. Palmer rose to take her leave. Evangeline walked her to the dining room door where the great lady paused to kiss her hostess lightly on the cheek.

"A most eventful evening, Engie. I'm pleased that we managed to prevent a very grave miscarriage of justice." She glanced briefly at her two servants. "Humphrey, Briggs, time to go."

The desk clerk bustled to open the front door for her while the porter ran down the stairs to summon her coachman.

Jack held the two suspects at gunpoint until Flint's officers came to collect them. The superintendent, with a belated sense of officiousness, decided to see them off to jail personally.

Before he left the room in custody, Blackthorne bowed to Evangeline and kissed her hand. "My compliments to the puppet mistress."

Evangeline studied his face for several seconds. "As you once observed, Jonathan, we are a great deal alike, you and I."

"*Au revoir, ma chérie,*" he added bitterly.

"You can be sure of that. I will see you again. When you hang!" And then in a whisper to herself, she added, "Perhaps somewhere in my nightmares, too!"

***

The only two guests remaining were Freddie and Mason. The latter whistled appreciatively. "Miss LeClair, I must say you really know how to throw a party!"

She smiled grimly. "Yes, a most interesting evening by any standard. We must all do this again sometime."

Freddie snorted in disgust. "When Hades freezes over will be soon enough for me!"

Evangeline linked her arm through Bill's and led him toward the door. "Mr. Mason, I believe you and I have a business arrangement to conclude?"

"Yes, miss," he assented guardedly.

"Would you not agree that I have given you the story to end all stories?"

"Nothing short of another mayoral assassination could beat it!"

"Well then, having kept my part of the bargain, these are my terms, which you agreed to uphold in advance."

"All right." He nodded. "Go ahead and give me the bad news."

"You may have exclusive use of this story for tomorrow morning's edition of the Tribune, as well as many other interesting details of the case that weren't revealed tonight, on one condition."

"And that would be?" He braced himself for the worst.

"On condition that you allow Freddie to pen the story and prevail upon your editor to offer him a job as a reporter."

Evangeline waited expectantly. Freddie held his breath.

Bill threw his head back and laughed. He slapped Freddie on the back. "Son, much as I might like to take credit for this scoop myself, I always knew you had printer's ink in your blood. This is your one chance, and I might as well be the one who gives it to you! Come on. We'll go over to the Whitechapel Club. After a few stiff belts, you'll see just how easy writing can be."

By now, the trio were standing outside on the front stairs. For the first time in their strangely enduring relationship, Freddie turned to Evangeline and, without hesitation, took her in his arms and kissed her on the lips. "Thank you, Engie," he whispered. "Thank you for everything!"

Evangeline smiled and pulled him by the ear. "Be off with you, young man. You have a story to write."

As the two men walked down the steps and into the street, Bill turned to observe, "Your performance tonight, Miss LeClair, puts me in mind of another clever lady who once furthered the cause of justice. To paraphrase the immortal bard." He spread his arms wide in a theatrical gesture and intoned, "'Most worthy *lady*, I and my friend have by your wisdom been this day acquitted. And stand indebted, over and above, in love and service to you evermore.'"

Evangeline, who still stood leaning in the doorway, laughed. "Ah, *The Merchant of Venice*. One of my favorites. I see you've taken a liberty with the gender as I will with the pronoun since Portia was, after all, a 'she' disguised as a 'he.' '*She* is well paid that is well satisfied; And I, delivering you, am satisfied and therein do account myself well paid.'"

Bill stared at her, speechless.

"Close your mouth, Bill," Freddie said laconically. "You're not the only victim of a classical education in this group."

"Well, I'll be." Bill chuckled and dug around in his pocket for a cigar as he turned back toward the street.

Evangeline called after them worriedly. "Freddie, don't drink too much or you'll wake up with a headache instead of a headline."

She shut the door and walked back into the foyer where Jack stood grinning at her. She smiled in return. "Yes, a most satisfactory evening in every respect. Now what to do about the leftovers?" She tapped her chin thoughtfully as she strode off to the kitchen.

28 – SINS OF OMISSION

When she came down to breakfast the following morning, Evangeline found a copy of the *Tribune* lying next to her coffee cup. The front-page headline blared, "Wealthy Banker Accused of Murder! Hull House Accountant Implicated in Scandal!"

Evangeline sipped her coffee and read the purple prose account of the apprehension of two dangerous felons penned by one Frederick Simpson. "Bill Mason, you are indeed a man of your word," she murmured approvingly as she digested both the story and her breakfast. Half an hour later, Evangeline went to the guest room where Rosa Grandinetti had spent the night. The two women then had a lengthy chat about matters past and future.

***

Once Evangeline finished restoring domestic order, she telephoned the Harrison Street police station to speak to Superintendent Flint. Since she'd allowed him to take credit for solving the crime, he was most forthcoming in giving her the details of the little scene that unfolded downtown after the arrest.

As Evangeline had expected, the weak link in the chain proved to be Sidley. Once taken into custody, he agreed to confess his own part in the crime in exchange for a lesser charge. He confirmed Evangeline's theories and added the appalling news that it was he, not Blackthorne, who had attempted to push her down the bluff in Lake Bluff. Equally appalling was his admission that he and Blackthorne both shared in the "sport," as he called it after their victims were drugged. For his part, Blackthorne admitted to being in Elsa's hotel room the night she died but insisted that she was still alive when he left via the fire escape. Both men denied murdering anyone including their first victim, the unfortunate Janet Stewart.

***

After satisfying her grim curiosity regarding the details of the crime, Evangeline wanted to satisfy her curiosity regarding Franz's release. She decided to go personally to Cook County Jail to see if he'd received the news yet.

As she came through the doors, she was amazed to see that the prison waiting room was swarming with reporters, police, firemen, and curiosity seekers. A uniformed guard was trying to hold the crowd at bay. Evangeline was startled to see Bill Mason at the head of a pack of newshounds yelping for information. She walked up to him and tapped him on the shoulder.

"Mr. Mason, what's happened here?"

The reporter turned with a worried scowl, which relaxed only slightly when he saw who was standing by his side. "I'm afraid it's bad news about your friend, Miss LeClair."

"Franz? What in God's name has happened now!"

Bill shuffled his feet uncomfortably. "Here, why don't we sit down." He led her to one of the benches in the waiting room. "You know how things operate in this town. The coppers are quick enough to round up suspects, but they drag their feet when it comes to letting them go. They call it 'paperwork.' Anyway, the guards were on their way up to his cell about an hour ago to process his release when they heard the explosion."

"The what?" Evangeline could barely force herself to grasp the inevitable conclusion.

"He's done away with himself."

"How?"

"Stuck a dynamite charge in his mouth and lit it. That's how." Bill shook his head in disbelief. "Of all the crazy, fool ways to die. He blew the top of his head clean off. From what the cops tell me, it was a mess."

"Like Louis Lingg," Evangeline whispered in shock.

"That's right, another crazy anarchist. The parallel wasn't lost on your friend either because he wrote a message on the wall of his cell before he died."

"Don't tell me, let me guess." Evangeline recalled the words sadly. "'The day will come when our silence will be more powerful than the voices you strangle today.'"

Bill nodded. "I covered the Haymarket trial and execution. Those were August Spies' last words from the scaffold before he was hanged."

Evangeline removed her gloves and distractedly twisted them around her fingers. "Why couldn't he have held on just a little while longer? Why was he so willing to believe that this was the only way out?"

Bill sighed and patted her hand comfortingly. "Miss LeClair, there are some men who are determined to die for a cause, even if they have to make one up out of thin air. Franz Bauer certainly seemed like the type."

"How ironic," she murmured, half to herself. "They were twins—Franz and Elsa. Twin destinies as well, it would seem."

"I just can't figure who would be crazy enough to smuggle explosives into his cell." Bill rubbed his chin speculatively.

"I can!" Evangeline's voice was bitter. "If you talk to Otto Schuler of the *Arbeiter Zeitung*, I'm sure he'll have a statement that he's eager to share with the world. I've no doubt he'll use the event to his political advantage somehow."

"Ah," the reporter said, drawing wordless conclusions.

Evangeline sat very still, feeling nerveless and limp.

Bill gave her a worried look. "Miss LeClair, would you like me to escort you back home? There's really nothing more you can do here. Nothing much anybody can do here now."

Despair threatened to engulf her, but she stopped herself. She could help no one by giving in to it. "You're right, Bill. There's nothing more to be done here." She stood up, declining the assistance of his hand. "Thank you for the offer, but I'll be fine. A walk will clear my head."

He rose to accompany her to the door.

"It would be better for me to salvage what remains." She drew on her gloves decisively. "As far as I'm concerned, there are now two deaths to lay at the door of Messrs. Sidley and Blackthorne. I intend to see them pay for this!"

211

29 – JUDGMENT DAY

Evangeline's grim wish for Sidley and Blackthorne was to be granted. By late January of 1894, the trial was over, and Blackthorne was convicted of murder and sentenced to hang. Sidley was convicted as an accessory to murder and sentenced to thirty years in Joliet State Prison.

The icy sleet of February gave way to the dogwood blossoms of April. These, in turn, gave way to the steam-wilted begonias of July, which in turn gave way to the scorched grass of August. During this interval, the Blackthorne family appealed the verdict to no avail. They even petitioned the governor for clemency but were turned down. An execution date was eventually set for Tuesday, August 28, 1894. In the prison courtyard, Jonathan Blackthorne would meet his death by hanging.

Evangeline belatedly made a decision to speak to him one last time. A week before his execution, she was admitted to a dim corridor in Cook County Jail to see what remained of Blackthorne. As she advanced down the catwalk that led to his cell, the only source of feeble light came from the glazed and barred windows above. There was no sound of other inmates because Blackthorne was caged on the fifth tier of the jail—an area normally reserved for prisoners in solitary confinement. When Evangeline approached the bars, the guard made no move to unlock the cell door. She motioned for the man to let her in.

"Are you sure, ma'am?" the guard asked in a shocked tone.

"Quite sure."

The guard undid the lock and announced the presence of a lady to the man in the cell. Then he shut the door behind him and drew back out of earshot.

Evangeline stood with her back pressed against the bars of the cage and peered into the interior. Her eyes hadn't adjusted yet to the dimness. She moved forward cautiously and strained to see into the shadows because the cell was narrow but very deep.

"Jonathan?" she whispered.

A darker shadow separated itself from the back wall and moved toward her. "Who's there?"

She said nothing.

As he moved into the light, he recognized his visitor. "Hello, *ma belle*. I hadn't expected to see you here. Did you fear the sight of me on a scaffold wouldn't afford you sufficient amusement, and you had to indulge in bating me personally before my execution?"

"That's not it at all, Jonathan." Evangeline instinctively retreated toward the door as she took note of the marked change in the man's appearance. Gone was the formality of a buttoned vest and precisely knotted cravat. Given the oppressive heat outside and the stifling, airless cell, she hardly wondered why. His hair had begun to gray prematurely. The hollow circles under his eyes suggested that sleep didn't visit him easily or often. However, his attitude seemed unchanged since their last meeting—still the same air of calculated composure.

He advanced and grasped the bars of his cell. "Then why have you come, Engie?"

Evangeline didn't move. She studied his face for several seconds before replying. "I want to know what happened the night Elsa died."

Blackthorne raised a corner of his mouth in a crooked smile. "You have pages and pages of trial transcripts to tell you that, my dear."

She shook her head. "No, that isn't what I meant, and you know it. I want to hear your version of events."

Blackthorne let go of the bars and walked toward the far wall. He threw his head back and laughed. Peering at his visitor from the shadows, he said, "I didn't kill anyone. Don't you believe me?"

"You tried to kill me."

Blackthorne strolled back toward her and leaned down until their faces were nearly touching. "You really do believe the worst of me, don't you? You're convinced that I orchestrated that disaster on the Ferris wheel along with everything else." He straightened his shoulders and retorted, "Perhaps you ought to ask yourself why I would attempt to kill a woman I love!"

"Love me!" Evangeline exclaimed in disbelief. "You're very free with that word! I'm sure you told Elsa you loved her, too. Why do you persist in lying even now when it can't possibly matter?"

Jonathan whispered urgently, "Why do you persist in believing I'm such a black-hearted rogue?"

"You'll have to forgive me for doubting your virtue." She folded her arms resolutely across her chest. "Your crimes are a matter of public record. Why would you stick at attempting to kill a woman who doubts your love when you showed so little restraint in killing one who believed in it?"

Blackthorne shrugged. "Assume whatever you like. But as you said yourself, *ma chérie*, I have no reason to lie now." He regarded her speculatively. "You want to believe I'm guilty because the thought of convicting an innocent man wouldn't fit into your tight and orderly universe. Evil is punished, and good is vindicated. Isn't that the way it's supposed to work?"

Evangeline stared back at him and said nothing.

He began to stroll around the perimeter of his narrow kingdom as he spoke. "I've always been amused by the naiveté of charity—by the benevolence of the well-intentioned ladies of the upper class. You believe you can save the world, don't you? If you read enough poetry to the poor, I'm sure you can, without resistance, eradicate the slums of Chicago. But nowhere in your benign philosophy of the universe have you left room for the devil." A ghost of a smile crossed his face. "Do you believe in the devil, Engie?"

She gazed back at him evenly. "I suppose I never really did until I came to know you."

"At the very least, I think you owe me a debt of gratitude for broadening your horizons," he replied caustically.

"Indeed, I'm most obliged to you for that lesson." Evangeline's voice was filled with pain. "The world has become a darker place to me because of it."

"The world was always a dark place, dear lady! It's no fault of mine you deluded yourself into thinking otherwise. The only reason you ever stumbled across events that were so wounding to your moral sensibilities is because you interfered in matters that didn't concern you. What was Elsa to you, after all, but another one of your many stray puppies!"

"She was far more than that to me!" Evangeline shot back angrily, advancing toward the center of the cell as she spoke. "All along you've made the mistake of underestimating both me and my motives."

"Not to mention my greatest mistake," Blackthorne added wearily, "which was falling in love with you. A mistake that is about to cost me my life."

"As loving you cost Elsa hers!" Scarcely registering his wounded expression, Evangeline forged ahead. "You think Elsa was no more than another object of charity to me? Another reason for me to feel sanctimonious and complacent at the end of each day?" She was practically shouting. "The one horrifying fact of which I've never lost sight is that I might have been her!"

"What?" For the first time, Blackthorne looked perplexed.

"Hasn't it occurred to you that this has become my nightmare? Do you really believe that you or I were born to a life of wealth because we are more worthy of that privilege that anyone else? We are the result of an accident of birth and no more. I'm painfully aware that without my fortune and education and the countless other advantages that protect me, I might have been lying in that coffin instead of Elsa. You're much mistaken if you think she was only one of my little projects. I've taken this matter very personally indeed!"

Blackthorne advanced toward her, his face assuming a look of wry satisfaction. "Why, Engie, that explanation had never crossed my mind. If you're being candid, then I've seriously underrated my ability to captivate you." He began to circle her in a languid manner, finally leaning down to whisper in her ear, "You must be a trifle unsure of your ability to withstand my advances, after all."

"Perhaps I once was," Evangeline replied in a faraway voice. "But not since I understood what your marriage proposal really meant. You never loved me. Your one true love is your own reflection in the mirror and in other men's eyes. You merely wanted to acquire me to arouse the admiration and envy of your friends. Like a new carriage or a thoroughbred horse, I would have been valued for a time before being discarded in favor of some fresh sacrifice to your vanity."

She glanced up at him contemplatively. "Why couldn't you have been a better man?"

He stepped back and swept his arms wide. "I am as God made me!"

Evangeline shook her head sadly. "God had nothing to do with what you've chosen to become!"

Blackthorne responded with a hollow laugh.

Changing the subject abruptly, Evangline said, "You really didn't have to kill her, you know. No one would have believed her story about you anyway. You, a respectable banker, and she, no better than she should be. An absurd attempt at blackmail on her part."

"Whatever the facts of the matter may have been," a cold smile played about his lips, "you'll never be certain, will you? And that's what you can't bear. Not to receive the final confirmation from me that you knew the truth. That you were right!"

Evangeline turned away and began to pace, her hands clasped behind her back. "Up until the very moment I walked into this jail cell, I might have agreed with you. But our conversation today has led me to an entirely different conclusion."

Blackthorne lifted an eyebrow quizzically.

"I no longer require your denial or assent. The truth isn't something that you control, Jonathan. Something you can grant or withhold. You didn't create it, and you can't destroy it. All you can do is admit to it. Sooner or later, we're all brought to that inevitable point of acknowledgement when there is nowhere left to run."

His eyes held a spark of defiance. "Dear lady, you may have failed to notice that there are precious few days remaining in which to effect my redemption."

Evangeline ventured closer. "This day or another. Here or hereafter. All men must converge to the same point at last."

He chuckled and shook his head in disbelief. "Engie, I'd always thought we shared a common contempt for Bible stories. I believe the worst I'll encounter at the end of my days is sweet oblivion, not the fiery furnace."

Evangeline stopped in the center of the cell and stared at Blackthorne. When she spoke, it was with a voice of utter certainty. "My notion of heaven and hell is hardly that simple. There's something more terrible for you to fear than that."

"Pray enlighten me," he drawled.

"Whether bidden or unbidden, truth abides!"

Abruptly, Blackthorne's temper flared. "Leave me!"

"Which do you suppose it will be, Jonathan? Endless night or relentless day. You will very soon be in a position to prove which of us is right."

He retreated a step. His demeanor, assured only a moment before, showed a flicker of something else—a faint tremor of doubt, followed by an even fainter tremor of dismay. He lashed out, "I told you to leave! Leave me this instant, or I will not be responsible for the consequences!" He walked to the back of the cell and resolutely turned his face toward the wall.

Evangeline stood looking at him silently for a long moment. He remained frozen in place.

"Good-bye, Jonathan," she whispered. "This is the last we'll see of each other." In a louder voice, she called, "Guard, you may let me out. Mr. Blackthorne wishes to be left to his own reflections."

***

Shortly before sunset that afternoon, Evangeline was kneeling in her garden cutting zinnias to make a bouquet for her breakfast table. Monsieur Beau sat nearby, supervising the effort. Evangeline heard someone walking across the lawn and looked up to find Freddie standing beside her.

"Well, did you talk to him?" he asked excitedly. "What did he say?"

Evangeline didn't reply at first. She quietly packed up her gardening tools and began to walk toward the house with Freddie beside her. She looked at her friend solemnly. "He said nothing of any importance, but he looked like a man who feared very much to die."

30 – TROMPE-L'OEIL

Blackthorne's last day on earth dawned muggy and sullen. Evangeline and Freddie took their places in the Cook County Jail courtyard to see their maiden voyage of amateur detection brought to a somber close with his execution. They said nothing to one another throughout the gruesome spectacle and, in unspoken agreement, quitted the spot as soon as it was over. Only about fifty onlookers had been allowed to attend: influential citizens, newspaper reporters, and members of the Blackthorne family.

When they reached the Dearborn Street gate, Evangeline noticed Blackthorne's mother being helped into a carriage by her coachman. The matron glanced briefly through red-rimmed eyes at the pair responsible for her son's death. In a pointed gesture of scorn, she lowered her black crepe veil and turned her back on them.

Evangeline made no attempt to speak to her. She whispered to Freddie, "Did you know Mrs. Blackthorne actually threatened me?"

Freddie raised his eyebrows in mild surprise. "With what, a hatchet?"

"No, with social ostracism."

"Oh, a blunt instrument."

Evangeline smiled grimly. "She said no respectable home in Lake Forest would ever receive me again."

The young man scratched his head in puzzlement. "I wonder what method she uses to measure respectability. Her son was hardly a model of propriety."

"I suppose all that matters is that he was her son and is her son no more." Evangeline sighed. "She's entitled to her grief."

Freddie flipped his notebook closed and placed it in his coat pocket. "Time I went back to the *Tribune* to write up the final chapter of this little saga." He added mordantly, "Readers love a good eyewitness account of a hanging."

Jack stood nearby, waiting to hand Evangeline into her carriage. She was about to climb in when Freddie nudged her. "Not so fast. I think there's someone here who wants a word with you." Following his gaze, she looked across the street where Patsy O'Malley stood. The girl was anxiously hopping from one foot to the other. She waved eagerly when she realized Evangeline had seen her.

"I'll leave you two to chat." Freddie tipped his hat in Patsy's direction and ambled up the street.

The girl skipped across to join Evangeline.

"Well, Patsy, this is indeed a surprise. Does your mama know you're here?"

The girl scraped the sidewalk self-consciously with the toe of her boot. "No, and it would be better if she didn't. She was pretty worked up last night because everybody kept reminding her the hanging was today."

"Why should she be concerned about it?"

Patsy shrugged. "Well, Ma says all the neighbors started bothering her with questions about Elsa again and stirring up gossip about whether we're respectable or not, and she doesn't want to talk about it anymore."

"Your family must have provided much grist for the gossip mill, especially after your papa ran away last fall." Evangeline thought back to her disturbing encounter with Patsy's father. "Are his whereabouts still unknown?"

"No. He came back home yesterday night." Patsy made the statement matter-of-factly. She hardly seemed thrilled that her father had returned. "Didn't say where he'd been or why. He was sober, but he was talking even crazier than he usually does when he's drunk."

"What did he say?" Evangeline was intrigued.

"Well, after ma started complaining about Elsa and the shame she brought on the house because of that terrible Mr. Blackthorne, Pa just smiled. He said that now he could stop looking over his shoulder and that maybe he'd finally get a good night's sleep."

"What do you suppose he meant by that?"

The girl fidgeted. "Don't know. When Pa says odd things, it's best not to ask too many questions."

Remembering the gin bottle thrown at her by the temperamental Mr. O'Malley, Evangeline silently agreed. She changed the subject slightly. "Did you come to see the execution, Patsy? Only a few people were allowed to witness it. I'm sorry if you came all this way for nothing."

"No, I didn't want to see it. I just wanted to be here to know it got done."

"Yes, it got done," Evangeline assured her succinctly. Not wanting to dwell on the image of how it got done, she changed the topic yet again. "You'll be in a new grade at school this fall, won't you?"

The girl perked up immediately. "Yes, and I can't wait. It was hard last year. Being in a class with all the little first graders because I didn't know how to read. Trying to keep up with everybody. It was nice of you to spend so much time at Hull House teaching me my ABCs."

"And what does your mama say about our arrangement now?"

Patsy gave a conspiratorial giggle. "The day your last check came in the mail, I heard her mumbling to herself when she didn't think I could hear. She said if you wanted to throw your money away on something as foolish as sending me to school, it was all right with her."

"Very good." Evangeline nodded approvingly. "You may rest assured that I intend to spend my money just as foolishly for many years to come."

Evangeline and her young friend had to step aside as more spectators emerged from the jail courtyard. "This probably isn't the best place to be standing now that the show, so to speak, is over." As she moved toward her carriage, she asked, "Can I drop you back at home?"

Patsy looked panic-stricken. "Lord no, Miss Engie! If Ma knew I was here at all, I'd be in big trouble." She reached into her skirt pocket. "Besides, I just wanted to give you this, and then I'll be going."

"What is it?" Evangeline unfolded a crumpled piece of paper. "It looks like a receipt of some sort."

"That's what I thought," Patsy beamed and added proudly, "now that I can read."

"Where did you find it?"

"It was jammed at the back of the dresser in one of the drawers Elsa used. I didn't see it when I packed all her things for you. Yesterday, I pulled the drawer out to shift some clothes around, and it just fluttered down on the floor. I don't know what it's for, but I know it was hers, and I thought you'd want to keep it with all her other things."

Evangeline frowned in intense concentration as she studied the receipt. A thousand questions leaped into her mind at once. She absentmindedly bid her young friend goodbye and stood on the sidewalk for several more moments just staring at the paper. When she finally looked up, she realized that all the other spectators had dispersed, and Jack still stood holding the carriage door open. She glanced down once more at the paper and exclaimed, "Good Lord!"

***

At the beginning of October in the somewhat tarnished year of 1894, Evangeline and Freddie stood near a gravesite in Graceland Cemetery. They were contemplating a tombstone newly placed over Elsa Bauer's grave.

"It was a year ago today, wasn't it?" Freddie asked.

Evangeline merely nodded, intent on some silent message she was communicating to the spectral world.

"What a difference from the last time we were here, eh?" Freddie attempted a humorous observation. "I remember Mrs. O'Malley doing her best to flatten me like a pancake."

219

Evangeline smiled at the memory. "I also recall that afterward you made a veiled death threat toward me, young man."

Freddie waved his hand dismissively. "Oh, that's just water under the bridge, Engie. The constant humiliation and aggravation to which you subjected me. Think nothing of it."

She looked up at her friend, her eyes twinkling mischievously. "I wouldn't say you exactly suffered by the arrangement, Mr. Reporter."

By this time, Freddie had become comfortably installed in his new line of work as a journalist. His Uncle Horace had sighed and washed his hands. Aloysius Waverly duly mourned the young attorney's passing, primarily because it meant the end of a lucrative side business in bribery. Freddie's mother had given him up as lost to all good society. And the young man's coverage of the Blackthorne affair had raised him in the estimation of his fellow reporters to such a degree that they only sent him out for lunch orders once a week instead of every day.

Freddie's voice softened. "Yes, I do owe you a debt of gratitude for that, old girl."

They stood together in silence for some minutes. The air was cool but clear, and a high breeze rustled in the massive oak tree above the grave.

"I take it this is to be some sort of private dedication ceremony of yours?"

"Yes, Freddie, some final unfinished business."

The young man studied the new headstone, topped by a large marble cross. He wrinkled his forehead, trying to understand the meaning of the epitaph. "An odd choice for a tombstone. And why isn't there any capstone?"

He pointed to the top of the central column of marble, which appeared to be hollow.

By way of reply, Evangeline opened her handbag and held out a marble capstone.

"Well, what are you carrying that around for?"

"Because there's something that has to be placed inside before we seal it," she replied mysteriously.

"Really, Engie, I had no idea I was attending an Egyptian burial service, complete with artifacts to be entombed with the dead."

Evangeline merely reached into the handbag again and withdrew another object. It gleamed of gold and rubies in the autumn light. She handed it to Freddie.

"The hair ornament! You got it back after the trial?"

Evangeline nodded. She took it back from him and turned the object over in her hands. "A fatal flaw in my character. I'm relentless so long as a twinge of doubt remains. Do you remember when Patsy O'Malley came to speak with me on the day of Jonathan's execution? She gave me a paper that she'd found in Elsa's dresser, thinking I would want it as a memento. It turned out to be a jeweler's receipt."

"A jeweler's receipt?" Freddie echoed.

"Yes. I knew that the hair ornament had been reworked at a later date to add the concealed knife. The original jeweler said he didn't know who had done the work. The paper Patsy gave me was the receipt from the second jeweler."

"But how did it get into Elsa's possession?" Freddie was beginning to feel uneasy.

Evangeline held up her hand to silence any further questions. "I'm getting to that. I took the receipt back to the jeweler's shop and questioned the man about the circumstances of the commission. He remembered modifying the ornament according to the instructions of a young woman who had been sent by Mr. Blackthorne. She said that the hair comb was meant as a gift for a lady who often carried a great deal of money with her, and who had occasion to go into some dangerous neighborhoods unprotected. The ornament was supposed to be a weapon that didn't look like a weapon. One that the lady could conceal on her person."

"It was a weapon all right, but one that was intended to be used on the lady, not by her," Freddie added ominously.

"When the jeweler's work was completed, the piece was picked up by the young woman who had given the design instructions on Jonathan's behalf. The jeweler said she spoke with a slight foreign accent. Her name was written on the receipt and on the back of the design sketch that he kept in his files. It was Elsie Farmer."

"And?" Freddie raised an eyebrow.

"Farmer is the English translation of Bauer. I showed the jeweler a photograph of Elsa and a group of her classmates. He identified her immediately."

"Good God, Engie! That changes everything! It means Blackthorne didn't kill her at all! He really was innocent!"

Evangeline shook her head. "No, not really." She took her friend's arm. "Shall we go over to that bench and sit down? This could take a while." She led him off toward a shady spot beneath an elm tree. Dusting off the leaves that had fallen, the two sat down, and Evangeline began her story.

"The more I uncovered about this, the harder it became to use words like 'guilty' and 'innocent' in the conventional sense. There were no tidy categories anymore."

Freddie said nothing. He was still attempting to recover his sense of mental balance.

"As nearly as I can tell, Elsa began to formulate a plan to confront Jonathan once she knew his real identity. She must have realized his part in the charade and also realized that she was in the early stages of pregnancy. This limited her options. She could hardly return to her old life as if nothing had happened. Aside from that, I don't think anyone ever considers the scars that remain on the heart after the kind of betrayal she suffered. I believe she cared desperately for him and that his abandonment left her without hope. The world offers very few options for a girl in her condition. I'm sure she had already sunk to such a level of despair that in her own mind the only alternatives were a life of prostitution or..." Evangeline hesitated.

Freddie completed the thought, "Or death. So, you think she went there that night intending to kill herself?"

"Not quite. She was going to let Jonathan decide. The outcome depended entirely on him. Though unfortunately, I think she had little doubt beforehand of what it would be."

Freddie looked at his friend in perplexity.

"Here's what must have happened. She made her arrangements ahead of time. Commissioned the hair ornament to be redesigned. Checked into the hotel anonymously weeks in advance of the rendezvous to judge the layout of the place. Even managed to find a source for the poison."

"How in the world would she have found a poison that exotic here?"

Evangeline smiled ruefully. "It was in her own backyard, so to speak. Hull House has many visitors passing through its doors. Some of them stay for extended periods of time. I recall a missionary who visited us sometime during August. He offered a very interesting lecture series on the natives of the Amazon."

"Good lord! Don't tell me he carried that stuff around with him."

"Several vials if I recall correctly. Elsa attended at least some of the lectures. She had free access to all the guest rooms at Hull House. I doubt he would have missed the minute quantity she required."

It took Freddie a moment to digest this new fact before he continued with his questions. "Well, the poison didn't cost her anything if she stole it, but the jeweler and the hotel visits would have cost money. Where did she get it?"

"Franz said his sister had many expensive items tucked into her dresser. I'm sure these were all gifts from Jonathan collected over the course of time. She pawned them for the money she needed. And when her plans were set, she wrote to Jonathan to arrange a meeting."

"How could she be sure he'd come?"

"She couldn't. It was a risk she took, but she guessed correctly that he would have done whatever was necessary to forestall the threat of exposure."

Freddie's uneasiness grew. "What about the handkerchief? Blackthorne said he never gave it to her."

"A young girl who is infatuated will fix on the most ridiculous mementos. On any number of occasions when they were together, he might have gallantly offered a handkerchief for her to use. Without a doubt, she would have kept it."

"You're saying she deliberately brought it with her that night."

"Yes, I'm certain she did. It would act as a clue to the murderer."

"Why do you keep calling him the murderer?" Freddie's uneasiness was rapidly deteriorating into irritation. "It's clear she planned this thing from start to finish. It must have been suicide made to look like murder."

"Suicide!" Evangeline laughed incredulously. "Freddie, how easy do you suppose it would be to achieve the proper pressure to trigger this knife at the proper angle while you're wearing it fastened to your hair?"

"Well, I don't know. I'd never be likely to wear one of those contraptions. You tell me."

"I think it would be very difficult to manage without some sort of assistance."

"Then what are you saying?" Freddie cried in exasperation. "That she walked up to Blackthorne and said, 'I'm having a bit of trouble with the murder weapon, dear, can you help me?'"

"I think he helped her, though without realizing that's what he was doing."

Freddie tapped his foot impatiently. He felt like a man lost in a maze who longs for a pair of hedge clippers.

His friend proceeded with her narration. "If you recall, I told you she'd probably gone to the hotel beforehand. Knew the layout of the rooms. Possibly she even requested a room of a certain type that would suit her requirements."

"Her requirements?" Freddie echoed.

"A room with a window leading to a fire escape. She was giving Jonathan one final chance to acknowledge her. The most painful part of her humiliation at his hands was that he would never admit that he knew her at all. Even if she had brought the matter to the police, all he had to say was 'I don't know her,' and the matter would have been dropped. If he had left by the door, things might have turned out differently."

"What on earth do you mean?" Freddie, having turned down a side row in the maze, had lost all hope of finding his way out unassisted.

"From start to finish, Jonathan's actions were secretive. He used a false name. Used an accomplice to do his pandering for him. Ruined the lives of others without technically ever killing them. I'm sure you would agree his behavior was elaborately calculated to prevent exposure."

"I certainly wouldn't argue the point."

"Then how would you expect such a man to behave in a room such as I have described, confronted by a woman he has wronged when a stranger knocks on the door?"

"I'd expect him to scuttle out of there as quickly as he could and leave as little evidence of his presence as possible."

"Quite right, Freddie. That's what I would have expected him to do, and I'm sure that's what Elsa, deep down, expected him to do as well."

"This is unbelievable!" Freddie exclaimed as the full force of her words hit him. "It was a deathtrap."

Evangeline nodded grimly. "Exactly so, my lad. But he had one chance left. If he had stepped forward and answered the knock on the door, it would have meant he at least had the fortitude to allow himself to be seen with her under his own name. That on some level, he had stopped denying her. As it was, he chose to betray her once more. He crawled out the window."

"Her body was found by the window. She must have been standing with her back to it when Blackthorne let himself out."

"Not standing next to it, Freddie, leaning against it. She rested her body on the sill and tilted her head back against the pane. And waited."

Freddie was horrified at the mental image she had conjured before his eyes. "She waited as he closed the window from the other side. The pressure of the sash coming down—"

"Would have caught the top of the weapon and released it, pressing the knife into her back," Evangeline completed the thought. "When her body fell away from the window, the knife would have sprung back into its hiding place, but there would have been enough blood to suggest a murder had been committed. All she had to do was wait for Jonathan to do the inevitable. Failing in every other recourse, she would finally force him out of the shadows through her death. While he might easily have denied seducing her and gotten away with it, a murder charge would have been less easily avoided. She planned it so that he wouldn't be able to run away from her, or from anyone else, anymore."

"What if he'd answered the door instead?"

Evangeline shook her head sadly. "Then we wouldn't be visiting this grave today. But I don't think she ever really expected him to do that. She already knew the sort of man he was."

Freddie rubbed his forehead in puzzlement. "It was such a long shot. How could she know someone would knock on the door at just the right moment?"

"Because she planned that, too. The knock wasn't an accident. All the rooms at the Palmer House are equipped with electric call buttons that send a signal to the housekeeper's station on each floor. She rang the call button in her room just before she opened the door to let Jonathan in. She calculated that it would take the maid between five and ten minutes to arrive. Plenty of time to say what she had to say. All she had to do was wait."

"It seems like a well-laid plan, but a few things went wrong along the way."

Evangeline sighed. "She didn't anticipate Sidley's involvement. Jonathan was never seen in the lobby as she planned he would be. I doubt she expected the police department would fail to track down the handkerchief or the hair ornament. Worst of all, she could never have foreseen the tragedy of her brother's role in all of this."

"She was lucky that you proved to be such a loyal friend to her. If not for you, it's possible that Blackthorne and Sidley would have gone free."

"Maybe so." Evangeline shrugged. "But I've always believed truth has a way of emerging over time, even though the path it takes may wind a bit." She studied the hair ornament, turning it in the light to let the jewels flash in the sun.

"What will you do with the evidence now?"

Without replying, Evangeline stood up and walked back to the gravesite. Freddie followed. She stood in front of the cross for a long moment and then turned to him. "The police and the court have had possession of it for a year. I believe I've given them an adequate grace period. The knowledge it contains is going to be buried with Elsa." She dropped the weapon into the hollow of the cross. It made a clattering noise in its descent and then was still. Evangeline took the capstone out of her bag and fitted it into place on top of the monument. "Jack is waiting for us to finish here. He's come under the guise of planting flowers, but his real purpose is to seal the capstone so that no one disturbs what it contains."

Freddie didn't interrupt as she performed her ritual. When she was through, he said, "You know, it's funny. If murder is defined by the intent to kill, then Blackthorne technically didn't murder her after all. He was telling you the truth. He was innocent."

"Innocent!" Evangeline looked at her friend with disbelief in her eyes. "He was technically innocent of the crime of which he was convicted but guilty of a multitude of others that never came to trial. And Jonathan depended on technicalities. Everything he did was calculated to keep him safe within the letter of the law." She sighed. "We honor the letter of the law, Freddie, never its spirit." Evangeline looked up as the wind shook loose a cluster of leaves over Elsa's grave.

"Would you have acted differently if you'd known in time?" Freddie asked gently.

"Known what?"

"About the jeweler's receipt. About Elsa's orchestration of her own death."

Evangeline sighed. "I don't believe I was meant to. Franz once said to me, 'Perhaps there is such a thing as fate—*schicksal*—after all.'"

Freddie contemplated the capstone of the cross, silently guarding its secret. He read the inscription on the tombstone aloud.

"Lo! o'er the city a tempest rose; and the bolts of the thunder
Smote the statue of bronze, and hurled in wrath from its left hand
Down on the pavement below the clattering scales of the balance."

Evangeline watched him intently. "Do you recognize the quotation, Freddie?"

The young man looked quizzically at his friend by way of reply.

"I thought it was appropriate since I became Elsa's avenging angel, perhaps as I was fated to be all along." She smiled grimly. "Both of us believed in a different kind of justice. The quote is from a poem by Henry Wadsworth Longfellow. It's called *Evangeline*."

ABOUT THE AUTHOR

"There's a 52% chance that the next Dan Brown will be a woman ... or should we just make that 100% now?" --Kindle Nation Daily

Nancy Wikarski is a fugitive from academia. After earning her Ph.D. from the University of Chicago, she became a computer consultant and then turned to historical mystery and adventure fiction writing.

She is a member of Mystery Writers of America, the Society of Midland Authors, and has served as vice president of Sisters in Crime - Twin Cities and on the programming board of the Chicago chapter. Her short stories have appeared in *Futures Magazine* and *DIME Anthology*, while her book reviews have been featured in *Murder: Past Tense* and *Deadly Pleasures*.

Her novels include the Gilded Age Chicago Mysteries set in 1890s Chicago. The series has received People's Choice Award nominations for best first novel and best historical. The award-nominated seven-volume Arkana Archaeology Adventure Series is an Amazon bestseller.

GILDED AGE CHICAGO MYSTERIES

The Fall of White City (2002)
Shrouded in Thought (2005)
The Black Widow's Prey (2021)

ARKANA ARCHAEOLOGY ADVENTURES

The Granite Key (2011)
The Mountain Mother Cipher (2011)
The Dragon's Wing Enigma (2012)
Riddle of the Diamond Dove (2013)
Into the Jaws of the Lion (2014)
Secrets of the Serpent's Heart (2015)
The Sage Stone Prophecy (2016)

Made in the USA
Middletown, DE
05 August 2022

70651331R00136